*The leaden sky leached everything
of color—except the blood.*

The faces of the corpses were white, the hair either black or a bleached non-color. The weapons, still clutched in stiffened hands or wedged in flesh, lacked shine. The circs of the priests were a dull white.

But the stains on them were luridly bright. Thick crimson oozed from wounds and slicked blades. Pools of it gathered under the dead like a morbid carpet. Trickles of it flowed down folds in the earth. It gathered to form streams. Pooled. Soaked into the soil, so that it bubbled to the surface at every step.

The sickened mud sucked at her feet. She took a few more steps, then found she could not move. The mud clung to her shoes. It gave beneath her. She felt herself sinking into it. She felt the cold moisture creeping up her legs and her heart began to race.

*"You killed us,"* hissed a voice.

She looked up to see corpses raising their heads to stare at her with dead eyes.

*"You,"* another said, his partly severed head lolling on the ground. *"You did this to me."*

# TRUDI CANAVAN

## Last of the Wilds

*An Imprint of HarperCollinsPublishers*

This is a work of fiction. The characters, incidents, and dialogue are drawn from the author's imagination and are not to be construed as real. Any resemblance to actual events or persons, living or dead, is entirely coincidental.

EOS
*An Imprint of* HarperCollins*Publishers*
10 East 53rd Street
New York, New York 10022-5299

This book was originally published in Australia in 2005 by Voyager, an imprint of HarperCollins Publishers.

First Eos paperback printing: May 2006

HarperCollins® and Eos® are trademarks of HarperCollins Publishers Inc.

Printed in the U.S.A.

10  9  8  7  6  5  4

*To my Nana, Ivy Dauncey,*
*who loves to tell stories*

# ACKNOWLEDGMENTS

Many thanks:
First to "The Two Pauls" and Fran Bryson, who read the roughest of all rough drafts. Also to Jennifer Fallon, Russell Kirkpatrick, Glenda Larke, Fiona McLennan, Ella McCay, Tessa Kum for their feedback. To all my readers, especially all my readers on Voyager Online. And, finally, to Diana Gill and the Eos team, and to Matt Stawicki for the fabulous cover illustrations.

ARBEEN

MIRROR STRAIGHT

AIME

GENRIA

NORTHERN
ITHANIA

PORIN    TOREN

THE OPEN

S I

BORRA                    PORTLE

SOUTHERN
OCEAN

JURAN

RIAN        MAIRAE

# Last of the Wilds

# PROLOGUE

Reivan detected the change before any of the others. At first it was instinctive, a feeling more than a knowing; then she noticed that the air smelled duller and that there was a grittiness to it. Looking at the rough walls of the tunnel, she saw deposits of a powdery substance. It coated one side of every bump and groove, as if it had been blown there from a wind originating in the darkness ahead.

A shiver ran down her spine at the thought of what that might mean, yet she said nothing. She might be wrong, and everyone was still deeply shocked by their defeat. All were struggling to accept the deaths of friends, family and comrades, their bodies left behind, buried in the fertile soil of the enemy. They didn't need something else to worry about.

Even if they hadn't been all scurrying home in the lowest of spirits, she would not have spoken. The men of her team were easily offended. They, like her, nursed a secret resentment that they had not been born with enough Skill to become a Servant of the Gods. So they clung to the only sources of superiority they had.

They were smarter than average folk. They were Thinkers. Distinguished from the merely educated by their ability to calculate, invent, philosophize and reason. This made them fiercely competitive. Long ago they had formed an internal hierarchy. Older had precedence over younger. Men had credence over women.

It was ridiculous, of course. Reivan had observed that minds tended to become as inflexible and slow with age as the bodies they rested in. Just because there were more men than women among the Thinkers didn't mean men were any smarter. Reivan relished proving the latter . . . but now was definitely not the time for that.

*And I might be wrong.*

The smell of dust was stronger now.

*Gods, I hope I'm wrong.*

Abruptly she remembered the Voices' ability to read minds. She glanced over her shoulder and felt a moment's disorientation. She had expected to see Kuar. Instead a tall, elegant woman walked behind the Thinkers. Imenja, Second Voice of the Gods. Reivan felt a pang of sadness as she remembered why this woman now led the army.

Kuar was dead, killed by the heathen Circlians.

Imenja looked at Reivan, then beckoned. Reivan's heart skipped a beat. She hadn't spoken to any of the Voices before, despite being part of the team of Thinkers that had mapped the route through the mountains. Grauer, the team leader, had made the task of reporting to the Voices his own.

She stopped. A glance at the men before her told her they hadn't noticed the summons, or that she was falling behind. Certainly not Grauer, whose attention was on the maps. When Imenja reached her, Reivan began walking again, remaining one step behind the Voice.

"How may I serve you, holy one?"

Imenja was still frowning, though her gaze remained on the Thinkers. "What is it you fear?" she asked in a low voice.

Reivan bit her lip. "It is probably underground madness, the dark upsetting my mind," she said hastily. "But . . . the air was never this dusty on our previous journey. Nor was there this much on the walls. The pattern of it suggests rapid air movement from somewhere ahead. I can think of a few causes . . ."

"You fear there has been a collapse," Imenja stated.

Reivan nodded. "Yes. And further instability."

"Natural or unnatural?"

Imenja's question, and what it suggested, caused Reivan to pause in shock and dread.

"I don't know. Who would do that? And why?"

Imenja scowled. "I have already received reports that the Sennons are causing trouble for our people now that the news of our defeat has reached them. Or it might be the local villagers seeking revenge."

Reivan looked away. A memory rose of vorns, mouths dripping with blood after a final "hunting" trip the night before they'd entered the mines. The good will of local villages hadn't been a priority to the army—not when victory was so sure.

*We weren't supposed to come back this way, either. We were supposed to drive the heathens out of Northern Ithania and claim it for the gods, and return to our homes via the pass.*

Imenja sighed. "Return to your team, but say nothing. We will deal with obstacles when we come to them."

Reivan obeyed, returning to her place at the back of the Thinkers. Conscious of Imenja's ability to read her mind, she kept alert for further signs of disturbance. It did not take long before she found them.

It was amusing to watch her fellow Thinkers slowly realize the significance of the steadily increasing amount of rubble in the passage. The first blockage they encountered was a small section of roof that had collapsed. It hadn't filled the passage, and it was only a matter of climbing over the mess to continue on.

Then these obstacles became more frequent and difficult to pass. Imenja used magic to carefully move a boulder here and shift a mound of dirt there. No one suggested a cause for the disturbances. All stayed prudently silent.

The passage reached one of the large natural caverns so common in the mines. Reivan stared into the void. Where there ought to be only darkness there were pale shapes faintly illuminated by the Thinkers' lamps.

Imenja stepped forward. As she entered the cavern her magical light rose higher and brightened, illuminating a wall of rock. The Thinkers stared up at it in dismay. Here, too, the roof had collapsed, but this time there was no way over or around the blockage. Rubble filled the cavern.

Reivan gazed at the pile of rocks. Some of the boulders were enormous. To be caught under a fall like that . . . she doubted there'd be time to comprehend what had happened. Crack. Squish.

*Better than a stab in the guts and a long, agonizing death,* she thought. *Though I can't help feeling a sudden death cheats you of something. Death is an experience of life. You only get one death. I would like to be aware it was happening, even if that did mean enduring pain and fear.*

A noise from Grauer caught her attention.

"This shouldn't have happened," he exclaimed, his voice echoing in the shortened cave. "We checked everything. This cave was stable."

"Keep your voice down," Imenja snapped.

He jumped, and dropped his eyes. "Forgive me, holy one."

"Find us another way out of here."

"Yes, holy one."

With a few glances at the Thinkers he favored, he gathered a small circle of men about him. They murmured for a small time, then parted to allow him to stride forward confidently.

"Allow me to lead you, holy one," he said humbly.

Imenja nodded to the other Thinkers, indicating that they should join him. The passage became crowded as the army doubled back on itself. The air became noticeably stale, despite the efforts of Servants to draw fresh air down vents and cracks in the mountain above. Servants, soldiers and slaves alike kept a worried silence.

The passing of time was hard to estimate underground. The months Reivan had spent here helping her fellow Thinkers map the mines, natural cave systems and mountain trails had given her a knack of guessing the time. Nearly an hour had passed before Grauer reached the side tunnel he wanted. He all but dove down the new route, rushing in his anxiety to prove himself.

"This way," he said, his gaze moving from the map to his surroundings over and over. "Down here." The Thinkers hurried after him as he turned a corner. "And then a good long walk along—"

There was a pause, then an echoing scream faded rapidly into the distance. The Thinkers hurried around the corner and stopped, blocking the passage. Reivan peered between two shoulders and saw a jagged hole in the floor.

"What has happened?"

The Thinkers stepped back to allow Imenja through.

"Be careful, holy one," one said quietly. Her expression softened slightly and she gave him a brief nod of acknowledgment before walking slowly forward.

*She must know already what happened to Grauer,* Reivan realized. *She would have read his thoughts as he fell.*

Imenja crouched and touched the lip of the hole. She broke off a piece of the edge, then rose.

"Clay," she said, holding it out to the Thinkers. "Molded by hands and strengthened by straw. We have a saboteur. A trap-layer."

"The White have broken their agreement!" one of the Thinkers hissed. "They do not mean to let us go home."

"This is a trap!" another exclaimed. "They lied about the traps in the pass so we'd take this route! If they kill us here nobody will know they betrayed us!"

"I doubt this is their doing," Imenja replied, her gaze moving beyond the walls of rock surrounding them. She frowned and shook her head. "This clay is dry. Whoever did this left days ago. I hear nothing but the thoughts of distant gowt-herders. Choose another leader. We will continue, but carefully."

The Thinkers hesitated and exchanged uncertain looks. Imenja looked from one to the other, her expression changing to anger.

"Why didn't you make copies?"

*The maps.* Reivan looked away, fighting down a rising frustration. *They went with Grauer. How typical of him to not trust others with copies.*

*What will we do now?* She felt a moment's apprehension, but it quickly faded. Most of the larger tunnels in the mines led toward the main entrance. It hadn't been the original miners' intentions to create a maze, after all. The smaller tunnels, which had followed veins of minerals, and the natural cave systems were less predictable, but so long as the army kept out of them it would eventually find its way out.

One of the team stepped forward. "We should be able to navigate by memory; we all spent considerable time here last year."

Imenja nodded. "Then concentrate on remembering. I will call a few Servants forward to check for traps."

Though the Thinkers all nodded graciously, Reivan saw signs of indignation in their manner. They weren't stupid or proud enough to refuse sorcerous help and she supposed they had also realized the Servants would share the blame if anything worse happened. Even so, the two Servants who stepped forward were ignored.

Hitte volunteered to lead and none of the others contested him. The hole was inspected and found to be a wide crack in the floor, ceiling and walls, but narrow enough to leap over. A litter was brought forward to use as a bridge, its burden strapped to the backs of already overladen slaves. The Thinkers crossed and the army followed.

Reivan guessed she was not the only one to find this slow pace frustrating. They were so close to the end of their journey through the mountains. The mines on the Hanian side were smaller and had brought them up to an otherwise inaccessible valley used by gowt-herders. A longer journey through large natural caves had avoided the necessity of climbing over a steep ridge. From there they had travelled for a day along narrow mountain trails. When passing this section on the way to battle they had travelled at night so the enemy's flying spies would not discover them.

Now they had only to find their way through these mines on the Sennonian side of the mountains and . . .

*What? Our troubles are over?* Reivan sighed. *Who knows what awaits us in Sennon. Will the emperor send an army to finish us off? Will he have to? We have few supplies left, and there's the Sennon desert to cross yet.*

She had never felt so far from home.

For a while she lost herself in early memories: of sitting in her father's forge shop, of helping her brothers build things. Skipping the brief time of hurt and betrayal after being given to the Servants, she remembered the relish with which she had learned to read and write, and how she had read all of the books in the monastery library before she was ten. She had fixed everything from plumbing to robes, invented a machine for scraping leather and a recipe for drimma conserve that earned the Sanctuary more money than all other monastery produce put together.

Reivan's foot caught on something and she almost lost her balance. She looked up and was surprised to see that the ground ahead was uneven. Hitte had taken them into the natural tunnels. She looked at the new leader of the Thinkers, noting the careful confidence of his movements.

*I hope he knows what he's doing. He seems to know what he's doing. Oh, for the Voices' ability to read minds.*

She remembered Imenja and felt a flush of guilt. Instead of staying alert and useful she had lapsed into reverie. From now on she would pay attention.

Unlike the tunnels higher up in the mountains, which were straight and wide, these were narrow and twisted. They turned not just left and right, but rose up and down, often sharply. The air was growing ever more moist and heavy. Several times Imenja called for a stop so that Servants had time to draw fresher air down into these depths.

Then, quite abruptly, the walls of the tunnel widened and Imenja's light illuminated an enormous cavern.

Reivan drew in a quick breath. All around were fantastic pale columns, some as thin as a finger, others wider than the ancient trees of Dekkar. Some had joined to form curtains, others had broken, and mushroom-like tops had formed over their stumps. Everything glistened with moisture.

Looking over her shoulder, Reivan saw that Imenja was smiling. The Second Voice walked past the Thinkers and into the cavern, gazing up at the formations.

"We will rest here for a while," she announced. Her smile faded and she looked at the Thinkers pointedly before turning away and leading the army into the enormous space.

Reivan looked at Hitte and the reason for Imenja's

meaningful glance became clear. His forehead was creased
with worry. As she watched, the Thinkers moved away from
the line of people entering the cavern and began talking in
hushed tones.

She moved closer and managed to catch enough words
to confirm her suspicions. Hitte didn't know where he was.
He had thought to avoid further traps by entering natural
tunnels, where interference by a saboteur ought to be more
obvious, but the tunnels hadn't joined with manmade ways
again as he'd hoped. He feared they were now lost.

Reivan sighed and moved away. If she heard any more
she might say something she'd regret. Winding her way
through the formations, she found that the cavern was even
larger than it first appeared. The sounds of the gathering
army faded behind her as she made her way between the
columns, climbing over uneven ground and wading through
puddles. Imenja's light cast all into either brightness or
inky shadows. In one place the floor widened and pools had
formed curved terraces. Reivan took note of openings that
might be tunnels.

While examining one of these a low, wordless sound
came from somewhere behind her. She froze and cast
about, wondering if someone had followed her. The voice
grew louder and more urgent, turning into an angry moaning. Was it the trap-layer? A local out for revenge—unable
to attack an army but not afraid to deal justice out to an
individual? She found herself panting with fear, wishing
desperately that she hadn't left the army or that her magical Skills weren't so small she could barely make one tiny,
pathetic spark.

If someone had followed her with ill intentions, however, they wouldn't announce their presence by moaning
loudly. She forced her breathing to slow. If this wasn't a
voice, what was it?

As the answer came, she laughed aloud at her own foolishness.

*The wind. It is vibrating through these tunnels like
breath through a pipe.*

Now that she was paying attention, she could detect a

stirring of air. She stooped to wet her hands in a pool, then moved toward the sound, holding her hands out before her. A breeze chilled her wet skin, leading her to a large opening at one side of the cavern where it became a stronger current of air.

Smiling to herself, she started back toward the army.

She was surprised to find she had wandered a long way. By the time she reached the army all five sections had arrived and were crowding about the formations. Something was wrong, however. Instead of wonder and amazement, their faces were tight with fear. For such a large gathering of people, they were too quiet.

Had the Thinkers let slip their situation? Or had the Voices decided to tell the army that they were lost? As Reivan drew near, she saw the four Voices standing up on a ledge. They seemed as calm and confident as they always did. Imenja looked down and met Reivan's eyes.

Then the moaning sound came again. It was fainter here and harder to distinguish as wind. Reivan heard gasps and muttered prayers from the army and understood what had frightened the men and women so much. At the same time she saw Imenja's mouth tighten with amusement.

"It is the Aggen! The monster!" someone exclaimed.

Reivan covered her mouth to hide a laugh and noted the other Thinkers smiling. The rest of the army appeared to give this idea credence, however. Men and women crowded together, some crying out in fear.

"We'll be eaten!"

"We've entered its lair!"

She sighed. Everyone had heard the legend of the Aggen, a giant beast that was supposed to live under these mountains and eat anyone foolish enough to enter the mines. There were even carvings of it in the older mines with little offering alcoves below—as if something that big could be satisfied by an offering that would fit into such a small space.

Or survive at all. No creature as big as this Aggen could possibly live off the occasional foolish explorer. If it could, then it was a lot smaller than the legends claimed.

"People of the Gods." Imenja's voice rang out in the

chamber and her words echoed into the distance as if chasing after the moaning.

"Do not fear. I sense no minds here other than our own. This noise is only the wind. It rushes through these caves like breath through a pipe—but not as tuneful," she added with a smile. "There is no monster here but our own imagination. Think, instead, of the fresh air this wind brings. Rest and enjoy the marvel that surrounds you."

The army had quietened. Now Reivan heard soldiers mimicking the noise or mocking those who had spoken their fears aloud. A Servant approached Reivan.

"Thinker Reivan? The Second Voice wishes to speak to you," the man said.

Reivan felt her heart skip a beat. She hurried after the man. The other Voices regarded her with interest as she reached the ledge.

"Thinker Reivan," Imenja said. "Have you discovered a way out?"

"Maybe. I have found a tunnel through which the wind is rushing. That wind may come from outside, but we will not know if the tunnel is passable until we explore."

"Then explore it," Imenja ordered. "Take two Servants with you. They will provide light and communicate to me if the tunnel proves useful."

"I will, holy one," Reivan replied. She traced the symbol of the gods over her chest, then moved away. Two Servants, a man and a woman, strode forward to meet her. She nodded to them politely before leading them away.

She found the tunnel again easily and entered it. The floor was uneven and they had to climb steep inclines in places. The moaning grew louder until the sound vibrated through her. The two Servants smelled of sweat though the wind was cold, but they said nothing of their fears. Their magical lights were perhaps a little too bright, but Reivan did not complain.

When the sound was at its most deafening she was dismayed to see the tunnel narrowed ahead. She waited for the wind to diminish, then moved sideways through the gap. The Servants stopped, looking uncertain.

The gap shrank until rock was pressing against Reivan's chest and back. Ahead it curved into darkness.

"Can you bring that light in further?" Reivan called.

"You'll have to guide me," came the reply.

The little spark of light floated past Reivan's head, then stopped.

"Where now?"

"A bit to the right," she called back.

"Are you sure you want to do this?" the other Servant called. "What if you get stuck?"

"I'll get unstuck," she replied, hoping she was right. *Don't think about it.* "Forward and a bit more to the right. That's it . . . now left—not so fast."

With the light near the end of the curve, she could see that the tunnel widened again. It might narrow later, but she wouldn't know until she got there. She pushed on, felt the constriction ease, shuffled around the bend . . .

. . . and sighed with relief as she saw that the tunnel continued to widen ahead. Within a few steps she could stretch her arms out and not touch either side. Ahead, it turned to the right. Her surroundings were no longer illuminated by the Servant's magical light, which was still within the narrow gap behind her, but by a faint light coming from beyond the turn. She hurried forward, nearly tripping over the uneven ground. As she reached the turn, she gasped with relief. The tunnel walls ended at a patch of green and gray.

Rock and trees. Outside.

Smiling, she walked back to where the tunnel narrowed and told the Servants what she had found.

Reivan watched as the army spilled out of the tunnel. As each man and woman emerged they paused to glance around, relief written in their faces, before starting along the narrow trail leading to the top of the ravine. So many had passed she had lost count of them.

Servants had widened the tunnel with magic. The White Forest, as Imenja had dubbed it, would no longer be haunted by moaning winds. It was a shame, but few in the army would have been able to wriggle through the narrow gap as Reivan had.

A team of slaves began to emerge. They looked as pleased to be out of the mines as the rest. At the end of this journey they would be freed and offered paid work. Serving in the war had earned them a reduced sentence. Even so, she doubted any of them would boast about their part in this failed attempt to defeat the Circlians.

*Defeat is probably far from anyone's minds right now,* she mused. *They're just happy to see sunlight. Soon all they will be worrying about is getting across the desert.*

"Thinker Reivan," a familiar voice said from close by.

She jumped and turned to face Imenja.

"I'm sorry, holy one. I didn't hear you approach."

Imenja smiled. "Then I should apologize for sneaking up on you." She looked at the slaves, but her gaze was distant. "I sent the rest of the Thinkers ahead to find a path down to the desert."

"Should I have joined them?"

"No, I wish to talk to you."

Imenja paused as the casket containing Kuar's body emerged from the tunnel. She watched it pass, then sighed deeply.

"I don't believe Skill should be an essential requirement of all Servants of the Gods. Most, perhaps, but we should also recognize that some men and women have other talents to offer us."

Reivan caught her breath. Surely Imenja was not about to . . .

"Would you choose to become a Servant of the Gods, if it were offered?"

A Servant of the Gods? What Reivan had dreamed of all her life?

Imenja turned to look at Reivan as she struggled to find her voice.

"I . . . I would be honored, holy one," she gasped.

Imenja smiled. "Then it shall be so, on our return."

# PART
## ONE

# 1

The man standing near the window all but reeked of fear. He hovered a few steps away from the panes, challenging himself to overcome his dread of heights and step closer, to look down from the Tower window at the ground far below.

Danjin did this every day. Auraya didn't like to stop him. It took a lot of courage for him to confront his fear. The trouble was, being able to read his mind meant that she felt his anxiety and was distracted from whatever she was trying to concentrate on—at the moment a long and boring letter from a trader asking for the White to enact a law that would make him the only man able to trade with the Siyee legally.

Turning away from the window, Danjin found her looking at him and frowned.

"No, you didn't miss something I said," she replied.

He smiled, relieved. Reading minds was a habit for her now. The thoughts of others were so easily detectable that she had to concentrate in order not to hear them. The normal flow of conversation felt frustratingly slow as a result. She knew what somebody was going to say before they said it and had to hold back from replying until the words were spoken. To answer a question before a speaker had the chance to ask it was rude. It made her feel like an actor, anticipating and delivering lines.

With Danjin, however, she was able to relax. Her adviser accepted her mind-reading as part of what she was and did not take offense if she reacted to his thoughts as if he had spoken them aloud. For that she was grateful.

Danjin moved to a chair and sat down. He looked at the letter in her hands.

"Have you finished?" he asked.

"No." She looked down and forced herself to continue reading. When she had finished she looked up at Danjin again. His gaze was distant and she smiled as she saw the direction his thoughts had taken.

*I can't believe it's been a year already,* he mused. *A year since I became an Adviser to the White.* As he noticed her watching him his eyes brightened.

"How will you be celebrating the end of your first year as White tomorrow?" he asked.

"I suppose we'll get together for dinner," Auraya replied. "And we will be meeting in the Altar, too."

His eyebrows rose. "Perhaps the gods will congratulate you in person."

She shrugged. "Perhaps. Perhaps it will just be us White." She leaned back in her chair. "Juran will probably want to review the year's events."

"Then he has a lot to review."

"Yes," she agreed. "I hope not every year of my life as a White is that exciting. First the Somreyan alliance, then living in Si, then the war. I wouldn't mind visiting other lands, or returning to Somrey and Si, but I would prefer it if I never had to go to war again."

He grimaced in agreement. "I wish I could say with certainty that it was unlikely in my lifetime." *But I can't,* he finished silently.

She nodded. "So do I." *We can only trust that the gods had good reason to order us to let the Pentadrian sorcerers live. With their strongest sorcerer dead, the Pentadrians are weaker than the Circlian forces—for now. They have only to find another to replace him to become a threat to Northern Ithania again.*

Once she would have been unconcerned. Sorcerers as powerful as the leaders of the Pentadrians were not born often—perhaps once every hundred years. That five had risen to power in Southern Ithania in the same generation was extraordinary. The White couldn't risk hoping that another hundred years would pass before the Pentadrians found a sorcerer strong enough to replace Kuar.

*We should have killed the four that survived,* Auraya thought. *But the battle was over. It would have seemed like murder. I have to admit, I would rather we White were known for our compassion than for ruthlessness. Perhaps that is the gods' intention, too.*

She looked down at the ring on her hand. Through it the gods heightened her natural magical strength and gave her Gifts that few sorcerers had ever possessed. It was a plain white band—nothing extraordinary—and her hand looked just as it had the year before. Many years would pass before it became apparent that she hadn't aged a day since she had put it on.

Her fellow White had lived far longer. Juran had been the first to be chosen over a hundred years before. He had seen everyone he had known before his Choosing grow old and die. She could not imagine what that must be like.

Dyara had been next, then Mairae and Rian, each chosen at twenty-five-year intervals. Even Rian had been immortal long enough that people who remembered him from before his Choosing must notice that he had not aged a day since.

"I have heard rumors that the Sennon emperor tore up the alliance he signed with the Pentadrians within hours of their defeat," Danjin said. "Do you know if it is true?"

Auraya looked up at him and chuckled. "So the rumor is spreading. We're not sure if it is true yet. The emperor sent all of our priests and priestesses out of Sennon after signing it, so none were there to witness if he tore it up."

"Apparently a Dreamweaver was," Danjin said. "Have you spoken to Dreamweaver Adviser Raeli lately?"

"Not since we returned." Since the war, she felt like someone had touched a healing wound whenever anyone mentioned Dreamweavers. Thinking of them always turned her mind to Leiard.

She looked away as a flood of memories overwhelmed her. Some were of the white-haired and bearded man who had lived in the forest near her home village—the man who had taught her so much of cures, the world and magic. Some memories were more recent, and were of the man she had made her adviser in Dreamweaver matters, defying the general prejudice of Circlians against those who followed the cult. Her mind then teased her with glimpses of more intimate moments: the night before she had left for Si when they had become lovers, the dream links in which they had communicated their desires, and the secret meetings in his tent as they both travelled separately to battle: her to fight; him to heal the wounded.

Finally she felt a chill as the memory of the brothel camp came. She had found Leiard there after Juran had discovered their affair and sent him away. She could still see it in her mind's eye, viewed from above, the tents bathed in gold morning light.

The thought she had read from his mind repeated in her own. *It isn't that I don't think Auraya's attractive or smart or good-natured. She's just not worth all this trouble.*

He had been right, in a way. Their affair was bound to cause scandal and strife if it became publicly known. It was selfish to pursue their own pleasure when people might suffer if it were discovered.

Knowing that hadn't lessened the shock of seeing no love or regret in his mind that day. The love she had sensed in him so many times, that she had risked so much for, had died, killed all too easily by fear. *I should thank Juran for that,* she told herself. *If Leiard was so easily frightened out of love, then something or someone else would have killed it sooner or later anyway. Anyone who loves a White has to be more resilient than that. I will know to avoid such weaknesses in a man next time, and the sooner I forget Leiard the sooner I will find a . . . a . . .*

*What?* She shook her head. It was too soon to be thinking of new lovers. If she fell in love again would it drive her into more irresponsible, shameful acts? No, she was better occupied with work.

Danjin was watching her patiently, and his suspicions

about her thoughts were far too accurate. She straightened and met his eyes.

"Have *you* spoken to Raeli?" she asked.

He shrugged. "Once or twice in passing, but not on this subject. Would you like me to ask her about it?"

"Yes, but not before tomorrow's meeting at the Altar. We're sure to discuss Sennon, and the other White may know the truth already." She looked at the trader's letter. "I will be suggesting we send priests and priestesses to Si."

Danjin did not look surprised. "As an extra defense?"

"Yes. The Siyee suffered such terrible losses during the war. Even with their new hunting harnesses they will never be able to repel an invader. We should at least ensure that they can contact us quickly if they need our assistance."

Thinking of the Siyee filled her with a different sort of longing and pain. The months she had spent in Si had been all too short. She wished she had a reason to return. Next to their honest, uncomplicated way of life her own people's demands and concerns seemed ridiculous or unnecessarily mean and selfish.

Her place was here, however. The gods may have given her the Gift of flight so that she might travel over the mountains and persuade the Siyee to become allies of the White, but that did not mean she should favor one people over others.

*Yet I must not abandon the Siyee either. I led them to war and death. I must ensure they don't suffer any more losses because of their alliance to us.*

"Most of their land is near impassable to landwalkers," Danjin pointed out. "That will slow down invaders and give them time to summon help."

She smiled at his use of the Siyee term for ordinary humans. "Don't forget the sorceress who entered Si last year and those savage birds she keeps. Even a few minor sorcerers could do a lot of harm if they slip into the country unnoticed."

"Even so, if the Pentadrians wanted to strike at us again, I doubt they'd bother with Si."

"Si is the closest of our allies to the southern continent. It has no priests or priestesses and the few Siyee who are Gifted have had little training. They are our weakest ally."

Danjin looked thoughtful, then nodded. "It's not like Jarime can't spare a few priests and priestesses. Whatever intrepid young fellows you send to Si ought to be good healers too. You want the Siyee to continue feeling grateful to you. In twenty years only the older Siyee will remember that you forced King Berro to remove the Toren settlers from their land. The younger Siyee will not understand the value of that act—or they'll convince themselves that they could have done it without you. They may even be convincing themselves of that now."

She shook her head. "Not yet."

"They might be. People can convince themselves of anything, when they want someone to blame."

She winced. *Someone to blame.* A few people had been driven by grief to blame the White, even the gods, for the death of their loved ones during the war. Being able to sense the grief of these and more rational people was another disadvantage of her ability to read minds. Sometimes it seemed every man, woman or child in the city was grieving over a lost relative or friend.

Then there were the survivors. She was not the only one tormented by unwelcome memories of the war. Every man and woman who had fought had seen terrible things, and not all of them could forget. Auraya shuddered as she thought of the nightmares she'd endured since the battle. In these dreams she walked a battlefield without end and the mutilated corpses of men and women pleaded to her for help, or shouted accusations.

*We must do everything we can to avoid another war,* she thought. *Or find a better way to defend ourselves. We White have great magical strength. Surely we can find a way to fight that doesn't cause so many deaths.*

Even if they did find one, it might be of no use if the enemy's gods were real. She thought back to a morning a few days before the battle, on which she had witnessed the Pentadrian army emerging from the mines. Their leader had called up a glowing figure. She would have dismissed it as an illusion, except that her senses had told her this figure was overflowing with magical power.

Circlians had always believed the Pentadrians followed false gods. That the Circle of Five were the only true gods who had survived the War of the Gods. If she had seen a real god, then how could this be?

The White had questioned the gods after the battle. Chaia had told them it was possible that new gods had risen since the War. He and his fellow gods were investigating.

She had discussed and debated the possibilities with her fellow White many times since then. Rian was reluctant to accept that new gods had come into existence. Normally fervent and confident, he was upset, even angered, by the prospect of new gods. She was beginning to understand that he needed the gods to be an unchangeable force in the world. A force he could rely on to always be the same.

Mairae, in contrast, was unconcerned. The idea that there were new gods in the world did not bother her. "We serve our five, that's all that matters," she had said once.

Juran and Dyara were not convinced that the "god" Auraya had seen was real. Yet they were more concerned than Mairae. As Juran had pointed out, real gods were a great threat to Northern Ithania. He had assumed that the Pentadrians had claimed that their false gods had ordered them to war in order to gain the obedience of their people. Now it was possible that these gods were real and had encouraged—perhaps even ordered—the Pentadrians to invade Circlian lands.

They had all agreed that if one Pentadrian god existed, then the rest probably did too. No god would allow his followers to serve false gods in tandem with himself.

Auraya frowned. *I'm convinced what I saw was a real god, so I must believe there are five new gods in this world. But surely that's . . .*

"Auraya?"

She jumped and looked up at Danjin. "Yes?"

"Did you hear anything I just said?"

She grimaced apologetically. "No. Sorry."

He smiled and shook his head. "You don't have to apologize to me. Anything that can distract you so thoroughly must be important."

"Yes, but it is nothing that hasn't distracted me a thousand times before. What were you saying?"

Danjin smiled and patiently began repeating what he had been telling her.

Emerahl sat very still.

From all around her came the sounds of the forest at night: rustling leaves, the chatter and whistling of birds, the creak of branches . . . and from somewhere not too far away, the faint sound of pattering feet.

She tensed as the sound came closer. A shadow moved in the starlight.

*What is it? Something edible, I hope. Come closer, little creature . . .*

It was downwind of her, but that should not matter. She had a magical barrier around her, keeping her odors to herself.

*And there are plenty of those,* she thought ruefully. *After a month of travelling, with no change of clothes, anyone would smell bad. How Rozea would laugh to see me now. Her whorehouse favorite covered in muck, sleeping on the hard ground, her only companion a mad Dreamweaver.*

She thought of Mirar, sitting by the fire several hundred paces behind her. He was probably muttering to himself, arguing with the other identity in his head.

Then the creature moved into sight and all thought of Mirar fled her mind.

*A breem!* she thought. *A tasty, fat little breem!*

A shot of stunning magic killed it instantly. She rose, picked up the little creature and began preparing it for cooking. Skinning, gutting and finding a good roasting stick took up all her attention. When it was ready, she started back to the campfire, stomach rumbling in anticipation.

Mirar was just as she had pictured him. He stared at the fire, lips moving, unaware of her approach. She chose her steps carefully, hoping to hear a little of what he was saying before he noticed her and fell silent.

". . . really matter if she forgives you or not. You cannot see her again."

"It matters. It might matter to our people."

"Perhaps. But what will you say? That you weren't yourself that night?"

"It is the truth."

"She won't believe you. She knew I existed within you, but never saw enough to understand what that meant. I stayed quiet while you two were together. Do you think I was doing it out of good manners?"

He fell silent.

*"She," eh?* Emerahl thought. *Who is "she"? Someone he has wronged, if this talk of forgiveness is a clue. Was this woman the source of all his troubles, or just some of them?* She smiled. *Typical Mirar.*

She waited, but he did not speak again. Her stomach growled. He looked up and she started forward as if just arriving.

"A successful hunt," she told him, holding up the breem.

"Hardly fair on the wildlife," he said. "Pitted against a great sorceress."

She shrugged. "No less fair than if I had a bow and was a good shot. What have you been doing?"

"Thinking how nice it would be if there were no gods." He sighed wistfully. "What's the point of being a powerful immortal sorcerer when you can't do anything useful for fear of attracting their attention?"

She set about propping the breem over the fire. "What useful acts do you want to do that would attract their attention?"

He shrugged. "Just . . . whatever was useful at the time."

"Useful to whom?"

"Other people," he said with a touch of indignation. "Like . . . like unblocking a road after a landslide. Like healing."

"Nothing for yourself?"

He sniffed. "Occasionally. I might need to protect myself."

Emerahl smiled. "You might." Satisfied that the breem was set in place, she sat back on her heels. "There will always be gods, Mirar. We just managed to get on their bad side of late."

Mirar laughed bitterly. "*I* got on their bad side. *I* provoked them. I tried to stop them deceiving people and taking control by spreading the truth about them. But you and the others . . ." He shook his head. "You did nothing. Nothing except be powerful. For that they've called us 'Wilds' and had their minions kill us."

She shrugged. "The gods have always kept us in check. You can still heal others without attracting attention."

He wasn't listening. "It's like being locked up in a box. I want to get out and stretch!"

"If you do, kindly do it somewhere away from me. I still like being alive." She looked up. "Are you sure the Siyee won't see our fire?"

"They won't," he told her. "It's not safe flying in these close parts of the mountains on moonless nights. Their eyesight is good, but not *that* good."

She readjusted the speared breem on its supports over the fire. Sitting back, she looked at Mirar. He was leaning back against a tree trunk. The yellow light of the fire enhanced the angle of his jaw and brows and turned his blue eyes a pale shade of green.

As he turned to meet her gaze, she felt a thrill of mingled pain and joy. She had never thought to see him again, and here he was, alive and . . .

. . . *not quite himself.* She looked away, thinking of the times she had tried to question him. He could not tell her how it was that he was alive. He had no memory of the event that was supposed to have killed him, though he had heard of it. This made the claims of the other identity—Leiard—more believable. Leiard believed that he carried an approximation of Mirar's personality in his mind, formed out of the large number of link memories of the dead Dreamweaver leader that he had received during mind links with other Dreamweavers.

*But this is Mirar's body,* she thought. *Oh, he's a lot thinner and his white hair makes him look a lot older, but his eyes are the same.*

Mirar believed his body was his own, but could not explain why this was so. Leiard, on the other hand, thought it merely coincidence that he looked similar to Mirar. When Leiard was in control he moved in a completely different way than Mirar did, and Emerahl wondered how she had managed to recognize him at all. It was only when Mirar regained control that she was sure the body was his.

So she had asked Leiard about the link memories. If what he said was true, how had this come about? How had he gained so many of Mirar's link memories? Could it be possible that Leiard, or someone Leiard had linked with, had collected Mirar's link memories from many, many Dreamweavers?

Leiard could not remember who he had picked up the memories from. In fact, his memory was proving to be as unreliable as Mirar's. It was as though they both had half a past each, but neither half filled the gaps in the other.

She had asked them both about the tower dream she had been having for months, which she suspected was about Mirar's death. Neither had recognized it, though it appeared to make Mirar uncomfortable.

It was frustrating. She wasn't sure what Mirar wanted from her. When she had found him on the battlefield he had been healing the wounded, just like all the other Dreamweavers, but obviously that disguise wasn't enough or he wouldn't have asked her to take him away. He hadn't said where she should take him, however. He had left that choice to her.

Knowing how good he was at getting into trouble with the gods, she took him toward the safest, most remote place she knew of. Soon she had discovered Leiard. He seemed to have accepted her company only because he had no choice in the matter. She could sense both Leiard's and Mirar's emotions. The realization that Mirar's mind was open and readable had been a shock to her. Belatedly she had remembered that Mirar had never been able to hide his mind as well as she could. It was a skill that required time and the assistance of a mind-reader to learn, and, like all Gifts, it must be practiced or the mind forgot it.

That meant that the gods would see his thoughts if they

happened to look his way, and through him they could see her. Mirar knew who she was.

Of course, they might not have any reason to pay attention to this half-mad Dreamweaver at all. One fact she knew about the gods was they couldn't be in more than one place at one time. Distances could be crossed in an instant, but their attention was singular. With so much to keep them occupied, the chance they would notice Mirar was slim.

If they did, who would they believe this person was? Leiard or Mirar? Mirar had told her something about the gods that she hadn't known before. They did not see the physical world except through the eyes of mortals. After a hundred years there were no mortals alive who had met Mirar before, so none would recognize him. Even those Dreamweavers with link memories of Mirar from predecessors might not recognize him now. Memory of physical appearance was individual.

The only people who could recognize him now were immortals: her, other Wilds, and Juran of the White. However, the Mirar they remembered had looked much healthier than this. His hair had been blond and carefully groomed. He'd had smooth skin and more flesh on his bones. When she had commented on how changed he was, he had laughed and described himself as he had appeared two years before. He'd had long white hair and a beard and had been even skinnier than he was now.

He had said he was more concerned about being recognized as Leiard, though he didn't say why. It appeared Leiard was as good at getting himself into trouble as Mirar had been.

Travelling was difficult and slow in the mountains of Si, but not impossible for those as Gifted as they. If they were being pursued their followers must be far behind them now.

Mirar yawned and closed his eyes. "How much longer?"

"That would be telling," she replied. She had refused to tell him where they were going. If he knew, the gods might read his mind and send someone ahead to meet them.

His lips twitched into a smile. "I meant until the breem is cooked."

She chuckled. "Sure you did. You've asked how long we have to travel every night."

"So I have." He smiled. "How much longer?"

"An hour," she told him, nodding at the breem.

"Why not cook it with magic?"

"They're nicer cooked slow, and I'm too tired to concentrate." She looked at him critically. He looked weary. "Go to sleep. I'll wake you when it's ready."

His nod was almost imperceptible. She rose and went in search of more firewood. Tomorrow they would arrive at their destination. Tomorrow they would finally be hidden from the gods' sight.

And then?

She sighed. *Then I'll have to see if I can sort out what's going on in that mixed-up mind of his.*

# 2

"These are beautiful," Teiti said, moving to the next stall. Imi looked up at the lamps. Each was a giant shell, carved with tiny holes so that the flame inside cast thousands of little pinpricks of light. They were pretty, but not *precious* enough for her father. Only something rare would do. She wrinkled her nose and looked away.

Teiti said no more about the lamps. Her aunt had been Imi's guardian long enough to know that trying to persuade her something was wonderful would only convince her it wasn't. They strolled to the next stall. It was covered in dishes brimming with powders of all colors, dried coral and seaweed, hunks of precious stones, dried or preserved sea creatures and plants from above and below the water.

"Look," Teiti exclaimed. "Amma! It's rare. Perfumers make wonderful scent out of it."

The stall-holder, a fat man with oily skin, bowed to Imi. "Hello, little Princess. Has the amma caught your eye?" he asked, beaming. "It is the dried tears of the giantfish. Very rare. Would you like to smell it?"

"No." Imi shook her head. "Father has shown me amma before."

"Of course." He bowed as she turned away. Teiti looked disappointed, but said nothing. As they passed several more stalls, Imi sighed.

"I can't see how I'm going to find anything here," she complained. "The most rare and precious things would have gone straight to my father and he uses all the best makers in the city already."

"Anything you give him will be precious," Teiti told her. "Even if it were a handful of sand, he'd treasure it."

Imi frowned impatiently. "I know, but this is his *fortieth* Firstday. It's *extra special*. I have to find him something better than anything he's been given before. I wish . . ."

She let the sentence hang unfinished. *I wish he'd agreed to trade with the landwalkers. Then I could find him something he's never seen before.*

That was something she wasn't supposed to know about. On the day the landwalker sorceress came to the city, Imi had been locked away in her room. She had sent Teiti to find out what was going on—but also so Imi could do something without being seen.

Behind an old carved panel in her room was a narrow tunnel just big enough for her to slither through. It had been blocked originally, but she had cleared it long ago. At the end of this was a secret room, lined with pipes. If she put her ear to a pipe, she could hear what was being said at the other end. Her father had told her about it once, and explained that it was how he knew about people's secrets.

The day the landwalker had come to the city, Imi had crawled through the tunnel to see if she could find out what had stirred up the guards. She'd heard this woman asking her father if landwalkers and Elai might become friends. Her people would get rid of the raiders that had killed and robbed the Elai for so long, forcing them to live in the underground city. In return the Elai would help her people if they ever needed it. They would also exchange other things. Her people would buy from the Elai, and Elai could buy from her people. It sounded like a good arrangement, but her father had refused. He thought all landwalkers were untrustworthy liars, thieves and murderers.

*They can't all be like that,* Imi thought. *Can they?*

If they were, then the mainland must be a horrible place where everybody stole from each other and people were murdered all the time. Maybe it was, because they had lots of valuable things to fight over.

Imi shook her head. "Let's go back."

Her aunt nodded. "Maybe there'll be something special next time."

"Maybe," Imi replied doubtfully.

"You still have over a month to find him a present."

The market was near the Mouth, the big lake that was the entrance to the underwater city. As they came in sight of the great dark cave filled with water, Imi felt a wistful longing. She had ventured beyond the city only a few times in her life, but always with many guards. That was the trouble with being a princess. You couldn't go anywhere without an escort.

She had learned long ago to forget about the armed guards that followed her and Teiti about. They were good at being inconspicuous and didn't get in her way.

*Inconspicuous.* Imi smiled. It was a new word she had learned recently. She said it under her breath.

They stepped out of the market into Main River. It wasn't really a river, since it carried no water, but all of the ways in the city were named rivers, streams, creeks or trickles. The larger public caves were called pools—sometimes puddles if someone was mocking the neighborhood.

Main River was the widest thoroughfare in the city. It led straight to the palace. She had never known Main River to be empty, not even late at night. There was always someone on it, even if it was just a courier hurrying to or from the palace, or the night guards patrolling the palace gates.

Today the River was crowded. Two of the guards following her stepped forward to ensure people moved out of her way. The noise created by so many voices, slapping feet, music and singing of entertainers was deafening.

She caught a thread of melody and paused. It was a new song, called "The White Lady," and she was certain it was about the landwalker visitor. Her father had banned anyone from playing it in the palace. Teiti caught Imi's arm and pulled her forward.

"Don't make the guards' job any harder," she said in a low voice.

Imi did not argue. *Can't show too much interest in the*

*song anyway, in case they guess I know about the land-walker*.

They reached the end of Main River. Teiti let out a sigh of relief as they stepped out of the crowd, through the gates and into the quiet of the Palace Pool. A guard stepped forward and bowed to Imi.

"The king wishes to see you, Princess," the man said formally. "In the Main Room."

"Thank you," Imi replied, managing to suppress her excitement. Her father wanted to talk to her in the middle of the day! He never had time to see her during the day. It must be important.

Teiti smiled approvingly at Imi's restraint. They walked down the main stream of the palace at a dignified but frustratingly slow pace. Guards nodded politely as she passed them. The stream was full of men and women waiting to see the king. They bowed as Teiti and Imi walked past to the open double doors of the Main Room.

As Imi stepped into the huge room she saw her father leaning on the arm of his throne, talking to one of four men sitting on stools arranged before him. She recognized her father's counsellor, the palace steward and the head clothes-maker. Her father looked up, smiled broadly and opened his arms.

"Imi! Come give your father a hug."

She grinned, tossed all decorum aside and ran across the room. As she leapt into his arms, she felt them wrap around her and the vibration of his laugh deep within his chest.

He released her and she settled on his knee.

"I have an important question for you to answer," he told her.

She nodded, making her expression serious. "Yes, Father?"

"What entertainments would you like to see at our party?"

She grinned. "Dancing! Jugglers and acrobats!"

"Of course," he said. "What else? Can you think of something particularly special?"

She thought hard. "Flying people!"

His eyebrows rose and he looked at his counsellor. "Do you think a few Siyee would agree to attend?"

She bounced up and down with excitement. "Would they? Would they?"

The counsellor smiled. "I will ask, but I can't make any promises. They might not like being underground where they can't see the sky, and they can't fly in small places. There isn't enough room."

"We could put them in our biggest, tallest cave," Imi suggested. "And paint the roof blue like the sky."

Her father's eyes lit with interest. "That would be a sight." He smiled at her and she searched for more ideas that might please him.

"Fire-eaters!" she exclaimed.

He winced, probably remembering the accident that had happened a few years before, when an overly nervous new fire-eater had spilled burning oil over himself.

"Yes," he said. "Is that all?"

She considered, then smiled. "A treasure hunt for the children."

"You're not getting too old for that?"

"Not yet . . . Not if we have it outside."

His expression changed to disapproval. "No, Imi. It's too dangerous."

"But we could bring guards and hold it somewhere—"

"No."

She pouted and looked away. Surely it wasn't *that* dangerous outside. From what she had overheard in the pipe room, raiders weren't circling the islands all the time. People went out every day to collect food or objects to trade. Whenever someone was killed, it was on one of the outer islands, or away from the islands altogether.

"Anything else?" he asked. She could hear the false brightness in his voice. She could tell when his smile was forced because the wrinkles around his eyes didn't deepen.

"No," she replied. "Just lots of presents."

The wrinkles appeared. "Of course," he replied. "Now, with all these suggestions to take care of, I have a lot of work to do. Go back to Teiti now."

She leaned forward and kissed him on the cheek, then slipped off his knee and walked back to Teiti. Her aunt smiled, took her hand, and led her out of the room.

In the stream outside stood a large group of traders. She heard them muttering among themselves as she passed.

". . . waiting for three days!"

"It has been in my family for three generations. They can't . . ."

". . . never seen such large sea bells. Big as fists!"

*Sea bells?* Imi slowed and pretended to brush something from her clothes.

"The landwalkers have discovered them, though. They guard them well."

"Could we arrange a distraction? Then we . . ."

The conversation became too quiet to hear as she moved away. Her heart was beating fast. Sea bells as big as *fists*? Her father loved sea bells. Could she ask one of these traders to get one for her? She frowned. It sounded like they were planning one big trip to gather lots of bells. When they did, bells the size of fists would be on sale everywhere. They'd be common and boring.

*Unless I get someone to sneak in and grab one for me before the traders get there*. She smiled. *Yes! I just need to find out where these sea bells are.*

Which would be easy. Tonight she would make a trip to the pipe room.

*:Auraya, are you coming?* Juran asked.

Auraya jumped at the voice in her mind. She dropped the scroll she had been reading—a fascinating account of a sailor who had been rescued from drowning by one of the sea people—and leapt out of her seat. Her sudden movement startled her veez. He gave a squawk, ran up the back of the chair he'd been sleeping on and scampered up the wall.

"I'm sorry, Mischief," she said, moving to the wall and stretching a hand out to him. "Didn't mean to startle you."

He stared at her accusingly, feet splayed firmly against the wall. "Owaya scare. Owaya bad."

"I'm sorry. Come down so I can scratch you."

He remained just out of reach, his whiskers now quivering in the way they did when he was living up to his name.

*:Owaya chase Msstf,* a tiny voice said in her mind. She shook her head.

"No, Mischief. I—"

*:Auraya?* Juran called.

*:Yes. I'm coming. Where are you?*

*:At the base of the Tower.*

*:I'll be right there.*

She sighed and left Mischief clinging to the wall. Setting a goblet on the edge of the scroll to stop it blowing off the table, she moved to the window, unlatched the pane and pushed it open.

An awareness of the world came to her as she concentrated. She somehow knew where she was in relation to the ground below, and the land and sky around her. Drawing magic to herself, she willed herself to change position slightly. A little higher, then outward. In a moment she was floating beside the window, nothing but air below her feet. Shifting her position again, she turned around and shut the window.

Below her lay the grounds of the Temple. Floating as she was, it almost looked as though one of her feet was standing on the round roof of the Dome, and the other on the hexagonal building known as the Five Houses where the priesthood was housed. Aside from the White Tower behind her, the rest of the Temple grounds were carefully tended gardens shaped into a pattern of circles—the circle being the symbol of the gods. Ahead and to her right she could see a thread of reflected sky where one of the many rivers of Jarime made its way toward the sea.

She willed herself to descend. When she moved like this, it did not resemble flying at all. She called it flying only because she could not think of another simple term to sum up what she was doing. "Moving in relation to the world" was a bit long-winded.

In addition to her awareness of the world was a new awareness of the magic in it. During the last moments of the battle, when she had gathered more magic to herself than ever before, she had become aware of magic in a way she had never been before. If she concentrated, she could sense it all around her.

Both Circlians and Dreamweavers agreed that the world was imbued with magic. All living things could draw in some of that magic and channel it out into the physical world. The uses it was put to were called Gifts and had to be learned, just as any physical skill must be learned. Most living things, including people, could draw only a little magic, and so had limited Gifts. Some, however, were stronger and more talented. If human, they were known as sorcerers.

*I was an unusually powerful sorceress even before the gods enhanced my powers to make me a White,* she reminded herself, looking down at the ring on her finger. *I wonder what sort of life I'd have lived in the days before Circlian priests and priestesses.*

She liked to think that she would have used her Gifts to help people, that she would not have become corrupt and cruel, like so many powerful sorcerers in the past. Sorcerers like the Wilds, who while powerful enough to achieve immortality had been more inclined to abuse their power and positions of authority.

Perhaps humans were not meant to wield that much power. Perhaps having physical form made them vulnerable. The true gods were not corrupt. They had no physical form, but were beings of pure magic that existed in the magic that imbued everything.

Auraya jolted to a halt.

*I can sense that magic. Does that mean I will be able to sense them?*

The possibility was both exciting and disturbing. She looked down. The ground was not far away. Descending again, she dropped until she was level with the top of the Tower entrance, then slowed to make a gentle landing.

Looking through the arches, she found the other White standing in the hall. Mairae saw her and smiled. At once the other White followed Mairae's gaze. Juran's expression softened as he saw Auraya. He started toward her and the others followed.

"Have you been taking a little early morning jaunt around the Tower?" he asked, indicating she should walk beside him as they started toward the Dome.

"No," Auraya replied. "I must confess, I forgot the time."

"You *forgot*?" Mairae exclaimed. "Your one-year anniversary?"

"Not that," Auraya said, chuckling. "Just the time. Danjin brought me a fascinating scroll to read on the Elai." She looked at Juran. "Will I be going back there to make a second offer of alliance?"

Juran smiled. "We'll discuss it at the Altar."

The priests and priestesses standing or walking about the Tower and Dome paused to watch them. Auraya had grown used to their stares of curiosity and admiration. She had learned to accept them as part of her role and was no longer embarrassed.

*Does that make me vain and spoiled?* she wondered. *This is no easy task. I work hard, and not for my benefit. I serve the gods, like them, but I happen to be more Gifted and good at what I do. And I am still capable of mistakes.* Leiard's face flashed into her mind and the usual pang of hurt followed. She pushed both away firmly.

They walked under one of the wide arches of the Dome, out of the gentle morning sunlight. The darkness inside took form as Auraya's eyes adjusted. In the center of the huge structure, upon a dais, stood the Altar.

The five triangular walls of the structure were folding down to the floor like an opening flower. Juran stepped onto one and strode up to the center, where a table and five chairs waited. The others followed. As they took their seats, the walls slowly hinged upward to meet above them, sealing them in what was now a five-sided room.

Auraya looked at each of her fellow White. Juran was taking a deep breath, preparing to speak the ritual words. Dyara sat calmly. Rian was frowning; he hadn't looked happy since the war. Mairae's arms were crossed and her fingers on one hand drummed silently against her arm.

"Chaia, Huan, Lore, Yranna, Saru," Juran began. "Once again, we thank you for the peace you brought to Ithania and the Gifts that have allowed us to keep it. We thank you for your wisdom and guidance."

"We thank you," Auraya murmured along with the others. She concentrated on the magic around them. If the gods were close she was not sensing them.

"Today it is a year since Auraya's Choosing, and a year more that the rest of us have served you. We will review the events of that year and consider how we shall proceed from here. If our plans divert from yours, please let your wishes be known to us."

"Guide us," the others murmured.

Juran looked around the table.

"Many small, peaceful alliances and one big war," he said. "That is one way to sum up the year." Auraya could not help a wry smile. "First let us deal with matters close to home." He turned to Dyara. "How are matters in Genria and Toren?"

She shrugged. "Very good, actually. King Berro has been remarkably well-behaved recently. King Guire is as sensible as ever. They're being gracious, acknowledging each other's part in the war and exchanging praise for the skills of their fighters." She rolled her eyes. "I'm waiting for all this male strutting about to turn into bickering again."

Juran chuckled and turned to Auraya. "How are the Siyee?"

She grimaced. "I have not heard from them since they left the battlefield." She paused. "It would be much easier to communicate with them if we had priests there. I did promise them that we would send some, as healers and teachers."

Juran frowned. "It is a difficult journey."

"Yes," Auraya agreed. "I'm sure we will find some young priests willing to make the effort for the chance to live in a place few landwalkers see. We could hire that explorer who delivered our first proposal of alliance as a guide."

"Yes. Arrange it, Auraya. And ask if any of the Si are interested in coming here to join the priesthood." He turned to Rian. "What of the Dunwayans?"

"A happy lot at the moment," he said. "Nothing pleases a warrior culture more than the chance to participate in such a grand battle. They're almost disappointed it's over."

Juran smiled crookedly. "What of the traps in the pass?"

"They're still in the process of removing them."

"How much longer will it take?"

"A few more weeks."

Mairae smiled as Juran turned to her.

"No complaints from the Somreyans. They left a week ago, as you know, and should reach Arbeem today or tomorrow."

Juran nodded. "Then that leaves the Sennons." To Auraya's surprise, he looked at Dyara. The woman was taking care of matters relating to two countries already, Toren and Genria. Surely she would not be taking on a third—especially when that country had sided with the Pentadrians and was likely to be difficult and time-consuming to work with.

"The emperor himself has sent messages proposing a 'new era of friendship,'" Dyara said, her disapproving expression telling them what she thought of this. "Rumor says he has torn up the alliance he signed with the Pentadrians."

"Good," Juran replied with satisfaction. "Encourage him, but don't be too eager." He looked at Rian and Mairae. "Since Somrey and Dunway aren't causing you much trouble, I want you to work with Dyara on this one. I doubt we will persuade the emperor to ally with us any time soon. He knows doing so would make his country the Pentadrians' first target if they declare war on us again. See how much you can get from him while he's feeling guilty about siding against us."

*Dyara, Rian and Mairae working together on Sennon,* Auraya thought. *What about me? The Siyee are no trouble . . . But of course. There is another country that we seek alliance with.*

Juran turned to her. She smiled.

"The Elai?"

"No," he replied. "I have another task for you, but we will deal with that later. Let us discuss matters beyond our shores. What should we do to avoid a Pentadrian attack in the future?"

The others exchanged glances.

"What *can* we do?" Rian asked. "We let them return to their home, where they are strongest."

"Indeed we did," Juran replied. "So what choices do we have now? We can do nothing and hope they will not regain their strength and attack us again, or we can work toward preventing it."

Dyara frowned. "Are you suggesting an alliance? They would never agree to it. They believe us heathens."

"In that they are wrong, and that is a weakness we can exploit." Juran interlocked his fingers. "Our gods are real. Perhaps the Pentadrians would abandon their false gods if they knew this."

"How would we convince them?" Rian asked. "Would the gods demonstrate their power if we asked it of them?"

"So long as we didn't keep asking them to make an appearance every time we met a Pentadrian," Juran replied.

Dyara made a small noise of disagreement. "Would the Pentadrians believe it, or conclude that we had conjured an illusion?"

Auraya chuckled. "Just as you and Juran have concluded that the Pentadrian god I saw was an illusion?" she asked lightly.

Dyara frowned, but Juran looked thoughtful. "Perhaps we would have been convinced, if we had been there."

"If their gods are real we will have to convince them ours are better," Mairae said.

Juran nodded. "Yes. For now we must make the Pentadrians change their mind about us. We must not only convince them that our gods are real, but that we are better befriended than invaded. Everything they dislike about us must be shown to be false. They think us heathens; we prove them wrong. They think us intolerant of other religions;" his eyes flickered to Auraya, "we prove them wrong."

Auraya blinked in surprise, but Juran did not pause to explain himself. He leaned forward and clasped his hands together. "I want you all to think about this carefully." He looked at them each in turn. "Find out what they loathe about us. Make befriending us beneficial to them. We do not want another invasion, and the last thing I fancy doing is conquering the southern continent and having the trouble of trying to rule it."

"If it is information we need, we should boost our network of spies," Rian said.

"Yes," Juran agreed. "Do it."

He turned to Auraya. "Now for your task."

She sat up straighter. "Yes?"

"The Pentadrians believe we are intolerant of other religions. I want you to continue your work with Dreamweavers. I was impressed with their healing efforts after the battle. Many of the healer priests and priestesses expressed admiration for their skills. They said they learned much just from watching the Dreamweavers. People in this city could benefit from Dreamweaver and Circlian cooperation. I want you to set up a place in which Dreamweaver and healer priests and priestesses can work together."

Auraya stared at him, wondering if he knew that this was exactly what she had thought of doing herself. Were his motives as noble as his words suggested? Did he realize the impact this might have on the Dreamweavers?

The Dreamweavers' continued existence relied on their unique healing abilities. People sought their help, despite distrust and intolerance, because Dreamweavers were better healers than Circlian healer priests. Most people who chose to become Dreamweavers did so in order to preserve that healing knowledge.

In doing so, they forfeited their souls. The gods would not take the souls of the dead who had not worshipped them in life. If Circlians knew as much about healing as Dreamweavers, fewer people would want to become Dreamweavers and fewer souls would be lost.

The cost was to weaken, perhaps even destroy, a people she admired. Yet, that cost didn't seem so high now. Saving souls was more important than preserving a heathen cult. And the living would benefit, too. There were more

Circlian priests and priestesses than Dreamweavers. They could save more lives.

For Juran to suggest she encourage Circlians and Dreamweavers to work together was extraordinary. He had, after all, killed Mirar at the gods' bidding. How far would his acceptance of their skills go?

"Do you mean to limit the kind of skills these healers learn from Dreamweavers?" she asked. "What of the whole range of mind-healing skills—of mind links and dream links?"

Juran frowned, obviously not comfortable with the idea. "Begin with the practical, physical information. If these dream-related skills prove themselves useful, we will consider taking them on."

She nodded. "I will begin making the arrangements tomorrow."

Juran looked at her, his expression thoughtful, then straightened and drew in a deep breath.

"Are there any other matters to discuss?"

A long pause followed. The four White shook their heads.

"Then that is all for today," Juran finished.

"So you decided not to call the gods?" Dyara asked.

Juran shook his head. "If they had discovered that the Pentadrian gods were real, they would have appeared and told us."

Mairae shrugged and stood up. The five walls of the Altar began to fold down. She smiled. "If they wanted to talk to us, the walls would stay closed."

As the White rose and left the altar, Auraya concentrated on the magic around her. There was no sign of the gods—nothing that she could sense, anyway. All she could sense was a stirring of magic where the walls met the floor of the altar.

"Auraya," Dyara said.

She looked at the older White. "Yes?"

"Are you planning to learn to ride?"

"Ride?" Auraya repeated, surprised. She thought of the Bearers—the large white reyner the other White rode. Her few attempts to ride ordinary reyner in the past had been uncomfortable and embarrassing, and she couldn't imagine riding the Bearers would be any easier. "Well . . . no. I don't need to."

Dyara nodded. "That's true. However, we had a Bearer bred for you so I can only assume the gods intended you to ride one, despite your ability to fly."

"It's possible they chose me long after the Bearer was bred," Auraya said slowly. "Before they knew they'd be choosing someone who didn't know how to ride. That may be the reason they gave me the ability to fly."

Dyara looked thoughtful. "To compensate?"

"Yes."

They heard a laugh from Mairae. "I think they might have over-compensated a little."

Juran chuckled and smiled at Auraya. "Just a bit, but for that we are immensely grateful."

## 3

At this time of year, in the dry and windy weather, objects in the distance looked ghostly—if they could be seen at all. As Reivan reached the Parade, the Sanctuary at its end came into full view. Her stomach twisted and she stopped, setting down her heavy bag with a sigh of relief.

The great complex of buildings covered the face of a hill at the edge of the city of Glymma. First there was a wide staircase leading up to a façade of arches belonging to a huge hall. Rising up behind this building were the faces of other structures, each a little more hazed by the dusty air. Whether they were joined together or separate buildings was hard to tell. From the front the Sanctuary was a convoluted mix of walls, windows, balconies and towers.

At the farthest point a flame burned, dimmed by the dusty air. This was the Sanctuary flame, lit by the mortal the gods had first spoken to a hundred years before. It had burned day and night since that day, maintained by the most loyal of Servants.

*How can I presume to think I deserve a place among them?* she asked herself.

*Because Imenja does,* she answered. The night after the army had emerged from the mines, Imenja had called Reivan to her during a meeting of the Voices and their counsellors to discuss the journey ahead. Reivan had waited for Imenja to give her an order, or ask a question, but neither came. It was only after the meeting, while lying sleepless and puzzled under the night sky, that she had realized Imenja had simply wanted her there to observe.

Throughout the rest of the journey Imenja had made sure Reivan was always close by. Sometimes she sought Reivan's opinion, other times she appeared to want only conversation. During the latter moments it was easy for Reivan to forget she was speaking to one of the gods' Voices. When Imenja put aside her demeanor of stern, powerful leader, she revealed a dry sense of humor and a compassion for other people that Reivan found appealing.

*I like her,* Reivan thought. *She respects me. I've been putting up with the Thinkers' derision for years. They've given me the most boring and menial of the jobs that came our way, afraid that a mere woman would prove to be their equal. They probably think keeping me poor will force me to marry someone, have children and stop being a nuisance to them. I'm sure Grauer sent me off to map the mines just to get me out of his sight.*

Now the former leader of the Thinkers was dead. Hitte, his replacement, hadn't spoken a word to her since she had led the army out of the mines. She wasn't sure if he was peeved at her for upstaging him by finding a way out or because he'd found out about Imenja's promise to make her a Servant of the Gods.

*Probably both,* she thought wryly. *He can stew all he likes. So can the rest of them. If they'd treated me better, as if I was worth listening to, I would have told them of the wind tunnel, not Imenja. We would have led the army out as a team, and they'd all have had credit for saving the day.* She smiled. *Imenja would have seen the truth anyway. She knows I saved the army. She knows I'm worthy of serving the gods.*

Shifting her bag to her other hand, Reivan started toward the Sanctuary. Climbing the steps, she stopped to catch her breath beside one of the arches. The Parade was unusually quiet for this time of the day.

She guessed that Glymma's citizens were at home, grieving for those who hadn't returned. Memories of the army's arrival in the city the previous day replayed in her mind. A crowd had gathered, but only a few subdued cheers had greeted them.

The army had been far smaller than the one that had set off to war months before. While the battle had claimed most, many slaves, soldiers and Servants had died of thirst and exhaustion during the return across the Sennon desert. Merchant caravans that had traded food and water before had been conspicuously absent. The guides that the Sennon ambassador had sent for the first crossing did not return, and only the Thinkers' maps, thankfully not among those lost with Grauer, had led them to water.

She had wondered if the people greeting the army would grow angry at the Voices for leading their loved ones to war, and at the gods for allowing them to be defeated. Any anger they felt must have been tempered by the sight of the casket the four Voices had carried between them, supported by magic. They, too, had suffered a loss.

Looking around, Reivan pictured how the homecoming must have looked from here. The army had been arranged into formation: the highest rank—the Dedicated Servants of the Gods—in front, ordinary Servants behind, then soldiers lined up in units. Slaves were moved to one side and the Thinkers had stood at the base of the stairs. The Voices had addressed the crowd from a place close to where she was standing now.

She remembered Imenja's speech.

"Thank you, people of Glymma, for your warm welcome. We have travelled far, and fought a great battle in the service of the gods. Our losses are also yours, as are our victories. For though we did not win this battle, we lost by the slightest of margins. So well matched were the armies of the Pentadrians and the Circlians that only chance could decide the winner. This time, the wind of change blew in their favor. Next time it could as easily blow in our direction."

She had lifted her arms, clenching her fists. "We know we are as mighty as they. We will soon be mightier!"

The crowd, knowing its role, had cheered, but the sound was lacking in enthusiasm.

"We have spread the names of Sheyr, Hrun, Alor, Ranah and Sruul throughout the world! The names of the true gods. The enemies of the Circlians will come here, to us. They will come to Glymma. Where will they come?"

"Glymma!" the citizens yelled half-heartedly.

"Those who wish to follow the true gods will come here. Where will they come?"

"Glymma!" The voices were louder.

"Where will they come?"

"Glymma!" Now there was some force behind the reply.

Imenja had lowered her arms. "We have lost much. We have lost fathers and sons. We have lost husbands and wives. We have lost mothers and daughters, sisters and brothers, friends and companions, mentors and leaders. We have lost our leader, First Voice Kuar."

She bowed her head. "His voice is silent. Let us now be silent in acknowledgment of all those who have died for the gods."

There had been a lump in Reivan's throat. Imenja's face had been lined with grief, and Reivan knew that this grief was real. She had seen it in Imenja's eyes and heard it in the woman's voice many times in the last month.

The silence had stretched out unbearably. Then, finally, Imenja had raised her head and thanked the crowd. She had told them a new First Voice would be elected after a month of mourning. The Voices and Servants had entered the Temple, the soldiers left and the crowd dispersed. Reivan had returned to the small room she rented at the edge of the city. Imenja had given her a day to settle her affairs before coming to the Sanctuary to begin her training as a Servant.

*And so I am here,* she thought as she turned to walk through one of the arches.

The large hall inside was also unusually quiet. Only a few Servants were present, standing in little circles of three or four. Their black-robed backs seemed to forbid inter-ruption. She stopped and waited. Servants were supposed to greet all visitors on arrival, whether they were from the highest or lowest part of society.

None of the Servants approached her, though in the

corner of her eye she noted that one or two were watching her whenever she wasn't looking in their direction. As time passed, she felt her confidence draining away. *Have I come at the wrong time? Imenja said to come here today. Should I approach the Servants? Would that be breaking protocol, or something?*

Finally one of the men stepped away from his companions and strolled toward her.

"Visitors do not come here during times of mourning," he told her. "Unless the matter is urgent and important. Is there something you need from us?"

"Ah." She managed an apologetic smile. "I did not know. However, I was told to come here this morning by the Second Voice."

"For what purpose?"

"To begin my training as a Servant."

His eyebrows rose. "I see." He pointed across the hall. Another wall of arches ran parallel to the entrance of the hall. "Cross the courtyard and enter the corridor. The Servant-novice quarters are to the right."

She nodded and thanked him, then walked out of the hall. The courtyard beyond was large and was dominated by a star-shaped fountain in the center. She walked around it to a wide opening in the building on the other side. This corridor sloped upward, the climb up the hill assisted by an occasional step or two. Servants were walking up and down. Before she had taken more than a few steps a middle-aged woman stopped her, face tight with suspicion.

"Where are you going?" she asked sternly.

"The Servant-novice quarters. I am here to begin my training."

The woman's eyebrows rose. "Name?"

"Reivan Reedcutter."

Somehow the eyebrows managed to rise higher. "I see. Follow me."

The Servant led her to a door on the left side of the corridor. Reivan paused, then shrugged and followed the woman in. They strode down a long, narrow passage, passing many doors. Finally the woman stopped at one and knocked.

The door opened. Inside a Dedicated Servant sat behind a desk. The woman looked up and, as she saw Reivan, frowned. A hand clasped Reivan's shoulder and pushed her inside.

"Reivan Reedcutter." The voice of her guide was heavy with disapproval. "Come to serve the gods."

Looking over her shoulder, Reivan glimpsed the Servant's expression, full of dislike, before the door closed. She turned back to face the Dedicated Servant and caught dismay, quickly smothered.

"So you came," the woman said. "Why do you think you can become a Servant when you have no Skills?"

Reivan blinked at the question. *Very direct,* she mused. *I gather "because Imenja said I could" won't be convincing this woman.*

"I hope to serve the gods in other ways," she replied.

The woman nodded slowly. "Then you must prove that is possible. I am Dedicated Servant Drevva, Mistress of Training." She rose and moved around the desk. "You will undertake the same training and tests that every other hopeful entrant takes. You will also live in the same accommodations. Come with me."

She led Reivan out of the room and farther down the passage. After a few turns the passages became even narrower. Finally she stopped outside a door and opened it.

Looking inside, Reivan felt her heart sink. The room was barely larger than the bed it contained. It smelled of dust and rot. Sand and dust lay in drifts on the floor.

"Do you allow your Servant-novices to live in such conditions?" she found herself asking. "The Servants that raised me would have had me whipped for such neglect."

"If it does not suit you, find a domestic to clean it," Drevva said. She turned on her heel and walked away, then paused and looked back. "Come to my room at the morning bell tomorrow and I will arrange for a Servant to begin your tests." Her eyes dropped to Reivan's bag. "What is that?"

"My belongings."

"Which are?"

Reivan shrugged. "Clothes, instruments, books . . ." She

thought of the books she had sold the previous day and felt a pang of loss. She had doubted the Sanctuary would appreciate her bringing a small library with her.

Drevva strode back and took the bag from Reivan. "Servants do not keep personal belongings. You will have all you need here at the Sanctuary. Clothing will be provided, and if you succeed in becoming a Servant-novice you will need no more than the robes."

"But—"

The woman silenced her with a stare. "But what?"

"But what if I fail the tests?" Reivan asked.

A tiny smile pulled at the woman's lips. "I will keep your bag in my room. It will be returned to you when you leave."

*When* you leave. Reivan watched the woman stride away, then sighed and went in search of a domestic. Her search took her a long way from her room, and she only realized she had reached the Servants' rooms when she finally found a domestic sweeping a corridor.

"I need someone to clean my room," she told him.

He gave her a sullen look. "All the domestics are busy cleaning out rooms of dead Servants," he told her, then turned his back.

She would have cleaned out the room herself but it was clear from Drevva's response that Servants considered such tasks beneath them. If the unSkilled newcomer behaved like a domestic she would be treated like one, Reivan guessed.

The domestics continued to claim their other tasks were more urgent. Eventually she followed a child domestic to a washroom where she bullied him into cleaning out her room and replacing the bedding. She felt a bit guilty about it, but knew from her extensive reading of philosophers and famous healers that to sleep in a grimy room was to encourage sickness in the body and mind.

This took the rest of the day. By the time the child had finished it was late and she was hungry. She went in search of food. Catching the aroma of cooking, Reivan followed it to a large hall full of Servants. Only a low murmur of voices could be heard and she decided that there must be a general rule against noise. Her footsteps drew several frowns as she entered. She looked around and was relieved to see one of the tables was occupied by young women and men in plain clothes. They must be other entrants. She took an empty place. The entrants regarded her curiously but said nothing.

A domestic thumped a bowl of a thin soup in front of her. She noted, with disappointment, that only a few crumbs of bread remained in the basket in the center of the table. When she had finished eating she met the eyes of the young man beside her.

"Is there a rule against talking?"

He nodded. "Only while we're in mourning."

At one end of the room several Dedicated Servants sat at a long table. She examined each of them as best she could. In a month's time, Servants from all over the world would choose one of the Dedicated Servants to be the new leader of the Pentadrians. Drevva was at the table. The woman glanced at Reivan, then looked away.

*This is hardly the reception I was hoping for,* Reivan thought. *These Servants are so cold they make even the Thinkers seem patient, kind and friendly.*

There were several empty places at the table. Reivan felt a chill as she realized why. The Dedicated Servants who had claimed those seats were probably dead, killed in the war.

*Perhaps this is why everyone at the Sanctuary is so unwelcoming,* she mused. *Defeat and loss has made them grumpy and distracted.* She could hardly expect them to be warm and cheerful toward her when they were grieving lost friends and colleagues.

A bell rang to mark the end of the meal, and Reivan followed the entrants back to their quarters.

Taking a firm grip of an outcrop of stone with his left hand, Mirar turned his attention to his legs again. Bending his left knee, he searched for a good place to wedge the toe of his right boot. He found a firm ledge and carefully shifted his weight onto it.

The constant pull of the rope around his chest eased as Emerahl played it out.

"Nearly there," she called, her voice unexpectedly close.

He paused and looked down. His feet were almost level with her head. She smiled.

*She's so beautiful,* he found himself thinking. The thought was Leiard's, however. So was the small pang of guilt that he might find a woman other than Auraya attractive.

*She* is *beautiful,* he told Leiard. *There's nothing wrong with appreciating that.*

*And you don't?* Leiard asked.

*I do. But I've known her so long that she no longer dazzles me.*

*You're friends,* Leiard stated.

*In a way. We have become . . . familiar with each other. We have mutual concerns.*

*You were lovers once.*

*Briefly.*

Leiard fell silent. Mirar shook his head. It was a strange situation, being with Emerahl. Like introducing two friends, one of whom he had already told everything he knew about the other. Which was a little unfair for Emerahl.

But it was nice to see her through fresh eyes.

Talking to Leiard made Mirar feel a little disorientated, however. He took a deep breath, cleared his mind, then continued his descent. Only when both feet were on the ground did he relax again.

Emerahl untied him, then let one end of the rope go and pulled on the other until it slithered down to tangle in the vegetation at her feet. She coiled it quickly and efficiently, swung it over her shoulder, then started along the bottom of the ravine. Mirar shouldered his pack and followed.

They were both familiar with climbing now. He had lost count of the number of times they had scaled walls of rock. This was typical Si territory. The mountains were steep and cracked, full of vertical slices of rock. They looked as if someone had dropped huge mounds of clay onto the world then stabbed at them repeatedly with giant knives. Even on a small scale the surface of exposed ground was fractured in this way, making walking difficult and dangerous. The bottoms of valleys and ravines were easier to traverse, as the cracks and crevasses had filled with soil over time to make a smoother floor. There they had only to navigate through the dense undergrowth of the forest.

No human had made tracks through this land. Not even the Si, who did not like to live this close to landwalker habitations. Animals occasionally did, and they had worn narrow, winding paths through the vegetation. Still, it was slow-going. He and Emerahl had been travelling for a month but had ventured only a little way into the northern part of Si. Before the Siyee had been created, this part of Ithania had been known as The Wilds.

*Now that's what Emerahl and I are classified as, according to the gods,* Mirar mused. *"Wilds." I wonder if they mean to imply that we are undomesticated? Uncivilized? Barbaric, perhaps.*

*Maybe unrestrained, disorderly, violent, dangerous,* Leiard suggested.

*None are true,* Mirar replied. In their day, he and Emerahl had represented great skill in magic. His Dreamweavers had provided order in a chaotic world. They were peaceful, non-violent and certainly not dangerous. Emerahl had been revered for her healing and wisdom.

There was another meaning for "wild." It could be a random force that could upset plans in either a beneficial or disastrous way.

*This, perhaps, is the true reason the gods chose that label for us,* Mirar thought. *Upsetting the gods' plans sounds like a worthwhile reason to exist. Trouble is, I have no idea what their plans are so how am I to upset them?*

The ravine had widened. He could hear the sound of water. Lots of water. They must be nearing a river. There was a lightness to Emerahl's steps now. He saw her emerge into sunlight ahead, turn to the left and smile.

*She's definitely pleased about something,* he thought. Lengthening his stride, he caught up with her. She was standing at the edge of a drop where the ravine ended abruptly. Following her gaze, he saw what she was smiling at.

*A waterfall.* Two steep slopes met far above it, channelling the river to a cliff edge. Water cascaded down into a wide, deep pool before chuckling eagerly over a rocky riverbed that curved below them, then away to their right. Mist billowed up from the fall, keeping the air dense with moisture.

"How pretty," he observed.

Emerahl gave him a sidelong look. "It is, isn't it? Let's find a tree to wind this rope around."

After several minutes they had both climbed down the drop, after first lowering their packs with magic. Emerahl crossed the river by jumping from rock to rock. When she started toward the waterfall, Mirar hesitated before following. After travelling through this rough country for a month and seeing plenty of grand and attractive natural scenery, he didn't feel any inclination to explore a waterfall. He'd rather reach their destination sooner and have a good long rest.

Emerahl moved closer and closer to the fall of water. The pounding was loud in his ears. She began to climb the smooth boulders beside the fall. He stopped to watch her. Looking back, she smiled and beckoned.

Shrugging, he followed. Scaling the boulders took all his attention. When he had reached a narrow length of flat pebbly ground he looked up and found her grinning. Then he saw what she had discovered. Behind the waterfall was a cave.

She moved inside. Feeling a mild curiosity, he followed. The cave dripped with moisture. It was larger than he expected, the back hidden in darkness.

He turned to look out at the wall of water. The constant, unvarying movement was hypnotic.

"Mirar."

Dragging his eyes away, he turned to find Emerahl looking over her shoulder at him. She had created a light and he could see his first impression had been wrong. There was no back to the cave. It was the beginning of a tunnel.

Curiosity grew and deepened. He moved to her side.

"You know this place?" he said.

"I've been here before."

"Is this our destination?"

"It might be. Or it might be a good place to stay for the night. Now, no more questions."

Her last words were firm. He smiled at her tone, then walked beside her as she moved down the tunnel.

Out of habit, he counted his steps. He had passed three hundred when they reached a large cavern. Emerahl's shoulders were tense as she started toward the center. Her steps slowed and she appeared to be listening to something.

After a moment she smiled. Her pace did not quicken, however. She moved steadily forward. Reaching the center of the cavern, she turned to face him.

"Did you sense it?"

He frowned. "Sense what?"

She took his arm, drew him back the way they had come for about ten steps, then stopped.

"Try to use one of your Gifts. Make a light like mine."

He reached for magic. Nothing came. He tried again with no success. Alarmed, he stared at her.

"What . . . ?"

"It is a void. A place in the world where there is no magic."

"But how is that possible?"

"I don't know." She put a hand on his shoulder and gently pushed him back toward the center of the room. He yielded reluctantly. Looking up, he noticed that her spark of light still floated above them.

"How are you doing that then?"

"I drew the magic for it before we stepped into the void," she told him. "Now try again."

He reached for magic and felt it flow into him. He channelled it out to form his own light.

"Good," she said, nodding. "It is still the same. There is magic in the center of the room. It is ringed by a void. The gods, who are beings of magic, can't cross the void, so they can't see you here. Not unless they look through the eyes of someone standing outside the void."

He moved around slowly. Now that she had drawn his attention to the void he could sense it easily. He started moving across to the other side.

"Don't leave!" Emerahl warned. "Come back. Now that you know what this place is, you can't leave it. If the gods are watching they might read your mind and . . . and . . ."

Her brow was creased with worry. He walked back to her side. "If they were watching me arrive, they'd know where I was anyway."

Her gaze was intense. "Do you think it's likely they were watching you?"

He grimaced and turned away. "It's possible. I don't know . . ."

"You still can't leave. If they don't know what this place is, I'd rather they didn't find out."

"You mean to keep me in here forever?"

She shook her head. "Only as long as it takes for me to teach you to hide your thoughts from them."

He considered her thoughtfully. He had learned that skill long ago, but had forgotten it when he lost his memory. It was difficult to relearn without the help of someone who could detect thoughts or emotions. Now *was* a good time to relearn it.

"And then?"

She shrugged. "I don't know. You asked me to take you away. You didn't say why or where. I guessed you wanted to go somewhere safe. I've taken you to the safest place I know." She smiled crookedly. "I'm also guessing that you need to sort out a few things in your mind. If you want help with that, I'll do what I can."

He looked around the cavern. It was not the cozy hut in the middle of the forest that he had been hoping for, but the void made up for that. It would have to do. Slipping the straps of his pack off his shoulders, he set it down on the hard stone floor.

"Then I guess we had better start decorating."

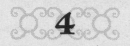

# 4

It was night. It was always night.

An eerie light hung about the ground. She could not see its source. It made the faces around her appear even more ghoulish.

Her path was blocked by a corpse. She stepped over it and moved on.

*I'm looking for something. What am I looking for?*

She thought hard.

*A way out. An end to the battlefield. Escape. Because . . .*

Movement in the corner of her eye set her heart racing with dread. She did not want to look, but did. All was still.

Another body blocked her path: a priest, his upper torso and head blackened and scorched. She stepped over him reluctantly.

*Don't look down.*

Something below her moved. Her eyes were lured downward. The priest stared up at her and she froze in horror. He grinned at her, then before she could step away, his scorched hand grabbed her ankle.

*:Owaya!*

She jumped at the urgent, unexpected shout in her mind. Suddenly she was staring at the ceiling of her bedroom. Her heart was pounding. Her skin felt hot and sweaty. Her stomach was clenched.

"Scare Owaya?"

A small form leapt onto the bed. With the moonlight behind him, she could see the distinctive fluffy tail and small ears of her veez twitching with concern.

"Mischief," she breathed.

"Owaya 'fraid?"

She drew herself up onto her elbows. "Just a dream. Gone now."

Whether he understood or not, she couldn't guess. Did veez grasp the concept of dreams? She had seen him twitch and mutter in his sleep, so she knew he had them. Whether he remembered them, or understood that they weren't reality, she couldn't guess.

He moved across the bed and curled up beside her legs. The pressure of his small body against hers was comforting. Lying back down, she stared up at the ceiling and sighed.

*How long will I have these nightmares for? Months? Years?*

She felt vaguely disappointed at herself, and at the gods. Surely being a White meant she didn't have to endure bad dreams as a consequence of a war in defense of Northern Ithania and all Circlians? Though the Gifts that they had given her protected her from age and injury, they did not appear to include protection against nightmares. Surely the gods didn't mean for her to suffer like this?

*Dreamweavers could help me.*

She sighed again. Dreamweavers. Now there was a matter to prick her conscience. She knew removing the Dreamweavers' influence over people by encouraging priests and priestesses to absorb their healing knowledge was ultimately the right thing to do. She would save the souls of people who otherwise turned from the gods. It just seemed too . . . too *sneaky*.

After the meeting at the Altar she had decided she'd better find out if any healer priests and priestesses were willing to work with Dreamweavers before approaching Dreamweaver Adviser Raeli. She had told herself she was being efficient—she could ask if any were willing to travel to Si at the same time—but she knew she was putting off the moment when she would have to start being sneaky.

Several volunteers had come forward. She had been expecting enthusiasm for the post in Si, but had been pleasantly surprised by the numbers interested in working with Dreamweavers. All had been impressed and humbled by what they had seen in the aftermath of the battle. Many were eager to learn from Dreamweavers, though for some it was out of a determination to match or surpass the heathens in knowledge and skill rather than because of any newfound respect for the cult.

She had delayed further by finding a location for them to work in. It needed to be a place where neither Dreamweavers nor Circlians had greater influence. She had found a disused storeroom near the docks, not too far from the edge of the poor area of the city. She had only to arrange for the building to be cleaned up and appropriately furnished and stocked, and decide what to call it.

Before then, however, she needed an answer from the Dreamweavers. Unable to put it off any longer, she had arranged to meet with Raeli.

Auraya rolled onto her side. She was wide awake now and doubted she'd get to sleep again for hours. Her heart was no longer pounding but it was still beating a little too fast.

She thought of the question she had asked Juran. *"What of the whole range of mind-healing skills—of mind links and dream links?"* He obviously did not like the idea of priests and priestesses learning those skills, but if Circlians were to replace Dreamweavers they would have to adopt all the heathens' practices.

She sighed. The nightmares she was having were proof of the need to have priests and priestesses learn dream-healing skills. She could understand why any ordinary man or woman would seek a Dreamweaver's help in stopping dreams like these.

*Perhaps I should seek a Dreamweaver's help. I'm supposed to be convincing people they're harmless. What would convince them more than if I used their dream-healing services?*

She could not see Juran approving of a White allowing a Dreamweaver into her mind—or even an ordinary priest or priestess exploring her thoughts and discovering their secrets.

Perhaps if she watched the mind of a Dreamweaver performing a dream healing on another person she would learn the knack of it . . . and be able to pass the knowledge on to one of the other White . . . and they could . . .

Her thoughts drifted. She was talking to Mairae, but it was nonsense. The other White kept laughing and saying they didn't understand. Frustrated, Auraya stepped out of the window to fly away, but she couldn't quite control her movements. A wind kept blowing her sideways. She floated into a cloud and was surrounded by a chill whiteness.

Out of that whiteness appeared a glowing figure. She felt her heart lighten. Chaia smiled and moved closer. His face was so clear. She could see every eyelash.

*My dreams are never this vivid . . .*

He leaned forward to kiss her.

*. . . or this interesting.*

His lips met hers. It was no chaste, affectionate brush of magic. She felt his touch as if he were real.

Suddenly she was sitting up on her elbows in bed again. Her heart was pounding, but not from fear. Lingering feelings of elation melted away, leaving her disturbed.

*What am I thinking? Gods, I hope Chaia wasn't watching me!*

She tried to gather her thoughts. *It wasn't intentional. It was just a dream.* She couldn't control her dreams. *Ah, if only I could!*

She lay back down, patting Mischief as he gave a sleepy whine at her movement.

*A dream,* she told herself. *Surely Chaia wouldn't have been offended by that?*

Even so, it was a long time before she fell asleep again.

It wasn't easy staying awake. Imi stared at the ceiling, tracing the marks made hundreds of years before by the tools of cave-carvers.

From the other side of the room came a soft wheezing.

*At last!*

She smiled and slowly began to climb out of the pool. It was one of Teiti's duties to stay close to her at night in case she fell ill or called for help. Curtains dividing the room gave Imi some privacy, but they did not block sounds.

Years before she had done something about that. She'd quietly complained to her father about her aunt's snoring and suggested walls be built around the guardian's sleeping pool. He had agreed, but she suspected only because Teiti had been the first guardian Imi had liked; he didn't want to have to find her a new one.

A single curved wall had been built beside the guardian's pool, not quite meeting the room's wall. Imi had told her father she been hoping for a complete room, including a door, but he only smiled and asked how Teiti was supposed to hear Imi call out for help if she was completely shut away.

Imi found that the curved wall did block noises enough to allow her to creep about without waking her aunt. Ironically, Teiti had not been a snorer in those days, but had recently developed the habit. Now Imi had two reasons to be grateful for the wall.

She brushed droplets of moisture off her skin, then paused to listen for Teiti's snoring. Earlier that day, Imi had sent her aunt on several errands—tasks that only the princess's guardian could carry out—in order to wear Teiti out. As she'd hoped, her aunt had wanted to retire early and had quickly fallen into a deep sleep.

The soft wheeze of Teiti's breathing continued. Imi walked over to a carving on the wall. Reaching behind, she found the bolt that held it fast and carefully pulled it aside. The carving swung outward like a door, revealing a hole in the wall.

A large box lay on the floor under the carving. She stepped on top of it, then climbed into the hole. Looking back, she wedged her webbed toes in a bolt loop on the back of the carving and pulled it closed.

It was utterly dark in the tunnel. Imi crawled forward, bothered less by the lack of light than by the closeness of the tunnel. She had grown quite a bit in the last year, and soon she would have trouble fitting into the small space.

When the sound of her breathing changed subtly, she knew she was near the end of the tunnel. She reached forward and touched a hard surface. Tracing her fingertips over it, she found the bolt and slid it open.

The hatch became visible as it opened and allowed in a faint light. She crept forward until her head was exposed. The inside of a wooden cupboard surrounded her. She paused to listen, then crawled farther forward so she could put her eye to the crack between the cupboard doors. The narrow room before her was empty and dim. Grabbing the frame of the hatch, she pulled herself out of the tunnel, unlatched the cupboard doors and stepped out.

She went straight to the door of the room and peered through the little spy-hole in its center. It was high up, and she had only recently been able to reach it. Before she had been forced to open the door a crack to check outside.

The passage beyond the door was empty. Satisfied, she turned to regard the room. The walls on either side were a mass of pipes. The end of each flared outward and were shaped like ears. Her father had told her long ago that he had a device that allowed him to listen into other people's conversations. He had never shown her this room, however: she had found it herself.

What he *had* shown her, years before, was the hole behind the carving in her room. He'd told her she was to hide there if the palace was attacked by bad people. She didn't know whether he feared attack by landwalkers or from bad Elai. The landwalker raiders that had robbed and attacked Elai in the past couldn't enter the city. They couldn't hold their breath long enough to swim along the underwater entrance.

If her father hadn't meant for her to discover the room, she reasoned, he wouldn't have shown her the tunnel behind the carving. For years now she had been venturing here every few weeks to listen in on conversations in and out of the palace.

Through the device she had learned a great deal about many important people, and that people in different parts of the city lived very different lives. Sometimes she envied the other children she overheard. Sometimes she didn't.

Though she knew her father used this room, he had never discovered her here. She was also lucky that Teiti had never woken and found her missing, or caught Imi entering the hole behind the carving.

Moving to one of the pipes, she put her ear to it. The voices that came whispering down the tube were quiet, but soon her hearing adjusted and she began to make out the words.

"... *not* marry him, mother! He is more than *twenty* years older than me!"

It was the voice of her cousin, Yiti. Imi frowned. Had she chosen the wrong pipe? No, she was definitely listening to the one that came from the jewellers' cave. She put her ear back to the opening.

"You will do as your father tells you, Yiti," a woman replied calmly. "You will marry him, have his children, and when he dies of old age you will still be young enough to enjoy yourself. Now have a look at this one. Isn't it pretty?"

"Young enough? I will be an old crone! Who will want me then?"

"You will be no older than I am now."

"Yes. An old crone with nothing to . . ."

Imi pulled away from the pipe. Though she sympathized with Yiti, she couldn't spend the whole night doing so. Her cousin and aunt must be visiting the jewellers' cave in order to buy something for the wedding.

She had tried the pipe to the jewellers' cave first because it was one of the places the traders might go to sell their wares. There was a good chance they'd talk about sea bells.

But they weren't there. She considered where else they might be. At home, perhaps. Moving to a pipe that came from one of the trader's homes, she listened carefully.

The pipe offered only silence. She tried a few more homes and even the Main Room of the Palace, but though she heard the voices of other members of the traders' families, or their servants, she heard nothing from the traders themselves.

Frustrated, she selected pipes at random. After hearing countless snatches of conversation, she caught a laugh that sounded much like one of the traders. It was a good laugh. One that put people at ease. Which was probably useful to a trader, she realized suddenly. He wanted people to relax, and relaxed people bought things. She'd noticed that about her aunt. If Teiti was annoyed or unhappy when she was at the market, she hardly looked at the wares in the stalls. If she was relaxed, she was much more likely to buy Imi a treat.

". . . wager?"

"Yes. Ten."

"Twenty."

"Twenty, eh? Matched!"

"You?"

A sigh. "Out."

"Settled? Yes? Turn."

There was a triumphant chuckle, and a groan, then the light sound of corrie shells clinking against each other. She recognized the voices of the traders she'd overheard, plus a few more. They were playing squares, she guessed.

For several more rounds the traders' comments related to their gaming, then they took a break to eat a late-night snack and drink drai. They began to talk of their families. She waited patiently for the talk to turn to their profession.

"Gili says he saw raiders off Xiti Island three days ago."

"Not raiders," a rough voice said. "Divers."

Several of the traders cursed.

"Knew we shouldn't have waited."

"It was a gamble we had to take. It takes time for sea bells to get big."

"And a lot less time for the landwalkers to steal them."

"Thin, pale-skinned thieves!"

Imi's heart skipped a beat. So the sea bells were somewhere near Xiti Island . . .

"Steal?" The one with the easy laugh gave a humorless chuckle. "It's not stealing if nobody owns it. Nobody owns anything they can't defend. We can't even defend our own islands."

"Huan made us the people of the sea. All treasures of the sea belong to us."

"Then why doesn't the goddess punish these divers? Why doesn't she punish the raiders? If she means for us to have all the treasures of the ocean, she would stop the land-walkers taking them, or make us capable of stopping them."

"Huan wants us to take care of ourselves."

"How do you know that?"

"Either she means for things to be this way, or we have made some error."

Imi sighed with frustration. *Stop talking about the gods!* she thought. *Talk about the sea bells again.* But the conversation fragmented into two different discussions.

"We should never have put aside so much of our knowledge of metallurgy. Or we should trade goods for swords from the mainland."

". . . lone swimmer might succeed where a group would not. The harvest was small, but better than . . ."

"What's the use? They rust away in . . ."

". . . dangerous. What if . . ."

". . . you care for them properly. You need to . . ."

". . . time it well. The right weather conditions . . . harder to see below the . . ."

". . . surface with something to prevent corrosion. The landwalkers . . ."

". . . won't dive during bad weather."

Imi's mind was spinning from the effort of deciphering the different conversations. The trouble was, she wanted to hear both. The traders' discussion of how a lone Elai might swim in and take some of the sea bells excited her, but she was also intrigued by the other traders' interest in trading with landwalkers.

A distant tapping caught at her attention. She reluctantly pulled away from the pipe, then felt her heart constrict as she realized she was hearing footsteps drawing nearer. She leapt away from the pipe and dove into the cupboard. Just as she pulled the doors closed she heard the sound of the main door opening. She froze.

Looking between the cupboard doors, she felt a thrill of apprehension as she recognized the broad shoulders of the man strolling up to the pipes. At the same time she could not help smiling with fondness. Her father was humming to himself. She recognized the song as a popular new tune by Idi, the beautiful new head of the palace singers.

He bent to listen at the pipe that led to the singers' cave. Imi watched, her heart racing. He was only a few steps away. Only the cupboard doors stood between them.

After a moment he straightened, smoothed his waist wrap, then swaggered out of the room.

Breathing a sigh of relief, Imi turned around. She grasped the frame of the hatch and pulled herself into the tunnel. Only when she had reached the other end did her heart stop racing.

She slipped out of the tunnel quietly, pushed the carving into place, and tiptoed back to her pool. Moving carefully to avoid splashing, she slipped into the water and felt the comforting coolness as it surrounded her.

*I know where the sea bells are now,* she thought. *All I have to do is find a way to get away from Teiti and my guards, and slip out of the city. There are only two ways out of the city: the staircase to the lookout and the Main Pool . . . When did I decide I'd go, rather than send someone?*

It wasn't until the next morning that she began to wonder why her father had been eavesdropping on the singers' cave.

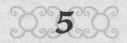

# 5

The old storehouse was full of tantalizing smells. The odors were of wooden shipping trunks and straw mixed with the variety of goods they had contained, spiced with the salty tang of the sea breeze coming in from the docks a few streets away.

In one room the pungent odor of hroomya, the dye that produced an intense blue, overwhelmed all other scents. In another the warm smell of oiled leather dominated. One room was highly perfumed, while another's stained floor reeked like a drink house. Goods from all lands of Northern Ithania had been stored here, from places Auraya had never seen.

A knocking brought her out of her reverie. She realized she had wandered far down the corridor and hastily turned back. As she reached the hall in which the former owner had conducted his business with customers, she stopped. *Am I ready to do this?*

She took a deep breath and made herself walk over to the main doors.

*As ready as I'll ever be,* she told herself. *All I can do is try to keep any less pleasant consequences as small as possible.*

She straightened as she reached the heavy wooden doors. Grasping the handles, she pulled them inward. They parted and swung open with a satisfyingly impressive creak. Auraya smiled at the woman in Dreamweaver robes standing behind them.

Raeli, Dreamweaver Adviser to the White, gave Auraya a wary look. She had never made any attempt to hide her distrust of the White, but had always been cooperative. Auraya read from the woman's mind that this strange meeting place had sparked both curiosity and wariness in the woman.

"Come in, Dreamweaver Adviser Raeli," Auraya said, beckoning.

"Thank you, Auraya of the White," Raeli replied. As she stepped inside her eyes moved around, taking in the storeroom's hall and the corridor that led away. "Why have you brought me here?"

Auraya chuckled. "You come straight to the point. I like that about you."

She indicated that Raeli should follow her, then, without waiting to see if she did, started walking slowly down the corridor. "Jarime is a large city and is growing ever larger. Until now the sick had to visit the Temple or send someone there to collect a healer priest when they needed the help of Circlian healers." She glanced over her shoulder and was pleased to see that Raeli was following. Slowing so that the Dreamweaver caught up, she gestured at the empty rooms. "It is a long journey for some. To alleviate that problem, we are going to turn this place into a hospice."

Raeli considered this news. *It is a good idea,* she thought. *It is about time the Circlians took better care of the poor living in this district. The distance to the Temple is a problem that some people overcome by consulting us Dreamweavers instead . . . Are the Circlians trying to take our custom away? Why has Auraya invited me here to tell me this? Her plans must involve Dreamweavers.* At once Raeli felt a rising suspicion.

"What do you want of us?" she blurted.

Auraya stopped at the entrance to the room that smelled of leather and turned to face the Dreamweaver. "To invite your people to join us. Dreamweavers and healer priests working together. I'd say it was for the first time, but it has happened before."

Raeli frowned. "When?"

"After the battle."

The Dreamweaver stared at Auraya. *So they admit we were useful,* she thought. *It would be nice if they thanked us. Or we got some kind of acknowledgment for our work . . . but I suppose this is an acknowledgment.* Her skepticism faltered for a moment and she felt a small thrill of hope.

Auraya looked away. "Of course, it might not work. Several healer priests have volunteered to work here with you, but they may find they are less tolerant and open-minded than they believe. The sick who come here might not accept your help. I doubt we will overcome more than a century of prejudice in a few weeks, months or even years. But," she shrugged, "we can only try."

The Dreamweaver moved into the opposite room, her nose wrinkling at whatever smell lingered there.

"I can't answer for my people. It is a decision for the Elder."

"Of course."

Raeli glanced back. "This place will need a good clean."

Auraya smiled ruefully. "Some rooms more than others. Would you like to have a look around?" She saw the answer in Raeli's mind. "Come then. I'll show you—and tell you my plans for modifications. I'd like your opinion on how we should change the water supply system."

This time, as she continued down the corridor, Raeli walked beside her. Auraya described how both cold and heated water could be piped through the building. Each room would be fitted with a drain to allow for easy cleaning. There were operating rooms for surgery, and storerooms for medicines and tools. Raeli made simple suggestions in a quiet voice and thought frequently of older, more experienced Dreamweavers who could give better advice.

When they had explored every room they returned to the main hall. Raeli was quiet and thoughtful, musing that she had always laughed at the title of Dreamweaver Adviser because she didn't believe the White would ever listen to her advice. Then suddenly she looked up at Auraya.

"Have you heard from Leiard?"

Auraya felt a jolt inside. She stared at Raeli in surprise.

"No," she forced herself to answer. "You?"

Raeli shook her head. Scanning the woman's thoughts, Auraya understood that Leiard had not just disappeared from her own life. No Dreamweavers had seen him since the battle. The Dreamweaver Elder, Arleej, was concerned about him and had asked all Dreamweavers to report to her if he was seen.

She felt a stab of worry and guilt. Had he fled everything and everyone out of fear that Juran or the gods would punish him for daring to be her lover? Or was he simply obeying Juran's orders? But Juran had said he had ordered Leiard to leave, not to disappear completely.

*He didn't order Leiard to sleep with a whore, either,* she reminded herself. She started toward the hallway and Raeli followed. *He must have known I'd read his mind the next time I saw him—whenever that might be—and see his infidelity.*

But he had decided the affair was over, so he wasn't actually being disloyal, she reminded herself. *That might have been forgivable if we'd been parted for a time, but we'd been separated for only a day.* She smothered a sigh. *Stop thinking about it,* she told herself. *It will get you nowhere.*

Opening the doors, Auraya stepped out into the sunlight. Two platten waited in front: the hired one that had brought Raeli, and the gold and white one that Auraya had travelled in. She turned to Raeli.

"Thank you for coming, Dreamweaver Adviser Raeli."

Raeli inclined her head slightly. "It was my pleasure, Auraya of the White. I will pass on your proposal to Dreamweaver Arleej."

Auraya nodded. She watched as Raeli climbed into the platten. As the vehicle trundled away a sound came to mind: the creak of a spring as an animal trap was set. *I am like a hunter,* she thought. *Knowing I need to set my traps for the good of others, but not liking it much.*

Holding a bucket out to the waterfall, Emerahl let it fill. Even with the vessel just touching the fall, the flow was strong enough to make her arm ache.

She had spent most of the last few days making the cave a more comfortable home. Felling a small tree, she had cut it up and bound lengths of wood together to make two simple beds and a screen behind which she and Mirar could attend to private matters. For those private matters, as well as for holding drinking water and other tasks, she had carved several wooden buckets out of sections of the trunk.

Since Mirar must remain inside the void, the fetching of water and gathering of food was her responsibility—but not one she minded. The forest was a bountiful place, full of edible plants, animals and fungi. Little had changed since she had last stayed here. Without magic and hundreds of years of accumulated knowledge, surviving would have been more difficult. And dangerous, too.

As many plants in the forest were poisonous as not. She had seen several beautiful venomous insects, but they lurked in nooks and holes that only a fool might stick his or her hands in. The larger predatory animals, like leramers or vorns, might have been a problem if she hadn't had magic to fend them off. She was alert to the beguiling effects of sleepvine, which used a telepathic call to lull animals into resting on its carpet of soft leaves, while slowly winding its limbs around them in a hold that eventually strangled and dismembered. Long ago she had met a plant breeder who had made himself rich selling a weaker dwarf variety to lords and ladies who had trouble sleeping.

The bucket was overflowing. She grasped the tough rope handle in one hand and picked up the second bucket. This was full of the afternoon's harvest. With both buckets swinging, she strode into the tunnel.

Emerging into the cavern, she saw that Mirar was lying on his bed, staring at the roof high above. There was an air of melancholy about him. He turned his head to look at her, then slowly sat up.

"Dinner," she said as she reached him. He said nothing. Setting the buckets down, she looked at the large, smooth boulder she had rolled into the cave two days ago. What had been a shallow natural depression in the stone was now a deep hollow. "Thank you."

He looked at her, but did not speak.

*Leiard must be in control,* she decided. It wasn't the melancholy that told her. Mirar was also prone to low moods, but he would have made a quip or comment as soon as she had appeared. Mirar was, by far, the more verbose of her two companions.

She poured some of the water into the hollow then began tearing the leaves into strips.

"You're not going to cook those, are you?"

She looked up to find him regarding the ears of fungi dubiously.

"No." She smiled. "I'll dry them later. For my new collection."

"Your collection of . . . ?"

"Medicines. Cures. Amusements."

"Ah." His brows rose. She sensed thoughtfulness, then disapproval. The latter, she guessed, was at the realization of what she meant by "amusements."

Talking to Leiard was like constantly reminding an elderly man of information he'd forgotten. No doubt he had accessed Mirar's memories about her even as she had answered, learning that she sometimes worked as a healer and had occasionally been a seller of concoctions for the entertainment of rich nobles. He could also be a bit judgmental.

It wasn't easy to make conversation with Leiard. He could not answer the questions she normally asked when she wanted to get to know somebody. Questions like: *"How long have you been a Dreamweaver? Where were you born? Parents? Siblings?"*

Her reluctance to believe he was a real person also held her back. He was probably an aberration—a personality that had somehow become grafted to Mirar's. Though Mirar could not remember why or how this had happened, or if he'd welcomed the grafting or not, he was clearly not happy with the situation. She worried that by talking to Leiard, she might strengthen his sense of identity and so make his hold on Mirar stronger, but she also doubted Leiard was going to go away if she simply ignored him.

*Perhaps I need to talk to him in a way that weakens him*

*instead. I could try to make him doubt his sense of identity. That might help Mirar regain full control.*

But what if she was wrong? What if Leiard was the real person and Mirar was just a residue of link memories—as Leiard believed? Was there any way of proving who was the true owner of that body?

She stopped working and stared at the stone depression full of water. Mirar's face was reflected in the surface, but the expression on it belonged to someone else.

*Mirar is a Wild. He has Gifts no ordinary sorcerer has. The ability to halt the aging of his body. The ability to heal perfectly, with no scarring. If he can still do these things then he must be Mirar.*

She could test him. A few exercises to prove he was a Wild might do it.

*Unless Leiard is a Wild too.*

She shook her head. While not impossible, it was too great a coincidence. What chance was there that a new Wild had been born looking just like Mirar?

Unless ... unless he *hadn't* been born looking like Mirar, but, having gained so many link memories that he was no longer sure of his identity, he had subconsciously started to change his appearance. Mirar had told her he had looked considerably different two years ago.

She shuddered at the thought. To have one's own personality slowly subverted by another's to that extent ...

Yet at the same time she felt a selfish elation. Did she really care if someone she didn't know lost their identity if it meant she got Mirar back?

*I am an evil, evil woman,* she thought.

She lifted the fungi out of the bucket and set it aside. In the bottom of the container were several freshwater shrimmi lying in a finger-width of water, their feelers still waving weakly. Drawing a little magic, she heated the water in the stone depression. When it was boiling rapidly, she grabbed the shrimmi and tossed them in the water, two at a time. They gave a high-pitched shriek as they died, but it was a quicker death than letting them slowly suffocate in the air.

Leiard recoiled slightly, then leaned closer. She sensed a sudden lightening of his mood and when he looked up at her and smiled she knew Mirar was back.

"Mmm. Dinner looks good. What's for dessert?"

"Nothing."

He pouted. "I sit here slaving over the cookware all day and you can't even find me a bit of fruit or honey?"

"I could get you some flame berries. I've heard they're quite sweet—on the tongue."

He grimaced. "No, thank you. I prefer to be blissfully unaware of my intestines and their function."

She lifted the shrimmi out of the water then added the shredded leaves. They wilted quickly. When they were cooked to her satisfaction, she picked up two wooden plates and divided the meal. From jars nearby she took some salt and toasted nuts and sprinkled them over the vegetable—a little seasoning for a bland but nutritious dish.

Mirar accepted a plate and ate with his usual enthusiasm. This was one habit Leiard also exhibited. They both appreciated food. Emerahl smiled. There was something lacking in a person who didn't enjoy good food.

"What else did you do while I was out?" she asked.

He shrugged. "Thought. Talked to myself." His nose wrinkled. "Argued with myself."

"Oh? Who won?"

"I did, I think."

"What did you argue about?"

He peeled a shrimmi and tossed its shell into a bucket. "Who owns this body."

"What did you conclude?"

"I do." He looked down. "I recognize it. You recognize it. Therefore it must be mine."

She smiled. "I thought I'd come up with a way to prove that today. If you could prove you were a Wild, you would know that your body was yours."

He chuckled. "And?"

"What if Leiard is a new Wild who has been infected with your link memories and you have been using his powers to change his body to make it look like your own?"

"Infected?" He looked hurt. "That's not a flattering way to look at it."

"No," she agreed. She met his eyes and held them.

He looked away. "It is possible. I don't know. I wish I could remember."

She sensed his frustration and felt sympathy. Then she felt a flash of inspiration. "Memory. Perhaps that is the key. You must regain those memories you've lost in order to know who you are."

Mirar looked uneasy. "If all I am is a manifestation of link memories there will be nothing to regain."

Standing up, she began to pace back and forth. "Yes, but if you are not, you will have memories that Leiard can't possibly have."

"Like what?"

She drew in a deep breath. "The tower dream. I suspect it is a memory of your death."

"A dream of death that proves I'm alive?" He smiled crookedly. "How would that prove this is my body? It might simply be another link memory. I might have projected the experience to another, who passed it on to others, who passed it on to Leiard."

"But neither you nor Leiard recall having this dream."

"No." He looked thoughtful. "Yet you believe I'm the source."

She sat down. "The dream grew stronger the closer I came to you. We are now far from other people, yet the dream is still vivid. I only dream it when you are also asleep."

"How could I be projecting a dream I don't know I'm having?" he asked, though from his tone she knew he already guessed the answer. He was, after all, well versed in the ways of dreams.

"We don't always remember our dreams," she reminded him. "And this is a dream you may not want to remember."

"So if I made myself remember the dream I might remember other things. Like why there is another person in my head."

"That shouldn't be so hard for the founder of the Dreamweavers."

He chuckled. "I have a reputation to live up to."

"Yes." She held his gaze. "A reputation that hasn't diminished over the last hundred years. If you are Mirar, the gods aren't exactly going to be declaring a festival day to welcome you back. It's time I started teaching you how to hide your mind. Shall we begin now?"

Nodding resignedly, he put aside his empty plate.

Dreamweaver Elder Arleej poured two glasses of ahm. She carried them to the chairs by the fire and handed one to Neeran. The old Dreamweaver accepted the drink gratefully and gulped it down.

Arleej took a sip and watched her old friend closely. He had said nothing at the news, just moved to a seat and collapsed into it. Lowering herself into the opposite chair, she set the glass aside.

"So what do you think we should do?"

Neeran pressed his hands to his face. "Me? I can't make this sort of decision."

"No. You can't. Last I recall, you weren't the leader of the Dreamweavers."

He removed his hands and gave her a withering look. "Then why do you always follow my advice?"

She chuckled. "Because it's always good."

He grimaced. "I want to advise caution, but a part of me wants us to snatch up this opportunity before it turns out to be another whim of Auraya's and she finds something else to occupy her."

Arleej frowned. Sometimes she almost regretted telling Neeran of Leiard's affair with Auraya of the White. It had lowered his opinion of Auraya. His disapproval reminded her to not be too enchanted by this White who favored Dreamweavers. When Neeran had declared Auraya was the source of Leiard's downfall, he was not far from the truth.

Though where Leiard was now, Arleej could not guess. He had disappeared after the battle and she had not been able to contact him via dream links. She had been forced to take on Jayim's training, though she hadn't regretted it yet. The boy was proving to be an adept and charming student.

Whether Auraya was the reason for Leiard's disappearance or not, it appeared she still wanted to encourage peace and tolerance between Circlians and Dreamweavers. This latest offer—to start a hospice in Jarime in which Dreamweavers and healer priests and priestesses worked together—was both startling and well-timed. Circlians had seen the good Dreamweavers had done for the wounded on the battlefield. The heathens had proven their worth to the healer priests and priestesses. It made sense that the best push toward peace and tolerance would be in the direction of healing.

"But what's the catch?" Arleej said aloud.

Neeran looked at her and smiled crookedly. "The catch?"

"Yes. Will Dreamweavers decide the Circlian way of life is better and leave us to join them?"

The old man chuckled. "Or will Circlians decide they prefer our way of life, and we'll have too many new students to teach?"

She picked up her glass, took a sip, then set it down again. "Just how closely will our people and theirs work? If they have suddenly decided that our medicines and healing methods are worthwhile, will they want to adopt them?"

"Probably. But we have never kept them a secret before."

"No. And I doubt their interest or tolerance extends to our mind-linking skills."

Neeran's nose wrinkled. "There is still a law against dream-linking in most of Northern Ithania. Dreamweavers should avoid linking in any way with their patients if Circlians are observing. I doubt the White's intention is to trick us into criminal acts so they can lock us away, but we should still exercise caution in these matters."

"Yes," she agreed. She turned to regard him. "It sounds as if you are advising me to agree to the offer."

He met her eyes, then looked away. Slowly he began to nod. "Yes. But . . . seek the agreement of the others."

"Very well. We will vote on it. I will dream link with leaders in other lands tonight." She picked up her glass and handed it to Neeran. "I will need a clear mind."

He took the glass from her, but didn't drink. Instead he looked at her, an odd expression on his face.

"I have a terrible feeling that we face a moment of great change. Either we will miss a wonderful opportunity to prove our worth to the people of Northern Ithania or we will make ourselves redundant."

Arleej shook her head. "Even if the Circlians surpass us in healing, even if they learn to heal through dreams and mind links, they can never be all that we are. Those that seek the truth will always come to us."

"Yes." He smiled and raised the glass. "Here's to link memories."

# 6

A week had not improved the mood of the Servants. Reivan found herself wondering several times a day if their coldness was directed only at her. Conversations ended when she drew near. When she approached a Servant with a question or request she was dealt with quickly and dismissively. Sometimes when she passed two Servants in a corridor, one would lean across to the other and murmur something.

She told herself she was simply not used to the Servants' ways. The Servants of the monastery she had grown up in had been quiet and reserved, but she had become accustomed to more stimulating company in recent years. The Thinkers might not have respected her, but she could always engage some of them in conversation—or at least a debate. She was used to being among livelier, friendlier people, that was all.

Dedicated Servant Drevva and the other Servants who were testing her knowledge and abilities were treating her fairly, acknowledging her strengths and not making too much of her weaknesses, even her obvious lack of Skills. The other hopeful entrants to the Sanctuary were politely friendly in that way young people were to those not of the same age.

The Sanctuary baths more than made up for her cramped little room. Cleanliness was considered essential for a Servant of the Gods, and an hour's soaking, scouring and rinsing each morning was deemed necessary for every man

and woman. Feeling refreshed, Reivan dressed in the plain
clothes the Sanctuary had provided her with, then stepped
out of the room. As she passed a doorway she overheard
a snatch of conversation from the steam-wreathed soaking
room within.

". . . ordain Imenja's pet."

"She passed the tests? I thought she was unSkilled."

"The order came from the Second Voice. I'm to allow
her through so long as she passed the other tests."

Reivan froze. *Imenja's pet?* They had to be talking about
her. None of the other entrants had any relationship with
Imenja, as far as she knew.

"I can't understand it," the first voice added. With a
shock, Reivan recognized Dedicated Servant Drevva.
"What's the point of making her a Servant when she has no
magical ability? Why not just make her a counsellor?"

Reivan's stomach sank.

"I heard it's what she asked for as reward."

"What! Being a Servant isn't something to be handed
out like sweets to a good child!"

"Hmm," a third voice said. "This makes me like her even
less. If she was meant to be a Servant, she'd have been born
with more ability."

The sound of approaching footsteps drew Reivan's attention back to her immediate surroundings. Aware that
anyone seeing her lingering by the door would suspect
her of spying—and she obviously did not need to give
the Servants any more reasons to hate her—she continued on.

Back in her room, she sat down on the edge of the bed
and sighed.

*So I wasn't being overly suspicious after all. They* are
*treating me differently. And it's because I'm unSkilled.*

Which wasn't a surprise, really. Being Skilled was what
set them apart. Just as being clever gave the Thinkers their
standing in society. It was ironic to discover that the Servants were as insecure about their superiority over others as
the Thinkers were.

*It's their weakness,* she thought. *Not a weakness I can*

*easily take advantage of, however. I'm not here to best the Servants at some challenge. I'm here to join them.*

The footsteps of someone in the passage outside her door suddenly stopped, and she saw something slide under her door. Rising, she stooped to pick it up.

It was a small scroll, slightly squashed where it had been forced under the door. She chuckled as she saw it was addressed to "Servant Reivan Reedcutter." *I'm not a Servant yet,* she thought, amused.

Turning the scroll over, she felt her amusement evaporate as she saw the seal of the Thinkers. Breaking it, she spread open the scroll and began to read.

> *Servant Reivan Reedcutter*
>   *It has been reported to us that you have entered the Sanctuary with the intent to become a Servant. Since this requires the full dedication of your time, assets and life to the gods, clearly you cannot fulfil the requirements of a Thinker. A man cannot be ruled by two masters. Your membership has been revoked.*
> *Prime Thinker Hitte Sandrider*

Reivan realized her heart was racing. She muttered a curse. If she didn't pass the tests and become a Servant she would leave the Sanctuary with no home, few assets and no legal means to earning an income from anything but menial tasks. She was risking her future—her life, even—on tests that she could not possibly pass.

*No,* she thought, taking a deep, calming breath. *Imenja has kept her word. She has ordered Drevva to ignore my lack of magical ability. I just have to hope I passed the other tests.*

A knock came from her door. She slipped the letter under her mattress then turned to open the door. Dedicated Servant Drevva stood in the passage, holding out a bundle of black cloth.

"Put this on and come to my room," she ordered.

Reivan closed the door and let the bundle unfold. It was a Servant's robe. Her heart jolted into rapid beating again and her hands shook as she quickly changed into it. Smoothing the cloth, she wondered how she looked in it. Did it suit her? Did it give her the look of authority she had admired in other Servants?

There was no star pendant of Servitude to go with it. That would be given to her when she finished her noviciate.

*I still have so much to learn,* she thought. *They're not going to make it easy for me, but perhaps that is for the best. Becoming a Servant shouldn't be easy. I need to prove I'm worthy of this.*

She straightened. *And I* will *prove it. Even if just to justify Imenja's decision.*

Holding on to that feeling of determination, she left her room. Other entrants were dressed in the black, excitedly running up and down the passage and knocking on each others' doors. One saw her and grinned. She smiled back.

This chaos quickly resolved into a line of black-robed entrants heading to Drevva's room. The Dedicated Servant was waiting outside her door. She looked at each of them closely, then nodded.

"It is time," she said. Turning, she led them down the passage to the main corridor, then began to ascend.

Reivan could not help thinking of Drevva's words in the baths as she followed the group. She felt vaguely betrayed. Until then Reivan had thought the woman the least unfriendly of the Servants she'd met. Drevva had hidden her true feelings well.

Their journey took them steadily uphill. The Lower Sanctuary was a maze of buildings but the corridor cut a straight line through them. Finally they reached the white rendered walls of the Middle Sanctuary. Drevva left them standing in a line before a narrow door through which she disappeared.

One by one the soon-to-be Servant-novices entered the room. When Reivan drew close enough to see through the door she caught glimpses of a large room with black walls. Black tiles covered the floor. Her heart began to race.

*This is the Star Room!*

She was about to enter the place where the most arcane

of ceremonies were held. The place where the Voices communed with the gods. Inside she could see dark-skinned Dekkans from the jungles of the south; pale-skinned, tall men and women of the desert races of Avven; broad-faced, sandy-haired people of Mur, and some that must have mixed bloodlines. All wore black robes. All would witness her become a Servant-novice. Reivan realized she was chewing her fingernails—an old habit from her childhood—and forced her hands back to her sides.

The youth in front of her stepped into the room. With her view now unblocked, Reivan could see the room properly. It had five walls. A channel of silver set into the floor formed the lines of a star, its points meeting the corners of the room. At its center stood a familiar figure. She felt her heart lift.

*Imenja.*

The Voice held out a hand to the young man, palm outward, fingers spread, and spoke the ritual words. He nervously placed his hand against hers. Reivan heard him murmur something, then Imenja's reply. Then the Voice made the sign of the star over her chest and the young man followed suit. He bowed his head and hurried away to join the small group of new Servant-novices standing nearby.

Imenja looked up at Reivan, smiled and beckoned.

Taking a deep breath, Reivan walked into the room with what she hoped was dignified grace. She stopped before the Voice. Imenja's smile widened.

"Reivan of the Thinkers," she said. "To you we owe much, but that is not why you are here today. You stand before me now because you wish to serve the gods before all else, and because you have proven yourself worthy of the task." She held out her hand. "Do you swear to serve and obey the gods above all else?"

Reivan pressed her palm lightly against Imenja's.

"I swear."

"Then from this moment you will be known as Servant-novice Reivan. You are welcome among us."

Their hands parted. Reivan was aware of every sound, every shuffle of feet and smothered cough from the watching Servants. Imenja made the sign of the star. Reivan's hand moved through the symbolic gesture as if it had a mind of its own. She bowed her head and stepped away. Her legs felt weak and shaky as she moved to stand with the other young Servant-novices.

"Today eight young men and women have chosen to dedicate their lives to the gods," Imenja said, her voice calm. "Welcome them. Teach them. Help them realize their potential. They are our future."

As she moved out of the center of the star, sounds began to fill the room. Servants stepped away from the wall, their sandals scraping and slapping on the floor. Some approached the new Servant-novices, who appeared to know them. The rest gathered into knots of discussion and voices echoed within the walls. To Reivan's dismay, Imenja strode to the door and disappeared.

She did not know what to do next, and when nobody stepped forward to instruct her she stood still, watching the people around her. None looked at her. She was surprised to feel a pang of loneliness.

Seeing several Servants leave the room, she decided she could probably slip away, too. She began to wander in the direction of the exit, hoping it would not be considered rude of her to leave.

"Servant-novice Reivan."

The voice was male and unfamiliar. Reivan turned to find a rather handsome Dedicated Servant approaching. He was Nekaun, one of the few whose name she had taken note of during the war. *It is always easier to remember the names of good-looking people,* she mused.

He smiled patiently as she respectfully made the sign of the star. "Welcome to the Sanctuary, Reivan," he said. "I am Nekaun."

She inclined her head. "Thank you, Dedicated Servant Nekaun."

"You will make a good Servant."

There was no hint of derision in his voice. She managed a smile, though she feared it looked more like a grimace.

"I hope so."

A frown creased his forehead. "I'm guessing you feel you don't fit in. Am I right?"

She gave a shrug. "I suppose so."

"Don't try too hard to do so," he told her. "Imenja didn't choose you because you're like everyone else."

She opened her mouth to reply, but couldn't decide on the right words to say. Nekaun smiled. Her heart skipped a beat.

*By the gods, he is even more good-looking close up,* she thought. Suddenly she didn't know what to say, but it didn't matter, as he was now looking around the room.

"So much chatter. Do you know what they're talking about?"

She shook her head automatically, then smiled as she realized she did know. "Who the next First Voice will be?"

He nodded. "They haven't stopped gossiping since we got back. It's only been a week and already I fear for my sanity." He shook his head, but there was a gleam in his eyes that belied his pained expression.

"I expect you'll all be trying hard to impress the rest of us in the next few weeks," she said boldly. Then she felt her face flush. *Am I flirting?*

"Am I that transparent?" He chuckled. "Of course I am, but do not think the reason I approached you was solely to gain your favor. I do wish you well, and I will be watching your progress with interest."

She felt herself relax a little at his frankness, though she was not sure why. "That's just as well. Since I am only a Servant-novice, I will not be voting, and you could hardly be seeking to raise your popularity in the Sanctuary by welcoming *me* so openly."

At once she regretted her words. *Silly girl. If you keep telling him you're unpopular he'll decide you're right and never talk to you again.*

He laughed. "I think you underestimate your position here. Or you are overestimating the power of jealousy to sway a vote. Imenja favors you. When the Servants have finished sulking about that, they will remember who brought you here. When that happens, you will have a whole new range of problems to overcome."

She could not hold back a bitter laugh. "Thanks for the reassuring words."

His shoulders lifted. "Just a friendly warning. Now is not the time to be complacent, Reivan. If Imenja intends to make you her confidant and counsellor—which I suspect she does—you will need to learn more about the Sanctuary than just law and theology. You will . . ." His gaze flickered over her shoulder. "It was pleasant talking to you, Reivan. I hope I have the chance to again."

"As do I," she murmured. He walked away. Looking over her shoulder, Reivan saw another Dedicated Servant staring at Nekaun.

*Interesting. I wonder what that was about? Is it one of the things he thinks I need to learn about in addition to law and theology?*

To her surprise, the suggestion that internal conflicts existed within the Sanctuary had sparked her curiosity. She looked at the faces around her with new interest. It would help if she knew their names.

*It is time I found out.*

Mirar woke with the distinct feeling that it was too early to be waking up. Then he heard gasping and alarm chased away the last dregs of sleep. He sat up, opened his eyes and created a spark of light.

Emerahl was propped up on one elbow, a hand to her chest as she forced her breathing to slow. She gave him a pained, accusing look.

"The dream?" he asked.

She nodded, then sat up and swung her legs over the edge of her bed.

"You?"

He shook his head. "Nothing. Are you sure I'm the one projecting them?"

"We woke up at the same time," she pointed out.

"Probably because you woke me."

She glared at him. "You're not taking this seriously."

He drummed his fingers against the frame of his bed. "I have no trouble controlling the dreams I'm aware I'm having. A forgotten dream is either extremely significant or completely insignificant." He rested his elbows on his knees, then his chin on his fists. "If I was my own patient, I would dream link with him. I'd encourage him to reveal and confront the dream by nudging him into it, and if I had seen snatches of it previously, that would be even easier."

"You want me to link with you?"

He looked at Emerahl. There had been the slightest hint of reluctance in her voice.

"Only if you are comfortable with it."

"Of course I'm comfortable with it," she said defensively. "You've rescued me often enough. It's time I returned the favor."

He smiled crookedly. "It is. Do you remember how to dream link?"

"Yes." She pursed her lips. "I'm a little out of practice."

"We'll manage," he assured her. He lay down again. "I'll link with you in the dream state. Once the connection is made, show me a little of what you've been dreaming. Not all of it. Your memory of it should act as a trigger in mine to start the original dream. If it *is* mine."

He closed his eyes. Emerahl's bed creaked as she lay down. For a while she tossed and turned. At one point she muttered darkly about not being able to get to sleep now that he needed her to, then her breathing began to slow and deepen. He let himself sink into a dream trance.

The state of mind he sought hovered between unfettered dreaming and conscious control. In that state he was like a child playing with a toy boat in a stream. The boat was his mind and it went wherever the current took it, but he could only direct it with gentle nudges or by stirring the water, though he could simply pick the boat up if it ventured where he did not want it to go.

*Emerahl,* he called. A long silence followed, then a groggy mind touched his.

*Mirar? Hmm, I am definitely out of practice. Shall I show you the dream?* she asked.

*Take your time,* he said. *No need to hurry.*

Instead of calming her, his words stirred a mixture of anxiety and agitation. Flashes of thought and images escaped her defense. He saw a scene that was unfamiliar in detail, but familiar in context. A sumptuous room. Beautiful women. Not so good-looking men in fine clothing appraising the women.

At the same time he sensed her desire to hide something from him, lest he be disappointed in her. He had seen enough to comprehend what that was, and felt a flash of anger. She'd done it again. She'd sold her body to men. Why did she do this to herself?

Then the familiar presence of another stirred in the back of his mind.

*She is a whore?* Leiard's surprise at this news was tainted with disapproval.

*She has been, from time to time,* Mirar replied defensively. *Always out of necessity.*

*And you . . . you have rescued her from that life before.*

*Yes.*

Mirar realized he had drawn away from Emerahl's mind. He had left the dream-trance state and was fully awake. From the other bed he heard a sigh, then the sound of the bed creaking.

"Mirar?" Emerahl murmured.

Drawing in a deep breath, he sat up and created a light. She was sitting on the edge of the bed, her shoulders drooping. Looking up, she met his eyes then looked away.

"You did it again," he said.

"I had to." She sighed. "I was being hunted. By priests."

"So you became a *whore*? Of all things, you had to choose such a demeaning . . ." He shook his head. "With your ability to change your age, why resort to that? Why not change into an old crone? Nobody would look twice at you? It's got to be easier to hide as an old woman than a beautiful—"

"They were looking for a crone," she told him. "An old

woman healer. I couldn't sell cures. I had to earn money somehow."

"Then why not be a child? Nobody would suspect a child of being a sorceress, and people would feel compelled to help you."

She spread her hands. "The change wastes me. You know that. If I'd gone back so far I'd have been too weak to fend for myself. The city was full of desperate children. I needed to be someone the priests wouldn't want to look at too closely. Someone whose mind they wouldn't attempt to read."

"Read?" Mirar frowned. "Priests can't read minds. Only the White can."

She looked up at him and shook her head. "You're wrong. Some can. One of the children I befriended overheard a conversation between priests about the one hunting me. They said he could, and that he was looking for a woman whose mind was shielded. The child wasn't lying."

Mirar felt his anger waver. If the gods could give the skill to the White, why not to a priest hunting a sorceress? He sighed. That did not make what she had done any less infuriating.

"So you became young and beautiful. A fine way to avoid drawing attention to yourself."

She looked up at him and he saw her pupils enlarge with anger. "Are you suggesting I did it out of vanity? Or do you think I'm greedy, that I could not get enough of fine dresses and gold?"

He met and held her eyes. "No," he said. "I think you could have avoided that life if you'd truly wanted to. Did you even try anything else?"

She did not answer. Her expression told him she hadn't.

"No," he said. "It is as if you are drawn to it, though you know it is harmful. I worry about you, Emerahl. I worry that you nurse some unhealthy need to hurt yourself. As if . . . as if you are punishing yourself out of . . . out of self-loathing, perhaps."

Her eyes narrowed. "How *dare* you. You tell me it's

harmful and disapprove of me resorting to it again, but you have never hesitated to buy a whore's services. I heard you once boast that you were such a regular customer at a particular whorehouse in Aime that they let you have every third night free."

Mirar straightened. "I am not like their regular customers," he told her. "I am . . . considerate."

"And that makes it different?"

"Yes."

"How?"

"Other men are not so considerate. They can be brutal."

"And I can defend myself."

"I know, but . . ."

"But what?"

He spread his hands. "You're my *friend*. I don't want you to be unhappy."

"I don't find it as miserable an existence as you think I do," she told him. "It's not the most enjoyable profession a woman can take—though some women do find it suits them well—but it's also not the worst. Would you rather I'd sat in the gutter, begging, or worked in some sewer or dump all day for a scrap of bread?"

"Yes," he said, shrugging.

She leaned forward. "I wonder what Leiard thinks." She looked into his eyes searchingly. "What do you think, Leiard?"

He had no time to protest. By addressing Leiard, she freed the other mind. Mirar found he had no control of his body; he could only observe.

"I think Mirar is a hypocrite," Leiard said calmly.

Emerahl smiled with satisfaction. "Really?"

"Yes. He has contradicted himself many times. He told me months ago that he did not want to exist, but now it appears he does."

She stared at him. "He did?"

"Yes. You believe that he is the real person, and I am not. So now he does too."

Her gaze wavered. "I'm prepared to accept that the opposite may be true, Leiard, but you must prove it."

"And if I can't? Would you sacrifice me in order to keep your friend?"

It was a long time before she replied. "Would you like it better that way?"

Leiard looked down at the floor. "I am of two minds." He smiled briefly at the unintended joke. "It might benefit others if I no longer existed, but I find I do not like the former leader of my own people. I am not sure if it would be wise to inflict the world with his existence again."

Her eyebrows rose, then she surprised both Mirar and Leiard by bursting into laughter.

"Looks like I'm not the only person here who hates themself! Are you casting your own shadows on me, Mirar?"

Mirar gasped with relief as control returned. Emerahl gave him an odd look.

"You're back?"

"Indeed."

"Saying your names does it. Addressing one or the other. Interesting." She looked up. "Why didn't you tell me this before?"

He shrugged. "You didn't address Leiard often. That left me in control most of the time."

"How am I supposed to help you if you aren't telling me everything?"

"I prefer being in control."

Her eyes narrowed. "Enough to destroy another person's mind?"

He did not answer. He had given her enough reasons to distrust him already tonight. She would not believe his answer, and he was not sure he'd believe it either.

"I'm going back to sleep," she announced. "And I don't want to be interrupted."

Lying down, she rolled over. Her back seemed to admonish him.

"Emerahl."

She did not reply.

"Priests can't read minds. They can communicate via their rings, but no more. You may have encountered an unusually Gifted priest, or the gods may have given him the skill, but once you were away from him you had no reason to—"

"Go to sleep, Mirar."

He shrugged, lay down and hoped she'd have forgiven him by the morning.

# 7

As the platten slowed again, Danjin let out a long sigh.

"To think that I used to enjoy the Summer Festival," he muttered. "How do the priests and priestesses endure this?"

Auraya chuckled. "We allow four times as much time to get anywhere as we normally do. Haven't you encountered festival crowds before?"

"On foot," he said. "Revellers don't block the streets where I live—or surround and stop every Temple platten when it passes."

She smiled. "We can hardly complain about that when their intention is to make a donation."

The clink of a coin in the platten's donation box emphasized her point.

Danjin sighed again. "I'm not complaining about that. I just wish they'd leave their donation at the Temple like everyone else, instead of holding up Temple plattens."

"Donate at the Temple like the wealthy and important?" she asked. "Poor drunken folk rubbing shoulders with rich drunk folk?"

His nose wrinkled. "I suppose we can't have that." He paused, then his eyes brightened. "There should be a donation day for wealthy donators and another for the rest."

She shook her head. "If there was, there would be such a large crowd in the Temple you'd never be able to leave the grounds. When people started approaching plattens years ago it was because the Temple was too crowded. It would be worse now." She shrugged. "Drunken revellers have always been gripped by a spontaneous need to give us money or gifts. It's hard to discourage them and trying usually means a longer delay. That's why we had the donation boxes attached to our platten. It is the best solution."

"But what would we do if we had to get somewhere urgently?"

"I'd lower the cover and ask them to clear the road."

"Would they? Half of them are drunk and delirious."

She laughed. "Yes, they are. It is a celebration, after all." Tugging aside the flap, she peered outside. "It's so heartening to see so many happy people. It reassures you that not everyone died in the war, and that people can be cheerful again."

Danjin subsided into his seat. "Yes, I suppose you're right. I hadn't thought of it like that. I guess I am too impatient."

Abruptly the platten began moving faster. It turned and the sound of coins entering the boxes ceased. Danjin lifted the platten flap on his side of the vehicle.

"At last," he muttered. "We've reached civilization."

On either side were mansions of the rich. The road to the Temple was the one thoroughfare the city guard kept clear of revellers. Instead it was filled by a long line of highly decorated platten. The wealthy disdained donation boxes, preferring instead to make a great show of their personal visits to the Temple.

"There's the Tither family," Danjin said, concern in his voice. "Look at the size of those trunks! They can't afford to be giving so much away!"

Auraya peered over his shoulder. Extending her senses she read the minds of the old couple in the Tither platten.

"The first trunk is full of pottery, the second of blankets and the third is oil," she told him. "Fa-Tither carries a modest amount of gold."

"Ah." Danjin sighed in relief. "It is all show then. I hope the gods do not mind."

Auraya laughed. "Of course not! They have never demanded or expected money from their followers. People came up with the idea themselves. We've told people that sacrificing income to the gods doesn't guarantee a place at their side after death, but they still do it."

"Just in case." Danjin chuckled. "The Temple would find it difficult if they didn't, though. How else would they feed, clothe and house priests and priestesses—and undertake charitable projects?"

"We'd work something else out." Auraya shrugged. "There are other benefits to the tradition, too. One of the farmers in my village gives most of his earnings to the local Temple in summer, then asks for most of it back when he needs it in winter. He says he'd spend it too fast otherwise, and that putting it in the care of the priest is his best protection against robbery."

"Because priests are likely to be more Gifted than anyone else," Danjin said.

He looked more relaxed now, Auraya noted. They had come from the hospice, in one of the poorer districts of the city. As a member of the city's upper class, he had good reason to be uneasy there. If he had been alone, dressed as he was, he would probably have been robbed.

At this time of year he had even more reason to be cautious. The Summer Festival was also referred to as the Festival of the Thieves. Robbers, muggers and pickpockets took advantage of worshippers when they could, either waylaying them on their way to make a donation or breaking into homes in search of the savings stored in preparation for the festival.

The previous year a cunning young thief had made himself a fortune by climbing in under the Temple plattens, drilling a hole into the bottom of the donation boxes, and pocketing the coins. His first successes has inflated his confidence and on the last day of the festival, after stories of the thefts had circulated, he had been caught and beaten to death by enraged worshippers.

"We can't be far away now," Danjin muttered, peering out of the platten cover again.

Auraya closed her eyes and searched the thoughts of those around them. From the driver's mind she read that they were nearing the Temple entrance, then she caught a snatch of anger from a vehicle in front. Looking closer, she learned that the occupant was Terena Spicer, matriarch of one of the most wealthy and powerful families of the city. Auraya was amused and a little disturbed to find the woman's anger was directed at herself.

Intrigued, she watched as the woman's thoughts churned. She barely noticed when Danjin informed her that they had passed through the arch and entered the Temple. Only when the platten stopped did she break her concentration. They climbed out. The paving before the Tower was crowded with plattens. Terena Spicer hadn't emerged from her vehicle yet. Indicating that Danjin should follow, Auraya strode into the Tower.

The enormous hall inside was full of priests, priestesses and the usual crowd of wealthy families talking and gossiping after having deposited their donations. As always, the entrance of a White sent a thrill of excitement through the crowd. Auraya kept her pace swift and her eyes on the room where the donations were presented. Despite this, a man stepped forward, intending to intercept her. To her relief, a priestess moved into his path to prevent him.

Danjin followed, full of unspoken questions. She considered stopping to explain, but there was too little time. As she neared her destination, she briefly looked into the minds of those within the donation room. A family had just made their contribution and were about to leave. She opened the door and stepped inside.

Her arrival caused the room to fall silent in surprise. A high priest and four lesser priests sat before a long, sturdy table. The family stood just within the door. Auraya smiled and nodded to all.

"Please continue."

"Fa Glazer was just leaving, Auraya of the White," the high priest said mildly, making the sign of the circle. "Having made a most generous donation."

"Indeed, I am," the older man of the family said with dignity. He made the formal sign of the circle with both hands, then ushered his family out. As the door closed, the priests turned to regard Auraya.

"I'm here to observe a visitor," she told them, moving to stand to one side.

The high priest nodded. Two of the lesser priests rose and, lifting the chests left by the family with magic, sent them floating through a door on the other side of the room. Auraya turned to Danjin. He could not stay here. The donations were meant to remain a secret.

"You had better wait in there," she told him, nodding at the door the trunks had been taken through. "I want you to listen, if you can."

He nodded and strode across the room to the door. It closed firmly after him. From his thoughts, she saw that he had pressed his ear to the crack of the door.

Three more visitors came and left before Terena Spicer entered. The woman's face was tight with disapproval. She strode forward and dropped a single small chest on the table with a thump, then she lifted her chin, swept her eyes imperiously over the priests and opened her mouth to begin the speech she had prepared.

As her gaze shifted to Auraya her haughty expression melted into one of horror.

Auraya smiled and nodded politely. The woman swallowed, looked away, then took a step backward from the table. The high priest leaned forward and opened the chest. His expression did not change, but the eyebrows of the other priests rose. One gold coin lay within.

Terena's mind was in turmoil. Clearly she could not give the speech she had planned now. Auraya's presence had reminded her that by protesting against a White's work she might be protesting against the gods' will. A small struggle followed, and the reason to stay silent won a narrow victory over her reason to speak out.

Auraya watched as the priests uttered their usual thanks. Terena murmured replies. The ritual over, she turned to leave.

*Not so fast,* Auraya thought.

"Ma Spicer," she said, keeping her voice gentle and concerned. "I could not help but sense your agitation on your arrival. I also sense that you intended to discuss the cause of your agitation with the priests here. Please do not hesitate to express your concern. I would not like you to harbor ill feeling toward us."

Terena flushed and reluctantly turned back. Her gaze flickered from priest to priest, then to Auraya. As the woman gathered her courage and anger, Auraya felt a wry admiration for her.

"I did intend to speak my mind," she said. "I have reduced my donation this year in protest at this Dreamweaver place you are building. Our sons and daughters should not be associating with those . . . those filthy heathens."

As the priests turned to regard Auraya expectantly, she laughed inwardly at their eagerness. This must be the most exciting event that had happened to them in days.

She walked forward until she was a few steps from the woman. "Leave us," she said to the priests. They rose and filed into the donation store room, unified in their disappointment. Once they were gone, Terena allowed her apprehension to show. She would not meet Auraya's gaze. Her hands were shaking.

"I understand your concern, Terena Spicer," Auraya said soothingly. "For a long time we have encouraged Circlians to avoid Dreamweavers. In the past this was necessary in order to reduce their influence. Now there are few who would choose that life, and Dreamweavers pose no danger to Circlians true to the gods.

"Those that do choose that life are often disillusioned or rebellious youth. Now, if these people are at all tempted by the life of a Dreamweaver, they will come to the hospice to see them. When they do they will see priests and priestesses as well. They will see that our healers are as skilled and powerful, if not more so, than Dreamweavers. If they are given a chance to compare, they will realize that one life leads to the salvation of their soul and the other does not."

The woman was staring up at Auraya now. She found herself approving, though reluctantly, of what Auraya was suggesting.

"What of those who still want the Dreamweaver life?"

"After seeing all that?" Auraya shook her head sadly.

"Then they would have sought and found it anyway. This way we can continue to seek their return. We will gently but persistently call them back, giving them no reason to hate and resist us. If they sought the *Pentadrian* way of life, however . . ." She let the sentence hang. Some people needed to hate others. Better they directed their animosity at the Pentadrians than at the Dreamweavers.

Ma Spicer lowered her eyes, then nodded. "That is wise."

Auraya lifted a finger to her lips. "As is keeping this to yourself, Ma Spicer."

The woman nodded. "I understand. Thank you for . . . easing my concerns. I hope . . . I hope I have not offended you."

"Not at all." Auraya smiled. "Perhaps you will be able to enjoy the party outside now."

The corner of Terena's mouth twitched into a half smile. "I think I will. Thank you, Auraya of the White."

She made the formal sign of the circle, then walked to the door, her shoulders stiff with pride again. Auraya of the White had confided in Terena Spicer. But then, why wouldn't she?

Auraya chuckled as the door closed behind the woman. She didn't believe for a moment that Terena Spicer would be able to resist relating what she had just heard to a few close and trusted friends. In a few days the story would be all over the city.

She moved to the side door and tapped on it. Danjin stepped out, his expression neutral. From his mind she confirmed he had heard most of what had been said.

The priests followed, a little miffed that Danjin had been allowed to eavesdrop, but trusting that Auraya had her reasons for asking him to. Auraya thanked them, then left the room.

"Are you sure you want people to know that?" Danjin murmured as they skirted the crowd and made their way toward the circular wall at the center of the hall.

"Ordinary Circlians won't accept the hospice unless they feel there is an advantage in it for us," she replied quietly.

"Plain old peace and tolerance isn't reason enough. Neither is the assumption that whatever I do is approved of by the gods."

"What if they hear of it?"

"The Dreamweavers?" Auraya smiled grimly. "They have already accepted my proposal. They voted on it, and won't go to the trouble of organizing another vote over a mere rumor. I'm hoping they're smart enough to realize that my lie about us being as skilled at healing means that we can't possibly have these intentions. If our aim was to prove ourselves better rather than equal to them, we would not set up this hospice."

"Unless your healers *become* as skilled as they. Do you really think they won't see that danger and guess at your true plan."

Auraya grimaced. "They will feel safe so long as we do not seek to learn their mind skills. By the time we do, in years to come, they will have become secure in the success of the venture and the danger will be long forgotten."

Danjin's eyebrows rose. "I hope you're right."

"So do I."

They reached the wall at the center of the hall. It encompassed a raised floor with a hole in the center through which large chains hung. To one side a staircase spiralled upward, but Auraya ignored it. She nodded at the priest standing at the bottom of the stairs. He made the sign of the circle.

Soon the chains began to move. A large disc of metal descended through the stairwell. As it passed the level of the ceiling the rest of a large iron cage slowly came into sight. The heavy chain it was suspended from extended up into the heights of the Tower. As the cage stopped the priest stepped forward and opened the door for her and Danjin to enter.

"Have you had any dreams about the hospice?" Auraya asked Danjin as the cage began to rise.

"Dreams? Do you . . . do you think they would try to find out your intentions from my dreams?" He looked appalled. "That would be breaking a law!"

"I know. So have you dreamed of this?"

Danjin shook his head.

"I have to consider the possibility that they might try. After all, I would risk it if I were in their position," she said. "I've spoken to Juran about it. I suggested that when we make a link ring to replace the ones the Pentadrians took, we include a shield for the wearer's thoughts in its properties. A shield that doesn't block my mind, of course, or there'd be no point in making the ring at all."

"So you intend for me to wear this ring?" He was unable to hide his discomfort.

Auraya resisted a smile. Since returning from the war, Danjin had enjoyed a renewed intimacy with his wife. He wasn't aware how often his thoughts drifted into reverie, and she didn't have the heart to point out that a link ring wouldn't reveal any more than she'd already read from his mind.

"Yes, the ring is for you," Auraya replied. "Though I may need you to pass it to others from time to time." The cage slowed to a stop. She opened the door and they stepped out. "Don't worry, Danjin." She winked at him. "I'll respect your privacy."

He flushed and hastily looked away. Auraya smiled and crossed to the door of her rooms.

Emerahl concentrated on Mirar's mind. At first she detected nothing, then a feeling of impatience and uncertainty touched her senses.

"I can sense you," she said. "You let your shield fall out of boredom."

He let out a sigh and rolled his eyes. "How long are we going to do this for? I'm getting hungry."

"The shield can't be temporary. You have to get to the point where it is there all the time, where you can hold it unconsciously. Now try again."

He groaned. "Can't we eat first?"

"No. Not until I can't detect your emotions at all. Do it again."

She sensed frustration, then stubbornness, then something strange happened. For a moment his emotions faded to nothing, then she sensed puzzlement. He shifted position from half-lying on the bed to sitting straight.

*Mirar never sits so . . . so symmetrically,* she thought. *He always lounges about.* Looking into his eyes she saw wariness and resignation.

"Leiard? Is that you?"

"It is I," he replied. Even the way he spoke was even and considered.

"How?"

His shoulders lifted. "I believe he wanted to not be present."

"He ran away?" She felt mirth well up inside her and let out a laugh. "Mirar fled from my lessons. Ha! What a coward!"

The corners of Leiard's lips lifted slightly, the closest he came to a smile. She sobered and considered him thoughtfully.

"I do not wish you to think I do not enjoy your company, Leiard, but I can't have Mirar playing truant like this every time he finds my lessons difficult. We are going to have to make sure he doesn't do this again."

Leiard's eyebrows rose. "How do you expect to persuade him otherwise?"

"By getting you to tell me about him. Tell me things he would not like me to hear. What terrible deeds has he been up to?"

As Leiard's expression darkened she felt a thrill of interest. Obviously there was much to tell.

"To do so would be to confess to my own . . . folly."

She blinked in surprise. "You? Folly? You do not seem the type to indulge in foolishness."

"Ah, but I have, and he will enjoy hearing me relate it, which will hardly achieve your goal."

She leaned forward, intrigued. "We can get to that later." She remembered the conversation she had overheard just before they had arrived at the cave. "Is this about a woman?"

Leiard started and frowned at her.

"He has told you."

"No. I'm a woman, remember. We sense these things. There's nothing like love to lead a man into folly. Perhaps . . ." She let her flippant tone rest. "Perhaps a woman's ear might be more sympathetic to your tale. I can't imagine Mirar would make a good listener."

Leiard let out a quiet snort. "He did not approve at all."

Mirar not approve of a woman? Interesting. "What would this woman's name be, then?"

The Dreamweaver looked up at her. His tortured expression was one she had never seen Mirar wear, and it made him look like a stranger. He considered her for a long time before he spoke again.

"You must swear to never allow another to know of it."

"I swear," she replied solemnly.

He looked down at his hands. She felt herself growing ever more tense as she waited for him to speak.

*Tell me!* she thought.

"The woman I loved . . . that I love . . ." he said, his voice barely louder than a whisper ". . . is Auraya of the White."

*Auraya of the White!* Emerahl stared at him. She felt a rush of cold, as if someone had just poured icy water over her head. The shock rendered her incapable of thinking for a moment. *One of the Gods' Chosen! No wonder Mirar did not approve!*

Now that the name had been admitted to, a dam against words within Leiard broke. The whole story flooded out: how he had been Auraya's friend and teacher when she was a child; how he had travelled to Jarime and been enchanted by the woman she had become; how she had made him Dreamweaver Adviser to the White, and the night of "folly" before she left for Si. He told of his resignation in order to preserve their secret; the growing presence of Mirar in his mind, the danger of terrible consequences should the affair be discovered, yet being unable to stop reaching out to her in dreams. He spoke guiltily of the resumption of their affair when Auraya joined the army, then of Juran's discovery of it, of fleeing and Mirar's suggestion he take over their body. Then discovering Mirar had hidden in a brothel camp. Finally he told of the dream link which had revealed that Auraya had seen him with a prostitute and now believed he had betrayed her.

When he had finished, he lapsed into a glum silence.

"I see," Emerahl said, for the sake of saying something. She needed time to consider this incredible story. "That is quite a tale."

"Mirar was right," he stated firmly. "I endangered my people."

Emerahl spread her hands. "You were in love."

"That is no excuse."

"It is excuse enough. What I don't understand is . . . Auraya must have seen Mirar in your mind. Surely this alarmed her."

"She knew the link memories in my mind had manifested into a personality I would occasionally converse with. She did not believe Mirar truly existed. She never observed him taking control."

"I can understand her wanting to believe that. Love makes us tolerate things we might not normally stand for. Juran, surely, would not have accepted it."

Leiard shrugged. "He did. Perhaps only because I was useful to him and Mirar did not show himself capable of taking control until later."

*He obviously didn't recognize Mirar's body,* Emerahl thought. *Has Juran's memory faded that much over the last hundred years? Had Mirar looked so different as to be unrecognizable?* She shuddered as she realized how close Mirar had been to discovery. *The gods must have looked into his mind, perhaps several times, yet they didn't recognize him. Unless . . . unless the gods did, but are unconcerned because they know Leiard is the true owner of his body.*

Even so, they would not have approved of this affair between their chosen one and any Dreamweaver. Why did they allow it? Maybe they feared to lose Auraya's trust and loyalty. Maybe they expected Leiard to confirm their low opinion of Dreamweavers. Auraya may now hate them because of Leiard's "betrayal."

She frowned as something else occurred to her. "You say she discovered you with a prostitute, but Mirar was in control. Surely if she hadn't observed him in control before, she should not have recognized you. Or rather, she should have realized it was him in control—not you."

He frowned. "I had not considered that. It is . . . puzzling."

"Yes. You must be alike enough for her to recognize both of you as the same person," Emerahl said slowly. "She might have noticed differences given the chance, but at that moment she would have been so shocked by what you had done. She may have decided she didn't know you as well as she thought."

"I would not have done what he did," Leiard stated, a little defensively.

Emerahl regarded him thoughtfully. "No. You are quite unlike Mirar in that regard."

"Why do you like him when he is so despicable?"

She laughed. "Because he is. He's a rogue, there's no denying it. While his morals may be a little questionable, he is a good man." She narrowed her eyes at him. "You know that, I think."

He looked away, frowning. "I know he was once more . . . restrained when it came to women. I think time made him change. He seeks physical sensation in order to assure himself he is still alive. That he is still a physical being. Not a god."

She stared at him in surprise, disturbed by what he was suggesting. The gods had accused Mirar of pretending to be a god. Now Leiard believed Mirar behaved as he did to reassure himself he *wasn't* a god.

"I believe you when you say joining the brothel was necessity," he added. "You believed the priests were more dangerous than they were. I also wonder if you unknowingly seek the same kind of assurance that Mirar seeks. You seek a reminder that you are a physical being, not a god. Whoring—"

"Mirar," she commanded. "Break's over. Come back to me."

He stiffened, then relaxed. As his gaze focused on her again his eyebrows lowered and he smiled at her slyly.

"I'm a rogue, eh?"

To her surprise, she felt her pulse quicken. *No, that's no great surprise. Mirar has always been able to stir my blood. It seems he still can, even after all this time. Or perhaps because so much time has passed.*

She could still sense his emotions, however, and could see he was just being playful. Trying to delay her from recalling her real purpose—mind-shielding lessons. She schooled her expression.

"Enough chit-chat," she said. "I don't intend to stay in this cave forever, so unless you want to end up stuck here by yourself, eating whatever insects find their way in, you had better get back to work."

His shoulders sagged. "Oh, all right then."

# 8

The staircase went on forever. Imi's legs ached, but she set her eyes on her father's back and pushed herself on, clenching her teeth to stop herself complaining.

*He warned me,* she thought. *He said it took hours to climb up to the lookout. Then you have to come all the way down again. Next time I won't have to come back. Next time I'll swim away and come back via the Mouth.*

The tunnel echoed with the heavy breathing of the adults. Teiti looked as if she was in pain. The guards, in contrast, appeared to be enjoying themselves. Those that regularly accompanied the king to the lookout were used to the exercise. Those who watched over Imi were enjoying a rare opportunity to visit a place that only a few were allowed to see.

Teiti began to gasp in the way she had each time she had been about to ask for a rest. Imi felt both annoyance and relief. She did not want to stop, she wanted the staircase to end.

"Not long now," her father tossed over his shoulder.

Her aunt paused, then shrugged and continued on. Imi felt her heart lift with expectation. The next few minutes seemed longer than the hours behind them. Finally her father slowed to a stop. She peered around him to see they had reached a blank wall.

There was no door. Confused, she looked at the others. They were gazing up at the small trapdoor set into the roof.

Her father moved to one side, where an alcove like the

ones they had passed on the way up held several pottery bottles of water. He passed them around. Imi splashed water over her skin gratefully, then drank. The water was stale but welcome after the long climb.

She looked up at the trapdoor, noting the rusty iron brackets in the back of the door. A heavy length of wood was propped against a wall nearby. She guessed this would be slipped into the brackets to stop the door opening if raiders found the tunnel.

At a signal from the king a guard reached up and knocked on the trapdoor. She noted the pattern—two quick knocks, three spaced ones, two more rapid ones. The trapdoor lifted. Two armored men peered down at them. Beyond them was the dazzling blue of the sky.

One of the watchers moved away, then returned carrying a ladder. He lowered it into the tunnel. The king sent two guards up first, then climbed it himself. As he stepped off it he peered down at Imi, smiled and beckoned.

She set a foot on the first rung and began to climb. Her sore feet protested after the long walk, but she gritted her teeth against the pain. As she reached the top her father grabbed her waist and hauled her out. She gave a laugh of surprise and pleasure.

Her father made a rueful sound. "You're getting a bit heavy for that," he said, rubbing his back. Straightening, he sighed and looked into the distance.

Imi examined her surroundings. She was standing in a dirt-filled space between several huge boulders. They were too high for her to see over. She jumped on the spot, and managed to catch glimpses of sea and horizon.

"Perhaps if I lift her, your majesty?" one of the king's more robust guards offered.

The king nodded. "Yes. Only so long as you can manage."

The guard smiled at Imi. "Turn around, Princess."

She did as he asked and felt his large hands grip her waist. He lifted her up onto one broad shoulder and held her there.

Now she had a better view than anyone else. She could see the edge of the sea all around, she could see the islands

of Borra forming a huge ring in the blue water, and she
could see the steep rock slope of the island she was standing on stretching down toward a fringe of forest and the
white of the beach.

"Can you get to here from the beach?" she asked.

Her father laughed. "Yes, but it would not be easy. The
ground is steep and the stony surface is slippery. This peak
is sheer smooth rock for a hundred paces on either side. You
need ropes and a wall anchor to get up here."

Imi felt her stomach sink with disappointment. Her plan
to bribe and cajole her way up here at night to "admire the
stars" then to slip away and run to the beach wasn't going
to work. Yet she was also relieved. It had been a long climb
and even if the outside had been as she'd imagined—a gentle
slope down to the beach—she'd have been too tired to run.

*I'll just have to come up with another plan,* she decided.

They lingered there for half an hour, while her father
pointed out landmarks. At the mention of raiders, Imi stared
hard at the horizon. She listened to the watchers describe
what a ship looked like, noting the details in case she
should come across one on her way to the sea bells.

After a while her skin began to feel unpleasantly dry. In
the corner of her eye she saw Teiti surreptitiously nudge
her father and give him a nod. He announced it was time to
leave.

Once they had all descended into the tunnel and wet
their skin again, the guard that had lifted her suggested she
might like to ride on his back. She looked at her father eagerly. He smiled.

"Go on. Just watch you don't knock your head on the
ceiling."

She climbed on the guard's back and rested her head on
his shoulder, pretending to be sleepy. Then, as her father,
aunt and the guard began to descend the staircase, she
started to put together another plan to escape her protectors,
and the city.

The curves of the paths within the Temple gardens were gentle and flawless. Whenever Auraya viewed them from her

room in the Tower she found herself a little repelled by the
overtly planned and ordered design of the gardens. In comparison to the natural wildness of the forest next to the village she had grown up in, or the magnificent disorder of Si's
wild territory, the interlocking circles and carefully spaced
plants seemed ridiculous.

From the ground, however, there was something reassuring about the tamed regularity of the gardens. There was no
danger of being stalked by leramers or vorns, or stumbling
upon sleepvine. Nothing was left around to rot, so the air
was fragrant with flowers and fruit. The curves of the paths
created one attractive vista after another, and led a walker
sensibly to where they needed to go without the temptation
of cutting across the carefully trimmed grass.

Today Auraya was not taking a walk for pleasure, however. She and Juran were bound for the Sacred Grove.

They passed one of the many priests and priestesses who
stood guard over the grove. The man appeared to be simply relaxing on a stone bench, reading a scroll, but Auraya
knew his main task was to prevent anyone but the select few
who tended the grove—and the White—from entering.

The priest made the sign of the circle and Juran nodded
in reply. The path took Auraya and Juran through a gap in a
wall of close-grown trees, then curved to the left. There it
wound through a grove of fruit trees tended by more priests
and priestesses before it reached a stone wall.

A wooden door filled a narrow opening in the wall. As
they reached it the door swung inward. Auraya shivered
as she stepped through. Though she had visited the grove
several times the previous year she still felt a thrill of awe
whenever she entered.

Four trees grew within the circular wall. They were the
only four survivors of the hundreds of saplings planted here
a hundred years before. Two had sprung up close to one
another, and where their branches met they had twined together sinuously. Another was small and stunted. The third
appeared to be crouching close to the ground, its branches
spread wide.

The leaves and bark of these trees were so dark they

were almost black. On close inspection the white wood beneath could be seen between cracks in the bark. The dark color was highlighted by the white pebbles that covered the ground, apparently to help retain moisture in the soil. The trees were better suited to a colder climate than Hania's.

The color of the trees was strange enough, but the growth of their branches was even stranger. They had grown in weird and unnatural ways. Most of the smaller branches had small disc-like swellings along their length, and several of these had developed holes within the swellings. Other branches higher up had formed many thin twigs that had woven themselves together to form a cup, or larger swellings containing small holes. As Auraya watched, a small bird landed in one of the cups. A fledgling head appeared and the parent began to feed it.

"Did you see that?" a priest said.

Auraya turned to see a high priest speaking to a young priestess. The woman, a trainee carer, nodded.

"It has grown into the shape of a nest," she said.

"Yes. If you climbed up there and put your hand inside you would find that the wood was warm. The bird has trained the wood not just to grow into a nest, but imprinted it with the Gift to convert magic into heat."

"Why does the tree do it?"

The old man shrugged. "Nobody knows. Maybe the gods made it that way."

"I can see now why it's called the welcome tree," the woman said. "I thought it a strange name for such an ugly tree."

Auraya smiled. It was an ugly tree, but only because of the use humans had put its magically malleable wood to. When Juran had first brought Auraya here she had been amazed to learn that these trees were the source of the priest rings. The swellings on the branches would eventually be harvested, each ring containing the Gift that allowed priests to communicate with each other.

The welcome trees contained great potential, both for good and evil, but when Juran had told her of their limitations she had wondered how the Circlians found a use for them at all. The trees were hard to keep alive. Groves of them were maintained in most Circlian Temples, though only the well-guarded one in Jarime was used for growing the rings of priests and priestesses. Those that tended the trees guarded the secrets to keeping them alive and healthy.

The branches must be "trained" every day. When she had helped create her first link ring, she had needed to visit the grove early each morning and sit with the tree growing her ring for at least an hour. Despite all the effort required to make a ring, the wood lost its qualities within a few years. Priest rings were constantly being grown to replace those that were no longer effective. They were also only ever imbued with the one simple Gift of communication. More powerful Gifts could be taught, but the more magic those Gifts required, the quicker the wood lost the imprint.

The only rings that did not have these limitations were the White's rings. They had grown spontaneously from the smaller tree, which otherwise stubbornly refused to be shaped by any will but the gods."

Another elderly priest appeared at Juran's shoulder.

"Juran of the White," he said, making the sign of the circle. "Auraya of the White. Are you here to begin your task?"

"We are, Priest Sinar," Juran replied. "Where should we begin?"

The priest led them to the larger of the lone trees and indicated a twig that had sprouted from one of the main branches. Auraya smiled wryly as she remembered a similar twig she had watched slowly swell and form a ring the year before.

"This may be suitable," the old man said.

"It is, thank you," Juran replied. He looked at Auraya. "We may need a few minutes free of distraction as we begin."

The priest nodded. "I will clear the grove."

He hurried away and herded the other priests and priestesses through the door in the stone wall. When the grove was empty Juran turned to regard her, an odd, pained look on his face.

"What is it?" she asked.

He grimaced. "We must discuss something first." He paused. "How . . . Have you forgiven me?"

She blinked in surprise. "Forgiven? For wh—? Ah." Her stomach sank as she realized he was referring to Leiard. "That."

"Yes. That." He chuckled. "I would have given you more time than this before bringing the subject up, but Mairae insisted we must talk before you make this ring." He sighed. "Years ago a priestess harvesting rings here suffered a terrible personal tragedy. Anyone who wore the rings she made began to feel sad, but nobody realized what was happening until a few priests and priestesses had killed themselves and people began to wonder why."

"You're afraid the same will happen," Auraya said. She could not help smiling. "I'm not bouncing about with happiness, Juran, but I'm not suicidal either."

"How are you feeling, then?"

"I've forgiven you." As she said it she felt a wave of emotion and realized it was true. "It has worked out for the best."

"Mairae thinks I handled it badly." He frowned. "She believes there would have been no harm in . . . letting you two see each other so long as it was not publicly known."

"But you don't agree."

His shoulders rose. "She has . . . made me reconsider."

Auraya's stomach constricted. *So I would still be with Leiard if Mairae and Juran had taken some time to think about it.* She tried to imagine what it would have been like to secretly meet with Leiard, with all the White knowing about it. *It would have been embarrassing. I would not have discovered how easily Leiard's eye was caught by another woman the moment he thought he couldn't be with me.*

She sighed. "No, I'm glad it worked out this way, Juran. It makes a lot of matters less complicated. Like the hospice."

He smiled and nodded. They both looked up at the tree in silence for a moment, then Juran let out a sigh.

"So how shall we approach this shielded link-ring idea of yours?"

The river was like a ribbon of fire below, reflecting the bright colors of the dusk sky. Veece sighed at the ache in his arms. He could feel his joints creak as he tilted his wings to follow the water. He had to rest. The younger ones would not like it. They would stamp about impatiently and worry about reaching their home by the following night.

While his old body was not as limber or robust as theirs, he was still their Speaker. They would not complain if he chose to land, though they might tease him. Such was the prerogative of the young. After all, they would be old one day. They might as well get in a little teasing now, before they became the subject of it themselves.

The river dropped over a small cliff. He felt the faint touch of moisture in the air, thrown up by the waterfall. Ahead he could see another smaller fall. He flew over it, and decided he liked the look of it. If he dove off the dry rock by the edge he could become airborne again without the exhausting effort of running and flapping.

Circling around, he led the others back to the stretch of river above the fall. Landing jarred all his bones, but a moment later the pain was made worthwhile as he let his arms fall to his side and felt the ache in them ease.

"We'll stop here for the night," he declared.

Reet frowned. "May as well gather some food," he said, stalking away into the forest. Tyve hurried after, muttering something about firewood. As Veece sat down on a boulder still warm from the sun, his niece, Sizzi, crouched beside him.

"How do you feel?" she asked.

"A bit stiff," he told her, rubbing his arms. "I just need to work it out a little."

She nodded. "And what of your heart?"

He gave her a reproachful look, but she stared back unflinchingly. Sighing, he looked away.

"I feel better and I feel worse," he told her. "No longer angry, but still . . . empty."

She nodded. "It was a good thing that the Circlians did.

The markers for the graves and the monument will ensure our help and our losses are never forgotten."

"It won't bring him back," he reminded her, then he grimaced at his words. It was unnecessary to point that out and he sounded like a sullen child.

"It won't bring back anyone's sons," she murmured. "Or daughters. Or parents. That cannot be undone. Nor should it, if it meant these Pentadrians won and came to slaughter us all." She shook her head, then stood up. "I heard that the Circlians are sending priests to us. They will teach us healing, and help us defend ourselves with magic."

He snorted. "No use to us, so far from the Open."

"Not straight away," she agreed. "If you send one of our tribe to learn from them, he or she will bring back that knowledge."

"And you would like to b—"

"Veece! Speaker Veece!"

Reet and Tyve dashed out of the forest and hurried to his side.

"We found footprints," one of them panted. "Big footprints."

"*Boot*prints," the other corrected.

"Must be a landwalker."

"And they're fresh—the prints, that is."

"Can't be far away."

"Should we track him?"

They looked at Veece expectantly, their eyes shining with excitement. Ready to rush into danger, despite their experience of war. Or perhaps because of it. He could see that surviving unscathed when so many had not might give a young man a sense of invulnerability.

Then he remembered the last time a lone stranger had been encountered in Si and felt his blood turn cold.

"We should be careful," he told them. "What if this is the black sorceress, returned with her birds to take revenge on us?"

The pair went pale.

"Then we can't leave without finding out," Sizzi said quietly. "All tribes will need to be warned."

Veece considered her, surprised but impressed. She was right, though it meant they must take a terrible risk for the sake of their people. He nodded slowly.

"We best leave and return tomorrow." He looked from Reet and Tyve to Sizzi. "In full light it will be easier to track this landwalker—or landwalkers. Hopefully we will be able to confirm whether magic has been used, or those black birds are present, without having to meet them."

"What if one of us is seen?" Tyve asked. "What if it's her, and she attacks?"

"We will do our best to avoid being seen," Veece said firmly.

"Most landwalkers make so much noise they can be heard a mountain away," Sizzi added.

Reet shrugged. "It's probably just that explorer who brought the alliance proposal from the White last year. They say he's a bit mad, but he's no sorcerer."

Veece nodded. "But we cannot gamble our lives on the chance that it is. We'll leave now and find another place to stay tonight—far enough away that a landwalker couldn't reach us if he or she walked all night."

He rose and flexed his arms, then walked toward the edge of the cliff, the others following.

# 9

The domestic led Reivan down a long hall. One side was broken by archways and as Reivan passed the first gap she saw that they led onto a balcony that gave an impressive view over the city and beyond.

*I must be close to the top of the Sanctuary,* she thought anxiously.

The domestic stopped outside the last arch, turned to face her, and gestured outside. Then, without saying a word, he walked away.

Reivan paused to catch her breath—and gather her courage. She was late. The Second Voice might not *want* to punish her, but she might be obliged to.

"Servant-novice Reivan." The voice was Imenja's. "Stop worrying and come in."

Reivan moved into the archway. Imenja was sitting on a woven reed chair, a glass of flavored water in one hand. She looked at Reivan and smiled.

"Second Voice of the Gods," Reivan said. "I . . . I apologize for my late arrival. I . . . ah . . . I got . . ."

Imenja's smile widened. "You got lost? *You*?" She chuckled. "I can't believe that *you*—the one who led us out of the mines—got lost in the Sanctuary."

Reivan looked down, but could not help smiling. "I'm afraid so. It's quite . . . humiliating . . . I wonder if I should draw myself a map."

Imenja laughed. "Maybe. Take a seat. Pour yourself a

drink. We'll have company soon, and I wanted some time to talk to you first. Are you settling in?"

Reivan hesitated. "More or less."

The past few weeks flashed through Reivan's mind as she moved to the seat next to Imenja. Being accepted and nominated a Servant-novice hadn't improved her in the eyes of the other Servants.

She found glasses and a jug of water on the floor. As she drank, thirsty after her long trek up staircases and along corridors, she remembered Dedicated Servant Nekaun. His words were the only truly welcoming ones she'd heard so far.

She had taken his advice and learned all she could of the internal politics within the Sanctuary—mostly by listening to other conversations. It was not difficult when everyone was discussing which of the Dedicated Servants might become First Voice.

"What do you think of Nekaun?" Imenja asked.

Reivan paused in surprise, then remembered Imenja's mind-reading Skill. During the journey home she had gradually grown used to having her thoughts read so easily. In the time since then she must have grown unaccustomed to it again.

"Dedicated Servant Nekaun seems nice," she replied. *And nice for the eyes, too,* she added.

Imenja's mouth quirked into a crooked smile. "Yes. Ambitious, too."

"He wants to be First Voice?" Reivan felt a spark of curiosity.

"They all do, for one reason or another. Even those who can't admit it to themselves. Even those who are afraid of it." Imenja took a sip of water, then nodded.

"Afraid of becoming the First Voice?"

"Yes. They fear responsibility without end. Or perhaps responsibility that leads to an unpleasant end—since that is what it brought Kuar. It is interesting watching their inner turmoil. Their desire to be nearer the gods fights with their fear of death, which would only bring them nearer the gods. Ironic, isn't it?"

"Yes."

"Then there are those that are afraid the gods will disapprove of them if they are motivated by ambition. They know to be a Servant of the gods one must put aside one's self interest and work for their benefit, so they tell themselves they do not want the position when they actually do."

"I thought it didn't matter what the gods think. The Servants choose the First Voice from the Dedicated Servants who pass the tests of magical strength."

Imenja's eyebrows rose. "Of course it matters. Imagine being chosen by the Servants, but rejected by the gods?"

Reivan grimaced. "Not a position I'd like to be in."

"What position would you like to be in?" Imenja asked.

The question surprised Reivan. She spread her hands. "I just always wanted to be a Servant of the Gods."

"Why?"

Reivan opened her mouth to reply, but closed it again. She had been about to say "to serve the gods," but she was not sure if that was true. *I'm no fanatic,* she thought. *I'm not sure I'd sacrifice my life without some explanation of why they wanted me to.*

*Then why did I harbor this dream for so long?*

She had always admired Servants. Their dignity, their wisdom. Their magic.

*Surely this isn't just about magic. Becoming a Servant won't give me stronger Skills. Ever.*

It must be more than that. Having to leave the monastery she had grown up in because she could not become a Servant had seemed so unfair. She had wanted to stay. She had been so sure she belonged there.

"It is the way of life," she said slowly. "We are guides and teachers. We are order in a chaotic world. Through ceremonies we mark the steps of people's lives and so give them a sense of value and place."

Imenja smiled, but there was no humor in it. "You speak like a village Servant. We also rule and extract taxes. We mete out justice. We lead men and women to war."

Reivan shrugged. "We do a better job at it than the old kings did, from what I've read."

The Voice laughed. "Yes. We do. If you have plans to become a village Servant, or work in a monastery, put them aside for your later years. I have other uses for you here, for now."

Reivan felt a pang of trepidation. "Then I hope I prove as useful as you expect."

"You will eventually, I'm sure. I want to make you my Companion."

After a moment, Reivan realized she was staring at Imenja and averted her eyes. *Me? A Voice's Companion?*

It meant she would have to advise and undertake errands for Imenja. Anyone who wanted to speak to the Second Voice would have to arrange it through Reivan. She would be replacing Thar, who had died in the war. Thar had been powerfully Skilled . . .

"I don't have Skills," she pointed out. "I'm only twenty-two."

"You have intelligence. I like the way you think. You can keep to protocol, and speak other languages. You'll do well. There is one obstacle, however. You must appear to earn the position. Few here witnessed your part in the army's escape from the mines, or know how much they owe you. Those who remained here during the war do not feel your act justifies changing a rule that has been accepted for so long that it is almost a law."

Though her heart was racing and her insides felt as if they had dropped somewhere below her feet, Reivan managed to nod. "Servants must be Skilled."

"Don't be disheartened. More here are willing to give you a chance than not, and not just because I wish it to be so. They will not protest if I take you to rituals and seek your advice, just as I would a Companion, but to make it official this soon . . ." She shook her head. "It could be many months before I can do so. I know you are more than able to convince them you are worthy, but do *you* feel up to the challenge?"

Reivan nodded slowly. "If I am to serve the gods well, then I had better put myself in a position where my abilities are useful."

Imenja smiled. "Good answer. Ah. Just in time, too. Here's Shar."

As the Fifth Voice stepped onto the balcony, Reivan felt her heart skip a beat. He may have been the least powerful Voice, but he was the most beautiful. His skin was unusually pale, and long, sun-bleached blond hair spilled down his back. His emerald eyes moved from Imenja to her.

"Ladies," he said, bowing.

"Do you mind if Reivan remains here to advise me?" Imenja asked him.

"Not at all." He smiled and bowed politely. She felt her face warm.

"Thank you, holy one," she replied, her voice coming out quieter than she had intended.

"Are we the last to arrive?" a new female voice asked.

They all turned as the other two Voices entered the balcony. Genza was as dark and sharp-featured as the birds she bred. Vervel, in contrast, was stocky and looked to be twenty years her senior. Both had been Servant-warriors during their mortal years, despite having powerful Skills.

"I'm afraid you are," Shar told them.

Genza looked at Reivan and nodded. "Welcome to the Sanctuary, Reivan Reedcutter."

Reivan felt her face grow even warmer. She murmured thanks. Two male Servants entered the room. She recognized Genza's and Vervel's Companions. The pair nodded to her respectfully, and she returned the gesture.

As the five new arrivals settled into woven reed chairs, Reivan felt her confidence wither. In the company of all the Voices and their powerful Companions, she felt unimportant and a little pathetic. She resolved to say as little as possible, and concentrate on listening. As if obliging her, the Voices began discussing the Dedicated Servants eligible to become First Voice.

To her surprise, they debated the merits and failings of each with an enthusiasm that was almost frightening. No aspect of any candidate's nature was spared their uncompromising scrutiny. She quickly realized why this was important to them. Whoever was chosen would be their leader.

They might be working with that person for centuries, or even millennia.

*I wonder why Imenja can't change to First,* she thought suddenly. *She seems a good enough leader to me.*

After some time two domestics arrived with a platter of dried fruits, nuts and other delicacies, and a jug of water. The conversation turned to minor matters. Reivan shivered as a cool breeze touched her skin. Looking over the balcony rail, she saw that the sun was near setting.

"There have been protests against holding the Rite of the Sun during a month of mourning," Vervel said quietly, his expression neutral.

Imenja nodded. "I was expecting there to be. We can't ask couples to wait another year for the next fertility ceremony. What is more healing to the heart than bringing new life into the world?"

The others nodded or shrugged. Imenja looked at each of them, then smiled.

"I think we have discussed enough for today. Shall we meet here again tomorrow, if the weather is pleasant?"

The other three Voices nodded.

Imenja rose and smoothed her robes. "I'll see you all at dinner." She looked down at Reivan. "Come with me, Reivan. We have much to discuss."

As she stepped away, Reivan rose and followed. Imenja asked Reivan a few questions about her lessons as they walked. After a few minutes they arrived at the threshold of a large room. Reivan looked around, noting the simple but luxurious furnishings.

"These are my rooms," Imenja said. "When you are my Companion you will be given your own private suite of rooms not far from here."

Reivan nodded, and thought of the small, dark room she'd been given after becoming a Servant-novice. "I'll look forward to that."

The Second Voice chuckled. "Yes. In the meantime, it may be useful for you to know how ordinary priests and priestesses live."

*And now I know how the Voices live,* Reivan thought as

she looked around the room again. *What is this room telling me about them? That they are powerful and wealthy, but in a dignified rather than excessive manner. I guess they need to impress any rulers that come here, and reassure their own people that they are in control.* She looked at Imenja, remembering her previous unanswered question.

"So why don't you become the First Voice?"

Imenja laughed. "Me?" She shook her head. "There are many reasons, but the foremost is strength. We need someone to replace Kuar who is as magically powerful, or more powerful than Kaur. That would make the new Voice more powerful than me, and it wouldn't do to have a less powerful Voice ruling over the rest, would it?"

Reivan shook her head. "I guess not."

"I don't fancy the position either," Imenja admitted. "I prefer to be less direct in my methods." She moved to a small gong. As she struck it a pleasant ring filled the room. "Now, I need to deal with a few matters I used to leave to Thar. Stay and listen, for you will be taking on these tasks soon."

Following the Second Voice to a set of reed chairs, Reivan resolved to learn as much as she could.

*I may not have magic, but that's not going to stop me from being a good Companion when the time comes,* she told herself.

Mirar closed his eyes and slowed his breathing, letting his consciousness sink until it hovered between wakefulness and sleep. In this state it was easy to become distracted, to wander into dreams. He kept a part of his mind set on his purpose. It was like the game he had played as a child, where one had to stay in contact with a tree or a rock with one hand while trying to "kill" the other children by touching them. They'd circle around him, darting in and leaping away. He'd stretch out, just one finger touching the tree . . .

*The tower dream,* he reminded himself. *I must see this dream Emerahl insists is mine.*

He called out to her, and felt her stir from sleep into dream.

*:Mirar?*

*:I am here. Show me the dream.*

*:Ah. Yes. The tower dream. How does it begin . . . ?*

The White Tower appeared. It loomed over her/him, as did a sense of impending danger.

*:Have you been to Jarime in the last hundred years?* he asked, gently and quietly so as to avoid disturbing her recollection. *Have you seen the White Tower?*

*:No.*

That was interesting. For her to have dreamed so accurately of something she'd never seen . . . but then she did believe this was not her own dream.

The dream was not as accurate as it first appeared. Clouds were cut apart as they passed the top of the tower; it was higher than it truly was. He felt dream fear wash over him. The urge to flee, but also the paralysis of fascination. The dreamer wanted to watch. Wanted to see, though it was dangerous. If he stayed too long *they* would see the dreamer. Discover who he was.

*"They"? Who were "they"?*

The tower seemed to flex. Cracks appeared. It was too late to run away, but still he tried. Looking back, he saw huge stone bricks falling toward him.

*Why didn't I run sooner? Why aren't I running sideways, out of the way of the long length of the falling tower?*

The world crashed around him. The noise was deafening. He felt his body covered. Crushed. Bones cracking. Flesh squashing, bursting. Chest collapsing under an enormous weight. Lungs burning as he slowly began to suffocate. No breath to cry out. Not even to give voice to the pain. He fought a numbness that was encroaching upon his mind. He tried to reach for magic, but there was none. The space around him was depleted. Despite that knowledge, he reached further, felt a trickle of it, drew it in. Used it to protect and sustain his head, his mind, his thoughts.

*It isn't enough.*

Not enough magic to repair his body. Not even enough to lift the rubble of the House piled atop him. Definitely not enough to face Juran again, which he would have to do if he managed to free himself.

*I could just let it go. Let myself die. Juran is right about one thing. A new age is beginning. Perhaps there is no place for me in it, as he claims.*

But what of the Dreamweavers?

*I am no use to them now. All I have done by resisting the gods' plans is make Dreamweavers an enemy of the people rather than a part of this new society. Nothing lasts forever. Perhaps it is time for them to end, too. I can't do anything for them now. If I can't save myself, how can I save them?*

He felt the little magic he had drawn dwindling, yet he reached out for more, stretching further than he had ever stretched before. If he could draw enough to sustain himself, he might survive. It was just a matter of being efficient. No need to realign bones or repair flesh. Just keep basic processes working. There was no food or water here under the rubble. He must slow his body down until it was barely alive. No need to think, just sustain the substance of his mind enough that it continued drawing magic and directing it to its purpose.

If he did not think, the gods would not see him. Would not know what he was doing. Would not know if he survived.

But they would know, once he recovered. They had only to read his mind.

*Let them not see me. Let them see another. One who will never be a threat to them. I will become another until . . . well, for as long as I'm able . . . or until I die.*

Slowly he let himself sink into darkness.

*:Mirar!*

The darkness veered away like a frightened reyner. Free from the dream, he remembered where he was and what he was doing, and the implications of the dream swamped him.

*:Emerahl. You were right. I remember.*

*:I saw it,* she replied. *You are the true owner of your body. The White Tower was a symbol representing Juran striking you. It was confused with the Dreamweaver House that you were buried under. You, Mirar.*

He felt awe and wonder at what he had done.

*:It worked. I survived. I created Leiard in order to keep the gods from seeing me, and it worked. I walked in their Temple, lay with their priestess and they didn't know me.*

*:You lost your identity,* she replied, appalled. *You may as well have been dead.*

*:But now I have regained it.*

*:Fortunate for you that you found a safe place to do so— and that I survived to teach you how to hide your thoughts.*

*:Yes, and to help me remember. Thank you, Emerahl.*

*:I doubt Leiard will thank me.*

*:Leiard? He is not a real person.*

*:He has become one.*

*:Yes,* Mirar agreed reluctantly. *He has had a hundred years to do so. At least he knows the truth. No wonder we were always at odds with each other. I made him opposite to me in many ways in order to strengthen my disguise.*

*:I wonder . . . Does he still exist? Should we wake up so I can try to call him forth?*

*:No,* Mirar replied. *Not yet. I have much to think about. I feel other memories coming.*

*:Tomorrow, then.*

*:Yes. Tomorrow.* Mirar pushed away a rising feeling of trepidation. What would he do if Leiard was still there in his mind? What could he do?

*:Good night,* Emerahl sent sleepily.

*:Good night,* he replied.

Their dream link broke. Alone, Mirar let himself drift into dreams and memories. Not all of them pleasant, but most of them filled with truths he had not known for a century.

# 10

Emerahl rose early and went in search of food. As she dug for edible roots and plucked fruit and nuts from trees she considered the revelations of the night before. What Mirar had done was extraordinary. She wanted to know how he had survived in his broken body as much as she wanted to learn how he had created Leiard and buried his own sense of identity. Was Leiard still in his mind? Could he temporarily slip into a Leiard state again if he knew the gods were watching? That might come in handy.

He was in a meditative pose when she returned. It was so uncharacteristic for him she felt a sinking dismay, sure that Leiard had taken control. As she put down her bucket one of his eyes opened and his lips twitched into a sly smile.

"What's for breakfast?"

*That's definitely Mirar,* she thought, relieved.

"Rootcakes. Fruit and nuts," she replied. "Again."

Unimpressed, he closed his eye again, leaving her feeling dismissed. He was shielding his mind well, too. She could not even guess at his mood.

Her stomach rumbled. She peeled the roots, chopped them finely and boiled them until they were soft. Straining them, she mashed them into a paste and began to shape them into flat circles.

"I remembered much last night," he said. "After you went to sleep."

She straightened to regard him. His eyes opened. He looked like a stranger, his face tight with emotions she had never seen him wear. Once again she wondered if she was talking to Leiard.

"Like what?"

His gaze dropped to the floor, but his eyes were focused beyond it. *On memories,* she guessed. *Bad memories from the look on his face.*

"Confusion. After I was found in the rubble I woke as if from a sleep. I didn't know who I was and nobody else did either. They didn't recognize me and assumed I was one of the ordinary Dreamweavers who had been caught in the collapse of the House. My body was twisted and misshapen. I couldn't walk. I couldn't feed myself. I was so ugly they hid me away so I didn't frighten women and young children."

He spoke softly, with no anger, but with a quiet horror. She shivered, appalled that her old friend had suffered so. Appalled that the great Mirar had been reduced to a cripple with no memory.

"I healed so slowly," he continued. "My hair fell out and grew back white. I couldn't cut it, and by the time I was able to I couldn't remember why I should want to. As soon as I was able to get my legs to move well enough to carry me, I fled Jarime. I was frightened of the city, but couldn't remember why. So I hobbled from town to town, village to village, travelling further and further away. Begging, scavenging, treated with charity in one place and driven away from others. The way I existed was pathetic, and it went on for years and years and years."

He sighed. "But still I grew stronger. My scars dwindled away. While some memories faded, others returned. I remembered that I was a Dreamweaver, but it was a long time before I dared to make myself a vest or offer my services. I stayed longer in each place, years instead of months. The longest I stayed was for more than a decade, and that was after . . ." He paused, then grimaced. "After I found a child with so much potential I could not help but stay and teach her."

"Auraya," Emerahl ventured.

He nodded. "She would have made a fine Dreamweaver."

Emerahl felt a mild surprise. "You think so?"

"Yes. She is intelligent. Compassionate. Gifted. All the right characteristics."

"Except for a certain preference for the gods."

He smiled ruefully. "Yes. Except for that. Once again, they ruined my plans. Or Leiard's, anyway." He frowned. "The Tower in the dream is the White Tower. It didn't exist then, but it was built where the Dreamweaver House stood. I think seeing that prompted my memories to return."

Emerahl leaned forward. "So, is Leiard still there?"

"I don't know." Mirar looked up at her, his expression unreadable. "I guess it is time to find out."

She nodded. "I guess it is." She paused, watching him closely. "Should I summon him?"

"May as well get it over with."

She drew in a deep breath.

"Leiard. Speak to me."

His eyes widened and his face contorted. Emerahl watched in horror and dismay as all signs of Mirar disappeared to be replaced by a mask of terror. His mouth opened, he sucked in a great lungful of air, then he covered his face and a tortured sound poured out—a thin cry of anguish and fear.

*Obviously Leiard's not gone,* she thought dryly.

He was rising to his feet. She rose hastily and moved closer.

"Leiard. Calm down."

The sound he was making faded to silence. His hands shifted to the sides of his head, as if he wanted to crush it.

"A lie," he gasped. "A lie—and she doesn't know! She doesn't know what she loved was . . ." He squeezed his eyes shut. "I'm not real."

Suddenly his eyes were open and staring at Emerahl. He took two steps toward her and gripped her shoulders. "But I *am*! If I wasn't, how is it possible that I can think? And *feel*? How can I not be real?"

Emerahl stared back at him. He looked half mad, half desperate. She felt a pang of sympathy. "He made you too well," she found herself saying.

He released her in one shove of rejection. She stumbled backward and one heel struck the bed. It hurt and she let out an involuntary gasp. Leiard did not notice, however.

"Why did he make me capable of love?" he railed. "How could he even do so, when he is incapable of it himself?" He paused, then spun about to stare at her accusingly. "Was this what he planned, then? Create another person, then kill him? He might as well sire a child, then murder it."

*He has a point,* she thought.

Then she shook her head. Leiard was not a real person. He had not been born. He had not grown up among a family. He had not formed this personality over time, it had been created. It made sense that Mirar would give his disguise a sense of self, or it would have no sense of self-preservation.

Suddenly he turned from her and began striding toward the cave entrance. Her heart stopped.

"Leiard!" she shouted. "Don't leave the protection of . . ." He kept walking. ". . . curse it. *Mirar!* Come back!"

He stopped. She watched as his shoulders straightened. He turned to regard her, his expression serious. It was impossible to tell if her summons had worked. To her relief, he walked back into the center of the room.

"That wasn't pleasant," he muttered as he sat down on the end of his bed.

"Mirar?" she asked tentatively.

"Yes, it's me," he confirmed. He stretched out on the bed, scowling. "So. What shall we try next, Old Hag?"

She snorted at his use of the name. The Old Hag. Provider of cures for ills or bad circumstances.

"Time," she prescribed. "I need to think. So do you." She stood up. "Can I trust you to stay put?"

"You can trust *me*," he said. "I won't be voluntarily handing the reins over to *him* again."

"Good," she told him. "Because I can't stay to watch you. We have to eat, and sleep. It'll become unpleasant in here if I can't empty those buckets."

He glanced toward his own waste bucket and grimaced

apologetically. "I hate to change an unpleasant subject to another, but I'm afraid I used mine while you were out."

She shrugged. Walking to the bucket, she picked it up. "I'll take care of it now—and see if I can find a more interesting breakfast."

"Thank you," he offered, then added a little sheepishly, "We need some fresh water, too."

She sighed, picked up the water bucket, and walked quickly out of the cave. Her footsteps echoed in the tunnel, but the sound was soon overwhelmed by the crashing of the waterfall. At the end of the tunnel she paused to stare at the falling water.

*He might as well sire a child, then murder it.*

Leiard's reaction had shaken her and his words had sent chills down her spine. He clearly understood what his fate would probably be—and he did not like it. He was going to fight for his existence.

*This isn't good,* she thought. *It can't be healthy to have two people struggling for control of the same body.*

No matter how cruel it seemed, Leiard was an *invention*. Mirar was the real person. They could not both continue to exist.

She sighed and moved outside the cave. The rain had stopped and the sun emerged from the cloud, reflected in water droplets everywhere. She paused to admire the effect. It was pretty. Romantic, even. She thought of Leiard's references to Auraya. It *was* interesting that an invention of Mirar's could feel romantic love. Surely that meant he was capable of it himself.

If that was so, then everything Leiard was, Mirar could be too. Mirar might not *like* those aspects of himself, but Leiard was evidence of them.

*This isn't a battle between Leiard and Mirar,* she thought suddenly. *It's Mirar fighting what he doesn't like or accept about himself.*

*In that case,* she thought, *he needs to—*

A fleeting emotion from an unfamiliar mind touched her senses. She froze, then made herself relax and search her surroundings. Somewhere to the left a male was watching her. From his emotions of concern and worry she gathered that he was alarmed by her presence here in Si. Was he alone?

Heart racing, she searched her surroundings and found another mind. Two minds—no, three. *Four!*

*So much for my brilliant hiding place,* she thought. *If we are discovered so easily . . . But who else would have ventured so far into Si?*

*The Siyee, of course.*

She felt alarm ease a little. There was always a chance that the gods were watching her through the Siyee, but the odds were small. She sensed curiosity as well as caution, and guessed finding her here had been a surprise to them.

They were, however, more fearful than she would have expected. Why they feared a lone landwalker woman, she couldn't guess. Perhaps they were worried that she wasn't alone.

*Well, I had better make an attempt to meet them. If I don't they are likely to bring back others, whereas if I convince them I'm friendly and don't intend to stay long they might leave me alone.*

She set the bucket down, then walked slowly along the water's edge, pretending to be looking for food. When she was close enough to the Siyee to be heard over the falling water she straightened and glanced deliberately in the direction of each of the four strangers.

"Greetings, people of the sky," she called, hoping their language hadn't changed too much.

There was a long, anxious pause during which one of the watchers—a male—considered what to do. As she sensed him become decisive she turned to face him and saw movement in the trees.

A gray-haired Siyee stepped into view. He stopped and uttered a series of sounds and whistles. Emerahl understood enough to know he was introducing himself.

"Greetings, Veece, Speaker of the North River tribe," she replied. "I am Jade Dancer."

"Greetings, Jade Dancer. Why are you here, in Si?"

She considered her answer carefully. "When I heard war was coming, I came here to wait until it is over."

"Then I bring good news," he told her. "The war was brief. It ended nearly two moon cycles ago."

She pretended to be delighted. "That *is* good news!" Then she added hastily: "Not that I don't like Si, but it is a bit . . . ah . . . hard on a landwalker."

He moved a few steps closer and she sensed a lingering suspicion. "The forest is dangerous and the journey here difficult for those without wings. How have you lived here? How is it you know our language?"

She shrugged. "I have lived many years on the edge of your lands," she told him. "I have knowledge and Gifts—and I once helped an injured Siyee, who taught me your language. I work as a healer, when I am among my people."

"You are not a priestess?"

"Me?" she asked, surprised. "No."

"I thought all Gifted landwalkers became priests or priestesses."

"No. Some of us don't want to."

His eyes narrowed. "Why not?"

*He's a nosy one,* she mused. "I don't want to tell others what to do, and I don't want them to tell me what to do."

For the first time, he smiled. "Forgive my questions. There are two reasons for them. We feared that you were a Pentadrian sorceress—a woman who once attacked our people. We are soon to have our own priests and priestesses so I was curious to know why someone might not want to be one."

*The Siyee are to have their own priests and priestesses?* The news saddened her. They had been free from Circlian influence for so long. *I suppose they need the protection now that there is the Pentadrian threat.*

She considered the old man. He was no longer radiating anxiety, though his curiosity was still tempered by caution. She felt certain he and his companions meant her no harm. They believed she was alone and that was how it must stay. She was not going to take any risks by introducing Mirar.

No, best she convince these people she was alone and harmless.

She crouched and washed her hands in the cold, swiftly running water.

"There's a basket-fruit tree just down the river from here," she said. "Would you stay and eat with me? I haven't had company for a long time."

He glanced toward his companions, then nodded. "Yes. We will. We cannot stay long, as we are already late in returning to our tribe, but we have time enough to talk and eat."

He whistled loudly. From among the trees stepped the other three Siyee: a middle-aged woman and two youths. They stared at Emerahl nervously as they approached. Veece introduced them. She smiled at them all, then rose and beckoned.

"Follow me. I don't know about you, but I always talk better when I'm not hungry."

And she led them down the river, and away from Mirar.

The sky was a roiling blanket of low black clouds. Lightning dazzled her eyes. There was no thunder, just silence.

*There was no storm the night after the battle,* Auraya thought as she stepped over bodies. *Well, there were no talking corpses either.*

She endeavored to avoid looking at the faces of the dead, having learned that this triggered them into movement. Not looking down made navigation of the battlefield difficult, however. The darkness between the flashes of lightning was absolute. The moment came when her foot caught on a corpse, and she found herself looking down.

Bloodshot eyes stared up at her. Lips moved.

"You killed me," the dead man wheezed.

*I used to wake up at this point,* she thought. *No more, however.*

"You killed me," another voice said. A woman. A priestess. Then another spoke, and another. All around her bodies were moving. Rising, if they could. Dragging themselves forward if they could not. Coming toward her. Chanting their accusation, louder and louder.

"You killed me! You killed me! You killed me!"

She ran, but there was no escaping them. They surrounded her. *I used to wake up now, too.* Reached out to her. Bore her down into a crush of putrid, rotting bodies. Faces pressed close to hers, spitting and dribbling blood and gore. She felt them press against her chest with their bony fingers, the pressure making it hard to breathe. All the time they uttered the same words.

"*Owaya! Owaya!*"

*What . . . ?*

Suddenly she was awake and looking into a pair of large eyes fringed with fine lashes. Eyes that belonged to a veez.

"Owaya," Mischief repeated aloud, this time with a definite note of satisfaction. He was sitting on her chest, shifting his weight from one paw to another.

"Mischief!" she gasped. As she sat up he leapt off her onto the bed. She took a deep breath and let it out slowly, then turned to regard the veez.

"Thank you," she murmured.

"Scratch?" he suggested.

She obliged him, enjoying the feel of his soft fur as she scratched all along his back. As he made small noises of pleasure, she considered her nightmares. They were getting worse, not better. What this meant, she couldn't guess.

*Perhaps I should consult a Dreamweaver.*

She considered the Dreamweavers who were going to be helping in the hospice. Would they agree to help her, or was that asking too much? *Of course they would. They're obliged to help anyone who asks for it.*

What would it be like, then? What did dream-healing involve? A mind link of some sort . . .

*Oh.*

She couldn't risk a mind link. Whoever she linked with might discover her true plans for the Dreamweavers.

*I can't do anything. I'm stuck with these nightmares forever.* Lying down again, she cursed under her breath. *Serves me right,* she thought. *How could I even contemplate asking the Dreamweavers for help when I'm working toward their downfall?*

Mischief made a sad noise, perhaps sensing her mood. She felt him move closer, then the weight of him against her hip as he curled up beside her. His soft breathing gradually slowed. She listened to it for a while, fighting sleep.

Then she found herself standing under a familiar, heavy black sky . . .

# 11

The Parade was full of people despite the heat of the morning sun. Their cheering was exhilarating. Reivan moved to join the other Voices' Companions, her heart beating a little too fast.

*When I am a Companion, experiencing crowds like this will become commonplace,* she mused. *I wonder how long it will take before it is no longer thrilling.*

The Voices descended the main stairs of the Sanctuary. At the base, four sets of four muscular slaves, each controlled by a slave master, waited beside litters. The Voices separated and stepped onto a litter each. As they settled onto the couches, the slaves hauled the litters onto their shoulders and set off down the thoroughfare.

The Companions fell into line behind the litters. None spoke. Reivan let out a sigh of relief as she found that, for the first time in a week, nothing was demanding her attention. She was finally free to think.

Reivan's days had become hectic and long. Imenja wanted her at her side for part of nearly every day. Sometimes Reivan was only required to observe a meeting or debate, other times she watched as Imenja undertook duties that Reivan would take over once she was given the responsibilities of a Companion. Duties like arranging Imenja's schedule, accepting or sending gifts or donations, refusing bribes and receiving reports of the tasks given to other Servants.

At the same time, her training continued. Imenja had

claimed all the time Reivan would have spent learning to use her Skills if she'd had any—and more. In the time that remained Reivan studied law, history, and the gods. Fortunately, her early years reading everything in the monastery she had grown up in were proving an advantage, and even Drevva admitted Reivan was more knowledgeable than the average new Servant-novice.

Reivan stayed up late and rose early. The list of duties she would have to take on as a Companion was so long now that she began to feel overwhelmed.

"How am I going to do all this?" she had asked Imenja.

Imenja had smiled. "Delegate."

"Give work to others? But how do I know who to trust?"

"I'll tell you if they're not trustworthy, and if I don't you'll soon find out who is and who isn't. I am not going to blame you for someone else's mistakes."

"And if nobody wants to do it?"

Imenja had laughed. "I think you'll find plenty of Servants willing and eager to help. Like you, they're here to serve the gods."

"Are you saying I can actually *reward* people with *work*?"

"Yes. So long as you don't make them see it that way. You are favoring them over others with a task few would be trusted with."

There were many rites and ceremonies that a Companion needed to be present at, even though they had no place in the rite. Reivan suspected that they attended in order to fetch and carry if such a need arose. Which was probably why nobody had protested whenever Imenja took her along.

Today she would attend the Rite of the Sun. She had never observed or participated in the fertility ceremony before. It was for married couples. Rich married couples. Only participants and Servants were present for the whole ceremony, but Voices attended the beginning of the rite.

The rite was the source of much curiosity for young Pentadrians—and all foreigners—because few ever talked about it. The Servants involved were sworn to protect the privacy of the participants, and participants were rarely willing to describe their experiences. Avvenans, as a people, considered talking of the intimacies of one's marriage to be crass and impolite.

This reluctance of Pentadrians to talk about the rite usually spurred foreigners into wild speculation. Reivan had encountered plenty of Sennons during her time mapping the mines in Northern Ithania who believed her people indulged in ritual orgies. She had explained that only married couples attended, but that did not convince foreigners there was nothing lewd about the rite.

*So long as it involves sex,* she thought, *they'll think it's depraved. Sennons are even more prudish than Pentadrians. I wonder if Circlians are the same.*

The curved wall of the Temple of Hrun appeared ahead. Reivan regarded the distant shadows of the arched entrance with longing. It was growing hotter, and she was discovering how uncomfortable her black robes could be in the full glare of the sun.

She looked enviously at the slaves walking before her, who wore nothing but short trousers. Their tanned skin glittered with droplets of perspiration. A rumor she had heard recently came back to her. One of the freed slaves of the army had married a Servant. She wondered what crime the man had done to earn himself a life of slavery in the first place. Surely the Servant wouldn't have married him if he was a rapist or murderer.

Were these men before her guilty of such evil deeds? She eyed them dubiously. Making criminals slaves of the Sanctuary was supposed to be better than imprisoning them in jails. All Servants were Skilled, therefore capable of defending themselves should a slave make trouble.

*Except me,* she thought. *I hope my fellow Servants remember that—or that my supporters do and my enemies don't.*

Imenja's litter reached the Temple doorway and disappeared inside. The moments before Reivan stepped out of the baking sunlight felt endless. Finally she was walking in cool shadows through a wide arched corridor. A delicious breeze cooled her. She looked ahead and drew in a breath in wonder.

Lush greenness lay beyond the end of the corridor. Two doors at the end had been opened to reveal a wide circle of grass and plants. A pool sparkled at the center and low garden beds and trees edged the grass. The roof was open to the sky, yet fountains kept the air moist. It was like an oasis in the middle of the desert.

Reaching the end of the corridor, she followed the slaves along a path that circled the garden, sheltered by a long, curved veranda. Open doors broke the inner wall of the Temple at regular intervals. She estimated that there were more than fifty of them.

The four litters were carried to the far side of the garden, where they were lowered onto the ground before a raised platform. A Dedicated Servant stepped forward to welcome the Voices.

As Reivan recognized the man she felt a thrill of pleasure. It was Nekaun, the Dedicated Servant who had welcomed her after she had become a Servant-novice. Only yesterday she had learned that he was among the Dedicated Servants still eligible for the position of First Voice after having their magical strength tested. She watched as he greeted the four Voices and invited them to sit. Four benches were brought for the Voices by Servants. As the other Companions sat on the edge of the platform, Reivan followed suit.

"Let the Rite of the Sun begin," Imenja said.

Nekaun inclined his head then turned to face the garden. He clapped his hands, and from a side door Servants began to file out. As they did they began singing. It was a tune both solemn and joyous, and Reivan made out phrases about love and children. Reivan guessed these were the Servant-guides who would attend to the couples participating in the rite.

Next came the couples. They all wore the same plain white clothing provided by the Temple and their feet were bare. Entering the garden, they walked out onto the grass and waited there. Some looked excited, others nervous. Their ages varied considerably. Some had barely reached adulthood. Others were middle-aged. Reivan noted some strange matches obviously made for money or position. Older men with younger women, ugly with attractive. Even an older woman with a young man—though both looked pleased with the situation.

*I don't envy the Servant-guides their duties,* Reivan thought.

The song ended. Nekaun stepped onto the grass.

"The Rite of the Sun is an ancient one," he told the participants, "begun by Hrun many thousands of years ago. Its aim is to teach the arts of pleasure, the skills of harmonious living, and aid in the creation of new life. Today it is taking place in temples all over Southern Ithania, and even in parts of Northern Ithania where our people are still welcome.

"For a month you will remain with us. You will feast so that the fire within the woman burns hot, and drink so the well within the man fills with the water of new life."

Reivan found herself scowling and quickly smoothed her face. Some of the great Thinkers of the last century had declared the old traditional belief that man was the source of new life and the woman literally an oven to warm it in—the hotter the better—was nonsense. Dissecting the bodies of dead women they had found no evidence of fire. No flame, no ash, no scorching. Fire needed fuel and air. There was no evidence that either existed within a woman's body.

By examining the internal organs of both fertile and infertile men and women, they had concluded that the woman grew seeds within her body and the man provided only nutrients. It was not a popular idea and only a few Thinkers had accepted it—not even when it was suggested that the more nutrients a man supplied, the stronger and more robust the child.

Nekaun was still addressing the crowd, speaking about exploration and learning, of challenges and rewards. She found her attention drifting.

*I suppose, as a Servant, I'll be expected to support the flame and water idea, when I'm more inclined, from reading and listening to those who have performed experiments and made dissections, to believe the seed and nutrient idea.*

*But . . . surely the gods would not allow their Servants to teach something that is wrong?*

Nekaun had finished speaking. He clapped his hands and from out of a side door came a stream of domestics carrying either pitchers or trays laden with small ceramic goblets. Two approached the dais, pouring drinks for the Voices, the Companions and Reivan, and finally Nekaun. The rest offered refreshments to the Servants around the garden.

The Servants took three goblets each, filled them, then moved into the grassed area to choose a couple. Reivan noted that the couples with an older participant tended to be chosen by older Servants. When all pairs had become trios, Nekaun lifted his goblet high.

"Let us drink to Hrun, Giver of Life."

"Hrun," all chanted.

As Nekaun lowered the goblet to his lips, the Voices, Companions and participants did the same. The drink was a surprisingly strong alcoholic brew full of the flavors of fruits, nuts and spices.

"Let us drink to Sheyr, King of Gods."

"Sheyr."

This was not the only ritual in which the first of the gods was mentioned *after* a lesser god. In the many rites of the Servant-warriors, Alor was recognized first. Nekaun now spoke that god's name.

"Let us drink to Alor, the Warrior."

"Alor."

Three mouthfuls had warmed Reivan's stomach. The drink was delicious. *Pity the goblet is so small*.

"Let us drink to Ranah, Goddess of the Moon."

"Ranah."

Now she felt the alcohol beginning to heat her blood. She regarded the dregs of it in dismay.

"Let us drink to Sruul, the Soul Trader."

"Sruul."

Swallowing the last mouthful, Reivan regarded the empty goblet wistfully. She wondered what this drink was called, and if it was sacred to the Temple of Hrun or could be purchased elsewhere.

"That's not part of the rite," Vervel murmured.

Reivan looked up to see that Nekaun was now moving among the couples, welcoming them personally.

"No," Imenja agreed. "The Head Servants of the Temple of Hrun have always been free to embellish the ceremony."

"I like what he's doing," Genza said, watching Nekaun. "It's reassuring them." She turned to regard Imenja. "What do you think, then?"

Imenja smiled crookedly. "Of him being First Voice? I think he would grow to fit the role."

Shar chuckled. "Rapidly, I imagine."

"He's popular," Genza said, turning to watch Nekaun again.

"Among the Servants. What about the people?" Vervel asked.

"They have no reason to dislike him," Shar replied. "It's hard to offend anyone when you're Head Servant of the Temple of Hrun."

"A role which he has performed well," Imenja added. She narrowed her eyes at Nekaun. "He is one of my preferred candidates. The others may be more experienced, but they are less . . ."

She did not finish her sentence. Nekaun was walking back to his place at the edge of the garden. He started addressing the couples again. Reivan did not hear what he said, instead catching a whisper behind her.

". . . charming?"

Reivan glanced back to see Genza raise one eyebrow suggestively at Imenja.

Imenja snorted softly. "Charismatic."

They both turned their attention to Nekaun. Reivan looked up and heard him say something about beginning lessons. The Servants began to sing again while leading their chosen couples out of the garden. Each headed toward one of the open doors of the inner wall. They stepped inside and the doors closed, ending the song. The garden was suddenly silent and empty.

Imenja rose, followed by the other Voices. As she followed suit, Reivan felt a little dizzy. A domestic approached to take their empty goblets. Nekaun walked back to join them, smiling with obvious satisfaction.

"It was a beautiful ceremony, Dedicated Servant Nekaun," Imenja told him.

He bowed his head. "Thank you, Second Voice. And thank you all for participating."

Imenja's expression became serious. "We have always done so. This year it is all the more important to take joy in the creation of new life as well as grieve loss and death. It gives us hope."

Nekaun nodded. "It does indeed. Will you be returning to the Sanctuary now, or would you like to stay for the feast?"

"We will return now," she replied. "As always there is much for us to do."

"Then let me escort you to the gate."

Reivan watched him closely. She tried to imagine him proud and all powerful like Kuar had been, rather than this friendly and obliging Dedicated Servant, and found she couldn't.

*One thing is sure,* she mused. *If he becomes First Voice he will be nothing like his predecessor. If that is better or worse, I cannot guess.*

As the platten turned into the street, Auraya was relieved to see that no crowd waited outside the hospice. Four guards stood beside the door, alert and ready to call for help from those that waited inside if there was trouble they could not handle on their own.

Extra guards had been employed after two had been overcome by street thugs a few nights ago, allowing a gang to break into the hospice. The intruders had smashed some of the furniture and stolen supplies, but had not damaged or taken anything that was irreplaceable. Nobody had seen the looters, but the thugs that had been hired to tackle the guards had been found. They claimed their employers were rich young men from the high end of the city.

A worker was touching up the paintwork, his movements hurried. Auraya read from his mind that someone had distracted the guards last night and painted a derogatory phrase about Dreamweavers on the wall. She smothered a sigh.

Resistance to the hospice was inevitable. People rarely gave up their prejudices overnight, even if it appeared the gods wanted them to. If they didn't like what the gods decided, they reasoned that the decision was simply a foolish human's misinterpretation of their will.

*And they could be right,* she mused. *My orders came from Juran, not directly from any god.* Yet even if the idea of starting a hospice had been Juran's alone, the gods would have put a stop to it if they disapproved.

The painter looked up. His eyes widened as he saw her. He made a few more jabs at the hospice façade with his brush, then hurried inside. As the platten pulled up before the door, the guards stood to attention and made the sign of the circle.

Auraya picked up the parcel lying on the seat beside her and stepped down to the pavement. She strode to the door of the hospice and pushed it open with magic. As she stepped into the hall inside, several faces turned toward her. She sensed the priests' and priestesses' relief that she had arrived and knew that they had been waiting in a tense silence. The cause of their awkwardness were five Dreamweavers standing calmly behind Raeli. Though these men and woman looked relaxed, Auraya detected anticipation, curiosity and fear.

She smiled at them all and, as always, was a little amazed at how the simple gesture could ease the tension in a room.

"Thank you for coming," she began, meeting the gaze of each person. "What we begin today is a noble task, but one not without dangers. Recent events have convinced me that a public ceremony to celebrate the opening of this hospice would only invite trouble, and I know you all agree. Instead we will mark the occasion quietly and privately. "Dreamweaver Adviser Raeli and High Priest Teelor, will you come forward."

The two approached her, both serious, both dignified. Auraya unwrapped the parcel, revealing a wooden plaque

inlaid with gold lettering: *For the benefit of all*. She sensed
the Dreamweavers' and healers' approval.

The plaque had been Danjin's idea, and he had come
up with the words. To him it was suitably ironic, since the
Dreamweaver policy of never refusing help was going to
lead to their downfall. For Auraya it was a reminder of why
she was doing this: to save souls that might turn away from
the gods.

Raeli and Teelor glanced back at the entrance to the corridor, where two sets of steps had been placed. A pair of
chains hung down from the top of the entrance, spaced at
the same distance apart as the hooks set into the top of the
plaque. Auraya held the plaque out to the pair. They took
hold of either end, carried the plaque together to the corridor entrance, climbed the stairs and attached the chains.
When the plaque hung in place, Auraya spread her hands in
a suitably dramatic gesture.

"I declare the hospice open."

The Dreamweavers and healers relaxed. Descending the
steps, Raeli and Teelor turned to regard each other. A smile
spread across Teelor's face and the corner of Raeli's lips
curled upward slightly.

"Everything is in place," Auraya said. "All we need now
is someone to treat."

The pair exchanged glances.

"Actually," Teelor said. "We have already. They came in
last night. A woman having difficulty giving birth and an
old man with lung sickness."

"The woman and babe are recovering," Raeli added.
"The old man . . ." She shrugged. "It is age as well as illness ailing him, I think. We have made him comfortable."

Teelor's eyebrows rose. "Turns out they can't cure everything," he murmured to Auraya.

Raeli's mouth quirked into a crooked smile. "Age is
not a disease," she told him. "It is a natural process of life.
After thousands of years of gathering knowledge, we have
no delusions about what can or cannot be achieved."

The high priest chuckled. "I would not be surprised if you
used that excuse for all the cases you fail to cure," he teased.

Auraya watched them both in surprise and amazement. These two appeared to have formed a bond of respect, perhaps even the beginnings of friendship. When had that happened? She looked closer and saw memories of a long night struggling together to save the mother and her child. It had been a learning experience for both of them.

She felt a stirring of hope, but it was stilled again by the recollection of what she was truly meaning to achieve here. Yet the nagging guilt was eased by the knowledge that, by learning from the Dreamweavers, the healer priests were going to be able to help many, many more people. Suddenly she saw the whole project in a different way. There was little in life that did not have bad as well as good effects. This hospice was one of them. All in all, the good outweighed the bad.

And that was a typically Dreamweaverish way to look at it.

# 12

"You're getting a bit old for this," Teiti said. "But I suppose it's good for you to have friends outside the palace, too."

Imi pulled a face. "Of course I'm not too old! There are children older than me here."

Her aunt looked out toward the other side of the Children's Pool and scowled disapprovingly. "I know."

Following her gaze, Imi saw that the usual crowd of older children had gathered by the edge of the deeper section. Unlike the young boys and girls splashing about in the rest of the pool, these lounged around as if they were above childish games. There were plenty of boys and girls in pairs, too, some with arms linked.

Not too far away, some slightly younger children mimicked the older ones. But most had not quite grown beyond their dislike of the opposite gender and their attempts at serious talk often dissolved into childish romping.

It was this group that Imi headed for once she entered the water. There was a boy called Rissi among them who often boasted of his travels outside the city with his trader father, and of knowing secret ways to smuggle things out of the city, and she wanted to talk to him.

The children regarded her with wary interest as she swam up to them. They always let her join in their romping and listen to their conversations. She hoped this was because they liked her, not because they didn't dare tell a princess to go away.

Rissi was among them. He grinned as she drew herself up onto the bank beside them.

"Hi, Princess," he said.

"Hi," she replied. "Been on any adventures lately?"

His nose wrinkled. "Father found out I skipped lessons. Won't let me go with him on the next trip."

She scowled in sympathy. "That's no fun."

"The king's birthday is in three days," one of the girls said to her. "Are you excited?"

Imi grinned. "Yes!"

"Decided who you're taking with you yet?"

This was the third time the girl had asked this question in the last few weeks. Imi hadn't understood why she might "take someone with her" at first, since she already lived at the palace. Then, last night, she had realized this girl wanted to come to the party, and hoped Imi would invite her.

"I haven't had a chance to ask father," Imi replied. She sighed. "He's very busy. I haven't seen him in a week."

They made sympathetic noises. The conversation turned to other matters. Imi listened and occasionally asked questions. Some of the questions she'd asked them in the past had been met with frowns or even smothered laughter, but the more she learned about their lives the easier it was to ask questions that made sense to them.

Teasing started, then the boys began wrestling. For once Rissi didn't join in, though he watched their antics with a grin. Imi moved closer and called his name. He looked at her in surprise.

"If your father won't take you out of the city, why don't you go on your own?" she suggested.

He stared at her, then shook his head. "I'd get into trouble."

"You're already in trouble," she pointed out.

He laughed. "You're right. I may as well do what I want. But where would I go?"

"I can think of a place. I overheard someone talking about it weeks ago. A place where there's treasure."

From the way he looked at her, she knew she'd caught his interest.

"Where?"

She swam a little away from him. "It's a secret."

"I won't tell."

"No? What if you were seen swimming out the main tunnel? They'd want to find out why."

"I wouldn't tell them."

"What if your father said he wouldn't take you out ever again? I bet you'd tell then."

He frowned and looked away. "Maybe. But I wouldn't go that way."

She feigned surprise. "What other way is there?"

"A secret way."

"There's another way into the city?"

He looked at her. "No. You can only go out that way 'cause of the currents."

She waded closer and lowered her voice. "If you show me the way out, I'll show you where the secret treasure is."

He paused and regarded her thoughtfully.

"It would be lots more fun than hanging around here all day," she said.

"Do you promise to show me the treasure?" he asked.

"I promise."

"On your father's life?"

The vow was a common one among the children, but it still made her pause.

"I promise, on my father's life, to show you the secret treasure if you show me the secret way out of the city."

He nodded, then grinned. "Follow me."

She blinked in surprise. "You want to go now?"

"Why not?"

She glanced back at Teiti, who was watching her closely.

"Wait. We'll have to trick my aunt or she'll stop me."

"No need," Rissi said. "You can get there from this pool. She'll see you dive, and not know where you came up. By the time she realizes you're not here any more, we'll be gone."

This was the opportunity she'd been waiting for, but still she hesitated. Teiti was going to be so angry.

Rissi's eyebrows rose mockingly. "What? Afraid of getting into trouble?"

She swallowed, then shook her head. "No. Show me."

He waded into deeper water, then dove under the surface. She took a deep breath, hoping that Teiti thought they were competing at how long they could hold their breath for, then followed.

Rissi headed for the deeper water near where the older children lounged. He swam quickly, forcing Imi to work hard to keep up. A tunnel entrance appeared, and she felt the current that kept the Children's Pool fresh pull her in after Rissi.

She had never swum into this tunnel before, and could only trust that Rissi would not have come this way if the tunnel didn't come out somewhere before they ran out of breath.

It was not long before she saw the rippled surface of the water above. Rissi swam up, took a breath, then dove down again. She followed suit, catching a glimpse of a poorer part of the city.

They swam through several more tunnels, the water and houses growing dirtier each time. She realized with distaste that they were in the outflow currents that bore waste out of the city, and made sure she didn't swallow any of the water.

The current grew ever stronger. Surfacing near a crumbling wall of a house, they clung to rocks at the edge to prevent themselves being swept on. Rissi looked at her, his expression serious.

"This is the last part. When we come out we'll be in the sea. The only way back in is through the main tunnel. Or we can climb out now and walk back."

She looked in the direction the current was surging. It would pull them through whatever tunnel lay ahead. If there was a blockage or she got caught somehow, she might easily drown.

"How many times have you done this?"

He grinned. "Once."

Her heart was racing. She realized she was terrified. "This is a bad idea."

"We don't have to go through," he told her. "I won't tell

the others you didn't go. I've shown you the way out, so you have to tell me where the treasure is."

She looked at him and felt a surge of frustration and anger. He hadn't said it would be so dangerous. But he had done it before and survived. How hard could it be? She just had to let the current take her through. She gathered her courage and forced herself to stare at him defiantly.

"Not until we get to the other side," she said.

He laughed then gave a whoop. "Let's do it! Try to keep in the middle of the flow. And take a really big breath. I'll hold on to you as long as I can. Ready? On three. One, two . . ."

Her heart was in her mouth, but somehow she managed to suck in a breath.

". . . three!"

They dove down into the current. He grabbed her wrist and held tightly as they rushed into darkness. She wondered how she was supposed to keep to the middle when she couldn't see, then she realized the walls rushing past them were faintly visible. Tiny curls of light decorated the surface.

*Glow worms,* she thought. Their presence indicated just how dirty the water was. She was too terrified to worry about getting sick, however. She had never travelled so fast before; she was sure she was going to be dashed against the wall before they made it out.

The tunnel began to curve this way and that. They had to swim frantically to avoid colliding with the occasional outcrop of rock. She glimpsed all manner of things stuck in cracks and dips of the surface—even, to her horror, a skull.

Just as her lungs were beginning to protest, she rounded a corner and found the current was sweeping her toward a slash of dark blue. Rissi let go of her and swam forward so he shot through the narrow gap. She kicked out and managed to slip through without touching the rock.

The current eased and died. She looked back to see a rock wall fading into a haze. Below she could see a vague hint of sea floor. In all other directions was a depthless blue that was somehow frightening in its potential.

The urgency of her need for air was more pressing, however. She swam toward the rippling surface above. As she broke through she gasped out the breath she had been holding then began sucking in another.

Before she could get a proper lungful of air, her head plunged under the surface again and she gulped in water. She kicked upward, broke through into the air again and coughed out the water. All the time she had to fight to keep her head above the surface.

"Rissi!" she called frantically.

"Imi," came the reply. There was a pause, then his head appeared.

"Why is it moving so much?" she gasped. "Is there a storm?"

He laughed. "No. This is normal. These are waves." He grinned. "You haven't been outside before, have you?"

"Yes! But it wasn't this . . . this *wavy*."

By keeping her legs moving, she found she was able to rise and fall with the waves.

"So where now?" he asked.

"What?"

"Where's the treasure?"

"Oh." She gathered her thoughts. "Xiti Island."

He stared at her in dismay. "Xiti!"

"Yes. Do you know the way?"

As he shook his head she felt a wave of disappointment. "Oh. I should have asked."

"I know where Xiti is," he told her. "But it's far from here. It would take hours for us to swim there."

She felt hope return. "How many hours?"

He shook his head again. "Three. Maybe four."

"That's not too bad. We could get there and back by tonight."

"How long will it take to get this treasure?" He frowned. "What *is* the treasure? I'm not swimming all day if it isn't worth it."

She smiled. "It's worth it. I overheard traders talking about sea bells. They said there were some there the size of a fist."

His eyes brightened. "Did they? Then why haven't they taken them?"

"Because . . ." Imi considered her answer. Would he change his mind if she mentioned the landwalkers? "Because they're waiting for them to get bigger."

"Bigger," he repeated. "I guess they wouldn't notice if a few went missing . . . But . . . we'd be stealing them, Imi. What if we got caught?"

" 'Nothing the ocean grows is owned by any man until it is taken,' " she quoted.

His lips twitched, then he began to grin. "I'll be rich!" He looked at her. "But you're already rich. What do you want sea bells for?"

She smiled. "A birthday present for my father."

"So that's what this is all about." He laughed. "We're outside the city and both already in trouble. We may as well keep going. Follow me."

He dove under the surface. Taking a deep breath, Imi plunged under the waves and swam after him.

Mirar regarded the growing contents of the makeshift table in surprise. A bowl of soup steamed in front of him. On a thick slab of wood lay something wrapped in leaves that smelled of roasted meat and herbs. A bowl of green leaves and fresh roots sat to one side of this and another of steaming cooked tubers on the other, and there was the usual bowl laden with ripe fruit.

"What's this?" he asked.

"A feast," she replied.

"Is this what's been keeping you busy all morning?"

"Mostly."

"What's the occasion?"

"We're celebrating."

"Celebrating what?"

She placed the two wooden cups he'd carved on the table then straightened. "I haven't detected your emotions in over a week. I think that's long enough to prove you've got the hang of hiding your mind."

He narrowed his eyes. "That's not all."

"What? Being free to leave the cave is not reason enough?"

She produced a leather pouch and lowered it to the cups. Out of the hollow stick that acted as a spout came a stream of dark purple liquid. The aroma was familiar, though he had not smelled it in centuries. Teepi, the Siyee's liquor.

"Where'd you get that from?"

"I traded for it. With the Siyee."

"They came back?"

"Yes, early this morning. I think they're concerned I'll perish. Or that I've decided to stay."

"Hmmm." He picked up the cup and sipped. The fiery liquor warmed his throat. "It's just as well I have learned to hide my thoughts. We can't stay here much longer."

"No," she agreed. She sat down and picked up her bowl of soup. "They also gave me a girri. I had to cook it today, so I thought I might as well make us a feast. Nothing much else for me to do now."

He watched her drink the soup. "You're getting bored with me, aren't you?"

She smiled slyly. "No. I have never found you boring, Mirar. In fact, I've always found you a little too interesting for my own good."

He chuckled. So. There it was. The invitation. He had noted the way she sometimes looked at him. Thoughtful. Curious. Admiring. The spark of attraction was still there for her. Was it for him?

He thought back to other times circumstances had brought them to each other's beds and felt an old but familiar interest flare. *Yes,* he thought. *It's still there.*

"I got to wondering today," she said, setting her empty bowl aside, "if any of the other Wilds have survived."

She looked up at him, seeking his opinion. He took another sip of Teepi, giving him time to slowly extract himself from pleasant memories.

"I doubt it," he replied.

She pursed her lips. Which reminded him of another time when she had paused and made that face, considering what they might do next. She had been naked at the time, he recalled. He shook his head to clear his mind.

"If you and I are still alive, why not them?" Emerahl insisted. "We know The Oracle was killed, and The Farmer, but what about The Gull? What of The Twins and The Maker."

"The Maker is dead. He killed himself when his creations were destroyed."

She looked at him in horror. "Poor Heri."

Mirar shrugged. "He was old. The oldest, apart from The Oracle—and she was half mad."

"The Gull and The Twins were younger," she said thoughtfully. "What about The Librarian?"

He shrugged. "I don't know. I doubt he still watches over the Library of Soor. That place was a ruin even before the gods' war."

She sighed. He considered her carefully. His interest in her was still there, though dampened by the conversation. She was too distracted. If he got her attention, what would she do?

"This is too morbid a conversation for a celebration," he told her. He reached out and took a piece of fruit, then carved a slice from it. She turned to watch him, but her gaze was still far away. Reaching across the table, he held the slice up to her mouth. "Life is too long to ignore opportunities for pleasure," he murmured.

Her eyes widened, then narrowed. "You said that . . ."

"A long time ago. I wondered if you would remember."

She took the piece of fruit. "I could hardly forget."

He looked meaningfully at the slice. "Are you going to share that?"

Her pupils widened and a smile slowly spread across her face. "It would be greedy of me not to." She rose and moved around the table, her eyes bright. Placing the slice of fruit between her lips, she leaned forward and offered it to him.

*Oh, yes,* he thought. He caught her waist, pulled her closer and bit into the slice. Their lips touched, their mouths met around the crisp sweetness of the fruit. He felt his teeth break through juicy flesh, felt her hands slide around his back, and the firmness of her back beneath his own palms.

His interest flared into desire. He felt her respond to it
with equal passion. Suddenly he wanted too much at once.
He was pulling her down onto his bed and trying to undress
her at the same time, but achieving neither. She laughed
and pushed him onto his back, then straddled him. Pulling
off her clothing, she tossed it aside. He caught his breath as
her breasts were uncovered. She was perfect, but how else
could she be when she could so easily change her age?

She brushed his hands away long enough to pull off his
vest and tunic. Her hand moved to the waist of his trousers.
The ties came undone. She tugged the waistband down,
then looked up at him and grinned. Then, without a word,
she sidled close and he felt the warmth of her begin to en-
velop him.

*No!*

The thought was not his. An emotion tore though him,
jangling his nerves. He could not put a name to it. Horror?
Anger? He gasped in confusion and shock. He felt as if his
entire being was sinking into misery. The fire in his blood
was doused by a chill that he could not shake, and a lingering sense of another will fighting his own.

Leiard.

"No!" he protested. He sat up, the sudden movement
causing Emerahl to lose her balance momentarily. "You
*bastard*!"

Emerahl braced herself and stared at him. "I trust that's
not me you're talking to," she said dryly.

He found he could not reply. It took all his will to keep
control of his body.

*I can't let you do this,* Leiard said. *I can't let you betray
Auraya again.*

*Auraya doesn't matter!* Mirar fumed. *You can't go back
to her. You don't even exist!*

Emerahl was watching him through slowly narrowing eyes. Mirar felt Leiard's will weaken. He took a deep
breath, trying to rein in the anger. "I didn't mean you," he
explained to her. "I meant *him. He* did it. He . . . *stopped*
me. I can't believe . . . I thought . . ."

"That if you didn't let him take control he couldn't

bother you any more?" She shook her head and climbed off his bed. "I told you it wouldn't be that easy."

"What am I supposed to do?" he exclaimed, standing up and yanking his trousers up to his waist. If it was possible to die of humiliation he felt he might have then. "Is he going to stop me from bedding any woman from now on, just because he feels loyal to . . . to that . . ."

"Auraya," she finished. She reached for her clothing and began to dress.

Her acceptance of his sudden impotence was somehow more mortifying than if she'd been amused by it. She could, at least, behave as if she was *surprised*.

"You have to accept that Leiard is a part of you," she said. "He cannot feel anything that doesn't exist in yourself."

"Obviously he can. *I* don't love Auraya."

She turned and smiled at him. "No, but a part of you does. A part you don't like, unfortunately. You have to accept that part and everything that Leiard proves that you can be. Otherwise . . ." She frowned and looked away. "I fear you'll never be whole again."

"You don't know that for certain."

"No, but I'd be willing to bet on it." She moved back to her table and sat down. Unwrapping the roasted girri, she began to tear off pieces of meat. "Eat. I'm not offended. A little frustrated. Perhaps a little embarrassed. But not offended."

"*You're* embarrassed," he muttered. "I'm *utterly* humiliated. I've never been unable to—"

"Let's just eat," she interrupted. "I don't need another tall story of your sexual prowess. Not now. And definitely not while I'm eating."

He shook his head. Anger had subsided into a sinking, dark emotion and he found he could not be bothered with it any more. He sat on the edge of his bed and glowered at the food. Seeing the skin of Teepi lying on the edge of the table, he topped up his glass, tossed the drink down, then poured himself another.

"They're not tall stories," he growled.

"I know," Emerahl said, in an overly placating way.

"I really—"

"Just eat."

Sighing, he did as he was told.

Teiti's legs shook as she stood on the bank of the Children's Pool. An hour had passed since Imi had disappeared. She could still remember the last glimpse she had caught of the princess as she dove into the water.

She and the guards had questioned the other children, but none had seen Imi leave. Teiti had sent out all of Imi's guards but one to ask people around the many entrances to the cave if they had seen the princess.

"She'll be back," the remaining guard soothed. "Most likely she gave us the slip so she could get a bit of private time with that boy."

*That doesn't reassure me at all,* Teiti thought. *She's too young to be interested in boys. If she was, I'd be just as alarmed that she was with some lowly trader's son.*

"Lady?"

She looked down to see a pair of girls standing in front of her.

"Yes? What is it?" she asked.

"Just thought you should know," one of the girls said. "There's a tunnel at the deepest part of the pool. It flows out into the city. I know Rissi's used it before, when he wanted to avoid getting beaten up by Kizz."

*Beaten up?* Teiti smothered a curse. *Why did I let Imi play with these ruffians?*

"Where is it?"

The girls pointed. "At the deepest place."

"I'll go and look," the guard offered. "If they're right, we're going to have to start searching the whole city."

The whole city. Teiti sighed. The chances that the king would not find out about this were dwindling rapidly. The longer Imi was missing, the less Teiti cared what the girl's father would say or do. What mattered most was whether Imi was safe.

"Go," she said. "Find it. Find out where it goes. I'll send for more assistance."

As he waded into the water she turned away and started toward the main entrance of the pool. One of the guards was there, questioning people. She would send him to the palace. It was time to inform the king of his daughter's disappearance.

# 13

The two veez circled each other slowly, their tails twitching. Auraya sighed and shook her head.

"They've forgotten they've grown up."

Mairae laughed. "Yes—they're like a pair of children who can only relate by wrestling with and insulting each other."

Stardust leapt on top of Mischief, and all detail was lost as the two became a blur of rolling, twisting fur, legs and tail.

Mairae chuckled. "How is Mischief's training going?"

"Well." Auraya grimaced. "There's not a mechanical lock that he can't open, and he's become much easier to link with now that he's matured a bit and I can actually hold his attention for more than a few moments. He speaks into my mind now, too."

The two veez separated. They stood apart and chattered at each other, then simultaneously affected boredom and began washing themselves.

"Have you met Keerim?" Mairae asked.

"No."

"He's a famous veez trainer, visiting from Somrey. Not bad-looking, too. You should arrange t—"

:Auraya.

The call was from Juran.

:Yes?

:The gods have called us to the Altar. Is Mairae with you?

*:Yes. I will tell her.*
*:Good. I will collect you both on the way down.*
Mairae was regarding her expectantly.

"What is it?"

Auraya rose. "We've been called to the Altar."

"The Altar?" Mairae's eyebrows rose. She stood and scooped Stardust off the floor. "How unusual. I wonder if the gods have an answer for us."

"On the existence of Pentadrian gods?" Auraya tried to pick up Mischief, but he darted away. She moved to the bell rope and pulled it. There was no time for chasing veez. A servant would have to take care of him.

They left the room, entering the circular staircase at the center of the Tower. Auraya heard Mischief speak her name telepathically, somehow managing to convey immense disappointment at her leaving so abruptly. Mairae put Stardust down.

"Go home," she ordered. The veez scampered down the stairs. "Good girl." Mairae straightened and looked up the stairwell.

"The cage is already descending."

"Yes. Juran said he would collect us on the way past."

They watched the base of the cage slowly drop toward them. As it drew level with their eyes it slowed. Dyara and Juran stood inside. When the cage stopped, Juran opened the door and stepped aside to let them in.

His expression was serious and perhaps a little pensive, but he managed a small smile. "No, I do not know why the gods have called us," he said before either of them could ask. "Let us hope it is good news."

Dyara looked at him and lifted an eyebrow. "We would hardly be hoping for bad news now, would we?"

The White leader chuckled. "No."

The cage began descending again. As it passed Rian's rooms, Mairae looked at Juran questioningly.

"Rian was in the city. He'll meet us at the Altar," Juran explained. He looked at Auraya. "How is the hospice faring?"

She nodded. "Remarkably well. There have been a few

differences of opinion, but that's to be expected. Our methods aren't going to be the same." She paused, wondering if that was the sort of information he really wanted. "We are learning much from the Dreamweavers," she added.

"And they from us?"

"Occasionally."

"Are the Dreamweavers holding back knowledge?" Dyara asked.

"Not yet," Auraya replied.

"I'm surprised," the woman said. "Who'd have thought they'd entrust their secrets to priests?"

"They've never considered their knowledge to be secret," Auraya told her. "That would give them a reason to withhold healing, which is against their principles. They never deny anyone aid."

"An admirable principle," Juran said. "One I think we should consider adopting."

Dyara turned to stare at him in surprise.

"Even if it meant healing Pentadrians?"

Juran smiled wryly. "It is possible that superior healing skills would help us win the favor of people of the southern continent one day."

The cage began to slow. "Not if their gods are real," Auraya pointed out.

"No," Juran agreed.

The cage stopped at the center of the hall.

"Then having plenty of skilled Circlian healers will be even more important," Juran replied. "We can't rely on a heathen cult to treat our wounded, no matter how skilled it is. Doing so would give them more influence than I would like them to have."

He led them out of the cage. Auraya considered his words. He obviously expected Dreamweavers to still exist in a century—not to fade away once their main advantage over Circlians had been taken away. Perhaps his reasons for asking her to start the hospice were a little different from what she'd assumed.

Juran reached the entrance of the Tower and led them out into bright sunlight. A covered platten had just pulled up outside the Dome. Rian stepped out and signalled to the driver to move away, then he turned to wait for them. As Auraya drew closer, she saw that his eyes were aglow with religious fervor. He said nothing as they reached him, just fell into step as they strode under the arches of the Dome.

After the bright sunlight the shade within the Dome was a relief. Auraya's eyes adjusted to the softer light and she saw the five triangular sides of the Altar opening. Juran led them across the building to the dais, then up into the Altar. As soon as all had taken their seats the points began to hinge upward again.

Juran paused, as he always did, to consider what he was going to say. But as he drew breath to speak, Auraya felt a movement nearby. Suddenly she was aware of the magic in the world around her, and that magic rippled and thrummed with a presence. She turned to face it.

"Chaia, Huan, Lore, Yranna, Saru," Juran began. "We—"

Auraya gasped as she realized what she was sensing was a god.

*:Hello, Auraya.*

A glow began to form in one of the corners of the Altar. Slowly it took on the form of a man. Auraya heard Juran take in a breath and the others make small noises of surprise.

"Chaia," Juran said, beginning to rise.

*:Stay,* Chaia said, raising a hand to halt Juran's movement.

Auraya felt the world around her vibrating with the arrival of the rest of the gods. She watched in awe as each became visible as a light that took on human form.

*:We have called you here to tell you the result of our search,* Chaia told them. He turned to regard Huan.

*:We searched throughout Southern and Northern Ithania,* Huan said, *but did not encounter other gods.*

*:That does not mean they do not exist,* Lore warned. *They may have evaded us. They may exist beyond those territories.*

*:We will continue our search,* Yranna assured them, smiling. *But it is best you do not leave Ithania all at once.*

*:That would leave you unprotected, should these gods exist and seek to do you harm,* Saru added.

Juran nodded. "Is there anything we can do to help?"

*:No,* Chaia replied. *I do not expect a confrontation with the Pentadrians for now*.

"We understand," Juran replied.

Chaia glanced at his fellow gods again, then nodded.

*:That is all. We will speak to you again when we have more answers*.

The five glowing figures vanished.

But they did not fade from Auraya's senses. She felt Huan, Lore, Yranna and Saru drift away. When they had gone she felt the lightest touch of Chaia's mind before he, too, moved away.

"Auraya?"

She jumped and found Juran staring at her. "What is it?" he asked.

"The gods. I felt them arrive and leave."

His eyebrows rose. "*Felt* them?"

"Yes. It was . . . strange."

"Has this happened before?" Dyara asked.

Auraya shook her head. "It is a bit like this sense I have of my position in relation to the world. I can sense the magic around me."

"And the gods are beings of magic," Mairae said, nodding.

"Yes."

The points of the Altar were hinging down toward the ground, but none of the others had begun to rise. Juran looked thoughtful and Dyara skeptical. Rian was scowling. As Auraya met his eyes his frown disappeared and he smiled—but it was forced.

"I am starting to expect these strange developments of yours, Auraya," Juran said. He chuckled. "As soon as you work out what this one means, let me know. For now," he glanced at each of the others, then stood up, "I suggest we return to our duties."

Auraya rose with the others, but hung back as they filed down the Altar points to the dome floor. She glanced back and concentrated, but sensed nothing disturbing the magic within the Altar.

There were small fluctuations in the distribution of it around her, however. Turning away, she kept her mind on the magic around her as she followed her fellow White back to the Tower. She noticed that the variations in magic were more pronounced at its base. Dyara and Juran began discussing Genrian politics, but Auraya was too engrossed in what she was sensing to pay any attention.

They reached the Tower and moved inside. The fluctuations did not lessen or grow stronger, and she was about to bring her attention back to her companions when she sensed a sudden change.

They had reached the cage at the center of the hall. In this place magic was considerably diminished. She would not have noticed it, even if she had drawn magic to herself, as there was enough about to make most Gifts possible.

But it was definitely spread a little thin.

*What caused this?* she wondered. *Did someone use up most of the magic here or is it a natural occurrence?*

She opened her mouth to tell Juran, but caught Rian watching her. He gave her another forced smile.

*I'll tell Juran another time,* she thought. *In private.*

Two giant elongated bowls bobbed in the water. They were made of wood, and it looked like tree trunks had been stripped of their branches and bark and set upright within the bowls. From the trunks hung a multitude of ropes, more beams of wood and what looked like large bundles of cloth.

"They're ships, aren't they?" Imi asked. "Father described them to me."

Rissi gave her an odd look. "Boats. You've never seen boats or ships before, have you?"

"No."

"If that's where the sea bells are then the landwalkers have got to them first," Rissi said, his disappointment obvious.

"That depends."

"On what?" He turned to frown at her.

"If they've got them all yet. They wouldn't still be here if they had, would they?"

Rissi looked thoughtful, but then he frowned and shook his head. "What are you saying? We sneak up and take a few? What if they see us? They'll kill us."

"Then we make sure they don't see us."

"But—"

She ducked under the surface and swam toward a rock that was closer to the boats. Coming up behind it, she carefully peered around at the landwalkers.

They were easier to see now. She watched them walking back and forth on what must be a flat floor just inside the bowl part of the boat. Ropes hung into the water.

She saw movement in the water—a landwalker's head. He floated beside the boat and she heard a distant guttural voice. One of the landwalkers in the boat reached down. The swimmer held up a bag, which the other man hauled up to the deck. The light brown skin of the diver's back disappeared as he dove beneath the water.

Rissi surfaced beside her.

"The sea bells must be there," she told him. "They're diving for them."

"Which means we can't sneak up on them," he told her.

"Not now," she said. "But they've got to stop some time. I've heard landwalkers can't spend long in the water, or their skin goes bad."

The landwalker's head reappeared. He floated only a moment before diving again.

"They can't hold their breath long, either," Rissi murmured. "Although we can't stay here long. It'll take us hours to get back and I don't want to swim in the dark."

"The dark . . . we could wait until night then sneak up while they're asleep," Imi said, speaking her thoughts aloud.

"No! I'm in enough trouble already! If I'm not back by tonight my father won't take me out with him ever again."

She looked at Rissi, but decided taunting him about being scared of punishment wouldn't change his mind. He was beyond bravado now.

Turning to regard the boat, she saw the swimmer climb

wearily out of the water and another dive in to replace him. They were diving in shifts. There was no chance they'd take a rest and give her an opportunity to sneak in and take a few sea bells.

A splash near the boat drew the landwalkers' attention. One pointed, and Imi saw a large arrow bird surface, a fish struggling in its beak. The bird tossed down its catch, then launched itself back into the air.

"A distraction," she said. "We need to distract them."

Rissi frowned. "How?"

"I don't know. Got any ideas?"

He looked at the boats. "Do you think they've seen Elai before?"

"Probably not."

"You could distract them while I get the sea bells."

"Me? No. This was my idea. *You* distract them while *I* get the sea bells."

"That's not fair. What if they've got . . ."

"What?"

"Spears or something."

She gave him a measured look. "So it's better that they spear me than you?"

He grimaced. "I didn't mean that. But it is a danger."

"Then . . . we give them something else to aim at. I know! I just thought of it. Something that will not only get them to look, but make the divers get out of the water too."

"What?"

"A flarke."

He paled at the mention of the fierce sea predator. "How are we going to find one of them and persuade it to eat them and not us?"

She laughed. "We don't have to. I've seen the singers' flarke costumes up close. They're made from spikemat spines. We'll find a big one and break off a few spines. Then we'll tie them to your back. You swim around like a flarke—far enough away that their arrows can't reach you. The landwalkers will be too scared to get into the water."

He was silent and she could tell that he was impressed. After a moment he gave her a big grin.

"Yes. That would be fun."

"Let's find us some spikemat fish," she said, and, not waiting to see if he followed, dove under the water.

Spikemat fish were common in every reef. It took them moments to find one with spines as big as a flarke's. Breaking them off was not easy, and she felt sorry for the creature as it slowly crawled away from them, bleeding from where they had ripped out the spines. The spines would grow back eventually, however.

She had expected that attaching the spines to Rissi's back would be the hard part, but he solved the problem by cutting himself a strip of wide leathery sea grass and making it into a vest shape. He drilled holes through the base of each spine with his knife, then pushed the spines through the back of the vest and secured them with another thinner spine threaded through the holes.

Out of sight of the boats, Rissi practiced swimming up and diving down again so that only the spines broke the surface.

"You're kicking your feet up out of the water," Imi told him.

"If I keep them together, it'll look like a tail fin," he replied, grinning.

"Flarke fins go sideways, not up and down."

His face fell. "Oh. Yes. That's right. I'll keep my feet down then."

"Are you ready?"

He shrugged. "Are you?"

She nodded. "Yes!"

"Let's go then—and be quick. Who knows how long they'll believe this for."

They swam back to the boulder and watched the landwalkers long enough to be sure they knew where each was. She looked at Rissi expectantly. He stared back at her, then nodded. Without a word, he sank under the water.

Her heartbeat began to quicken as she watched for him surfacing again. When the spines finally rose out of the water she held her breath and looked to see if the landwalkers had noticed.

They were all hard at work.

The spines broke the surface again, but still the land-walkers didn't notice. Rissi moved back and forth, sometimes slowly, sometimes diving under the surface abruptly. Imi realized he had probably seen a flarke before and was mimicking its behavior.

A shout drew her attention back to the landwalkers. They had finally noticed the spines. She grinned as they stopped working and milled anxiously about in the boat. One pounded on the outside of the boat with a hard object. She could hear the dull sound of it. A head appeared beside the boat and she felt a surge of triumph as the swimmer hastily climbed aboard.

*My turn,* she thought.

Taking a deep breath, she dove under and swam hard in the direction of the boats. Her heart was pounding with excitement, fear and exertion by the time she saw the elongated shadows above her.

Looking down, she almost let her breath out in amazement.

Her father had once taken her outside the city to show her a forest. She had looked up into a tangle of branches and leaves. It was a sight she had never forgotten. Now, gazing down at the branches of the sea-bell plants swaying gently in the sea current, she knew what it was like to look down on a forest from above.

It was also like looking at the night sky. Growing from every twig and stem were faint pinpoints of light. Swimming closer, she realized that these were the sea bells. Each was filled with tiny grains of brightness.

She hadn't known that they glowed. As she reached the swaying strands and their burdens of light, she stretched out and touched one. It was surprisingly soft—nothing like the hard translucent bells she had seen before. She took the knife Rissi had loaned her and carefully cut through the stem.

As soon as the bell was severed from the stem, the light died. She felt a pang of guilt and sadness. It seemed a shame to disturb the plants. They were so pretty.

She then thought of her father and all that she had gone through to get here. She began cutting more bells. While Rissi had been making his flarke costume she had made a rough bag out of another leaf of sea grass curled into a cone and pinned with short lengths of spine. She put the bells in this.

A splash above her drew her attention upward. She saw a silhouette of a landwalker and her heart stopped.

*The diver's back!*

She held the bag closed with one hand and dashed away.

*They must have worked out they were being tricked! Or maybe the costume started falling apart. Or—*

Something pressed into her face. It slid across her skin, enveloping her before she could react. Rope. Fine rope woven into a net. She threw out her arms but felt the net curl around them.

*Don't panic!* she told herself. Now that she was caught she was conscious of the growing need for air. She had heard stories of Elai that had drowned, tangled in landwalkers' nets, but also others of how people had freed themselves. She knew if she thrashed about, she'd only become more tangled. *I must stay calm and work my way free.*

Looking at the net, she saw that the spaces in the weave were wide enough that most fish could swim through. It extended to either side in a curve that suggested it surrounded the sea-bell plants. What that implied set her heart racing again. Had these landwalkers put it there to keep off predators, or Elai?

She did not want to find out. In one hand she held the bag of sea bells. In the other she held Rissi's knife. She needed both hands to cut through the net. Holding the bag in her mouth, she sawed at the net until she had made a hole big enough for the bag. She pushed it through and let it go. It slowly sank to the sandy bottom.

Now she began to cut her arms free. Just as she had released one arm, she felt a tug through the net.

She looked up, her heart sinking with dread as she saw the net was slowly moving upward.

*Not yet!* she thought, as she set to sawing at the weave

frantically. Another tug came and she felt the strands tighten around her. She slashed at them. An easing in water pressure told her she was moving upward. She realized more of her was outside the net than in it. Yet still the tangle of it around her legs pulled her upward, feet first. She saw the surface rapidly approaching. Felt the looming hulk of the boat nearby. Heard voices.

She felt a surge of panic and hacked at the net. Something caught the blade and it slipped from her grasp. She twisted and grabbed for it, but her fingers closed on water. Sunlight flashed on the blade once before it sank out of sight.

The net tightened on her legs as she was hauled upward. *No!* She shrieked into the water and twisted about to claw at her legs, but the next pull lifted her into air. She gasped in a fresh lungful then tried to reach up to her ankles again. Free of the buoyancy of the water, she didn't have the strength to reach them. She heard voices above her. Angry voices. One of them barked a word.

Then hands were clawing and pulling at her. She struggled and struck out, shrieking in terror. The hard edge of the boat rolled under her, then she fell onto a flat surface.

The hands left her. She stopped shrieking and stared up at her captors, panting with fear. They stared back at her, their pale, wrinkled faces twisted with disgust.

Words passed between them. One narrowed his eyes at her, then barked at the others. They eyed him with sullen respect, then all but one moved away.

She guessed the barker was the leader. He began to talk with the one who'd stayed. Imi turned her attention to the net still tangled around her ankles. The rope had drawn painfully tight. If she could free herself, she had only to spring up and leap over the side of the boat to get away.

But the rope would not loosen. She felt a shadow fall over her and realized the leader was bending down. Seeing the knife in his hand, she shrank away, sure that he was going to kill her. She heard herself whimpering with fear.

The knife moved to her ankles. With a few careful cuts he freed her.

He was going to let her go. She felt a surge of relief and found herself thanking the man. He looked at the second man, who smiled.

It was not a friendly smile. Imi felt her stomach twist. The leader barked again, and one of the other men tossed him a short length of rope. As he moved toward her ankle again she realized what he was going to do. Relief evaporated and she tried to leap up, but his hand closed around her leg firmly. The second man grabbed her shoulders, shoved her down onto her back and held her there. She shrieked again, and kept shrieking as the leader tied her ankles together. They rolled her onto her front in order to tie her hands together behind her, then dragged her to the center of the boat where they tied her hands to a metal ring.

"What are you doing?" Imi cried desperately, struggling into a sitting position. "Why won't you let me go free?"

The two men exchanged glances, then turned and walked away.

"You can't hold me here. I'm . . . I'm the Elai king's daughter," she declared, feeling anger growing. "My father will send warriors to kill you!"

None of the landwalkers paid any attention. They did not know what she was telling them. They did not understand her words any more than she understood theirs. How could she tell them who she was?

One of the landwalkers nearby upended a bag. Its contents spilled out. She stared at the green mess, and as the men set to plucking small objects out of the tangle she realized that the limp strands she was looking at were the fragile branches and roots of the sea-bell plant.

The landwalkers had ripped the plants out of the sandy floor of the sea.

She felt a wave of nausea at the thought of what they'd done. There would be no crop of bells next year for this plant. They had killed the plant outright in their haste to harvest them.

*How can they be so wasteful?* she thought. *And so stupid! If they left the plants intact, they could come back next year and gather more bells.*

Her father was right. Landwalkers were horrible. She twisted her hands about, but there was no way she was going to be able to get to the knot to untie it.

*Rissi,* she thought. *He's got to tell father where I am.* She struggled to her feet and searched the water. After an eternity she thought she saw something move. A head, perhaps.

"Rissi!" she screamed. "Tell father where I am. Tell him I'm a prisoner. Tell him to come—"

Something struck her face. She staggered to her knees, her face aflame. The leader was standing over her. He barked out a few words, pointing at her with his long, webless fingers.

Though she could not understand a word, the warning was clear. Stunned, Imi watched him walk away.

*Father will come,* she told herself. *He'll save me. When he does, he'll spear every one of these horrible landwalkers, and they'll deserve it.*

# 14

It was pleasantly warm outside the cave, now that the late summer sun had set. The sky was free of cloud, and the stars were a dense carpet above. Emerahl sighed with appreciation.

"That's better," Mirar murmured.

They had decided the rock wall was the most comfortable place to sit two nights ago, when Mirar had first ventured outside. Though she hadn't caught a hint of Mirar's thoughts for many days now, he wasn't invisible to physical eyes so he only emerged at night. The Siyee thought she was alone and she did not want them to find out otherwise until she and Mirar had decided what they wanted to do next.

There was little to do at night but admire the stars and talk. She heard Mirar draw in a breath to speak.

"I've been thinking about the other Wilds today. It is possible some are still alive."

She turned to look at him. His face was faintly lit by starlight. "I've been thinking about them, too. I've been asking myself whether it would be better or worse for us if we found them."

"Worse if it leads to the gods discovering our existence."

"How would they?" She paused. "Do you think the others would betray us?"

"They may not mean to. The gods may read their minds."

Emerahl smiled crookedly. "If their minds were readable, the gods would have found and killed them long ago," she pointed out.

Mirar shifted his position. "Yes. Probably."

She looked up at the stars. "Still, the others might need our help."

"I'm sure if they've survived this long they don't need our help."

"Oh? Like *you* didn't need *my* help?"

He chuckled. "But I'm just a young fool a mere thousand years old. The other Wilds are older and wiser."

"Then they might be able to help *us*," she replied.

"How?"

"If I was able to teach you to hide your mind, imagine what they might be able to teach us. Perhaps nothing, but we can't know that until we find them."

"You want me to come with you on this search?"

Emerahl sighed. "I'd like you to, but I don't think it would be wise. If you are right about ordinary priests not being able to read minds . . ."

"And I am."

". . . then I will be safe enough, unless I have a moment of exceptionally bad luck and bump into the priest with the mind-reading ability who was looking for me before."

"While there are far more people who might recognize Leiard," he finished.

"Yes."

"If the gods are looking for me, they may have instructed priests and priestesses to call for them if they see me. Dreamweavers are probably also watching for me. The gods could be watching their minds, too." He groaned. "There are so many people who could recognize me. Why did Leiard agree to become Dreamweaver Adviser to the White?"

"I'm sure he thought it was for the best."

"Dealing with the gods never turns out for the best." He sighed. "How long am I going to have to hide for? Am I going to have to stay in this cave until no one is left alive who might recognize me?"

"If you did, you'd never leave. Unless you plan to have someone assassinate the White."

"Is that an offer?"

She smiled. "No. You are going to have to do what I did—become a hermit. Avoid all but the most ordinary, unimportant people."

"So if I stay here for a lifetime I'll only have the White to worry about."

"If you want to avoid all people you can't stay here. I told the Siyee I would return home now I knew the war was over," she said. "They will keep coming back to check if I am still here."

"Do you know of any other hiding places?"

"A few. I don't think you can or should avoid other humans completely, however. You need people about or the rift in your identity might widen again."

"I have you."

She smiled. "Indeed you have. But I am a person who Mirar relates to strongly. I may be inhibiting your ability to accept Leiard. You need to interact with people who have no prior relationship with you. These Siyee will do you no harm. You said you hadn't met any of them."

"Who will I tell them I am? I can't tell them I am Mirar."

"No. You will have to pretend to be someone else again."

"Leiard?"

"No," she said firmly. "Give yourself a new name and appearance, but don't invent new habits or personality traits to go with them. Be yourself."

"What name should I use, then?"

She shrugged. "I wouldn't choose a name you dislike."

He chuckled. "Of course not." She heard him drumming his fingers. "I'm still a Dreamweaver, so I'll name myself after one. On the journey to the battle I met a young man not unlike myself. Opinionated and smart. His name was Wil."

"Wil? Isn't that a Dunwayan name? You don't look Dunwayan."

"No. I'll add a syllable, then."

She chuckled. "How about Wily? Or Willful?"

He sighed. "In a thousand years your sense of humor hasn't improved much, Emerahl."

"I could have suggested Wilted."

He made a low, disapproving noise. "I will call myself Wilar."

Emerahl nodded. "Wilar, then. Wilar what?"

"Shoemaker." He lifted one foot. The sandals he had made were just visible in the faint light.

"Useful skill, that one," she said.

"Yes. Leiard did learn some new ones for me. I never needed to make my own before then. People were always happy to give them to me."

"Ah, the good old days," she said mockingly. "How we miss the unending adoration and generosity of our followers."

He laughed. "Except it wasn't unending."

"No. And I don't miss it."

They were silent for a long time. Mirar finally stirred, and she braced herself in preparation to stand up. But instead of suggesting they go back inside, he only turned to regard her.

"You are going to leave, aren't you?"

She looked at him, and felt pulled in two directions. "I do want to find the other Wilds," she said. "But it can wait. If you need me to stay, I will."

He reached out and touched her face. "I want you to stay," he told her. "But . . . you're right about your effect on me. You're an anchor that I'm afraid to let go of. I should do as you suggest and seek out other people."

She took his hand and closed hers around it. "I can stay a little longer. There is no hurry."

"No, there isn't. Except I feel restless already. I think I'll soon become unbearable to be around if I don't find something to do. I'd come with you if I could. I wish you had a plan in mind that I could assist with, but I'm glad you're trying to find them." He paused. "We must stay in contact."

"Yes." As she said it, she felt her wish to find the Wilds harden into determination. "We will dream link. I can tell you how my search is going."

"And keep an eye on me?"

She laughed. "Definitely."

He drew his hand away and leaned back on the rock wall again. His head tilted as he looked up at the stars.

"So beautiful," he said. "Will you change your appearance again?"

She considered. Being good-looking gave one an advantage when gathering information, but being beautiful—and young—usually proved a hindrance when travelling. People tended to notice and remember beautiful women. They asked too many questions or, if men, tried to seduce her.

"Yes. I'll add about ten or twenty years I think."

He murmured something. She caught the words "missed out" and smiled. It was nice to know he was still attracted to her. Perhaps once he had accepted Leiard and become whole again there would be another opportunity for a dalliance.

She smiled. *The sooner I leave, the sooner he'll sort himself out and the sooner we can explore those possibilities. If I have doubts about going, I'll just remind myself of that.* Still smiling, she rose and headed back into the cave to start preparing for the long process of changing her age.

Imenja poured another glass of water, then topped Reivan's glass up.

"One more to go," she murmured. "It'll be over soon."

Reivan nodded and tried not to look too relieved. When she had first entered the room and realized that she would be included in the final stage of an event as momentous as the election of the First Voice she had been dizzy with awe and amazement.

She had watched in fascination as each of the Voices closed their eyes, communicated with Head Servants in regions all over Ithania, and spoke aloud the tally of votes for each Dedicated Servant. The Companion for each Voice had marked the tally on a huge sheet of parchment. When Imenja had indicated that Reivan should do the same for her, she had been overwhelmed. As she'd taken up the brush her hands had been shaking with excitement.

At the end of an hour the endless repetition of the tallying had turned fascination to boredom. After two hours she was dismayed to find they had collected tallies for only a sixth of the regions on the parchment. It was going to be a long day.

Domestics brought an endless variety of delicacies and drinks as if to make up for the monotony of the day. All conversation was undertaken in quiet murmurs, so as to avoid distracting whichever Voice was collecting information.

"That is all," Vervel said. "All votes are cast. Will you do the first count, Imenja?"

The Second Voice rose and moved to the sheet of parchment. She ran her finger down the first column slowly, her lips moving as she added up the numbers. When she reached the end of the column she took the brush and inked in a total, then she started counting the next column of numbers.

This was also a slow process, but Reivan felt a growing anticipation. When Imenja was done, they would know who was to be their new leader. She glanced at the Companions. They, too, were watching with rapt expressions.

Imenja's finger made a soft scraping sound as it moved down the parchment. Each time she paused to ink in the result Reivan studied her face. Reivan had memorized the order of the names and knew which Dedicated Servant her mistress was counting the tallies of. She also knew from the tallies she had written down which candidates were most favored. But when Imenja's eyebrows rose at one result, and frowned at another, Reivan could not guess whether her mistress was pleased, dismayed or merely surprised.

When Imenja had finished, she straightened and looked at Vervel. He returned her gaze, then shrugged. Karkel, Vervel's Companion, half rose out of his chair, but sat down again as Vervel looked at him and shook his head.

*So they're not going to tell us now,* Reivan thought. *Will they tell us when the others have confirmed the count? Or will we have to wait until they make the public announcement?*

Vervel now began to count the votes. Unable to stand the suspense, Reivan looked away. A plate of nuts and dried fruit lay on the table beside her. She began to eat, though she was far from hungry. The plate was half-empty by the time Shar announced his count finished. Imenja rolled the parchment up then smiled at the four Companions.

"Let's go and give one Dedicated Servant some good news and a lot of people something to celebrate."

The Companions stood. Reivan noted the expressions of resignation on their faces. *So we have to wait like everyone else,* she thought, smiling to herself. *So much for being Imenja's favored pet.*

They followed the Voices out of the room. Two domestics approaching the door with trays of food paused and bowed their heads as the small parade of importance passed. Looking back, Reivan saw them exchange meaningful looks, then hurry away.

Soon she was noting other domestics and a few Servants peering around corners or doors at them. She caught excited whispers and running footsteps. A feeling of growing expectation began to fill the Sanctuary. Distant shouts and calls could be heard, muffled behind walls or doors. A bell rang somewhere, then others. The Voices left the intimate passages of the Upper Sanctuary and started down the main corridor of the Middle Sanctuary. Reivan could see Servants ahead hurrying to join those waiting to hear the announcement. Others formed a small crowd that followed at a discreet distance.

The corridor of the Middle Sanctuary ended at a large courtyard. Imenja and the other Voices strode across this, the Companions following, and entered an airy hall. A crowd of black robes filled the room. Reivan recognized the faces of many Dedicated Servants. She wondered how long they had been waiting here.

The sound of chatter died and all heads turned toward the Voices, but the Pentadrian leaders did not stop. They crossed the hall and emerged at the top of the Main Stairs. As they appeared a roar of voices greeted them. The people of Glymma, and those who had travelled here to witness the election of the new First Voice, formed a great mass of upturned faces and waving arms.

The four Voices formed a line. Standing behind them, Reivan could not see their expressions. She closed her eyes and let the great sound of the cheering crowd wash over her.

"Fellow Pentadrians," Imenja called, her voice rising above the noise.

The cheering dwindled reluctantly. Looking past Imenja, Reivan saw many overly bright eyes in the crowd, and bottles and mugs clutched in several hands. She chuckled quietly to herself.

*It was a long wait. I guess they had to entertain themselves somehow.*

"Fellow Pentadrians," Imenja repeated. "We have gathered the votes of Servants from all over the world. The day has been long, but this was too important a task to be hurried. The tally has been counted." She held up the impressively long roll of parchment. "We have a new First Voice!"

The crowd cheered again.

"Come forward, Dedicated Servants of the Gods!"

From the hall behind, men and women filed down the stairs. They began to form a long line across the bottom, turning to look up at the Voices.

*One of these people has convinced most of the Servants of the Gods that he or she will be a good leader,* Reivan thought. She considered all the histories she'd read, of philosophical discussions on the qualities of a good leader. *Do any of these candidates have the right qualities? What if none of them have? Would the gods intervene?* She frowned. That would be quite a slap in the face. It would imply that most Servants didn't know how to choose a good leader.

*Perhaps they don't.* She suddenly felt uneasy. *How would they have chosen?* She considered what she would have done, if she had been a Servant living far from Glymma. *I guess I'd have dismissed anyone who's caused trouble or made big mistakes. It would help if one of these people had proven his or herself capable of leading and making good decisions already. I think I'd prefer someone who'd fought in the war to one who hadn't, but ultimately*

*I'd have to take a gamble, based on the information I had.
I wouldn't choose anyone I didn't like. Nobody's going to
vote for someone they dislike.*

The last of the Dedicated Servants joined the line.
Imenja held up the roll of parchment. She waited until all
was silent—or as quiet as a half-drunk crowd could manage. Then she let the parchment unroll.

"The Servants of the Gods have chosen Dedicated
Servant Nekaun as the new First Voice. Come forward,
Nekaun."

As the crowd erupted in cheering again, Reivan felt her
heart lift. She thought back to the man who had offered both
congratulations and advice at her ordination, and smiled.

*Oh, good,* she thought.

Peering past Imenja's shoulder, she watched Nekaun
step forward. He looked composed and calm, but his eyes
burned with excitement. *I would have chosen him,* she
thought. *He's never made any great mistakes, has run the
Temple of Hrun for a few years as well as fought in the war.
He's likeable and kind. And to top it off, he's good-looking.
That's got to be an advantage in a leader! What more could
the gods want?* She watched in admiration as he stopped a
few steps before Imenja and made the sign of the star.

Imenja handed the parchment to Genza, who began to
slowly roll it up again. From within her robe Imenja produced a star pendant. She held it up. The crowd slowly
quietened.

"Accept this symbol of the gods," she said, "and you
accept an eternity of servitude to them and to their people.
You will become the Voice with which they speak to mortals. You will become the Hand that toils for our benefit,
and strikes down our enemies."

He slowly reached out to take the chain, then bowed his
head.

"I accept the burden and the responsibility," he said.

He closed his eyes and draped the chain around his
neck. Reivan saw him stiffen and an expression of wonder
crossed his face. He straightened, looked up at Imenja and
smiled.

"And the gods have accepted me."

"Then take your place among us," Imenja finished.

Still smiling, he stepped up beside her and turned to face the crowd. Imenja gestured toward him, while regarding the crowd.

"People of Glymma and beyond. Do you welcome Nekaun, First Voice of the Gods?"

The crowd responded with a roar of approval. Imenja turned her head to regard him. "Will you address the people?"

"I will." He paused and waited until all was quiet. "My people. As I stand here before you I feel both joy and sadness. Joy that I have been gifted with the greatest opportunity to serve the gods that a man or woman may be given. Sadness that I take the place of a man I admired.

"I willingly take on the same responsibilities that he bore, because our aims are the same. We must rid the world of the heathen Circlians. But do not fear that I will lead you into another war. That has been tried, and through ill chance or the will of the gods it failed.

"I see another way to achieve our goal. We must show them their mistake and lead them to the true gods. We must draw them to our side gently, through persuasion and reason. For I believe truth and understanding are powerful forces, and they are forces we have in our favor. Using them, we cannot fail." He raised his arms. "With them, we will conquer Northern Ithania!"

*It's not the torch to the oil of glorious war that Kuar's kill-and-take speech was,* Reivan mused. The crowd roared anyway, fired up by the excitement of this momentous event, as well as drink and perhaps relief that there would not be another war for now.

As Imenja addressed the crowd again, Reivan considered Nekaun's goal. *So he wants to convert the Circlians,* she thought. *I wonder how he plans to do that? Will he send Servants into Northern Ithania to woo the people there? I can't imagine they'll be given a warm welcome.*

Imenja finished. Nekaun glanced at her, then began to lead the Voices back to the hall. Reivan and the Companions followed. As they moved indoors, Servants crowded around, offering congratulations to their new leader. Reivan wondered how many of them had realized what Nekaun's plan might mean for them. Travelling into Northern Ithania to convert Circlians might prove to be more dangerous than marching to war.

*I don't envy them that task,* she thought. Abruptly she realized she was not disqualified from it. *But shouldn't I want to go? Shouldn't I be willing to do anything for the gods?*

*I'm unSkilled and only a Servant-novice. I'm of more use here, serving Imenja.*

Yet she might not have any choice in the matter. What if Nekaun asked her to go? What if she ended up in a situation where he wanted her out of the way? She could see no reason for that now, but this was the world of politics and favor. Anything could change.

*Then there's only one thing I can do,* she decided. *Make sure I give him no reason to want me gone.*

# 15

The cave was dark when Mirar woke. Only a faint light was visible at the entrance. Emerahl usually woke earlier than he did and ventured outside to empty the buckets and bring in fresh water. He could not hear her breathing, so he guessed she had gone. Creating a spark of light, he strengthened it until the whole cave was illuminated.

Emerahl was still in bed.

At once he remembered. She was in the process of changing her age. He got up and moved over to her bed.

He could only see her face, but it showed subtle signs of change. Skin that had been fresh and firm with youth now hung slightly looser on her cheekbones. The faintest lines had formed around her eyes and mouth. Strands of hair had fallen out, forming a golden coating on the rough mattress she had made.

He picked up a few strands. There were stripes of variation along the first hand span of its length. Successive dying, he guessed. Weaker each time. Why would she have dyed her hair?

*She said she had been an old woman before this,* Leiard reminded him. *Her hair could have been white. It must have stayed that way, despite the rest of her body changing to a more youthful form, but from then on it grew in her natural color.*

*Yes,* Mirar agreed. He looked at the strand. *She must have dyed the white, first with cheap pigment then with better dye that that brothel provided.*

The brothel. He sighed and shook his head. She was so Gifted. Why must she resort to selling herself whenever she needed to hide?

*Because she had no choice,* Leiard said.

*Of course she had a choice.* Mirar scowled. She could have become a washer-woman or a fish-scaler.

*The priests would have looked over all women's trades that an old crone might take up. By practicing a trade only young women could practice she could be sure she would never be examined by a priest.*

It made sense, but Mirar didn't like it. The risk of discovery must have been small. Only one priest had been given the ability to read minds by the gods.

*She didn't know that,* Leiard reminded him.

Mirar almost wished he hadn't told her that the gods did not make a habit of giving priests that Gift. Now that Emerahl knew she was safe she wanted to roam about the world in search of other Wilds. He looked at her and felt a stab of concern.

*I should go with her,* he thought.

*You can't,* Leiard pointed out. *There's a greater risk that I'll be recognized than her. I'd only put us all in danger.*

Mirar nodded in agreement. Even in sleep there was a strength in her expression. Or perhaps he only imagined that. *She'll be fine. I doubt she's suddenly become a risk-taker,* he told himself. *No, she'll be as cautious as she has always been.* He sighed and looked away. *And me? I'm supposed to seek out people in order to cure myself. How foolish is that?*

Perhaps not overly foolish. He would seek out the Siyee—or most likely linger here until they found him.

*What excuse will I give them for coming here?* he asked himself. *Why would a Dreamweaver come to Si?*

*To offer healing services, of course,* Leiard replied.

Healing was what he had always done best. Even as a child he'd had an unusual understanding of healing. Years of study and work had refined the Gift. Each time he had thought he had reached the limits of his powers something caused him to stretch himself further and he discovered he could do more. One day it had all culminated in a sudden flash of understanding in which he comprehended how his body might be sustained in a healthy, youthful state indefinitely.

It had been the moment he had achieved immortality. Emerahl, too, had come to the same understanding. She did not have the intuitive aptitude with healing that he had. Instead, her innate Gift was this ability to change her age.

*And the other Wilds?* He thought of the extraordinary people who had once roamed free in the world. The Farmer had been famous for his understanding of growing and raising crops, stock and all manner of produce. His innate Gift had probably related to that somehow. The Seer's ability had been to predict a person's probable path in life, though she had admitted to Mirar once that she did not see the future, she just saw the nature of mortals too well.

The Gull had understood everything to do with the sea. He could find shoals of fish, warn against storms and was rumored to be able to change the weather to a limited degree. The Twins . . . Mirar had never been entirely sure what their abilities were. He had never met them, but someone had once told him they understood the duality of everything in the world, that they perceived connections and balances where nobody else could.

Where the magic was in that talent, he didn't know. Most likely he would never find out. They had probably been killed a century ago, when the Circle of Gods had decided to tidy up their new world.

*The gods are probably the only beings that know,* he thought.

*You could ask them,* Leiard suggested.

He chuckled. *Even if calling on them wasn't likely to result in our death, I doubt we could trust their answer.*

He looked at Emerahl again. She hadn't moved while he'd been watching her, except to breathe. The rise and fall of her chest was so slow he had to watch patiently to see the change.

*I'll miss her.* He frowned, surprised at the wistful emotion that came with the thought. It was not that he didn't expect to feel this way, just that it was stronger than he had anticipated.

*You didn't feel like this about her before?* Leiard asked. *Do you love her?*

Mirar considered. He felt affection and concern. He would not like her to be harmed or feel pain. He enjoyed her company, had always enjoyed her physical company the few times they had been lovers—but he was still sure he did not feel anything like romantic love. Emerahl was a friend.

*Yes. You have missed the company of an equal.*

*Perhaps I have,* he conceded.

Looking away, he considered the cave. He was hungry. She had told him there was enough food to last him for the few days she would be changing. It was mostly nuts, fresh and dried fruit, some dried meat and a few tubers.

*Hardly inspiring fare,* he thought. He glanced at the cave entrance, thinking of the shrimmi she had caught and cooked once before. *I think it's time I saw a little daylight. If the Siyee fly past and see me, so be it. I doubt they'll be any danger to Emerahl. To be sure I'll tell them she has already left. I don't think I need to stay in here every moment of the next few days. Perhaps I can find her something decent to eat when she wakes up.*

Picking up the bucket she had used when collecting food, he started toward the tunnel and daylight.


Erra considered the strange child curled up on the deck. She was completely hairless as far as he could see. Between the fingers and toes of her enormous hands and feet was a thick webbing. Her skin was unnaturally dark—a bluish black. It had been glossy yesterday, but now it looked dull.

"She bring trouble," Kanyer warned. "She child. Adults come for her. Slit our throats in our sleep."

"That's what you said last night," Erra replied. "No one came."

"Why you keep her?"

"A hunch. My da used to say you can find something useful in everything that comes out of the sea."

"How she useful? You think sea folk trade for her?"

"Maybe. I have another idea. Silse said he saw her taking the bells. Said she must have been there for a while."

Kanyer looked at the girl with interest. "It true they breathe water then."

Erra shook his head. "Nah. She hasn't got gills. See the size of her chest. Big lungs. Prob'ly means she can hold her breath a long time." He rubbed his stubbly chin. "That'd be useful to us."

"You want her get bells for us?"

"Yes."

"She won't."

"She will if we give her a reason."

Erra strode across to the girl and cut the ropes around her ankles. She didn't wake up so he nudged her with his foot. Her whole body jerked as she came awake and she turned her head to stare up at him. Her lips were cracked and the film across her eyes was red. He guessed that being out of the water was doing her harm and felt a small pang of guilt. *Well, she shouldn't have tried to steal my bells.*

He reached over to the lamp ring and untied the end of the rope that tethered her.

"Get up."

She moved slowly, her expression wary and sullen.

"Come over here."

He tugged her to the baskets of sea bells and waved to the last empty one. He indicated the level of the full one next to it, then held his hand over the empty basket at the same place. She watched him intently. He pointed at her, then at the sea, then indicated the full level of the empty basket again. Finally he pointed to the ropes and made a cutting motion, then pointed to her and then waved out at the sea.

She glared at him, obviously understanding but not liking what he was proposing. Nevertheless, she did not resist as he tugged her over to the side of the boat. The crew watched, still chewing on their morning meal.

He turned her around and untied the rope binding her wrists. Then he tied a long length of new, dry rope around her neck. It would swell when it got wet, and be impossible to untie. He nudged her and pointed at the water.

She stared at him resentfully for a moment, then jumped into the water. At once she began struggling with the rope.

"Silse," Erra called.

The swimmer strolled over.

"Get in the water and keep an eye on her. If it looks like she's going to get free, let me know. We'll haul her back out."

The man hesitated. Using the girl like this probably pricked the fool's conscience. Or was he worried about losing his share of the profits?

"What are you waiting for?" Erra growled.

Silse shrugged, then jumped into the water. The girl's struggles stopped. She looked at Silse floating nearby. After staring at him for a long time, she suddenly dove into the gloom, the rope running into the water after her.

Silse watched her. After a moment he raised his head out of the water.

"She's doing it, but she's cutting them one by one."

"Let her," one of the other crewmen said. "It'll save us some work."

Erra nodded. There'd be less trouble later, when it came to dividing the profits, if the others couldn't claim Silse had done less work than them. He pointed to one of the bags the swimmers had used to haul up the sea-bell plants.

"Give me that."

They tossed it to him. He dropped it into the water beside Silse.

"When she comes up again, give her that," he told the swimmer. He sat down to wait.

She reappeared sooner than he expected, but her hands were overflowing with sea bells. Silse awkwardly began trying to explain to her about the bag's use. She ignored him. Tipping the bells onto the deck, she grabbed the bag and disappeared into the depths again.

Silse looked up at Erra and shrugged.

The crew began to lounge about. A few started a game of counters. The girl came to the surface about three or four times to take another breath. Each time the bag was emptied into the basket and handed back.

After the fourth time, Erra decided his idea was working well. He may as well have a drink and enjoy himself. He looked for the youngest of his crew, Darm, and found the boy was at the top of the mast.

"Darm!" he bellowed.

The boy started. "Yes capt'n?"

"Get down here."

The boy uncurled his thin legs from the mast and began to climb down. Erra reached into his pocket for some smokewood.

"Capt'n?"

Erra looked up. The boy had stopped halfway down the mast and was pointing toward the bluff at one side of the bay.

"Sails," he said. "Someone's coming."

At once all the crew were on their feet. Erra moved toward the mast, determined to have a look himself, but he didn't need to. The bow of a ship was now gliding into sight beyond the bluff.

It was a battered but sturdy trading vessel, larger than the fishing boats. Erra narrowed his eyes. He could just see men on board, lined up along the side. As the rest of the ship came in sight, the strangers all raised their arms and waved.

Erra felt his stomach drop. They were waving swords.

"Raiders!" Darm yelled.

Erra cursed. Even if the sails had been hoisted and they hadn't been cornered in the bay, his boats could never have outrun the ship. They would have to abandon them—but perhaps not their hoard. He turned to the crew. They looked pale and ready to bolt.

"We've got to swim for shore!" one cried.

"No!" Erra bellowed. "Not yet. We've got a bit of time before they get here." He pointed to the baskets of sea bells. "Bind them closed, tie on weights and throw them in. *Then* we'll swim for it. Anyone who doesn't help, doesn't get a coin."

A flurry of activity followed. With heart pounding, Erra grabbed anything that would do as a weight and roped it to the baskets. He bullied the crew with feigned confidence. Two baskets splashed into the water, then another. They sank into the depths.

"They're coming fast!" Darm wailed. "We won't make it to shore!"

Erra straightened to look. The ship was approaching quickly. He judged the distance they had to swim.

"Right. Leave the rest. They'll want to feel they got something, or they'll come after us for sport. Swim!"

Not waiting for the others to follow, he dove into the water. Fear lent him strength and speed. When he finally reached the sand he dragged himself upright and glanced back. The ship was bearing down on the boats. His crew were emerging from the water. He cursed then started running toward the forest.

Only later, when he stared down at the smoking hulls of the boats from a rocky bluff, did he remember the sea girl. Had she been smart enough to hide or escape, or had they found her? He sent Silse back to look, but the swimmer found no sign of her. Only the cut end of the rope.

The small pang of guilt Erra felt was easily brushed aside. He had more important things to worry about now.

Like how he was going to get off this island.

The leaden sky leeched everything of color—except the blood.

The faces of the corpses were white, the hair either black or a bleached non-color. The weapons, still clutched in stiffened hands or wedged in flesh, lacked shine. The circs of the priests were a dull white.

But the stains on them were luridly bright. Thick crimson oozed from wounds and slicked blades. Pools of it gathered under the dead like a morbid carpet. Trickles of it flowed down folds in the earth. It gathered to form streams. Pooled. Soaked into the soil, so that it bubbled to the surface at every step.

Auraya tried to walk gently, tried to keep to the dry areas, but the blood welled up to coat her sandalled feet. The sickening mud sucked at her feet. She took a few more steps then found she could not move. The mud clung to her shoes. It gave beneath her. She felt herself sinking into it. Leaning on one leg to try and free the other only sent her deeper. She felt the cold moisture creeping up her legs and her heart began to race.

"*You killed us,*" hissed a voice.

She looked up to see corpses raising their heads to stare at her with dead eyes.

*Not now,* she thought. *I've got enough problems.*

"*You,*" another said, his partly severed head lolling on the ground. "*You did this to me.*"

She tried not to hear the voices, concentrating instead on getting free of the mud, which did not want to let her go. Red bubbles and froth foamed the surface. She leaned forward, desperately trying to find something to grab hold of to stop herself sinking. Something to use to lever herself out.

*I'm going to drown,* she thought, and fear surged up within her. *I'm going to suffocate, my mouth and lungs full of bloodied soil.*

There was nothing but a sea of corpses reaching out to her with clawed hands. She shrank away, felt herself sink further, then forced herself to reach out to them.

"*It's your fault I'm dead,*" a woman hissed.

"*Your fault!*"

"*Yours!*"

*:No.*

Everything stilled. The corpses froze in position. The sucking of the mud stopped. Auraya peered around in confusion. The corpses' eyes swivelled about in search of the voice.

*This doesn't usually happen,* she mused.

*:It is not her fault you are dead. If you must blame someone, blame me. Either way, you are wrong. Neither Auraya nor I dealt the blow that killed you.*

A shining figure appeared. The corpses rolled or shrank away from him. He looked down at Auraya and smiled.

*:Hello, Auraya.*

"Chaia!"

*:Yes.*

He walked to the edge of the mud and held out a hand. She hesitated, then reached out to take it. Firm, warm fingers gripped her own. He pulled, and she felt the mud relinquish its hold on her legs.

*:Let's return to your room,* he said.

The battlefield vanished. Suddenly she was sitting on her bed, Chaia beside her. He smiled and reached out to her face. The touch of his fingers as he traced them along her jaw sent a shiver down her spine. He leaned toward her, and she knew he was going to kiss her.

*Uh oh,* she thought, drawing away. *It's all very well conjuring him up to rescue me from the nightmare, but dreaming up erotic encounters is definitely going too far.*

*:You resist. You think this is wrong. Disrespectful.*

"Yes."

He smiled.

*:But how can it be disrespectful, when I am the one kissing you?*

"You're not real. The real Chaia might be offended."

*:I'm not real?* His smile widened. *Are you sure?*

"Yes. The real Chaia can't touch me."

*:I can in dreams.*

*As Leiard had,* she thought. The memory of him brought an uncomfortable rush of different emotions. Pain at his betrayal. Shame that she had taken to bed someone whom this god probably didn't approve of. And despite this: longing. Her dream links with Leiard had seemed utterly real. She felt a flush of remembered pleasure, quickly followed by embarrassment and shame again as she remembered whose presence she was in—even if he was only a dream shadow of the god.

*:Do not regret your past,* Chaia told her. *Everything you do teaches you something about the world and yourself. It is up to you to draw wisdom from your mistakes.*

She considered him warily. He was so forgiving. But of course he was. This wasn't Chaia. The real Chaia would . . . what? Scold her like a child?

Chaia laughed.

*:Still convinced I'm a dream?*

"Yes."

He slid his hand behind her neck and leaned close.

*:Open your eyes.*

She stared at him. "What if I dream of opening my—"

He sealed her mouth with his. She stiffened with surprise. Suddenly he and her room disappeared. She was lying down, covered in blankets. In her bed. She saw only darkness. Her eyes were closed.

Awake.

But her lips tingled. She opened her eyes. A luminous face hovered over hers. The mouth widened into a smile. One eye winked.

Then the apparition vanished.

# PART
# TWO

# 16

A salty breeze told Emerahl she was approaching the coast long before she saw the sea. Yet it was only when she crested a rise and saw the wide gray strip of water in the distance that she felt she was close to her destination.

At the sight of water, she sighed with relief. She sat down on a fallen log while she caught her breath. Two months of walking had made her lean and given her stamina, but the hill she stood upon was steep and it had been a long, relentless climb to get to this place.

*Rozea wouldn't recognize me now,* she thought. It was not just her age that she had changed. She kept her hair dyed black now and wove it into a simple braid each morning. The dress she had on was plain and practical and over it she wore an eclectic mix of tawls, drapes, beaded jewellery and embroidered pouches. The aromas of herbs, essences and other ingredients for her cures surrounded her.

It had never been necessary to mention her trade to anyone. She simply entered a village or town, enquired of the first person she met if there was safe and decent accommodation to be found, and by the time she had settled into the suggested place the first customer arrived.

Most of the time, anyway. There had always been, and always would be, places where strangers were treated with suspicion, and healer sorceresses with outright hostility. The first priest she had met had been unfriendly, which hadn't helped to ease her fear of being found by the gods. To her relief he had simply ordered her out of his village.

For days afterward she had expected to find herself being hunted again, but nobody had followed her.

However, in most places she was welcome. Village priests and priestesses did not usually have strong Gifts or more than a basic knowledge of healing. The best of their healers worked in cities, and Dreamweavers were rare, so there was a great demand for her services. Having the appearance of a thirty- to forty-year-old woman also helped—nobody would have believed she had much healing knowledge if she'd remained a beautiful young woman.

The road ahead wove in and out of sight behind hills and forests. She traced it to the sea's edge. Buildings clustered around the middle of a bay like stones in the bottom of a bucket. According to the owners of journey houses, helpful drinking companions, and a copy of a rough map given to her by a trader, this port was called Dufin.

It had grown and prospered in the last forty years due to its position near the Si border. Or rather, due to the Toren people's inclination to ignore the border and settle wherever they saw good fertile soil or mineral deposits. The "inlanders" she had spoken to had told her gleefully how the White had forced the Toren king to order his people out of Si. It would be interesting to see what effect—if any—these orders had made on the people of Dufin.

Hearing a sound behind her, she turned to regard the road. A single arem was pulling a small tarn up the hill toward her. She stood up. Though the driver was too far away for her to read his expression, she was sure he was staring up at her. She could sense his curiosity.

She considered how far away he was, the lateness of the hour and the distance between her and Dufin. Sitting down, she waited for the tarn to reach her.

It took several minutes. Long before then, when the driver was close enough to see, she had exchanged a smile and a wave. As the arem hauled the tarn up to the rise, Emerahl stood up and greeted the man.

He was in his forties, she judged. His weathered face was pleasant—plenty of smile wrinkles. He pulled the arem to a stop.

"Are you going to Dufin?" she asked.

"I am," he replied.

"Have you room for a tired traveller?"

"I always make room for fine young women in need of transportation," he said jovially.

She cast about, as if looking for another. "Where is this woman you speak of? And how selfish of you to leave a tired old woman by the side of the road in favor of a more youthful companion."

He laughed, then gestured to the tarn. "It is no grand covered platten, but if you don't mind the smell you could sit on the furs."

She smiled in gratitude, then climbed on board. As soon as she had settled onto the furs he urged the arem into a walk again. There was a distinctly fishy smell underlying the animal odor of the furs.

"I am Limma Curer," she told him. "A healer."

He glanced back at her, his eyebrows rising. "And a sorceress, I guess. No ordinary woman travels these parts alone."

"A fighting woman might." She grinned and shook her head. "But I am no warrior. Who might you be, then?"

"Marin Hookmaker. Fisherman."

"Ah," she said. "I thought I could smell fish. Let me guess: you deliver fish to inlanders and bring back furs and ..." she looked at the rest of the tarn's contents ". . . vegetables, drink, wood, pottery and—ah—a pair of girri for dinner."

Marin nodded. "That's right. Makes a nice change for me and the inland folk."

"I used to live by the sea," she told him. "Caught my own dinner plenty of times."

"Where'd you live?"

"A remote place. Didn't have a name. I hated it. Too far from anything. I left and travelled to many places and learned my trade. But I always like to be near the sea."

"What brings you to Dufin?"

"Curiosity," she replied. "Work." She paused. Should she begin her search for The Gull now? "I've heard a story. An old story. I want to discover if it is true."

"Oh? What story is that?"

"It's a story about a boy. A boy who never ages. Who knows everything there is to know about the sea."

"Ah," Marin said, the sound more like a sigh than a word. "That *is* an old story."

"Do you know it?"

He shrugged. "There are many, many stories about The Gull. Stories of him saving men from drowning. Stories of him drowning men himself. He is like the sea itself: both kind and cruel."

"Do you believe he exists?"

"No, but I know people who do. They claim to have seen him."

"Tall tales? Stories of old folk grown fanciful in their retelling?"

"Probably." Marin frowned. "I've never known Old Grim to tell something any way but as it was, and he says he crewed with The Gull as a boy."

"I'd like to meet Old Grim."

"I can arrange that. You might not like him, though." Marin looked back at her and grimaced. "He has a foul mouth."

She chuckled. "I can handle that. I've heard some words come out of the mouths of women in childbirth that would burn the ears of most folk."

He nodded. "So have I. My wife's a quiet one most of the time, but when she's in a fury . . ." He shuddered. "Then you know she's a fisherman's daughter."

They had reached the bottom of the hill now. Marin was silent for a while, then he gave her another fleeting glance.

"So you want to discover if The Gull exists. What would it take for you to believe in him?"

"I don't know. To meet him, perhaps."

He laughed. "That would prove it."

"Do you think it's likely I'll meet him?"

"No. What would you do if you did?"

"Ask him about cures. There are many cures that come from the sea."

"Of course."

"I might never find him, but I've got plenty of time. So long as there are people there are always people who need cures. I'll work my way along the coast, perhaps buy passage on ships."

"Most likely you'll meet some lucky man, have lots of pretty children and forget all about The Gull."

She grimaced. "Hmph! I've had enough of foolish romance."

He chuckled. "Have you, then?"

"Yes," she said firmly. As the tarn turned between two smaller hills and the buildings of Dufin came into sight, Emerahl shifted into a more comfortable position.

"So tell me some of these stories about The Gull," she prompted.

Marin, as she'd guessed, was happy to oblige.

Auraya leaned against the window frame and looked down. The Temple grounds were striped and patched with the long shadows cast by the late afternoon sun. Where the rays touched the gardens they set bright drifts of autumn leaves glowing. Juran, as First of the White, occupied the rooms of the Tower's topmost floor. The view was little different to her own, the extra height only giving a slightly greater vista.

"Try this," Juran murmured.

She turned away and accepted a goblet from Juran. Inside was a pale yellow liquid. As she sipped a familiar tartness filled her mouth, followed by the flavor of spices.

"It tastes a little like Teepi," she said.

Juran nodded. "It is made from the berries of the same tree the Siyee use to make Teepi. When the first Toren settlers entered Si, the Siyee treated them as visitors. The Toren took particular interest in Teepi, and learned to make a stronger version of their own."

As he handed the other White glasses of the drink, they each took a sip. Dyara grimaced, Mairae smiled, and Rian, who had no liking for intoxicating drinks, shrugged and set the glass aside.

"It's simpler," Auraya said. "There's no flavor of nuts or wood."

"They brew it in bottles, not barrels. Which is just as well. Wood is scarce in Toren."

"So they plan to continue making it?"

"Yes. One of the more enterprising of the settlers took a few bottles to Aime. The wealthy have acquired a taste for it, and since there's not much about it is selling for a high price. Many of the settlers brought cuttings and saplings of the tree back with them, which are also selling for a high price."

"Good. Many of these Torens ordered to leave Si have left nearly all their assets behind them. This trade will ease the trials of displacement," Dyara said quietly.

"And end any opportunity of the Siyee selling Teepi to the Toren," Auraya added.

"It is not the same drink," Juran said. "The Torens may come to like Siyee Teepi too. There is a demand here that the Siyee could still take advantage of."

Auraya nodded slowly as she began to consider how she might suggest this idea to the Siyee, but something caught her attention and suddenly she was aware of the magic about her. A familiar presence drew close and she felt an equally familiar anxiety returning.

*:Good evening, Auraya.*

*:Chaia.*

*:Why so anxious?*

*:You distract me—sometimes at the least convenient moment,* she confessed. As soon as her mind formed the words, she felt ashamed and apologetic. A bubbling wave of amusement came from Chaia, but it did nothing to dispel her unease.

*:Do not fear to think, Auraya. Your reaction is spontaneous, so how can I be offended by it? I prefer you to treat me like a mortal companion. Or one of your fellow White.*

*:But you're not. You're a god.*

*:That is true. You will have to learn to trust me. You are free to be angry with me. Free to question my will. Free to argue. I want you to argue with me.*

*And he wants more than that,* she thought.

This time she felt herself flush with embarrassment, and

she turned back to the window to hide her reaction from the other White. There was no hiding from Chaia, however. Another wave of amusement washed over her.

*:That is also true. I like you, Auraya. I've been watching you for a long, long time. I have been waiting until you had grown enough that I could tell you without causing you distress.*

*This isn't causing me distress?* she thought wryly. She remembered the kisses she'd evaded. For a being that had no physical form, he could be surprisingly sensual. He often drew close to her as if to compensate for his lack of body. His touch was the touch of magic, yet it was not an unpleasant sensation.

*It's not causing me as much distress as it ought to,* she thought. *I should just admit to myself that I miss Leiard. Not just his company, but the . . . nights. Sometimes it is so tempting to let Chaia have his way.*

She suddenly felt intensely uncomfortable. How could she feel desire for, of all things, a *god*? It was *wrong*.

*:Don't I get to decide what is right or wrong?* Chaia asked.

She felt a tingling along the side of her face and caught her breath. It was a brief touch. She sensed his attention shift abruptly.

*:I must go,* he said.

The luminous presence flashed away. She had an impression of incredible speed, leaving her with no doubt that he could cross Ithania in a heartbeat.

"Auraya!"

She jumped and turned to look at Juran. To her surprise the others had gone. They had left, and she hadn't even noticed.

Juran stared at her, clearly annoyed. She grimaced in apology and his expression softened.

"What is going on, Auraya?" he asked quietly. "Your attention has been straying of late, even during important meetings. It is not like you."

She stared back at him, unsure what to say. *I could make up some excuse. It would have to be a good one, though.*

*Only something important could justify how I've been lately.* As the silence between them lengthened she realized she could not think of an excuse good enough—except the truth.

Still, she hesitated. Would Chaia want Juran to know he spoke to her all the time?

*:Chaia?*

As she expected, there was no answer. The god was nowhere near. Juran watched her expectantly.

*He never said I should* not *tell Juran,* she thought. She took a deep breath.

"It's Chaia," she murmured. "He talks to me. Sometimes at . . . inconvenient times."

Juran's eyebrows rose. "Since when? And how often?"

She thought back. "Two months, and at least once a day."

"What about?"

He looked annoyed. She was not surprised. He was the leader of the White. If Chaia was going to favor anyone with daily visits, surely it ought to be Juran.

"Nothing important," she said hastily. "Just . . . conversation." As Juran frowned, she realized this had not helped. It sounded too evasive. "He advises me on the hospice," she added.

Juran nodded slowly and she was relieved to see he was mollified by this. "I see. That would make sense. What else?"

She shrugged. "Just friendly conversation. I think . . . I think he's trying to get to know me. He had over a hundred years to get to know you. Even Mairae's been around for twenty-six. I've only been here a short time."

"That's true." Juran nodded and his shoulders relaxed. "Well. That is a revelation. What you didn't hear me say was that a trio of Siyee have been sighted flying toward the Tower. The others have gone up to the roof to greet them."

Auraya felt her heartbeat quicken. "Siyee? They would not fly this far without good reason."

He smiled. "Let's go up and find out what it is."

It was only a short climb up the stairs to the roof. The sun now hung just above the horizon. Auraya looked beyond the other White and scanned the sky. Three figures were gliding toward the Tower.

The White were silent as the winged trio drew near. Two of the Siyee were middle-aged, Auraya saw. The other was a little younger and wore a patch over one eye. The Siyee formed a line and landed in unison. The younger man stumbled, but caught his balance. They were clearly exhausted.

Three pairs of eyes fixed upon Auraya. She glanced at Juran, who nodded. Smiling, she stepped forward to greet the arrivals.

"Welcome, people of the sky. I am Auraya of the White." She indicated each of her fellow White, introducing them. The Siyee with the eye patch made the sign of the circle.

"Thank you for your welcome, Chosen of the Gods," the man replied. "I am Niril of the Sun Ridge tribe. My companions are Dyni and Ayliss of the Bald Mountain tribe. We have volunteered to remain here in Jarime as representatives of our people."

"We will be honored to have you among us," she replied. "You must be tired from your journey. I will escort you to rooms where you can rest, if you wish."

Niril inclined his head. "We would be grateful for that. First I have news that the Speakers are anxious for me to deliver. Ten days ago a black ship was seen off the coast of southern Si. The Siyee who investigated sighted several groups of Pentadrian men and women disembark and travel inland. They saw the star pendant on some of the Pentadrians' chests, and they saw birds."

Auraya felt a chill run down her back. The Siyee had lost too many fighters in the war. Did the Pentadrians know this? Did they think the Siyee vulnerable?

"That is bad news," she acknowledged. "But it is fortunate your people saw them arrive. That gives us time." She glanced at Juran and the other White. "We will decide what can be done about it."

"Yes," Juran agreed. "We will meet at the Altar. Auraya

will take you to your rooms first. We will discuss our conclusions with you when you are rested."

Niril nodded, his shoulders dropping with weariness. Auraya smiled in sympathy and beckoned.

"Come with me."

## 17

Imi floated in a forest of sea-bell trees. They swayed softly, stirred by a current. Glowing, tiny bells moved in dizzying patterns around her. She reached out to touch one. The delicate cup swayed closer, as if eager to be plucked.

Then rows of teeth appeared, and the bell lunged toward her hand.

She snatched her hand away, horrified. A shadow slid over her, smothering all but the glowing bells in darkness. Dread gripped her. She looked up.

The hulk of an enormous ship loomed overhead. Ropes descended like snakes, seeking her out. She wanted to flee, but could not move. Only when the ropes had tangled about her did she regain control, but by then it was too late. The ropes drew her upward, and her struggles made no difference.

Still she fought them, knowing what awaited her on the surface. Raiders were there. Cruel, cold men. In comparison to these landwalkers, the fishermen who had caught her taking the sea bells had been kind and generous. The fishermen would have let her go once she had finished harvesting the bells for them.

Once free she would have swum to the sea floor to retrieve the bells she had collected for her father before heading home. She wouldn't have given them to him straight away. He would be too angry at her to enjoy them. No, she would have accepted his punishment for slipping away and been thankful that she had escaped.

That wasn't what had happened. As the ropes drew her to the surface she braced herself for the memory of what had come next, but before she broke free of the water, something hard rammed into her ribs. The pain jolted her awake. She gasped and opened her eyes.

Light filtered down through a wooden roof. From the cool sensation around her legs she knew there was more water sloshing around her than there had been when she had fallen asleep. Her nose caught the smell of fresh fish. As always, the crew moved about at their tasks, visible through the open section of the deck. One stood in the hull, facing her. Her ears registered a rough male voice barking at her. The words were strange, but she knew their meaning well.

*Back to work.*

Her hands found the bucket and she stooped to fill it. The man stopped barking. She poured the contents into another bucket hanging from a rope through the hole in the deck. Something dropped from the man's hands into the water at her feet. He climbed up onto the deck to bark at the crew instead.

Imi looked down. Two small fish floated in the seawater. She managed to grab and eat them without pausing in her task.

Raw fish had been served to her many times before in the palace, but it had always been sliced up into delicate pieces and accompanied by salted seaweed or pickled kwee bulbs. Nobody had ever shown her how to scale a fish and she had no sharp object to help her. She had learned to strip off the scales with her teeth and spit them out again.

It wasn't healthy to live on raw fish alone, just as Teiti had told her she couldn't live on just sweets. Teiti had always said a healthy diet was one with many different kinds of foods, including many Imi didn't like. Thinking of her aunt make her heart ache. She missed Teiti so much. Her heart ached more whenever she thought of her father. How she wished she hadn't left the city. She should have bought her father something from the market. She should have listened to Teiti.

Imi worked steadily. The hull of the ship let in water slowly and the raiders didn't seem to mind how fast she scooped it out, so long as she, and whoever hauled the other bucket up out of the hull to empty it, kept at it. They didn't care that she splashed herself from time to time, or slept in a pool of it at night. Without the constant immersion in water her skin would have dried out and she would have suffered a slow and painful death.

After the raiders had pulled her out of the sea they had tied her up in the open at first. The hot sun had been unbearable. Her skin had dried out and she had suffered from a terrible thirst despite the water they had given to her to drink. Pain had begun in her head and spread to the rest of her body until she could only lie slumped on the wooden floor.

The next thing she remembered was waking up in the hull, water swirling around her body as the ship rocked back and forth. Terrifyingly loud sounds came from outside the ship, deafening her. Rain, which she had seen only twice before, and the occasional wave cresting the deck, had begun to fill the hull at an alarming rate. Several of the raiders had begun bailing out the water, and when one pressed a bucket into her hands she had joined them, terrified the ship would sink and she would drown, tied to it by the rope around her ankle.

Later a raider came and tossed fish at her. She had been so hungry, she had eaten the scales, bones and flesh.

Slowly she had recovered some of her strength. The raiders' leader had made it clear he wanted her to keep bailing out the water. She had refused at first. She was a princess. She didn't do menial work.

So he had beaten her.

Shocked and frightened, she had given in. He had watched her work for a time, menacing her if she slowed. Finally, satisfied she was cowed enough, he had left her to it.

It was endless, tiring work and she was always hungry. They gave her so little food. Her body was thin. Her arms looked like muscle, skin and bone, and nothing more. Her shift hung from her, dirty and torn. She didn't know how long she could keep doing this. So many days had passed. She clung to the hope that her father or one of the young fighters of her home would rescue her. It was better not to think too much about it, however. If she did, she could see too many reasons why rescue was unlikely.

*Something will happen,* she told herself. *I'm a princess. Princesses don't die in the hulls of ships. When my rescuer comes, I'll be alive and ready.*

The five walls of the Altar met above the White. Juran spoke the ritual words to begin the meeting and Auraya joined the others to speak the short phrase that was their part. When all were silent, Juran looked at each of them, his expression troubled.

"We are here to discuss what to do about these Pentadrians in Si," he began.

"Does this mean we are at war again?" Mairae asked.

Juran shook his head. "No."

"But the Pentadrians have invaded one of our allies."

"They have trespassed," Juran corrected. "As far as we know, they have not harmed anyone within Si."

"Because the Siyee aren't foolish enough to approach them," Auraya pointed out. "We must find out why they are there."

"Yes," Juran agreed. "That will take time. I will send the priests who have recently arrived at the Open to meet them."

"Priests?" Auraya repeated, surprised. "Why risk their lives and subject the Siyee to such a delay? I can reach Si in a day."

Juran exchanged a glance with Dyara before meeting Auraya's eyes.

"That may not be wise."

Auraya blinked in surprise. She glanced at Mairae and Rian, who looked as puzzled as she. "How so?"

He placed his hands on the table. "We know the Pentadrian leaders are powerful sorcerers. We know the remaining four are close to us in strength."

"The one they call Shar—the vorn rider—is weaker than I," Rian interjected.

"Yes," Juran agreed. "You are the only one of us to face a Voice in single combat." He paused, looking at Auraya. "The only one who has faced a still-living Voice, that is," he added. "Fortunately, Rian overcame Shar. We can't test ourselves against the others without risking that one of us will prove weaker, and be killed."

"Then I will not approach if I see either of the two more powerful Voices," Auraya said. "The weaker two should not be a problem."

Juran smiled grimly. "Your courage is admirable, Auraya."

"Why? We gained some idea of their strengths during the battle."

"Some, but not a definite idea. We don't know if the weaker two were engaged in defenses we were unaware of at the time. They may be stronger than they seemed."

She shrugged. "If Rian could defeat Shar then I can too. We know the bird woman—Genza—is next in strength. I'm willing to take the risk that I can overcome her alone."

"And could you defeat them both at once?"

She hesitated as doubts rose.

Juran spread his hands. "Do you see the danger now? Think of our own vulnerabilities." He looked at them one by one. "What if you were all absent, and the remaining four Pentadrian leaders attacked Jarime? I could not stop them alone. What if they are watching our movements, planning to ambush and kill us individually if we separate?" He shook his head. "When we are alone we are vulnerable."

Mairae made a small noise of disbelief. "Surely you don't mean for us all to stay in Jarime from now on? How can we defend other lands? What of our alliance agreements?"

Auraya nodded in agreement. Travelling to Si was a risk, but one worth taking. *What do you think of this, Chaia?* she found herself thinking.

Juran grimaced. "Our priests and priestesses can deal

with most threats. We will send them out to gather information before tackling anything ourselves."

"That's hardly going to work in Si," Auraya pointed out.
"They'd never arrive in time."

"When we have Siyee priests and priestesses that will no
longer be a problem."

"Which won't happen soon enough for this threat. It will
be years before any are—"

A sudden shift in the corner of her eye distracted her.
She looked around and realized the movement was not
physical, but magical. A familiar presence brushed her
senses.

*:Hello, Auraya.*

She suppressed a sigh. Her celestial admirer had returned, and as usual it was at a time when she didn't need
the distraction.

"What is it, Auraya?" Dyara asked quietly. "What do
you see?"

Auraya looked at Dyara. "You don't sense him at all?"

Dyara shook her head. Auraya quickly glanced at Mairae and Rian, who looked bemused. Juran was frowning.
Then all expressions changed to awe and pleasure and their
eyes shifted to a place behind Auraya. She looked over her
shoulder to see a glowing figure standing there.

*:Juran,* the god said in greeting. *Dyara, Auraya, Rian
and Mairae.*

"Chaia," the others replied reverently, making the sign
of the circle. Auraya hastily followed their gesture. She had
grown so used to Chaia's presence, it was easy to forget
the formalities the White usually followed when any of the
gods appeared.

The god began to walk around the table slowly.

*:As you know, we prefer to allow mortals to choose their
own paths most of the time. Occasionally we steer your
course, as we have a responsibility to guide your actions
when they do not agree with our purpose.* He stopped and
looked at Juran. *I must intervene now.*

Juran's eyebrows knitted together. He looked down at
the table.

*:Your purpose is to protect our followers, not only your-selves,* Chaia said.

Juran flinched. "Protecting ourselves at the expense of others was not my purpose," he said, looking up at the god. "It is the long-term protection of Circlians that I am concerned with. If one of us dies, all Northern Ithania will be vulnerable."

Dyara nodded. "I agree. If Auraya dies in Si it may lead to more deaths in the long term."

Chaia smiled.

*:If Auraya dies, then we will chose a replacement—though I doubt we would find another so talented or Gifted.*

Despite the praise, Auraya felt a chill. She had thought herself ready to risk her life for the Siyee. Now, knowing that the gods had intended her to take that risk, she felt fear stirring somewhere deep inside her. She felt . . . expendable.

*Just like any soldier,* she thought. *Well, that's what we are. Powerful, immortal, Gifted soldiers in the service of the gods.* The irony of what she had just thought struck her. *We are called immortals only because we do not age. If we face the sort of conflict Juran fears—if we must constantly risk our lives in order to protect Circlians—then we may prove shorter lived than ordinary mortals.* She straightened her back. *So be it.*

"I chose to serve the gods and I don't intend to stop anytime soon, though it would be a joy to join them," she told the others. "I will not take any unnecessary risks. And remember—I can be back here in a day if you need me."

Juran met her eyes and held them, then nodded and turned to Chaia.

"Thank you for your wisdom and guidance, Chaia," he said humbly. "I will send Auraya to Si."

The god smiled, then vanished. Auraya felt him move out of the reach of her senses. When she looked at Juran again he was regarding her with an unreadable expression.

"The gods have favored you with unusual Gifts," he said. "I should have seen that they intended you to use them. Be careful, Auraya. It is not just your unique abilities we would sorely miss if we lost you."

She smiled, touched. "Thank you. I will."

Juran looked at the others. "That is decided. We had best inform our guests." He looked at Auraya.

"I'll tell them," she said.

As they rose and the sides of the Altar began to unfold, Auraya thought of Chaia's appearance. She had wondered what he would think of Juran's argument. Had she called to him without realizing it? Had he been close enough to hear their conversation before then while still beyond the limit of her senses?

These were questions she would have to think about later. For now, she had best consider how to approach these Pentadrians in Si without putting herself, or the Siyee, in danger.

Old Grim looked up as the woman entered the room, and kept looking. High cheekbones, hair black as night, a good figure—though it could do with a bit more flesh on it. As the lamplight caught her eyes he saw that they were green. Wrinkles appeared around them, betraying her age as she smiled at her companion.

*Would have been a beauty when she was younger,* he thought. *Who's that she's with? Ah, Marin. Can't help himself. Got to have a look at anything new. I can remember him picking over the beach as a boy, looking for things washed up by the tide.*

Marin introduced the woman to his regular drinking companions but didn't stop. To Grim's surprise the man looked up at him, winked, then guided the woman across to Grim's table.

"Evening," Marin said. "This is Old Grim," he told the woman. "Grim, this is Limma Curer."

"Evening," Grim said, nodding at the woman. She smiled easily. He caught the smell of herbs and something earthier. The family name was probably an accurate description of her trade.

"Limma is interested in stories about The Gull," Marin said. "I told her you'd met him. She actually believes me."

"Does she?" Grim felt an old resentment begin to simmer, but when he tried to glare at the woman his anger faded again. She met his eyes steadily. There was something about her manner. She wanted something from him. He couldn't imagine he had anything to offer—apart from his story.

Intrigued, he lifted his goblet. "A long story needs a wet mouth."

Limma laughed and reached under her tawl. He glimpsed many pouches underneath and the smell of herbs and cures grew stronger. Turning to the drinkhouse owner, she tossed him a coin. He caught it neatly, and nodded as she told him to keep their cups full. Marin and Limma settled onto the bench opposite.

"So you've met The Gull," she said. "How long ago?"

Old Grim shrugged. "I was young, barely more than a boy. Thought I'd see a bit of the world, so I got work on boats moving up the coast to Aime. When I got there, I found work on a trading ship. It wasn't what I expected. It's always hard work, but I learned then that the bigger the boat, the more concerned people get about making sure everyone knows who takes orders from who. I was pretty low in the beating order, so to speak." He grimaced at the memory.

"There was a boy on the ship. He didn't have a name. Everyone called him "boy." One day it came to me that nobody ever bothered this boy. He gave them no reason to, but on this ship being quick at your job didn't save you from a beating.

"I started watching this boy. He was a fair lad, but none of the bullies had a go at him. In fact, they acted like they were scared of him.

"One day he sat down beside me during the meal break. He told me this wasn't the right ship for me. He said I needed a smaller boat and I'd make a good captain. I was better off setting myself against the sea than other men.

"Deep in my heart I knew he was right, but I wanted to see the world, you see, and he was just a boy. What did he know? So I stuck it out.

"A few weeks later, when we were about to leave the

port of Aime, he spoke to me again. He pointed to a smaller ship and said they were looking for crew. I thanked him for telling me, but stayed on. Others got off and I felt proud of myself for not giving in."

Old Grim stopped as a serving boy placed three fresh goblets on the table. He drank deeply, sighed, then scratched his head.

"Where was I?"

"The boy warned you a second time," Limma said.

He stared at her in surprise. She smiled knowingly, but said nothing. Grim wiped his mouth and continued on.

"We were only out at sea a few days when the sky turned black and the wind began to scream at us. We couldn't see more than a few strides. I heard the boy telling the captain that they were headed for rocks and should hove to starboard. He said it with such . . . authority. The captain cursed the boy and told him to get below decks.

"Next thing the boy appeared right in front of me. I could see he was angry. Furious as only an adult can be. It was such a strange thing to see in the face of someone so young."

Grim paused. The memory was so vivid. He could still feel the ice in the wind and the fear in his guts, and see the boy's face. Gulping a mouthful of drink, he concentrated on the comforting warmth it brought. The two listeners waited patiently.

"The boy dragged me to the dinghy. When I realized he wanted me to help him cut loose, I protested. He straightened up and looked me in the eye . . ." Grim mimicked the boy, fixing the woman with what he hoped was a convincingly firm stare, ". . . and he said: 'I've warned you twice. I will warn you only once more. Leave this ship or you will not live another day.'

"And at that moment one of the bullies—a big hulk of a man—saw us. He gave a roar and went to strike the boy. His fist never found its target. The boy made the smallest movement, and the bully went backward. His head hit something and he stayed down."

Grim smiled. "I stood there gaping at the boy. He gave

me a big shove so I fell into the dinghy, then the ropes went and untied themselves. Next thing the dinghy and I were falling. We hit the water. I just lay there, more than a little stunned, looking up at the boy as the dinghy moved away from the ship like something was pushing it."

Old Grim shook his head. "Never saw him again. The next day a flock of gulls followed me as I rowed to shore. That's when it hit me who he was. Later I heard that the ship ran up on the rocks. Most of the crew died, but no one saw any boy. Not dead or living."

The woman was smiling now. It gave Old Grim a bit of pleasure to see that. *She enjoyed my story,* he thought. *I guess it doesn't matter if she believes it or not.*

"You're a lucky man," she said.

He lifted his mug and drank. "That I am. My luck changed from that day. By the time I'd worked my way home I had enough to buy a boat of my own."

"So you did become a captain, after all," she said, raising her mug to her mouth.

"Sure did."

"But nobody believed your story."

"None but my wife."

"Are you sure?" Her eyes narrowed. "Have you never encountered anybody at all who knew the truth of your tale?"

He paused as he realized what he'd said was not entirely true. "There have been a few who seemed to take my word for it. Travellers, mostly. A young sailmaker told me recently he'd heard a trader up north tell a story like mine."

"This trader met The Gull, too?"

"So he said. Reckoned he was attacked by raiders and a boy saved him."

"Did he give you the trader's name?"

"No, but the sailmaker lives up the coast from here." He leaned forward. "Why are you so interested in The Gull?"

She smiled. "I want to find him."

He laughed quietly. "Good luck. I get the feeling he's the type who finds you, not the other way around."

"I hope so."

"What d'you want from him, then?"

"Advice."

From her expression, he could tell she wasn't going to say any more. Shrugging, he held up his empty mug. "Another drink, and I might remember the names of more travellers who believed me."

As he'd hoped, she laughed and turned to wave at the server.

# 18

As Reivan followed Imenja onto the balcony she saw that the other Voices were already there. All but Nekaun were seated in the reed chairs, sipping cool drinks, and all but Nekaun were accompanied by a Companion.

He had not chosen one, yet. Only two months had passed since he had become First Voice and a Companion ought to be chosen carefully, Reivan reasoned. It wouldn't be fair if he chose and dismissed Companions until he found someone he liked and trusted.

Nekaun turned to nod at Imenja as she sat down, then his eyes shifted to Reivan and he smiled. As always, he smiled as if she was a friend he was happy to see, which always made her feel a little self-conscious. She felt flattered such an extraordinary man paid her any attention at all.

Everyone adored him. He was charming and thoughtful. When he spoke to people he gave them his full attention. He laughed at their jokes, listened to their complaints and always remembered their names.

*I guess it only seems like he remembers,* Reivan reminded herself as she took a seat beside her mistress. *He doesn't have to memorize anyone's name. He can pluck it from their minds whenever he needs to.*

The way the Voices behaved as a group had changed. While she had never seen Nekaun angry or forceful she had no doubt that he was in control. He always sought the others' opinions and advice, but ultimately decisions were made by him.

*Of course, the others can't object when they gave him the advice that led to his decision,* she mused.

When Imenja had handed the responsibilities of leadership over to him she expressed neither relief nor regret. Since then she had said little about Nekaun's actions. If she found fault with Nekaun's decisions, Reivan had seen no sign of it.

*She can't say anything to me. He would read it from my mind. She won't tell me anything that she doesn't want him to know.*

Nekaun had begun to pace the railing. Now he shot her an unfathomable look. She felt her face flush.

*What am I thinking? I'm being cynical again. I must stop that. I hope he knows it's just a habit and I don't actually think there is fault in his decisions or—*

"Since we're all here, we may as well begin," Nekaun said.

"Yes," Imenja agreed. "Who will—or should I say where will—we consider first?"

Nekaun smiled. "Shar and Dunway first, I think."

The handsome blond Voice cleared his throat. He had brought one of his tame vorns with him and the beast lay panting beside the chair. "The shipwreck plan appears to have worked so far. The survivors are being treated well. The second boat is still trapped in Chon's harbor. As we expected, the Dunwayans are reluctant to allow our people to disembark."

Nekaun nodded. "Genza?"

The fourth Voice flexed her lean, muscular arms. "My people have been travelling for eleven days, but even with the help of our birds in surveying the land their progress is slow. They have seen Siyee in the distance a few times, but the flying people do not approach them."

"No sign of the one they call Auraya?"

"No."

"Good." Nekaun turned to Vervel. The stocky man shrugged.

"My Servants have arrived. The Torens don't seem to care about their nationality, so long as there's something to buy from them. A pragmatic people. The second boat has not yet reached Genria."

Nekaun turned to Imenja. "And your Servants are still at sea?"

She nodded. "Yes. They were delayed, along with yours, by that storm. Now that the weather has cleared they should arrive in Somrey in a few days."

"Is it wise for our people to arrive at their destinations at the same time?" Vervel asked. "The Circlians may notice and grow suspicious of our intentions."

"If they are paying attention," Nekaun said. He looked at Genza. "It is unlikely that your people will remain unnoticed, since people enter Si so rarely. However, the Siyee have no priests or priestesses of their own, so they may prove easier to sway."

"It will not be as easy finding potential Servants among normal humans," Vervel said. "My people tell me that nearly all Skilled men and women of Northern Ithania become priests or priestesses."

Nekaun smiled and glanced at Reivan. "And no unSkilled do. That rule has been our weakness in the past, too. Would unSkilled Northern Ithanians abandon their heathen gods and embrace the true gods if they knew there was a chance they might gain power and authority by becoming Servants?"

The others looked thoughtful. "The power and authority you offer is only valued here," Imenja murmured.

"For now."

"How many unSkilled will you allow to become Servants?" Vervel asked. "How will you choose?"

"I would not set a number to begin with," Nekaun replied. "They would have to prove themselves worthy."

"Good. We don't want to make a mockery of the gods by ordaining complete fools," Genza muttered.

"No," Nekaun agreed. He suddenly looked at Reivan. "We are in no danger of that yet. What do you think, Reivan?"

She blinked in surprise. "I . . . uh . . . I can't help thinking there must be an easier way to convert Northern Ithanians. The Circlians believe our gods aren't real. They would flock to us if you proved them wrong."

"How do you suggest we do that?"

"I don't know. Perhaps only the sight of the gods would convince them."

He smiled crookedly. "We may call upon the gods for guidance or approval from time to time, but even then they do not always appear at our request. It is unlikely they would agree to appear and demonstrate their powers for every doubting Circlian each time a Servant requested it."

Reivan looked down. "No, that would be too much to ask. But . . . it is a pity the Circlians did not see Sheyr appear when we emerged from the mines. If they had seen that magnificent sight, they might not have fought us, but instead joined us. Would the gods agree to appear before a gathering of Circlians?"

"I guess if that were possible they would have done it already," Imenja said.

"What prevents them?" Reivan asked.

Silence followed. She forced herself to look up at the Voices. To her surprise, the Voices wore thoughtful expressions. Nekaun was frowning, as if troubled by her words. His gaze shifted to hers and he smiled.

"Ah, Thinkers. They have a way of asking unanswerable questions. We all wish to understand the gods, but I doubt any of us ever will. They are the ultimate mystery."

The others nodded. Nekaun rubbed his hands together and glanced around the room. "Shall we move on to other matters?"

"Yes," Genza agreed. "Let's."

"I hear there has been another duel between Dekkan nobles."

Genza rolled her eyes. "Yes. Same old families. Same old grudge."

"We must do more to prevent these confrontations."

"I'd love to hear any suggestions you have."

Relieved that their attention had moved from her, Reivan picked up a glass of water and drank deeply. Nekaun often asked for her opinion during these meetings, whereas he rarely spoke to the other Companions. Though it was flattering that he sought it, she did not always enjoy the experience. Sometimes, like today, she suspected she had made a complete fool of herself.

Fortunately, the others did not appear to mind. Instead they discouraged reticence. Reivan had shied away from giving her opinion once and Nekaun had pursued her with a ruthless patience until she gave in.

*They were disturbed by my question, though,* she thought, looking at the other Voices. *It seems I am not the only one who wonders why the gods are so reluctant to show their power or influence more. If they had, would we have lost the war? Would they have advised us against attacking the Circlians? Surely Kuar would not have led us into battle unless the gods had approved.*

*After all, Sheyr would not have appeared and encouraged the army to fight if he knew the battle was a hopeless cause. I can only conclude that he either knew we'd lose, or couldn't discover enough about the enemy to see the danger. Either way, he must have known there was a risk of failure.*

Reivan shook her head. *At least I'm not the only person mystified by the gods. Even the Voices don't know everything about them.*

Mirar stood before the wall of falling water. He reached out and touched the sheet of liquid. The smooth, rippling surface broke around his fingers and cold droplets ran down his bare arms, chilling him.

*Get it done quickly,* Leiard suggested.

Closing his eyes, Mirar leaned forward and plunged his head into the water.

The water was bone-chilling cold. He scrubbed at his scalp and beard, moving quickly to combat the chill and hasten the rinsing. A step backward and he was back in the air again, water trickling down his bare chest as he straightened.

Running his hands through his hair, he was pleased to find none of the stickiness of the dye was left. He didn't relish the thought of ducking into the cold water again. The prospect of it had discouraged him from reapplying the color for several days.

*"Don't forget your eyebrows,"* Emerahl had said. *"If people see pale eyebrows and dark hair, they'll know you've been using dye.'* He smiled at the memory as he carefully washed the remaining dye away with water cupped in his hands. She hadn't said anything about dying the hair on his chest, or anywhere else, but who would see it anyway? Nobody, while Leiard had any say in it.

A piece of cloth was all he had to dry himself with. He started back into the cave, rubbing at his skin to warm it.

"Wilar?"

He stopped and turned back to the fall. The voice was familiar. A Siyee was silhouetted in the entrance.

"Reet?"

"It is Tyve."

*The brother,* Mirar thought. *They sound so alike.* "Give me a moment," he called.

He hurried into the cave, quickly finished dressing, then returned to the fall with his bag of cures. A young Siyee male was waiting at the gap between the edge of the fall and the rock wall. He grinned as Mirar appeared.

"Have we come at a bad time?"

"No," Mirar assured him. "Your company is always welcome."

The Siyee hid a smile. Their language had come back to Mirar quickly, but he did not always understand the words or phrases they used. He suspected he used an old-fashioned way of speaking that they found amusing, and that the puzzling phrases and words they used were recent inventions of the last century or so.

He'd met the pair some weeks ago, giving them the explanation he and Emerahl had come up with: he had agreed to meet her here and she had communicated the way to the cave via dream links, but when he arrived she had already left.

They understood what a Dreamweaver was. He was pleased to learn that the Siyee still remembered Mirar through stories in which he was a benevolent healer and wise man. To his amusement, they assumed all Dream-weavers were male and magically powerful.

He and Tyve walked out from behind the fall and down to the edge of the pool, where another young Siyee was waiting.

"Greetings, Wilar. I brought you some food," Reet said, holding up a small bag.

"Thank you," Mirar replied. He lifted his bag. "Have you come for more cures?"

"Yes. Sizzi says your remedy worked. She wants some more. Speaker Veece's joints are paining him now that it's getting colder. Do you have anything that would help?"

Mirar smiled. "He didn't tell you to ask, did he? You're asking for his sake."

Reet grinned. "He's too proud to ask for help, but not so proud he doesn't complain about it all the time."

Sitting down on a rock, Mirar opened his bag and considered the contents. "I'll have to make something up. I have the wound powder and pain ease here." He drew out a carved wooden jar and a small bag of pellets. "The pain ease is in the bag. Use no more than four a day, and never more than two at once."

Reet took the bag and jar and stowed them in a pouch strapped to his chest. Mirar picked up the bag of food. It was surprisingly heavy, and he heard the faint sound of liquid sloshing inside.

"Is there . . . ah!" He drew out a skin of Teepi.

"A gift from Sizzi," Tyve explained.

Mirar regarded the two Siyee. "Are you in a hurry to return?"

They shook their heads and grinned. Unplugging the skin, Mirar took a sip of the liqueur. A tart, nutty flavor filled his mouth. He swallowed, savoring the warmth that filled his stomach and began to spread to his limbs. He handed the skin to Tyve.

"Any news?" he asked.

Tyve drank and handed the skin to Reet. "Priests have reached the Open. They're going to teach the Siyee who want to become priests and priestesses."

Mirar sighed. The Siyee had been free from all but Huan's influence for centuries, and the goddess hadn't meddled in their lives much since she had finished creating them. Once the Siyee had priests and priestesses they would be encouraged to worship all five gods, some of which were more inclined to mess about with people's lives.

"You don't look pleased to hear it," Reet observed.

Mirar looked at the young man, then shook his head. "No."

"Why not?"

"I . . . I don't like the thought of the Siyee being ruled by the gods, and their landwalker servants."

Tyve frowned. "You think that is what will happen?"

"Maybe."

"Is this a bad thing?" Reet asked, shrugging. "The gods can protect us."

"You were safer when you were apart from the rest of the world."

"The world invaded us," Reet reminded him.

"Ah, you're right. The Toren settlers did, in their fashion. I guess you could not have remained separate or safe forever."

"You do not worship the gods?" Tyve asked.

Mirar took the skin from Reet and put it aside. He shook his head. "No. Dreamweavers do not serve gods. They help people. The gods . . . don't like that."

"Why not?"

"They like to be worshipped, to control all mortals. They don't like that Dreamweavers don't worship or obey them. When we help others, they think we reduce their influence on those we help."

Tyve frowned. "Do they punish you for it?"

Memories of crushing stone and a crippled body crept close. Mirar pushed them away. "They ordered Juran of the White to kill our leader. At their urging, Circlians turned against Dreamweavers. Many were killed. Though this does not happen now, those few of my people who brave the life of a Dreamweaver are scorned and persecuted by Circlians everywhere."

The two Siyee regarded Mirar in dismay. "The Circlians are our allies," Tyve said. There was neither defensiveness nor alarm in his voice. "If you're an enemy of the Circlians, then are you our enemy, too?"

"That is up to your people to decide," Mirar said, looking away. "Most likely this alliance will do your people much good. I would not sow doubts in your minds."

*Liar,* Leiard accused, his voice a whisper in the back of Mirar's mind.

"Why don't you worship the gods?" Reet asked.

"For several reasons," Mirar told him. "Partly it is because we feel we should have a choice in the matter. Partly it is because we know the gods are not as good and benign as they would like mortals to believe they are." Mirar shook his head. "I could tell you of the exploits of the gods in the past, before their war reduced them to five, that would make your skin turn cold."

*Just exploits of the five remaining gods, in their bad old days?* Leiard asked.

*No,* Mirar replied. *That would be too obvious. I'll mix them with stories of other gods.*

"Tell us," Tyve said seriously. "We should know, if we are going to be ruled by them."

"You might not like what you hear," Mirar warned.

"That depends whether we believe you or not. Old tales are usually just exaggerations of the truth," Reet said wisely.

"These are not stories. They are memories," Mirar corrected. "We Dreamweavers pass on our memories to our students and each other. What I tell you is not an exaggeration or embellishment, but true recollections of people long dead."

*Or not so dead,* Leiard added.

Mirar paused. *Are you admitting I am the owner of this body?*

There was no answer. The two Siyee were watching him intently. He could sense their curiosity. *What am I doing?* he thought. *If these tales spread among the Siyee, the gods will take note of them and seek the source.*

Stories were powerful. They could teach caution. The thought of Siyee becoming priests and priestesses and of the gods controlling and changing them spurred him on. They should not accept such a fate without knowing some of the truth.

"I will tell you tales of dead gods as well as those of the Circle," he said. "Have you ever heard of the whores of Ayetha?"

The young men's eyes brightened with interest. "No."

"Ayetha was a city in what is now Genria. The most popular god or goddess of that city was . . . no, I will not speak her name. The people built a temple for her. She held power over them through an exchange of favors. Any family that needed her help must surrender a child to the temple. That child—male or female—was taught the arts of prostitution and made to serve those who came and donated money to the Temple. They did not even need to be full grown to begin service. If they ever tried to leave their temple, they were hunted down and killed. The babes born of these women . . . they were sacrificed to this goddess."

The interest in the young men's eyes had changed to horror.

"This was before the War of the Gods?" Reet asked.

"Yes." Mirar paused. "Do you wish to hear more?"

The pair exchanged glances, then Tyve nodded. Mirar considered their grim, determined expressions, then continued.

"She was not the only god to abuse her followers. One seduced young girls from all over Ithania. Some parents feared him and kept their daughters hidden, but in vain as the gods can see the minds of all people, everywhere. Others valued the regard of a god too much and foolishly dreamed their own child might be chosen.

"This god favored innocence and craved complete devotion. When he found a girl who fulfilled his requirements, he pleasured them with magic in a way that left them unmoved by ordinary physical sensation. They lost interest in eating and neglected themselves.

"Innocence dies easily and the girls inevitably questioned what had been done to them. When they did, he abandoned them. They did not live long after. Some killed themselves, some starved, some became addicted to pleasure drugs. I tended some of these girls, and was never able to save one."

"You?" Tyve asked. "Surely this was before the War of the Gods, too."

Mirar shook his head. "I'm sorry. I was speaking as the one whose memory I have called upon."

Reet was frowning. "It is strange."

"What is?"

"The gods . . . they are not physical beings. Why would one want . . ." He flushed. ". . . girls."

"There are many tales of the gods falling in love or lusting after mortals. They may be beings of magic, but they crave physical closeness. There was a famous tale of a goddess—old even a thousand years ago—who fell in love with a mortal, and struck down any woman he happened to see and feel the briefest admiration for. Eventually he went mad and killed himself."

"So if they feel love, do they feel hate?"

Mirar nodded. "Oh, yes. You would never have heard of the Velians. That is because one of the gods hated them so much he had his followers slaughter them, right to the last half-breed child. It took centuries, but he destroyed that race completely."

Tyve shuddered. "If the gods can destroy a whole people, it would not be wise to become their enemy."

"You do not have to be their enemy to suffer from their meddling. The Dunwayans were a peaceful race of farmers and fishermen until a war god decided to turn them into warriors. A long century of starvation followed because so many of them had become fighters that too few were growing crops or raising stock. Many thousands died."

"Not all gods are bad, though," Reet pointed out.

"No," Mirar agreed. "There were some good ones. Like Iria, the goddess of the sky. She could be called upon to predict the seasons, and would appear to warn of unfavorable weather or impending disasters. There was a sea god,

Svarlen, who helped sailors navigate or warned them of storms. And Kem, the beggar god, whose followers cared for those without homes or anyone to care for them. It was a terrible thing, losing them."

"They died in the war." Tyve frowned. "Who killed them?"

Mirar held the young man's eyes for a short while before answering.

"Who knows? The victors, perhaps."

Slowly Tyve's face changed as he comprehended what that meant.

"The five," he gasped. "Surely not! These good gods must have been killed earlier in the war by someone else. The five might have killed their killers."

"That is possible," Mirar agreed. "It is also possible that one or more of the five killed them."

"They wouldn't have," Tyve insisted. "They are good. If they were evil, the world would be a terrible place. It is peaceful now . . . it is in Northern Ithania, anyway."

Mirar smiled. "Then we are all safe," he said. "But remember this: two of the first gods I mentioned—the ones whose abuses I listed—are still with us. Perhaps they have changed their ways, but knowing what I know I will never trust them to have mortals' best interests at heart."

The pair looked distressed. Mirar felt a pang of guilt. *Is it fair of me to shatter their illusions about the gods? What choice do they have?*

He picked up the skin and handed it to Tyve. "Drink, and forget what I've told you. It is all in the distant past. As you said, we are in better times now. That is all that matters."

# 19

Once the servants had left her rooms, Auraya began to pace. In a few hours she would be in the air, heading to Si. There were only a few arrangements to make before she was free to go.

Mischief romped around the room, infected by her excitement. She hoped this burst of energy would tire him out and keep him quiet later. As a presence touched the edge of her senses, she glanced at the veez. He didn't react. As far as she could tell, he was completely unaware of Chaia's visits.

:Are you ready? Chaia asked.

:Yes. I've been up since dawn, driving my servants to distraction.

:That's unlikely. You're taking little with you, so there was barely any packing for them to do. They did not even dress your hair.

:No point, she replied, touching the clasp that bound her hair into a tail. It will only come out in the wind.

:You could protect it from the wind with magic.

:I like the feel of the wind.

:I like how you look with your hair dressed.

She felt a flush of pleasure at the compliment.

:It is a mere physical detail. You cannot see it, she pointed out

:I see it through the eyes of others.

:Ah, she replied. Do you like it because they do, or—

A furry shape leapt onto the table. She turned in time to see the veez seize a circular object in its teeth.

"Mischief!" she gasped, leaping toward him. "Put that down!"

The veez's ears flattened against his head. He evaded her easily, jumped off the table and darted behind a chair. She followed and found him crouching in the narrow gap between the chair and the wall, staring at her defiantly.

"Mnn," he said around the ring.

"Not yours," she said firmly. She held out her hand. "Give it to me."

"Nf yrs," the veez mumbled. *Mine!* he sent telepathically, giving up on trying to vocalize around the ring.

"Give," she ordered. "Now."

The veez blinked at her. She shuffled forward and reached toward him. As she expected, he darted away, behind another chair.

She stood up and sighed. Testing her like this was his current bad habit. Mairae assured her all veez did this and eventually grew bored with the game, but in the meantime Mischief's behavior was annoying. Most of the time Auraya managed to ignore it, but this morning she didn't have the time to indulge him.

He was moving around the room now, avoiding her. She did not like to use magic on him. It was always better to use persuasion.

"Give Auraya ring or Mischief no fly," she said.

There was a pause, then a muffled word. He did not emerge.

*I have used that threat before,* she thought ruefully.

"Auraya go away," she said. "Not take Mischief. Leave Mischief alone long time."

The pause was longer, then there was a whimper that twisted her heart, and he came bounding out. He raced across the room, ran up her circ and wrapped himself around her neck.

She held out her hand. The ring dropped into it. Mischief's head drooped onto her shoulder and he sighed.

"Owaya stay."

"Auraya and Mischief fly," she said.

"Fly now?"

"Later."

She moved to a chair and sat down. At once he climbed down into her lap and demanded scratches. As she obliged him with one hand she held up the ring in the other. Abruptly she remembered Chaia. She could still sense him.

*:Sorry about that.*

She felt a wave of amusement from him.

*:I am used to interruptions,* he replied.

She considered the ring.

*:What happened to the old ring?* she asked Chaia.

*:The Pentadrians still have it. They do not completely understand its properties, or they would have used it against you.*

She shuddered at the thought. It had been bad enough witnessing the Siyee spy harried out of the sky by the Pentadrians' black birds into the enemy's midst. She could imagine how much worse it could have been. If the wearer was tortured, for example. She did not have to watch, but knowing that something like that was occurring because of her would be awful.

*:Can you destroy the ring?* she asked.

*:Only through another. Its power will diminish eventually.*

*:Can you speed up . . . ?*

A knock at the main door interrupted her. She reached out to the mind of the person behind it and smiled. Drawing a little magic, she willed the door open.

Danjin stepped inside.

"Good morning, Auraya of the White," he said, making the sign of the circle.

"Good morning, Danjin Spear," she replied. "Come in and sit down."

He moved to one of the chairs. Mischief looked at the adviser, his whiskers twitching, then curled up and went to sleep.

"I'll be leaving in a few hours," she told Danjin. "Before I go, I have something to give to you. Catch."

She tossed the ring toward Danjin. He caught it neatly. As he examined the ring his expression remained mild, but she could read the lingering misgivings in his mind.

*I can't help feeling reluctance at having someone in my head again, even though it's only Auraya. This is a necessary requirement of my position, however.* He slipped the ring on his finger.

"It will shield your mind from Dreamweavers who might try to invade your dreams," she told him.

He looked at her. "So I can work with them on your behalf."

"Yes." Auraya thought of the hospice, and felt a nagging worry return. "It won't be as difficult a job as you might expect. Dreamweavers and healers alike are being as cooperative as possible. I have another task for you. The Siyee ambassadors have asked for someone to teach them our language and we need people here who can speak theirs. Would you like to be one of those people?"

He smiled. "Of course. I managed to pick up a few words during the weeks before the battle."

"Mairae is translating for them," she told him. "Which is keeping her busy. You'll be her favorite person in all Jarime if you learn fast."

"I consider myself warned."

Auraya laughed. "Don't set your hopes too high."

"Me? I'm not nearly pretty enough for Mairae. Besides, my wife would kill me."

"She would. How is she?"

He nodded. "Well." His smile widened. "You know your life is good when it wouldn't make a thrilling tale. I've come to relish that."

"I hope it stays that way. Now, is there anything you think I need to do before I go? Anything that can be done in an hour, that is."

As Danjin considered he turned the ring around and around. Auraya felt a twinge of guilt. She had not told him the entire truth about it. The ring would blanket his mind from all minds but Auraya's, which was not exactly what had been intended. It wasn't supposed to shield the wearer's mind from the other White, but it did. The White and the welcome-tree tenders had never tried to make a ring like this before, and by the time they had realized the error it had been too late to grow another one. The decision had been made for Auraya to leave for Si and she needed the ring now.

Juran had told her to keep the flaw from Danjin. *He might still work it out,* Auraya thought. *Circumstances might make him realize the other White can't read his mind.*

*:I doubt he would take advantage of the situation,* Chaia said. *He can be trusted.*

*:Yes.*

*:Even so, the ring should be destroyed when you return.*

She smothered a sigh. Once again she would have to visit the grove every day, no matter the weather or how busy she was, to encourage the growth of another replacement link ring.

"The only matter we haven't dealt with is Mischief," Danjin said suddenly. He looked down at the veez. "Would you like me to visit every day, as before?"

She grinned and shook her head. "He's coming with me."

"Really? That will be a treat for the Siyee." His voice was heavy with irony.

"And for him." She picked up Mischief and put him on the seat, then stood up. "Thank you for your help these last few days, Danjin. If there's anything else, speak to me via the ring."

"I will," he replied. They moved to the door. "Have a safe journey and be careful in Si."

She opened the door. "Of course."

He smiled and stepped outside. Closing the door, Auraya turned to regard the room. She didn't know how long it would be before she returned to it. At least this time she would not have to worry about poor Mischief pining away on his own—or tormenting Danjin.

He looked up at her, whiskers twitching.

*:Fly?*

"Yes, Mischief," she said. "We have a long way to travel and it's time we began."


Whenever Reivan had the chance she explored a part of the Sanctuary she was not familiar with in the hopes that she would eventually know all its corners and routes. She was glad that she had this morning. A fast route from the Baths to the Star Room obviously hadn't been a priority for anyone involved in constructing the Sanctuary buildings. There were two choices: a long but less convoluted route down to the Servants' quarters then back up to the Middle Sanctuary, or a twisting route through storerooms, the kitchens, a minor library and what smelled like a tannery.

Why she was headed to the Star Room was a mystery. The messenger hadn't explained. There was probably another ritual about to take place that Imenja needed her to attend.

As she drew closer to her destination she felt her stomach flutter. Though she had been in the Star Room many times she always felt a thrill when entering it. Turning a corner, she saw the narrow entrance to the room ahead and paused to take three slow breaths. Straightening her back, she smoothed her robes and moved through the entrance.

Standing within the silver star set into the floor was a handsome black-robed figure. Reivan's heart lurched as Nekaun looked at her and smiled. He motioned toward a group of Servant-novices. As she moved to join them she looked around the room, noting the Servants and Dedicated Servants lining the walls. Seeing Imenja standing among them, she felt a moment's relief.

Then it evaporated as Nekaun began to address the room.

"Today eight men and women are to be ordained as Servants of the Gods. These Servant-novices have worked hard, each earning the right to serve the gods to the best of their abilities. They have passed the required tests and satisfied their teachers. Today they will take the vow we all have spoken. Today they will wear the symbol of the gods over their hearts. Today they join us as sisters and brothers."

He turned to the novices and spoke a name. A man stepped forward. Reivan realized her mouth was open and closed it quickly. She had been gaping at him in surprise. Now she felt her stomach flip over.

*They're making me a full Servant!*

But it took years to become a full Servant. She looked at the Servant-novices around her. They were all in their early twenties—closer to her age. The entrants that had begun their training with her were all in their mid to late teens.

*Magic is the reason,* she thought. *Or my lack of it. Drevva did seem to be running out of other things to teach me. I guess all the years of training must be mostly in Skills.*

"Servant-novice Reivan."

Her heart skipped a beat and she looked up to find Nekaun beckoning. Taking a deep breath, she stepped forward into the center of the star.

"You have been a novice for only a few short months," he said, "but your knowledge of Pentadrian laws and history has proven to be exemplary. We have decided you are ready to take on the full responsibility of a Servant of the Gods."

*Why didn't Imenja warn me that they were planning this?* She glanced in the Second Voice's direction and saw the woman's lips twitch into a smile.

"Servant-novice Reivan," Nekaun repeated. "Do you wish to dedicate your life to the service of the gods?"

She met his eyes. "With all my heart."

"Are you willing to sacrifice all for the Five?"

"I am."

"Would you forfeit love, wealth and even your life for them?"

"I would."

"Then take this symbol of their power and unity. Wear it always, as it is your link to the gods and their Servants."

He opened his hand. On his palm lay a silver five-pointed star. A chain ran through one of the points and was now spilling through his fingers.

Reivan reached out and picked up the star. It was lighter than she had expected. Taking the chain, she lifted it up and draped it over her head.

"My eyes, my voice, my heart and my soul are for the Five," she said.

"May you serve them gladly and truly," Nekaun finished. The young man who had been ordained before her now stood on the other side of the star in the floor. Reivan moved to join him. As she watched the next Servant-novice come forward to face Nekaun she felt a strange sensation. Something was tickling her brow. She scratched her forehead, but the sensation was coming from somewhere *within* her head. Closing her eyes, she concentrated on the sensation. At once it became something she understood.

*:Welcome, Reivan.*

She opened her eyes and turned to stare at Imenja. The voice was definitely that of the Second Voice, but she knew she hadn't heard it with her ears. The Second Voice smiled.

*:Yes, we can speak to your mind now.*

Imenja's mouth had not moved.

*:I . . . I can talk to you in return?*

*:Yes.*

*:So this is what using magic is like?*

Imenja's smile widened.

*:It is, and it isn't. Nobody is truly devoid of Skills, Reivan. The pendant relies on you having some magical ability to work. Everyone has magical ability, even those we consider unSkilled. You are not consciously drawing magic or willing it to fulfil this task, and you have not needed to practice a Skill in order to do this, so in that way it is not like using magic at all.*

Reivan nodded.

*:You could have warned me.*

*:About the ceremony? Then you would have had a sleepless night. I need you to be awake and alert this afternoon.*

*:You do? What do you have planned?*

*:Oh, just another boring meeting with a Murian diplomat.*

The last of the Servant-novices had received her star pendant. As she joined the group around Reivan, Nekaun spoke again, welcoming all the new Servants. When he had finished those standing around the room came forward to offer congratulations. Though Reivan was welcomed by all the teachers she'd worked with, she noted there wasn't the warmth they offered to the other new Servants.

*There just hasn't been time to win them over,* she thought

wistfully. *Even if they didn't resent me, I haven't had the chance to make friends.*

Then Imenja approached and she was amused to watch the change in their manner. Some became quiet while others gushed. The Second Voice thanked them for their hard work in teaching the Servant-novices.

*Why aren't I intimidated by Imenja?* she wondered.

*:Because fawning isn't part of your nature,* Imenja's voice said in her mind. *You're much too clever for all this nonsense.*

*:If everyone was the same you'd never get anyone to follow your orders.*

*:No. So why do you follow my orders?*

*:I don't know. You're a Voice. You're wise and, er, sensible. You'd burn me to a pile of ashes if I didn't?*

Imenja chuckled, mystifying the other Servants. She said something about needing Reivan's help and somehow neatly extracted them from the crowd. As they left the Star Room Imenja chuckled again.

"I think you follow my orders because I am the closest thing to the gods you have," Imenja said quietly. "You are drawn to the gods not just out of a wish to serve, but because you are—or were—a Thinker. Mysteries fascinate you."

Reivan nodded. "I guess it's a good thing that I can't solve this mystery or I might get bored and look for something else to wonder about."

Imenja's eyebrows rose. "Indeed."

"But I'd still . . ." Reivan stopped. Something stirred at the edge of her mind, distracting her. She wondered if she imagined it even as it resolved into a distinct feeling of another presence. A presence that she did not recognize.

*:Welcome, Servant Reivan.*

In the next moment the presence was gone.

"Wh . . . what was that?"

She looked around the room, then at Imenja. The Second Voice was staring at her in surprise. Surprise was not an expression Reivan had often seen on Imenja's face.

"I believe Sheyr just indicated his approval of your elevation to Servant," the Second Voice murmured.

*Sheyr? One of the gods spoke to* me*?* The corridor seemed to tilt, then right itself. Reivan looked at Imenja. She felt utterly overwhelmed. *What does this mean?*

Imenja smiled. "I think you may need a little celebratory drink. Let's find ourselves a domestic and send for a bottle of Jamya."

"Jamya? I thought that was only served during ceremonies?"

"And sometimes after ceremonies." With one hand still resting on Reivan's shoulder, Imenja steered her toward the Upper Sanctuary.

For a long time now Imi was sure that something had changed. The ship no longer rocked as much and she had bailed all but a shallow puddle of water out of the hull. The muffled shouts of the raiders were different. They held a note of anticipation.

Wondering and listening had taken her mind from the ache in her arms and shoulders. Yet she feared what the change meant, and instead of boredom and exhaustion making the hours turn gradually, fear and anxiety now made their passing unbearably slow.

Suddenly the ship lurched. She dropped the bucket and fell to the floor. The seawater was warm, but welcome. Closing her eyes, she gave in to weariness.

She must have fallen asleep. When she woke again the piles of boxes and large pottery jugs stored in the hull were gone. She listened to rapid footsteps and shouted orders above. By the time the sounds subsided the patch of sky she could see had changed from blue to orange to black. It was quieter than it had been in weeks. She felt herself drifting toward sleep again . . .

. . .then she jerked awake as light filled the hull. Dragging herself up, she grasped the bucket and stooped to fill it. A pair of legs appeared, moving down the ladder into the hull. She felt her mouth go dry as she saw this was the man who led the raiders. The hull was empty except for her. What did he want?

When his feet reached the hull he stepped back. He

looked at her, then back up at the deck. Another pair of legs were descending. These were covered in cloth as black as seatube ink and belonged to a man she had never seen before. As this stranger stepped off the ladder onto the uneven floor he swayed unsteadily, obviously unused to even the gentle movement of the ship.

He looked at her and his eyes widened in surprise, then he grinned at the raider. The pair began to talk as they made their way toward her.

They stopped a few steps away. She averted her gaze, disturbed by the way the stranger stared at her. His eyes moved from her feet to her head and back again. The conversation grew more animated. Suddenly the pair grasped each other's wrists. They turned their backs and walked away.

As they disappeared onto the deck, Imi let the bucket go. She sighed and collapsed into the puddle again.

Sounds came from the ladder again. Two of the raiders entered the hull and came toward her. She scrambled to her feet, heart thundering as they loomed over her. One held a bundle of roughly woven cloth.

The other grabbed her arm and dragged her forward. As the first held out the cloth in both hands she realized it was a sack and that they intended to put her in it.

She tried to wriggle out of the first man's grasp, but his hands were large and strong and she was too weak. Dizziness overcame her and she lost her balance. The sack went over her head. Strong hands held her as it was pulled down to her ankles. She was lifted in the air and felt the bag drawn closed below her feet.

They carried her between them. She had no energy left to struggle.

*Where are they taking me? Do I care? Somewhere different to here. Perhaps somewhere better. Couldn't be much worse than this.*

Blood rushed to her head as they turned her upside down, probably to carry her up to the deck. Cooler air reached her through the sacking. She heard the sounds of footsteps on wood change to footsteps on a harder surface.

The sound of many, many voices came to her, growing louder until they were all around her.

A musty stink followed. She was dropped onto a hard surface and a door was closed, muffling the voices. Someone close by said something tersely. There was a mumbled reply then footsteps moved away.

A voice barked a word. The surface below her shifted abruptly, then she felt motion. Whatever she lay upon began to sway gently. It was nothing like the ship's movement. She drifted into a half-conscious state, too tired to pay attention to the strange noises around her. So many voices could only mean she was among many, many landwalkers. She ought to be frightened, but she had no energy left for fear.

The voices slowly died away. For a long time there was only the sound of rhythmic steps close by. The sound of doors opening and closing eventually roused her. She felt hands lift her up, then lower her to the ground again.

Silence followed. She was vaguely aware of something fussing about near her feet. The cloth around her pulled tight, lifted her up, and she gave a yelp of surprise as she slid out of the bag.

She plunged into cool, welcome water. It helped to clear her head. Surfacing, she took in her surroundings. She was in a round pool in the middle of a round room with a domed ceiling. In the center of the pool was an odd little sculpture of a woman with a fish tail instead of legs. Like landwalkers, she had hair growing from her head.

*A fish woman. Is this supposed to be an Elai?* She snorted with disgust.

The man the lead raider had brought down into the hull to see her was standing nearby, smiling. Raising his arms, he gestured to her surroundings. She couldn't guess what he meant.

He gazed at her for a while, then backed away through an arched entrance. Reaching to one side, he grasped a gate made of metal bars and swung it closed. Still smiling, he walked away.

Imi waited until his footsteps had faded away completely, then she hauled herself out of the pool. It was not easy—the level of the water was an arm's length below the floor and she was so tired. The effort exhausted her and she lay on the floor, panting, until her head stopped spinning.

Eventually she dragged herself to her feet and walked to the metal gate. Grabbing it, she pushed. It did not move. She examined the latch. It was held closed by some kind of metal lock. All was dark beyond it.

*Of course,* she thought. Sinking to her knees, she turned to regard the pool and its ridiculous sculpture. *This is my prison now. I'm a decoration, like that statue. The staring man will probably come to look at me all the time.*

She crawled to the edge of the pool. There was nowhere shallow to lie. If she tried to sleep in there, she would drown. She would have to wake every few hours and wet her skin, or risk drying out and . . . She reached down and cupped some water in her hand. Bringing it to her mouth, she sipped.

*Plain water,* she thought. *I wonder how long it will be before I start to sicken.*

She shook her head. *I'm too tired to think about it.* Lying down on the cool stone floor, she fell into an exhausted sleep.


Looking up from her work, Emerahl squinted into the fine rain. *A dismal day,* she thought. *But the captain is happy. We netted a fine catch.*

The high wall of the Toren cliffs loomed over them on the right. They had been much farther out to sea when they had passed the lighthouse the day before. Looking at the distant white tower, Emerahl had expected to feel regret. She had spent so long living in that remote ruin. Instead she felt repelled.

*All those years living in isolation with only lowlife smugglers for neighbors. I don't know why I didn't die of boredom. It's so good to be among decent, hard-working people again.*

Emerahl began to turn back to the fish-gutting but a light caught her eyes and drew her attention back to the cliff. As a fold of the rock face drew back, more lights appeared. This was their destination. Yaril.

There—so she had been told—lived a young man who had been saved from drowning by The Gull but six months before. She had heard many tales of the mysterious sea boy now. Everyone who lived on the coast knew someone who could relate an encounter with The Gull. These same tales were repeated in every town. Perhaps nobody was related to the heroes and the tellers were just claiming to know them in order to tell a better tale, but these towns were small and it was possible they all knew each other, even if distantly.

In fact, it was amusing to think of them all linked by these stories.

Yaril was in plain sight now. To the fishermen it was merely a good place to sell their catch. She turned her attention back to gutting the fish. The captain had only agreed to take her to Yaril if she made herself useful. She didn't mind the work. It kept her hands busy while she thought about all she'd learned.

As the boat drew closer to the town, the crew left the preparation of the catch to Emerahl while they navigated into a shallow bay. She hurried through the last of the fish then rose and gathered her belongings. Her clothes stank of fish and her skin was sticky from sweat and salt water. As soon as she was ashore she would book a room and wash herself and her garments.

The crew guided the boat up to a short jetty. The moment it was close enough, she leapt off. Turning back once, she gave the captain a nod of thanks before striding into Yaril.

Unlike most of the towns on the coast of Toren, Yaril did not sit at the top of the cliff. Behind the fold in the rock wall a narrow river had worn the sheer drop into a steep, broken slope. Houses had been built on this out of the same stones as the cliffs—right up to the edge of the cascading river.

It was a town with no roads, just staircases going up and down and narrow paths running across the slope. Emerahl paused to smile at a man walking down the stairs who was staring at her with open curiosity.

"Good day to you. Would there be lodging for travellers here?"

The man nodded. "The Widow Laylin has a room for rent. Number three, third level. That's the next level up. It's on the right."

"Thank you."

She continued up the stairs and turned on to one of the narrow walkways. Stopping at a house with a large number three carved into the door, she knocked. The door opened and a large middle-aged woman looked Emerahl up and down.

"I hear you have a room to let," Emerahl said. "Is it available?"

The woman's eyes brightened. "Yes. Come in. I'll show it to you. What is your name?"

"Limma. Limma Curer."

"Curer by trade as well as by name," the woman observed.

"That's right."

The widow led her into a long, narrow room with a view of the bay. It was simple, but clean. Emerahl haggled the price down to a reasonable rate, then asked for water to wash in.

The woman sent her daughter away to fetch it, then turned to regard Emerahl with shrewd eyes.

"So what brings you to Yaril?"

Emerahl smiled. "I'm looking for a young man named Gherid."

"Gherid? We have a Gherid here. Use to fish with his father until all on the boat drowned but he. Now he works for the stonecutter. Is that the one?"

"Sounds like it."

"What you want him for?"

"I hear he tells an interesting tale."

The woman chuckled and shook her head. "Used to. He got fed up with people picking holes in his story and won't say a word now."

"No?"

"Not a word. Not for money or favors."

"Oh." Emerahl looked around the room as if wondering what she was doing there.

"You've come a long way," the woman soothed. "You may as well try. Perhaps you'll get something out of him. I'll take you to see him when you're done washing."

She left the room and the girl arrived with a pitcher of water and a large bowl soon after. Emerahl washed herself and changed into her second set of clothes, then washed her first set and dried them by drawing magic and using it to warm and stir the air around them.

When they were dry, Emerahl draped them on a chair, then tied her collection of pouches around her waist, wrapped her tawl about her and left the room.

The next room was as narrow as hers, but even longer. The space was divided into sections by screens and the farthest proved to be hiding a kitchen. There she found the widow.

"Ready?" the woman said.

Emerahl nodded.

"Come along, then. He'll be at the stonecutter's place."

She followed the woman to the door, then out into the cold air. The houses, built of the same black stone, seemed to hunch against the rock wall as if afraid they might slide off into the sea below. It gave the town a sinister, anxious look, yet all the people Emerahl and the Widow Laylin passed smiled and greeted them cheerfully.

The staircase grew steadily steeper as they neared the top of the cliff. The widow had to stop three times to catch her breath.

"Wouldn't think I lived here, would you?" she said after the third rest. "You're doing well enough."

Emerahl smiled. "Travelling makes you fit."

"Must do. Here we are at last. They live at the top because it's easier to carry his wares down than to bring them up again."

Instead of a road there was a rubble-strewn "yard." Emerahl followed the woman through this to where two gray-haired men were chipping away at large slabs of rock.

"Megrin," the Widow said.

One of the men looked up. He appeared surprised to see Emerahl's companion.

"Widow Laylin," he replied. "Don't often see you up here. Need any work done?"

"No, but my guest wants to have a chat with Gherid about The Gull."

The man looked at Emerahl and straightened. She smiled as she sensed his admiration. The second man had turned to face them. He had a surprisingly young face, though it was set in a scowl. Emerahl looked closer and had to suppress a laugh. The gray in his hair was dust. He was just old enough to be considered a man.

"This is Limma," the widow continued. "She's a curer."

Megrin turned to regard the young man, whose scowl deepened.

"Why do you want to talk about The Gull with me?" Gherid asked.

Emerahl met and held his eyes.

"I heard you met him."

"So?"

"I would like to hear your story."

"Go on, Gherid," the widow urged. "Don't be rude to a visitor."

He looked at the woman, then the stonecutter. The older man nodded. Gherid sighed and shrugged in resignation. "Come with me . . . Limma, wasn't it?"

"Yes."

She followed him back to the stairs, then upward. Intense emotions began to spill from him as they climbed. Guilt and fear combined. She caught snatches of his thoughts.

*. . . I can't kill her! But I must, if she . . .*

Alarmed, she hesitated, then drew magic and formed a shield around herself. Why would he think he might have to kill her? Did he think she would try to harm him? Or take something from him? Surely he didn't think she could force him to give up any information he didn't want to give.

*I'm a curer. A sorceress. Both might mean I have the power to make him tell me things he doesn't want to, either through drugs or torture.*

Either way, he obviously had something to protect. They reached the top of the cliff. He walked along the edge, saying nothing. Emerahl watched him closely. She sensed he was taking a precaution of some kind. When they stopped, she realized they had moved past the edge of the town. She now stood above a precipice. *Does he plan to push me off?*

"So, what do you want to know?" he asked.

She met his eyes. "Is it true you've met The Gull?"

"Yes," he replied. "Everybody knows that."

She sensed that he was telling the truth and felt a pang of sympathy for him.

"Nobody believes you, do they?"

"And you do?"

She nodded. "But that's not why you don't tell the story any more, is it?"

He stared at her, his anxiety and guilt increasing. No amount of talking was going to reassure him. She decided to take a gamble.

"You made a promise," she stated. "Did you break it?"

He flushed. She began to guess how it had been for him. Saved by a mythical being and needing to explain what happened, he had told as much of his tale as he knew it was safe to tell, until one day he had let some detail slip that he hadn't intended.

"Why do you want to know?"

She frowned as if in worry. "I don't *want* to know, I *need* to know. The Gull's secrets must be safe."

His eyes widened and he turned pale. "I thought you . . . They didn't understand what I told them. I'm sure they didn't understand."

"What did you say?"

"I . . . I told them about the Stack. They put something in my drink." He looked at her pleadingly. "I didn't mean to. I didn't tell them where it was. You don't think they can find it on their own, do you?"

She sighed. "I don't know. I don't know where the Stack is. We all end up with different secrets to keep and that was yours. Have you warned him?"

His eyes widened. "How?"

She blinked as if surprised. "You don't have a way to contact him?"

"No . . . but I suppose if I went back . . . but it's so far away and I don't have a boat."

"Neither do I, but I could buy one." Shaking her head, she turned toward the sea and pretended to think. "You'd better tell me everything, Gherid. I'm a long way from home and my way of contacting him doesn't work here. We need to get a message to The Gull. It may be that the only way we can do that is for me to go to the Stack and leave a message for you."

The surge of gratitude that spilled from him sent a pang of guilt through her. She was manipulating the poor boy. *It's not like I have malicious intentions,* she told herself. *I want to find The Gull so we can help each other.*

He moved to a nearby rock to sit down. "It's a long story. You'd better sit down. Have you sailed a boat before?"

Emerahl smiled. "Many, many times."

# 21

Devlem slipped the last slice of fruit into his mouth then licked the sweet juice off his fingers. One of the three servants standing nearby stepped forward and held out a tray made of gold. Taking the neatly folded damp cloth from it, Devlem cleaned his hands, then dropped the cloth back on the tray.

The sound of running footsteps echoed in the courtyard. A servant raced up to Devlem's table and bowed.

"The shipment has arrived."

*Only two days late,* Devlem thought. *If I threaten the dyers a little I may make the market before Arlem does—but only if the stock hasn't spoiled.*

He rose and strode out of the courtyard. An arched corridor took him through to the front of the house. He followed a paved path to the plainer buildings that housed his wares.

Tarns waited outside. Men were already carrying the large rolls of cloth inside, watched by his overseer.

Entering the building, Devlem ignored the servants and examined the shipment. The waterproof wrapping of one bolt of cloth was torn.

"Open it," he ordered.

Servants hurried to cut the wrapping away.

"Careful!" Devlem bellowed. "You'll damage the cloth!"

Their movements became slower and more cautious. As they worked they cast nervous glances in his direction. *Good,* he thought. *The whipping I ordered has finally taught them to be more respectful. They were getting more like Genrian women every day, whining and complaining.*

The wrapping parted, revealing clean, undamaged cloth. He moved closer as more began to appear.

"Master Trader!"

The room echoed with running footsteps. He glanced up, annoyed at the interruption. The intruder was one of the lawn clippers. She was ugly for an Avven woman and he had sent her out to work in the garden so he didn't have to look at her.

"Master," she panted. "There is a monster in the pool house!"

He sighed. "Yes. I put it there."

She bit her lip. "Oh. It appears to be dead."

"Dead?" He straightened in alarm.

She nodded.

Cursing in his native Genrian tongue, he strode past her out of the warehouse and hurried toward the gardens. The pool house was at the center of a large lawn. The lawn clippers had gathered in a crowd around the entrance.

"Get back to work!" he ordered.

They turned to stare at him, then scattered. As he reached the gate of the house he drew out the key to the lock. Inside, he could see the youngling sea creature lying on the floor.

He hadn't had much time to examine his purchase closely last night. The raider had claimed it was a girl child, but the only evidence of that was the lack of male organs. Devlem had ordered his servants to remove the dirty rags that had hung off the creature's shoulders. Looking her over, he decided the raider was right, and wondered if she'd develop breasts like humans.

Perhaps, when she was mature, he would purchase a male. If they produced offspring he could sell their young for a fortune.

The lock clicked. He pushed the gate open and walked over to the creature. Why had she climbed out of the water? Crouching down, he saw that she was still breathing.

The more he looked at her, the more concerned he grew.

Her breathing was labored. Her skin was dull and cracked. If she had been human, he would have said she was dangerously thin. She also smelled foul. All animals smelled bad and he had assumed that the reek was natural, but now he wasn't so sure.

He took her chin and turned her head so he could examine her face. At the touch her eyes fluttered open, then closed again. She gave a faint moan.

*I paid a lot of money for her.* He rose and stared down at her. *If she's sick I need to find someone to cure her. Who will know what's wrong? I could bring in an animal healer, but I doubt they've ever seen one of the sea people before. I doubt anyone has. Unless . . .*

He smiled as he realized there were people in Glymma who might know about the sea people. Turning away, he quickly locked the gate and hurried toward the house, shouting for a messenger.

Mirar lifted a rock. Nothing. He put it down again and lifted another. A creature scurried away. He made a grab for it, but it shot straight into a crack between two much larger and heavier boulders.

*Curse it. How does Emerahl catch these shrimmi? If I could just—*

"Wilar! Dreamweaver!"

He jumped in surprise and looked up. Tyve was circling above him. Mirar caught a powerful feeling of anxiety and urgency from the boy. Standing up, he shaded his eyes and watched the Siyee land.

"What is it?"

"Sizzi is sick. So are Veece and Ziti. Others are sickening, too. Can you come to the village? Can you help us?"

Mirar frowned. "Did the Speaker send you to me?"

"Yes."

This was not entirely the truth, if the uneasiness Mirar sensed in Tyve was any indication. He narrowed his eyes at the young Siyee.

"Did he really?"

Tyve shot Mirar a guilty glance. "Not exactly. He is too sick to speak. I suggested to the rest that I ask you for help, since you're a healer. They agreed."

This, Mirar sensed, was the truth. He nodded. "I will come. What are the symptoms?"

"You'll see when you get there," Tyve said impatiently. "We should leave now, if you're to arrive before . . . It's a long way."

"Therefore a long way to return to get the right cures," Mirar pointed out. "I need to know what this illness is so I can pack my bag. Tell me about it."

Tyve described what he had seen. As he did, Mirar felt his stomach sink. It sounded like a disease called Hearteater which occasionally spread among landwalkers. Most likely a Siyee had caught it during the war and brought it back to the tribe. Mirar hadn't considered that diseases might be an inevitable consequence of the Siyee mixing with outsiders. He cursed the White silently.

*You can't be sure the White knew this would happen,* Leiard reminded him.

*But there's no happiness greater than having someone to blame,* Mirar replied.

"I know this illness." he told the young Siyee. "I can help your tribe overcome it, but I cannot promise that all will survive."

Tyve went pale. Mirar laid a hand on his shoulder. "I'll do all I can. Now give me a little time to pack my bag, and you can guide me to your village."

The Siyee sat down on a rock to wait, his expression anguished. Walking up the river, Mirar considered his store of cures. When he had left the battlefield with Emerahl he had been carrying his Dreamweaver bag, but it had been near empty. It was full now. First Emerahl then he had spent many hours in the forest finding and preparing cures, drawing on their knowledge of the plants there. Not all of the cures were as potent or acted in quite the same way as those they replaced. Some were more effective, some less so.

Moving behind the fall, he walked down the passage into the cave. He looked at the objects piled or stacked around the walls. Rope would be essential but bedding would be too cumbersome to carry. He would sleep in his clothes on the ground, which meant he would need some warmer clothes now the weather was turning cold.

*Food, too,* Leiard reminded him

*Of course.* He smiled crookedly and moved around the room, gathering what he would need. When he had finished he gave the cave one last look.

*Will I return here soon, or will this crisis of the Siyee lead me away indefinitely?* He shrugged. *I don't mind either way. If Emerahl is right, being among people will do me good.*

Turning away, he hurried out to rejoin Tyve and begin another arduous journey through the Si mountains.

The sun was low in the sky by the time Auraya saw the Open in the distance. She had not flown as fast as she'd intended, having discovered that Mischief grew apprehensive if she flew beyond a certain speed. He would shiver and mew in terror, but so long as she kept below this speed he was happy to crouch within the bag strapped between her shoulder blades.

Because of the delay, she had not stopped to talk to any of the Siyee she had seen once she reached Si. They hadn't attempted to meet her either; they could probably see she was moving too fast for them to intercept. Now, as she slowed to approach the long stripe of exposed mountain slope that was the main Siyee gathering place, the sky people flew up to join her.

She felt Mischief shift position on her back.

"Fly!" he declared. "Fly! Fly!"

He had no words to tell her of the strange winged people gliding around and behind her, but she could sense his excitement.

"Siyee," she told him. "They're Siyee."

He fell silent for a moment.

"Syee," he said quietly.

Some of her impromptu escort she recognized, some she didn't. She exchanged whistled greetings with them all.

Their thoughts were full of relief and gladness. They knew why she was here, however, and worry made their welcome subdued compared to previous ones.

She descended steadily, heading for the large, level area in the middle section of the Open known as the Flat. Several Siyee stood around the outside of this and she could hear the sound of greeting drums. Two white-clothed men drew her eye. Like most landwalkers they were nearly twice the height of the Siyee and their white priest robes made them doubly conspicuous.

She turned her attention to a line of men and women standing near the outcrop known as Speakers' Rock. As she drew closer she made out enough detail to identify each of them. All were Speakers—leaders of a Siyee tribe—but only half of all Speakers were present. That was no surprise. Some would not want to leave their tribe while invaders roamed within Si, and others lived too far from the Open to travel here for every unplanned meeting. Representatives of each tribe lived in the Open, however, and would be waiting among those at the edge of the Flat.

Speaker Sirri, the Head Speaker of all tribes, stepped forward as Auraya dropped to the ground. She smiled and held out a wooden cup and a small cake. As Auraya took them Sirri spread her arms wide. Sunlight filtered through the membrane of her wings, illuminating a delicate tracery of veins and arteries between the supporting bones.

"Welcome back to Si, Auraya of the White."

Auraya smiled in return. "Thank you, Speaker Sirri, and thank you to the people of Si for their warm welcome."

She ate the sweet cake then sipped some water before handing the cup back. Sirri's gaze flickered to Auraya's shoulder and her eyes opened wide.

"Syee," Mischief whispered at her ear.

Smothering a laugh, Auraya gave his head a scratch.

"Speaker Sirri," she said, "this is Mischief. He's a veez. The Somreyans tamed them long ago, and keep them as pets."

"A veez," Sirri said, coming forward to stare at Mischief. "Yes, I remember catching sight of this animal in the war camp."

"They can speak, in a limited fashion." Auraya looked at Mischief. "This is Sirri," she told him.

"Seeree," he replied. "Syee Seeree."

Sirri chuckled quietly. "He is an appealing animal. I had better make sure none of the Siyee decide he will make a nice meal." She straightened. "The Speakers have requested that I call a gathering in the Speakers' Bower as soon as you arrived, but we could delay if you are tired."

Auraya shook her head. "The Pentadrians travel deeper into Si every moment that passes, and I'm as anxious to deal with them as I am sure you all are. I will meet with the Speakers now."

Sirri nodded in gratitude, then gestured to the other Speakers. As they moved forward to join Sirri, Auraya looked toward the two priests. They made the sign of the circle. She inclined her head in reply.

Seeking their minds, she saw that they were eager to talk to her, though neither had any matter they urgently needed to discuss. Though they had found the Siyee welcoming, they also felt their ways were a little strange.

*They need reassurance from me that they're doing well,* she realized.

Turning away, she followed Sirri into the forest, the other Speakers and tribe representatives following. They passed many of the Siyee bowers—frames of wood with a membrane stretched between, built around the bases of the enormous trees growing around the Open—and many curious Siyee. Sirri did not hurry, despite the other Speakers' impatience. She knew that her people would be reassured by the sight of the gods' Chosen One.

Once they entered the unoccupied forest around the Speakers' Bower, the Head Speaker quickened her pace. They wound through narrow paths to a large bower and filed inside. Carved tree-stump stools had been arranged in a circle. The Speakers took their places. Auraya set her pack down on the floor beside her. Mischief peered out, then decided it all looked uninteresting and curled up to sleep.

"As we all know," Sirri began, "a Pentadrian ship was seen off the coast of southern Si fourteen days ago. Several

Pentadrians landed and separated into groups, which have been travelling inland. It appears they are using their birds to guide them toward Siyee villages." She looked at Auraya. "We sent a request for help to the White and Auraya has come back to us. Before we begin discussing how to deal with the Pentadrians, do you have any questions, Auraya?"

"How often have you received reports on the Pentadrians' movements?"

"Every few hours. My son, Sreil, has organized for groups of watchers to follow the Pentadrians and report back regularly."

"Have any of these watchers seen one or more of the Pentadrian sorcerer leaders among them?"

"No."

*That doesn't mean they're not with them.* Auraya drummed her fingers together. "Have the Pentadrians harmed anyone?"

"Not yet."

"Have they spoken to anyone?"

"No—all Siyee have been told to keep away from them."

"Have they attempted to make a permanent settlement?"

The Speakers looked surprised. She read from their minds that none had considered the possibility.

"The watchers say they have been travelling constantly," Speaker Dryss replied.

Auraya considered all that they had told her. "I have no more questions for now. Does anyone have questions for me?"

"Yes," one of the representatives replied. "What will you do?"

She brought her hands together and interlocked her fingers. "Advise and assist you. I am not here to decide a course of action for you. I will protect you if they attack, and drive them out of Si—if I can—should you decide I must. I will also translate for you if they wish to communicate. It is possible they wish to make peace with you."

The Siyee exchanged glances, many scowling.

"Never!" one of the representatives hissed.

"Do not dismiss the possibility," one of the older Speakers told the young man. "The Pentadrians are not a people about to die out. Better we be at peace with them than not."

"So long as we are not forced to compromise too much for it."

"Of course not."

"There is another possibility," Auraya continued. "One that disturbs me. They may hope to convert Siyee to their cult."

"They will be disappointed," Speaker Sirri said firmly. "There is not one Siyee who does not grieve the loss of a family or tribe member. None would betray us to join the enemy."

"I believe that is so," Auraya replied. "If they come with such intentions, it is best all are alert to the possibility and prepared to resist sweet words of persuasion."

"They will not have a chance to utter them," the young representative declared. "They will go home or we will kill them."

"We will send them home, whatever their intentions," Sirri agreed. "Even if their purpose is peaceful, it is too soon after the war for us to welcome Pentadrians in Si."

The other Speakers voiced their agreement.

"If that is what you mean to do," Auraya said, "the Pentadrians need to hear it from you, not me. They need to know it is your decision and that you are not merely doing what the White tell you to do."

Silence followed her words. She sensed their fear and reluctance.

"What if they attack us?" a Speaker said in a thin voice.

"I will protect you. We will retreat and, when you are safe, I will return to drive them away."

"Must we all go?" Speaker Dryss said. "I am not so quick with the winds these days and I fear I may hamper you if we need to retreat quickly."

"There is no need for you to all go," Auraya said. "Choose three from among you."

Sirri cleared her throat. "I would prefer to ask for volunteers."

As she glanced around the room, Auraya noticed many

averted gazes. The young representative did not flinch away. Auraya felt her heart sink as he straightened in preparation to speak. *He's a bit headstrong for this*.

"I'll go," he offered.

"Thank you, Rizzi, but this is a task for Speakers," Sirri said. "How seriously will these Pentadrians take our words if they aren't spoken to by tribal leaders?" She spread her hands. "I will go. If no others volunteer, I will be forced to call for nominations, or have names drawn from—"

"I will go—if I am not too old."

The volunteer was a middle-aged Speaker, Iriz of the Green Lake tribe.

Sirri smiled. "There are many years in you yet, Speaker Iriz."

"And I," another Siyee woman offered. Auraya recognized the Speaker of the Sun Ridge tribe, whose members had been attacked by the Pentadrians' trained birds months before the battle.

"Thank you, Speaker Tyzi," Sirri said. "That makes three."

The relief of the other Siyee washed over Auraya. She resisted a smile. Sirri slapped her knees decisively. "We will leave at first light tomorrow. Are there any other matters to raise with Auraya?" She looked around the room, but none of the Siyee spoke. "Then this gathering is over. Speakers Iriz and Tyzi, could you stay? We must discuss preparations for the journey."

As the Siyee filed out of the room, Auraya looked down at Mischief. He was still asleep. She smiled and turned her attention to the remaining Siyee. At once she felt a twinge of apprehension. If she found herself facing one of the more powerful Pentadrian sorcerers it would not be easy to protect these Siyee. She must ensure she had a good look at the intruders before they saw her.

For now, she must show the Siyee no sign of her own doubts and fears.

# 22

The sea surged under the boat as if it regarded the vessel as an irritating pest that it must shake off. As a wave threatened to capsize it, Emerahl drew magic and used it to press the hull back against the water. A gust of wind drove rain into her face and she cursed.

She realized she was cursing the sea in a language long forgotten, from a time when fishermen and sailors worshipped gods of the seas. It was easy to imagine the thrashing expanse of water was still ruled by a greater mind—one who wanted to be rid of this trespasser—especially when she considered how quickly the storm had blown in.

Emerahl snorted. *The old gods are dead. This is just bad weather. I should have taken the boat seller's advice, bought a bigger boat and waited a few weeks for the season to change.*

She had once known this stretch of coast well and had been able to read the signs of bad weather. Much could change in a thousand years, however. The currents as well as the weather were different. Even the shape of the shoreline was unrecognizable in places. As she had travelled along the Toren coast she had experienced an odd succession of familiar and unfamiliar sights. Fortunately the hills that marked the border between Toren and Genria were still where they ought to be. From there she had turned her back to the coast and sailed straight out to sea, as Gherid had instructed.

A wave broke over the boat, soaking her. She scooped

the water out of the hull with magic. The rain was so thick now she could barely see the other end of the vessel. There was nothing for her to do but endure. She could not raise the sail in these conditions. She could not see where she was, let alone find her destination, or return to the mainland.

She cursed again as another wave nearly toppled the boat. The wind sounded like an inhuman voice. She could not help feeling a twinge of superstitious fear. Perhaps she should not be cursing the god of the sea.

*Why not? He can't harm me,* she thought. *He's dead. Like all the old gods. Well, all but the Circle.* Could it be that one of the remaining five had learned to influence the sea? Was one playing with it right now?

The thought was not comforting. If the gods were causing this, what purpose did they have? Were they aware of her? Were they trying to stop her reaching her destination? She clung to the rudder. Though rain and cloud lay thick between herself and the sun, a thin gray light struggled through to her. Suddenly the light failed and she moved into shadow. She looked around, holding back a growing dread. When she saw the source of the shadow her heart froze. Something tall and dark loomed over her.

Fear melted away as she realized what it was.

*The Stack!*

Through sheer luck, the boat had been driven by the storm to the very place she wanted to be. Now, however, the current was drawing her away from it. Casting about, she considered the oars clipped to the sides of the boat.

*No. They'll be of no use. I was lucky the sea didn't throw the boat against the Stack. Even if I manage to row closer, I can't tie up the boat. It'll be dashed to pieces. This calls for magic, and a lot of concentration.*

Drawing in a good deal of magic, she sent it out around the boat. She would have to act quickly once she had hold of the vessel or the next wave would wash right over her.

*Lift.*

Her stomach sank as the boat soared upward, carrying her with it. She stared ahead, where she knew the Stack stood, now hidden by the rain.

*Forward.*

It was not a smooth ride. Moving the boat demanded the unwavering focus of her mind. Every gust of wind or shift in her thoughts caused the boat to tilt or sink. Even her relief at seeing the Stack emerge from the rain caused the boat's movement to waver.

*Closer.*

She stopped when she could see the rocky surface before her.

*Higher.*

The sound of the churning waves crashing against the rocks diminished as she lifted the boat up. Tufts of hardy sea grass appeared, growing in cracks and nooks, then a blanket of it became visible. She had reached the top of the Stack.

*Forward.*

She moved the boat over the sea grass, then, several paces from the cliff edge, lowered it to the ground.

There was no time to feel relief. The wind threatened to toss the boat back off. Jumping out, she removed her belongings, turned it over, rammed pegs into the ground and lashed the vessel to them.

When she was sure it was secure, she straightened and looked around. It was possible she had just landed on a promontory of the coast and not the Stack the boy had described. Leaving the boat, she walked carefully to the edge. The sea below was hidden by the dense rain.

She marked her position by pulling up three handfuls of grass to reveal the pale sandy soil beneath, then she paced around the edge. After fifty paces, she found the uprooted grass. To be sure she hadn't encountered a natural repetition of her marker, she walked away from the edge. The boat appeared, and she nodded to herself.

*I'll know this is the Stack the boy described if I find the cave.*

She walked around the cliff edge again, looking for the beginning of the staircase that led down to the cave, but found no sign of it. After the fifth circuit of the island, she gave up and returned to the boat.

Sitting down, she drew enough magic to form a shield against the rain. Her clothes were soaked and heavy. She channelled a little more magic to warm and dry herself. As the water misted out of her clothes and hair she shivered.

*This had better not be one of those three-day storms,* she thought. *If it goes for more than a few more hours, I will try to find that staircase again.*

And if she didn't find it? She would have to stay and wait the storm out. Even if she used magic to keep the boat afloat and propel it through the water, she still had no way of knowing which direction to go to return to the coast.

With a resigned sigh, she opened her bag and brought out some dried fruit to chew on while she waited.

Early morning sunlight set the membrane walls of the bower glowing. Auraya looked around the little house and sighed with pleasure. It was good to be back in Si.

*Why does this place feel like home?* she asked herself. *I feel better today than I have for months. And I had no nightmares last night,* she realized. She felt as if she had left a lot of troubling things behind her. Nightmares. The hospice. *I hadn't realized how much the hospice was bothering me.*

She thought back to her previous stay in Si. She'd always woken up feeling good here. *But was that because of my dream links with Leiard?* she suddenly thought.

Leiard. Did she imagine that the pang of hurt that always came at the thought of Leiard was weaker? He seemed a part of someone else's life now. Perhaps soon she would feel nothing at all.

*:I hope not,* a familiar voice spoke into her mind. *It would be terrible indeed for you to feel nothing. Neither joy nor sorrow. Neither pleasure nor pain.*

*I meant feel nothing about Leiard,* she told Chaia. *You know that.*

*:You will always feel something in regard to him. Time will dull the pain. There is nothing that eases it as well as immersing oneself in new feelings.*

*Yes,* she thought. *New challenges. Like getting these Pentadrians out of Si.*

*:That wasn't what I had in mind.*

She smiled crookedly. *I thought not. But as they say: work before pleasure.*

*:I'll hold you to that.*

His presence abruptly vanished. Auraya shook her head. Sometimes she did not understand Chaia, but then he was a god and she wasn't. She rose and moved to the hanging that covered the bower entrance.

"Owaya fly?"

She looked back at Mischief, who had decided one of the baskets hanging from the bower roof was an acceptable sleeping place. Only his nose was visible over the lip.

"Yes. Auraya fly alone. To a dangerous meeting. Mischief stay here. Safe."

Mischief considered this for a long moment, then his nose withdrew from sight. Since being kidnapped before the battle, he took all warnings of danger seriously.

"Msstf stay," he murmured.

Relieved, Auraya moved outside and took a step toward the Speakers' Bower. At once a small crowd of Siyee children erupted from the forest and surrounded her. She laughed in surprise as they showered her with flowers. A few daringly reached out to touch her hands. Suddenly one gave a piercing whistle and they scampered away. Auraya caught enough from the jumble of their thoughts to learn they were prudently fleeing the approach of an adult. She turned to see Speaker Sirri walking toward her.

The Siyee leader was smiling. "You've become a figure of legend since you last visited. The singers among us have made up a song called 'The White Lady,' in which you defeat the Pentadrians single-handedly."

Auraya chuckled. "That's a little unfair on the other White."

Sirri shrugged. "Yes. It certainly looked like you struck the killing blow, however."

"It was more . . . complicated than that," Auraya told the Speaker. "The others were attacking in less visible ways. It just happened to fall to me to take advantage of the enemy's mistake."

"When the sorceress became distracted?"

"Yes." Auraya saw Sirri's crooked smile and looked closer. What she saw amused and surprised her. "*Tryss* was the distraction? He *attacked* her?"

Sirri nodded. "So he says, and I have no reason to doubt him."

"How incredibly brave," Auraya breathed, thinking of the shy young inventor of the Siyee's hunting harness.

"Not many know of it. He does not want to be treated like a hero when so many died. The war has changed him. I think he feels guilty for having made something that enabled the Siyee to join a war that killed so many of us. I try to tell him it was not his fault, but . . ." She looked up at Auraya and frowned, suddenly wondering whether Auraya, too, felt the burden of guilt. When Auraya met her eyes Sirri looked away. "I've come to tell you that the volunteer Speakers are waiting in the gathering place," Sirri said.

Auraya frowned. "Am I late?"

"No. They are early. Anxious to get it over with, I suspect."

"Then let's oblige them."

Sirri led Auraya to the edge of the forest then leapt into the air. Auraya followed and they glided down to the Flat, where the two speakers, Iriz and Tyzi, waited. Several hunters wearing harnesses waited nearby. Sirri had decided they should accompany them in case the Speakers were separated from Auraya, and the Pentadrian birds attacked.

Iriz and Tyzi radiated both fear and determination as they exchanged greetings with Auraya.

"Which Pentadrian group will we meet first?" Iriz asked.

"Which do you think we should approach?" Auraya asked in reply.

"Whichever is closest," Tyzi answered. "The sooner we tell them to leave, the better."

"The one travelling northeast then."

"The north group is closer to a tribe," Iriz pointed out. "If the Pentadrians decide to attack, we might not be able to send a warning in time."

"The north group won't know what the other group is doing," Tyzi said. Then she looked at Auraya doubtfully. "Or will they?"

"They have a way of communicating with each other as Circlian priests and priestesses do," Auraya said.

Tyzi frowned. "Then we should meet the north group."

"By the time we get there, the Pentadrians travelling east will be close to a tribe, too," Iriz said.

"Scouts are watching the enemy," Sirri said. "All Siyee know to avoid them, and have made preparations to leave their home if they have to. No tribe is going to sit and wait around to be attacked."

Iriz and Tyzi nodded in agreement. "The closest tribe then," Iriz said.

"We should reach them by this afternoon," Tyzi added.

Auraya looked at Sirri. "And return tomorrow, if all goes well."

The Speaker smiled grimly. "Let us delay no longer."

She moved to the lower edge of the Flat, where a short drop divided the rocky slope. As Sirri leapt off the edge, the other Speakers and hunters propelled themselves after her. Auraya drew magic and sent herself up to join them.

As she drew level with Sirri, she felt another presence at her side.

:*You're back.*

:*I am,* Chaia said.

:*Do you know what these Pentadrians are up to?*

:*Yes.*

:*Are you going to tell me?*

:*No.*

:*Why not?*

:*It is up to you to find and deal with them.*

:*So you won't even tell me where they are.*

:*There is no need. You will find them easily enough.*

:*What's the point in talking to you if you won't tell me anything useful?*

:*Does there have to be a price? Isn't my company enough?*

She sighed.

*:Of course there doesn't have to be a price. I just wish I knew how dangerous these Pentadrians are. I would not like these Siyee to be hurt or killed.*

*:Then you should be taking every precaution.* Chaia's tone was no longer playful. *Do not be complacent just because I am present now and then. I cannot be everywhere at once, or with you all the time. If I could, and if the world was full of highly Gifted mortals willing to do my will, we would not have needed to make you what you are.* He paused. *Have you taken every precaution?*

*:I have,* she answered. *At least, I hope so.*

As he moved away, she felt a twinge of anxiety. Once more she started to consider all the possible outcomes of this meeting with the Pentadrians.

Dedicated Servant Renva grasped the hand of Servant Vengel and held tightly as he hauled her up over the top of the ridge. He steadied her as she struggled to stand. The ground was a mess of grooves and sharp protruding stones and there was no flat surface to stand on.

When she had caught her balance, she looked around. The ridge was high enough to give her a view of the terrain ahead. She groaned as she saw exposed ridges and shadowed ravines extending toward the mountains ahead.

*This is a nightmare!* she thought. *Surely only winged creatures can live here. It's as if the land is doing its best to repel us.*

She wished she could oblige it, but she had her orders to follow. The Siyee were primitive folk, she had been told. Simple people with simple ways were easy to impress. Whether she could persuade them to worship the Five Gods depended on how impressed they were with the Circlians and their false gods.

*But we've got to reach them first.*

It would be much easier if they came to her. She had glimpsed them in the distance from time to time. Often she had the feeling they were watching her and her companions, yet they never came within hailing distance.

*Simple people are often fearful,* she reminded herself.

*We were their enemy a few months ago. They will regard us as invaders.*

Turning away from the view, she began making her way along the ridge top.

"Dedicated Servant Renva," Vengel called.

She turned to see him staring into the distance. He glanced at her, then pointed. Looking in the direction he indicated, she searched the sky, but saw nothing.

"What is it?" she asked.

"Siyee," Vengel replied. "Flying low. Between the trees and us."

She looked lower, but it took some time before she saw them. Flying shapes too large to be birds glided among the tree tops, too far away for her to make out details. There were more than ten of them and they were coming directly toward her.

"I see them." She considered her position. Whether the Siyee were coming to talk or fight, she ought to be with her people. Since the others wouldn't make it to the ridge in time, that meant returning to the narow ravine below.

She walked back to Vengel's side and leaned over the edge.

"Go back down," she called to the Servant climbing the rope. The man frowned and started to descend. She looked at Vengel. "Stay here and see if you can get their attention, but be ready in case they attack."

Vengel nodded. His face was grim, but he said nothing as she started to descend. He had enough Skill in magic to protect himself from arrows.

Once she had reached the floor of the ravine, Renva gathered the others together.

"There is a group of Siyee heading our way," she told them. "They may be coming to meet us; they may not be aware of us at all. We should be prepared for an attack, just in case."

The unSkilled carriers and less Skilled Servants moved to the center of the group. All were silent as they waited. Vengel gave a shout and all looked up to search the sky.

Winged shapes flashed behind the tops of the trees.

Renva caught glimpses of eyes staring down at her suspiciously. They circled overhead, their confidence not a little intimidating. She saw a larger figure—wingless and white—and her throat went dry.

*The White sorceress. Nekaun warned me that she might come.* She touched the star pendant hanging against her chest.

*:Nekaun!*

The pause that followed was short, but felt like an eternity.

*:Renva. I see you have met the Siyee.*

*:In the process of meeting,* she corrected. *The White sorceress accompanies them.*

*:That is no surprise. So long as no violence is done, she won't attack you. Proceed.*

Renva swallowed. *I hope he's right.* She took a deep breath and forced herself to call out.

"People of the Sky. Siyee. We do not wish to harm anyone. Come down so we may speak to you."

The forest echoed with the flying people's whistles. Strange words were mixed with the piercing calls. They were talking, she guessed. She did not expect them to understand her, but hoped they'd hear peaceful intent in her voice. The White sorceress probably did understand. It was said they could read minds.

"I am Dedicated Servant Renva and these are my companions. We have come a long way in the hopes of becoming your friends," she told them. "We have . . ."

Leaves stirred as three of the Siyee dove through the tree tops. They landed on branches high above and stared down at Renva and her people. She heard a voice behind her.

"If your intentions are peaceful, why did you not learn the local language before you came?"

Renva spun around. The White sorceress stood on a lower branch of a tree, not far away.

"There was no one to teach us," Renva replied. "Or we would have."

The White sorceress looked upward and spoke a string of strange words. One of the Siyee above replied. The White sorceress smiled faintly, then met Renva's eyes again.

"I am here as protector and translator only. Speaker Sirri, leader of the Siyee, wishes to know why you have entered Si uninvited."

Renva looked up at the Siyee who had spoken. *A woman leads them. Interesting.* "We come to make peace with the Siyee."

The White sorceress translated. *Or at least I hope she is,* Renva thought. *How will I know if she mistranslates my words in her favor?*

*:Take care how you phrase your questions,* Nekaun advised.

The Siyee leader spoke.

"Speaker Sirri says: 'If you wish to make peace, leave us be. Leave and do not return,' " the White sorceress said.

"Will you not give us a chance to mend the rift between our people?" Renva asked.

Another of the Siyee responded.

"The rift is too wide. How can you expect us to forgive those who invaded our allies' lands and murdered so many of our fathers and sons, mothers and daughters?"

"Must we then remain enemies always?"

"Friendship must be earned," the Siyee leader replied. "Trust is not gained when an enemy enters a house uninvited."

"How may we win your trust? How can we even learn your language if we can't . . . Will you come to Avven instead?"

The Siyee exchanged glances.

"Perhaps one day, if we were sure we would be safe."

"I swear, on the Five Gods, it will be so," Renva said earnestly.

At that the Siyee looked uneasy. The older man spoke. The White sorceress looked surprised, and paused before translating.

"Speaker Iriz says: 'If you attempt to persuade any Siyee to worship your gods you will fail. Huan created us and we will never turn from her.' "

*They believe their gods created them?* Nekaun murmured.

*:It appears so,* she replied.
*:Do as they say,* he told her. *Leave.*
*:Yes, holy one.*

Renva bowed her head. "Friendship was our reason for coming here. To prove our trustworthiness, we will leave as you bid us. I hope, in the future, another chance will come to make peace between us."

The White sorceress translated, then the Siyee voiced their approval. They leapt from their perches and swooped out of the trees. The White sorceress lingered a moment, watching Renva as though measuring her up.

"Scouts will watch you," she warned. "We will know if you do not leave."

She floated upward, gaining speed so quickly that the leafy canopy of the tree vibrated at her passing. Renva shook her head in awe. It was incredible that someone could be so skilled in magic that they could defy the pull of the earth.

*And depressing knowing what we're going to have to travel back over to get to the coast again.*

*:Take your time,* Nekaun said in her mind. *Your situation may change between now and then.*

*I hope not,* she thought. She felt a little guilty at thinking this. She was supposed to be willing to face and endure anything in order to serve the gods.

*:But you don't have to enjoy it,* Nekaun told her, his communication light with humor. She laughed. As her travelling companions turned to stare at her, she composed herself again.

"We'll retrace our steps until dusk," she decided, "then find a good place to stop for the night." She looked up at the ridge. "You may as well come down," she called to Vengel, who was leaning over the edge, peering down at her. "We're going home."

# 23

Pain and movement assailed Imi as she woke. Her skin burned, her joints ached, and her stomach clenched. Someone was lifting her. A voice drew her attention—a male voice speaking quietly and soothingly. It sounded like her father.

She jolted toward full awareness. Could it be? Had he come to rescue her at last? Opening her eyes, she stared up at a strange face. The man's skin was pale and fur grew from both face and scalp.

He was a landwalker, but not the landwalker who had put her here. He stared back at her, the two furry lines above his eyes drawing close together as he frowned. There was a sloshing sound below her and she realized he was standing in the pool. He began to lower her. She felt a moment of panic and struggled weakly. The pool was too deep and she had no strength to drag herself out again. She would drown.

A moment after she felt water on her back she felt the solid surface of the pool's bottom. The landwalker let her go, but remained squatting beside her. He began to splash water over her. It stung her skin, then cooled it. There was a good smell in the air—the smell of the sea. It came from the water. She lifted a hand to her mouth and tasted it.

*Sea water. They're trying to make me well again.*

The thought ought to have been a relief, but it brought only fear, heightened by the realization that she was naked. Where was her shift? Would they give her new clothes? What would they do with her once she was healthy? What would they make her do? Maybe it would be better if she didn't get well. Maybe it would be better if she died.

*No. I have to get well,* she told herself. *I have to get better and be ready when father comes . . . or when I get a chance to escape by myself.*

The landwalker stopped splashing her with water. He stood up and moved to the side of the pool. Picking up a large platter, he sloshed back to her side.

He began to speak again, his voice quiet and cheerful. Taking something from the platter, he held it out to her.

It was raw fish. She grimaced. At once he returned it to the platter.

Next he offered her a piece of cooked fish. She felt her stomach growl and reached out to take it, then hesitated.

*What if it is poisoned?* she thought. She looked at the man suspiciously. He smiled and murmured more strange words. Trying to reassure her.

*What does it matter?* she thought. *If I don't eat, I'll die anyway.*

She took the morsel and put it into her mouth. It tasted wonderful. She swallowed and a deep relief spread through her body.

The landwalker offered her more, piece by piece, then set the tray aside. She was still hungry, yet her stomach felt too . . . busy . . . for much more. He moved closer. She felt a stab of fear as he kneeled in the water beside her. He spoke earnestly, then glanced over his shoulder at the closed metal gate of the room. Turning back, he stared into her eyes and spoke again. This time his voice was quiet, but strong with emotion. She recognized anger, but knew it was not directed at her. He gestured at the room. He pointed at her, then himself, then waggled his fingers like two pairs of walking legs.

The meaning swept over her like a current of cool water. He was going to rescue her.

She felt tears come to her eyes. Overwhelmed with gratitude, she threw her arms around him and began to sob. At last. He might not be her father, but he was going to rescue her. She felt hands patting her back like her father did when she was hurt or upset. The thought brought more tears.

Then she felt his back stiffen, and he gently pushed her away. She wiped tears from her eyes. As her sight cleared she saw a figure standing outside the metal gate, and her blood went cold.

It was the landwalker who had put her here, and he was scowling.

Had he heard the nice landwalker talking of rescuing her? She searched the nice landwalker's face. He patted her gently on the shoulder and gestured at the tray, inviting her to eat more, then he turned to face her captor. They exchanged words. The nice landwalker climbed out of the pool and walked to the gate.

They exchanged more words. She could hear the restrained anger in their voices. Lying down in the water, she felt her hopes begin to shrivel up as the two men's voices rose in what was clearly going to be an argument.

Thunder grumbled ominously in the distance as Auraya, Speaker Sirri and the other Siyee landed in the Open. They were welcomed by an anxious crowd, including the Speakers and tribe representatives who had stayed behind.

"The Pentadrians are leaving," Sirri announced. Whistles and cheers followed and she had to raise her voice to be heard over the noise. "They claim to have entered Si in order to make peace with us, but Auraya saw in their minds their true intent. They wished only to persuade us to worship their gods. We have sent them away."

"How can we be sure they will not turn back and attack us?" a Speaker asked.

"We can't," Sirri answered. "We have scouts watching them. We are as prepared to deal with an attack now as before, except we now have Auraya's help."

Auraya managed to avoid frowning at this. Now that the Pentadrians appeared to be leaving would Juran want her to return to Jarime? As the Speakers crowded around she leaned closer to Sirri.

"They'll want the whole story," she murmured to Sirri, "but you, Iriz and Tyzi are exhausted. Why not suggest we gather later tonight to tell the tale over dinner?"

Sirri glanced at her and smiled crookedly. "Good idea," she said out of the corner of her mouth. "It has been a long journey," she said to the crowd. "For now, I think my fellow travellers would appreciate some time to rest and refresh themselves. Shall we meet again after dinner, in the Speakers' Bower?"

The tribal leaders nodded and murmured agreement. Auraya sensed a wave of relief from Iriz.

"We will speak to you then," Sirri finished.

The crowd began to disperse. As Auraya started toward her bower Sirri joined her.

"I feel like I could sleep for a week," Sirri admitted when they were out of the crowd. "I'm not used to travelling long distances. My position keeps me here." She paused. "Despite that, I doubt I'll sleep at all."

"I wouldn't sleep well if my son was leading the scouts watching the Pentadrians. However, Sreil is a sensible young man. He will not take any risks."

Sirri looked at Auraya anxiously. "Do you think the Pentadrians will leave?"

Auraya shook her head. "I can't be sure. I caught a mind conversation between the leader and her superior. His orders were to leave, but he did warn her that his orders might change. I do not think it likely. I doubt they'd start another war by attacking Siyee, but I would not dismiss the possibility completely."

Sirri sighed. "I don't like that we won't know of an attack for days."

Auraya nodded. "I don't like it either."

"The sooner we have priests and priestesses the better."

"Yes."

They had arrived outside Auraya's bower.

"Do try to rest at least," Auraya told the Siyee leader gently. "Even if you have to slip away to a hiding place to get some peace."

Sirri chuckled. "Might have to." She glanced around. There were few Siyee around. "Yes. That's another good idea. I'll see you after dinner."

Auraya smiled as Sirri strode away, heading deeper into

the forest. She pushed past the hanging of her bower and stepped inside. As she moved toward the seats in the center of the room she focused her mind on her ring.

*:Jur—*

Something fell onto her shoulders. She jumped, then gasped in relief as a high voice spoke uncomfortably close to her ear.

"Owaya! Owaya! Owaya!"

"Yes, Mischief," she said, unwinding him from around her neck. "I'm back. I'm alive and safe." He clutched her arm, whiskers quivering. "And, yes, I'd like to play with you, but right now I need to talk to Juran."

As she sat down he let go of her and curled up in her lap. Taking a deep breath, she sought Juran's mind again.

*:Auraya? I thought that was you.*

*:Yes. I have just reached the Open.* Juran had watched the confrontation telepathically. *I thought about what I learned there all the way back. Are you free to discuss it?*

*:Yes. So what were you thinking?*

*:This woman we met believes her superior—Nekaun—is the leader of the Pentadrians. They have elected a replacement for Kuar already.*

*:It appears so,* Juran agreed. *Either the Pentadrians breed powerful sorcerers at a frightening rate, or they have elected a less powerful sorcerer in order to regain their people's confidence.*

*:The latter does seem more likely. These Pentadrians were sent to Si to befriend the Siyee in order to turn them from the Circle of Gods to their own five gods. Would he have sent similar groups to other Ithanian lands for the same purpose?*

*:It is possible. We will have to be watchful.*

*:I would say they had little chance of success if I was sure the Pentadrian gods did not exist. Have the gods discovered anything more?*

*:They have not spoken of it. What of Chaia? Is he still "chatting" with you?*

*:Yes. He has said nothing on the subject, however.*

*:Have you asked him?*

*:Yes, but he is remarkably good at ignoring questions he doesn't want to answer.*

*:He would tell you if he could.*

*:Do you think so? He can be a frustrating companion at times.*

*:You are fortunate that he favors you with his presence so often. He regards you highly, Auraya. Enjoy it; it may not last forever.*

She winced. Was she being ungrateful? She couldn't reveal the reason she found Chaia's visits so . . . so . . . She could not think of a word to describe the mix of annoyance and curiosity she felt.

*It's all very well for Juran to tell me to enjoy Chaia's visits. He's probably never had a god murmuring seductively in his ear before,* she thought. Then she frowned. *Or has he?* She shook her head. *Get back to the subject,* she told herself.

*:I would like to stay here until we are sure the Pentadrians have left Si.*

*:Yes, you should.*

She sighed with relief. After his earlier resistance to her going to the Siyee's aid she had expected him to order her back to Jarime.

*:I will return when they are gone.*

As she drew back from Juran's mind, she paused to scratch Mischief. She should see how Danjin was faring next. Something in the room had changed, however. Just as she realized what it was, a voice spoke in her mind.

*:Danjin is busy,* Chaia said. *And as you said yesterday, work comes before play. You have done enough for now—or are you going to work without pause for the rest of eternity?*

Auraya smiled.

*:Not unless you want me to.*

*:That was never my intention. Our Chosen ones ought to enjoy themselves from time to time. Even better if we enjoy each other's company.*

She felt a fleeting touch of magic on her shoulder. It sent a shiver down her spine. It was impossible not to think of the potential such sensations might have if they were stronger, or if they roamed from her neck to other places . . .

*:You need only ask, and I will show you.*

She thought of Juran's words. *You are fortunate that he favors you . . . Enjoy it; it may not last forever.*

But he could not have meant *this.*

*:No, but he is right about one thing: I do favor you as no other.*

An invisible finger touched her lip and slowly traced a line down her neck and chest to her stomach . . . then faded away. She found she was breathing quickly.

*A god,* she thought. *Why not? Am I resisting just because I don't want to attract another inappropriate lover?*

*:Not inappropriate,* Chaia corrected. *Unusual, perhaps, but nothing to be ashamed of.*

*Not like Leiard,* she thought. *But still . . . complicated.*

*:Not as complicated as you fear. I will not run away from you as he did, Auraya.*

She felt his touch on her shoulders and closed her eyes.

*:Send him to the past to be a memory you can look back on fondly,* Chaia whispered.

His invisible fingers ran down the sides of her breasts.

*:Come with me into that place between dreaming and waking . . .*

She felt his mouth against hers. At first it was the faint touch of magic, but it became something more tangible as she sank into the dream trance.

*: . . . and begin a new time with me.*

*:Yes,* she whispered, reaching for the luminous figure before her. *Show me how it could be.*

A wave of pleasure more intense than she had ever experienced swept over her.

# 24

Reivan yawned as she pulled out the chair behind her desk. She'd stayed up late helping Imenja access a trade agreement and now she was late starting her duties of the morning. A nagging headache remained from the previous day and the constant whine of the dust storm outside—which had been blowing for days—was beginning to annoy her.

Becoming a full Servant might have ended her training, but the time she'd spent in lessons was quickly taken up by new duties. Imenja had given her more responsibilities. She now organized Imenja's schedule. This involved interviewing people who wanted an audience with the Second Voice and deciding if their purpose, or status, was important enough to allow a meeting to take place.

She was given a room near the front of the Sanctuary in which to interview these people. It had two entrances: a public and a private one. The private one allowed her to come and go without being accosted by the people waiting outside the public one.

She had also been given an assistant, Servant Kikarn. He was an ugly man, so skinny he looked perpetually stern, but she was discovering that he had a sharp wit and intelligence. As she sat down he placed a particularly long list on her table and she suppressed a groan. *The corridor must be crowded today,* she thought wryly.

"What did the wind blow in this morning?"

Kikarn chuckled. "Everything from gold dust to litter,"

he replied. "The merchant Ario wishes to bribe—er, *give* the Second Voice a large donation."

"How much?"

"Enough to build a new Temple."

"Impressive. What does he want in return?"

"Nothing, of course."

She smiled. "We'll see. What else?"

"A woman who was a palace domestic in Kave claims the High Chieftain's wife has taken to worshipping a dead god. She says she has proof."

"She must be sure of it, or she wouldn't approach Second Voice Imenja."

"Unless she is ignorant of the Voices' mind-reading skills."

"We shall see." She looked down the list and stopped at a familiar name. "Thinker Kuerres?"

"He is here to see *you*."

"Not Imenja?"

"No."

"What does he want?"

"He won't say, but he insists that it's an urgent matter. Someone's life may depend on it."

*Someone's life would have to be at stake before the Thinkers deigned to speak to me again,* she mused.

"And the others."

"Not as important as the first two."

"The first two will take some time. Send Kuerres in. I've never known him to exaggerate or lie. Most likely they want to know what I did with my books and instruments."

Kikarn bowed his head. As he moved to the door she considered what she knew of Kuerres. He was one of the quieter Thinkers. He'd never been unkind to her, though he hadn't paid much attention to her either. She frowned as she searched her memory for facts that might prove useful. He had a family. He kept a menagerie of exotic animals.

That was all she could remember. She recognized the middle-aged man who entered the room, but his manner was nothing like she remembered. He glanced around the room nervously, his face pale and his hands clasped together.

"Thinker Kuerres," she said. "It is good to see you again. Sit down."

"Servant Reivan," he said, tracing a star over his chest. He eyed Kikarn, then stepped forward and dropped into the chair.

"What brings you to the Sanctuary?" she asked.

"I . . . I have a crime to report."

She paused. She'd assumed he was nervous about being in the Sanctuary and talking to people of importance. Now she began to wonder if he'd got himself into some kind of trouble.

"Go on," she said.

He took a deep breath. "We—the Thinkers—were approached by a trader yesterday. A rich trader who wanted information and was willing to pay generously for it." Kuerres paused and met her eyes. "He wanted to know about the Elai."

"The sea people? Some of the Thinkers don't even believe they exist."

"Yes. We told him all we knew, but he wasn't satisfied. He asked if any of us knew much about keeping wild animals and I offered my services."

Reivan smiled. "Let me guess: he'd bought some kind of large, strange sea creature and thought it might be the origin of the legend?"

Kuerres shook his head. "Rather the opposite. I offered to help him. I was curious. He took me to his home. What I found there was . . ." he shuddered ". . . horrible. A sick, frightened child—but a child like none I've ever seen before. Thick black skin. Entirely hairless. Large hands and feet with webbing between fingers and toes."

"Feet? No fish tail?"

"No fish tail. No gills either. But definitely a . . . a being of the water. I have no doubt this child is one of the Elai."

Reivan felt a thrill of excitement, but suppressed it out of habit. Thinkers did not allow their reason to be overtaken by emotion. It was too easy to convince oneself of something if one wanted to badly enough.

"Did this merchant say where he found her?"

"No. He complained that she'd cost a fortune and talked about her like she was an animal." He shook his head in disgust. "She is no animal. She is a human. He is breaking our laws by buying and keeping her."

"Enslaving an innocent." She nodded. "Who is this trader?"

His nose wrinkled. "Devlem Wheelmaker. He is a Genrian. He changed his name before the war."

Reivan nodded. "I know of him. I will bring this to the Second Voice's attention later today and I'm sure she will have someone—"

"You have to do something *now*!" he interrupted. "I'm sure he suspects that I will report him. He might get rid of her—kill her—before you get there!"

He stared at her earnestly, obviously deeply concerned for the safely of this sea girl. Reivan pressed her palms together and considered.

If the merchant believed the child was an animal he would reason that he hadn't committed any crime. Nevertheless, he wouldn't take the risk that others would come to the same conclusion as Kuerres. The punishment for enslaving an innocent was to be enslaved. *He'll either kill her or move her somewhere else, depending on how much she cost him. Either way, the faster we act, the more likely it is we will find the girl before he does anything to her.*

But leaving the Sanctuary to rescue a child wasn't part of her duties, and she didn't have the authority to search the man's property. She needed Imenja's help. Was this important enough to interrupt the Second Voice?

*Am I simply curious to know if this child is an Elai?*

*Whether she is an Elai or not, she is being kept like an animal. Imenja will want to do something about that.*

Taking a deep breath, she placed a hand on the pendant and closed her eyes.

*:Imenja?*

She waited, then called again. Not having much Skill in the use of magic, it often took several attempts before she managed to get the pendant to work. Finally an answer came.

*:Is that you, Reivan?*

*:It is.*

*:Good morning. What has you calling me so early?*

*:A report of a crime.*

*:Tell me.*

She related Kuerres's story of the sea girl.

*:That is appalling. You must free her. If the girl is not there, bring the merchant to me. I will read her location from his mind.*

*:I will. I think I may need assistance.*

*:Yes. Take Kikarn. Contact me as soon as you find her.*

*:I will.*

Opening her eyes, Reivan found Kuerres staring at her. She smothered a smile at his curiosity.

"We will deal with this right away," she told him. Servant Kikarn made a small noise of protest. She guessed he was thinking of the visitors still waiting to be seen. "Servant Kikarn. Tell the Dekkan domestic to wait until I return but let the others know I have urgent and unexpected business to attend to and will see to them tomorrow morning. Assure Ario he will be first."

He smiled and bowed his head. Reivan rose and Kuerres jumped to his feet.

"Do you want to accompany me?" she asked him.

He hesitated. "I should return to my home," he said doubtfully.

She moved around the desk. "Then go. I will send news to you when we return. I will use an ordinary messenger, not one from the Sanctuary."

He looked relieved. "Thank you, Reivan—Servant Reivan."

She smiled. "Thank you for bringing this information to the Sanctuary, Thinker Kuerres. You are a good man and I hope this action doesn't work against you."

"There are those who will support me," he assured her. He turned to the door, then paused and looked back. "Just as there are those who support you."

Surprised, Reivan watched him leave, wishing she could bring herself to ask who her supporters were, but knowing he would say no more.

*     *     *

With Tyve constantly advising him on the terrain ahead, Mirar had been able to travel faster than he and Emerahl had during their journey into Si. The boy circled above, warning of dead-end ravines and guiding Mirar to valleys that provided easy travelling. Each night Tyve slipped away to visit his village and each morning he returned more worried than ever. More of the tribe had fallen ill. A young baby had died, then its mother, weakened by a difficult birth. Veece was failing fast. At each report Mirar grew more certain the Siyee were facing a plague. He travelled from first light to dusk, stopping only to drink and eat, knowing that the situation in the village was worsening every hour.

He had seen many plagues before. Injuries, wounds and minor diseases were easy enough for a sorcerer with healing knowledge and magical strength to treat, but when a disease spread quickly it was not long before there were too few healers capable of fighting it to treat all victims—when they were not battling the disease themselves.

*And here in Si you are the only one,* Leiard added.

Mirar sighed. *If only I could have prevented Siyee from leaving the village and spreading the disease.*

He'd sent this advice ahead, but the news Tyve brought back had been alarming. Some families had fled to other villages already. Messengers had been sent to the Open.

*They're already panicking,* Leiard said. *You'll have as much work dealing with their fear of disease as the disease itself.*

Mirar didn't answer. The rocky slope he was descending had become an enormous, roughly hewn staircase that took all his attention. He jumped from rock shelf to rock shelf, each landing jolting his entire body.

The steps became steadily shallower as the trees around him grew larger. Soon he was walking on smooth leaf-covered ground, surrounded by the trunks of enormous trees. The air was moist. A stream trickled slowly nearby, dividing and rejoining and forming pools here and there.

It was a peaceful place and would have made a pleasant camping site—apart from the lingering smell of animal feces. The area must be a thoroughfare for forest creatures. Remembering the reason for his journey, he quickened his pace again.

Then he heard a Siyee whistle a call of warning and he halted.

Looking up, he blinked in surprise as he saw that platforms had been built between many of the tree branches overhead. Faces peered over the edges of these, gazing down at him, and he sensed fear, hope and curiosity.

He had reached the village.

From the right a Siyee glided down to meet him. It was Tyve.

"Some have hung ropes for you to climb," he told Mirar. "Others are too suspicious. They'll change their minds once they hear you've cured some of us."

Mirar nodded. "How many are ill now?"

"I don't know. Ten the last time I counted."

"Take me to the sickest, then fly to all the people and find out how many are sick or are showing the first signs of it."

"Yes. I will. Follow me."

Tyve walked through the trees for several hundred paces. A rope hung down from one of the platforms. Mirar tied the end of the rope to the handles of his bag.

"Who lives up here?"

Tyve swallowed and looked up. "Speaker Veece and his wife and her sister."

*The old man.* Mirar smothered a sigh. *Even among land-walkers, Hearteater most often claims the old and the very young.*

He took hold of the rope and began to climb.

It was a long climb. Halfway up he looked down and considered what would happen if he slipped and fell.

*I'd definitely be injured. Probably badly. Probably to a point that would kill mortals.*

But he would not die. His body would repair itself, though gradually.

*Like it did after they took me out from under the ruined Dreamweaver House in Jarime. I was a bag of broken bones, not quite dead, not quite alive.* Mirar shuddered. *A mind fixed only on keeping alive enough to regenerate, parts of me decomposing while others healed . . .*

*Think of something else,* Leiard suggested.

Mirar drew in a deep breath and concentrated on hauling himself upward. When he reached the top he pulled himself onto the platform and lay on his back, panting. Once he had caught his breath he rolled over and found two elderly Siyee women hovering nearby.

*They have it,* Leiard observed.

He was right. Their faces were pale and shone with sweat, and their lips were tinged with blue. Despite the name of the disease, it actually attacked the lungs. As it ate away at them the victim was less and less able to breathe, causing their blood to weaken. In some places it was known as the White Death.

He stood up. A bower had been built on top of the platform. From his high position he could see bowers on most platforms—and many Siyee watching him. He looked at the two women.

"I am Dreamweaver Wilar. I will try to help Speaker Veece, if you wish me to."

They exchanged a quick glance, then nodded.

"Thank you for coming. He is inside," one croaked. She lapsed into a wracking cough.

Mirar nodded. "I will bring up my bag of cures, then I will go in and see what I can do for him."

He turned away and began to haul on the rope. It seemed to take hours to bring up the bag. Untying it, he carried it inside the bower.

On a blanket in the middle of the room lay the Speaker. Though Mirar hadn't met the man before he doubted he would have recognized him if he had. Pale, bloodless skin stretched over the man's bones. His lips were a deep blue and his breath came quickly and painfully.

*He's near death,* Leiard murmured.

*Yes,* Mirar agreed. *But if I don't save him, will the rest of the tribe trust me?*

*Maybe. Maybe not. You best get to work.*

Mirar opened his bag and began sorting through its contents. A thump outside distracted him. He looked up to see Tyve standing in the doorway.

"Twenty are sick, twelve are feeling ill, and the rest say they're well," the boy reported.

Mirar nodded. *I wish Emerahl had remained here. I could do with her help.* "Stay close," he told the boy. "I might need you to . . ." He frowned and looked at Veece's wife. "Where do you get your water from?"

The woman pointed at a small hole in the floor. Next to it was a bucket and a coil of rope. "We bring it up from the creek below."

He thought of the winding path of the creek and the smell of feces.

"Where do you put your bodily wastes?"

She pointed downward again. "It washes away."

"Not quickly enough," he said.

Her shoulders lifted. "It used to, but a slide upslope diverted some of the water away."

"That should be cleared, or you should move the village," he said. Tyve, fetch me some water from far above the village. Don't use the same vessel as any that has been in the stream."

The boy nodded and flew away. Mirar sensed annoyance from the woman. He met her gaze.

"Better to be sure," he said.

She lowered her eyes and nodded. Turning away, Mirar moved to Veece's side and began his work.

# 25

The crowd surrounding the two priests consisted mostly of children. From the minds of the few adults present, Auraya read that the pair were a great source of entertainment for the youngsters in the Open, but the adults also listened attentively, conscious that what these landwalkers were teaching would influence their people's future.

Sitting behind the priests were four Siyee, all listening attentively. They noted not only the stories and lessons, but the way in which they were told. The oldest was a woman of thirty-five, the youngest a boy of fifteen. All had hopes and ambitions of becoming priests or priestesses.

Auraya felt a surge of pride. If they learned well and passed the tests, their dreams would come true. They would be the first Siyee priests and priestesses.

The priest who was speaking—Priest Magen—finished his tale and made the sign of the circle. He glanced at Auraya, then told the audience that their lesson was over. Disappointment flowed from the children, but as they rose and began to discuss with their guardians what they might do next the feeling dissipated.

Auraya walked forward to greet the priests. They made the formal two-handed sign of the circle as they greeted her—something the trainee priests and priestesses noted with curiosity.

"A bigger crowd today," she noted.

Danien nodded. "Yes. A few new children from a visiting tribe, I believe."

"Come inside," Magen urged. "Have you eaten yet? A woman just sent us several roasted girri as thanks for treating her broken ankle."

"I haven't," Auraya replied. "Is there enough?"

Magen grinned. "More than enough. The Siyee are nothing less than generous."

The priest beckoned to the trainees then led them all inside the large bower that had been provided for the land-walkers. They sat on wooden seats in the center of the room and passed around the food.

"You've learned the Siyee language quickly," Auraya observed.

Danien nodded. "When you know a few languages it gets easier to pick up new ones. The Siyee tongue is not that hard once you see the similarities between it and land-walker tongues."

"We were assisted by a young man here—Tryss," Magen told her.

"Ah, Tryss," Auraya said, nodding. "Clever boy."

"Your advice about taboos, customs and manners was helpful, too," Danien added. "I was thinking of—"

"Auraya of the White?"

All turned to the doorway. Speaker Sirri stood in the opening, radiating concern. A young Siyee male stood beside her. He had brought bad news, Auraya read. A sickness . . .

"Speaker Sirri," Magen said, rising. "Welcome. Will you and your companion join us?"

The Speaker hesitated, then stepped inside. "Yes. Thank you. This is Reet of the North River tribe." The young man nodded as each of the occupants was introduced.

"Come and sit down," Magen said, rising to usher them to seats.

Sirri did not smile as she sat down. "Reet has come to the Open seeking help," she told them. "His people have sickened with an illness they have never heard of. Our healers have not seen such a malady either, so we have come to ask you if you know it."

"Can you describe it, Reet?" Auraya asked.

She concentrated on the young man's mind as he told of the illness that had come upon his family and relatives, and felt a chill as she recognized the symptoms.

"I know it," she interrupted. The boy stared at her hopefully. She turned to regard Magen. "It is Hearteater."

"The White Death," Magen said, his expression turning grim. "It appears among landwalkers from time to time."

Sirri looked at Auraya. "Do you have a cure?"

"Yes and no," Auraya replied. "There are treatments that ease the symptoms, but they do not kill the disease. The patient's body must do that. Magical healing can help boost a patient's strength, but it cannot kill a disease without the risk of harming the body."

"Babies and young children are in the greatest danger as well as the elderly and weak," Magen added. "Healthy adults spend a few days in a fever, then slowly recover."

"But they're not," Reet interrupted. "My second cousin died the day before yesterday. She was twenty-two!"

The room fell silent as all exchanged looks of dismay. Danien turned to Auraya. "Could Hearteater have grown more potent?"

"Perhaps. If that is so, we must be extra careful to make sure it doesn't spread," she warned. "Has anyone from the village other than you left it? Have outsiders visited since the illness began?"

Reet stared at her. "Other than me? Two families left after it started. One went to the North Forest tribe. The others came here. We'd had no visitors, when I left."

*The newcomers among the children!* Auraya thought suddenly. A moment after the danger occurred to her she heard Magen's indrawn breath and knew he'd thought of them too.

She looked at Sirri. "You need to find this family and isolate them from others, and find out who they've met since they arrived and isolate those Siyee too."

Sirri grimaced. "They may not like that. What of the North River and North Forest tribes?"

"Send someone to the North Forest tribe to see if anyone is sick. As for the North River tribe . . ." Auraya considered. It would be better to treat them in their village, but could she leave the Open? What if the Pentadrians attacked? Any report of an attack would come to the Open first. She looked at Danien and Magen. They could contact her through their rings. "I will go to them," she said. "Danien and Magen will be my link to you. Anything you want me to know, tell them. They will communicate it to me."

Sirri nodded. "I will. When will you leave?"

"As soon as I can. You may need me to help you explain to the families the reason they must isolate themselves. I would like to gather some medicines. You have some that will help."

Sirri rose. "Tell me what you want and I'll send someone for them. You had best come with me now. The sooner we isolate these families the better. What of Reet?"

Auraya turned to regard the boy.

"You, too, may carry the disease," Auraya said gently.

"It is spread by touch," Magen said. "And by the breath. Who have you spoken to since you arrived, Reet?"

"Only Speaker Sirri. I didn't touch her."

"Will I have to isolate myself?" Sirri asked. "Who will direct the tribe in my place?"

Auraya considered. "If you are careful not to touch anyone . . . Magen can put a magical shield around you so your breath doesn't reach anyone. In a few days, if you haven't developed symptoms, you can conclude you haven't caught it. The same applies to everyone here." She looked at the trainees. "Reet may have infected you, if he has the disease. Keep away from others unless you have a priest shielding you."

"Can I return to my tribe?" Reet asked.

"I can't see why not," Auraya said. "So long as you stay there."

"Rest and eat something first," Magen said.

"Yes." Auraya stood up. "I had better get started." She nodded at the priests in farewell, then hurried out of the bower with Sirri.

\*       \*       \*

Though Imi had been in the room for hours she knew nothing about her new surroundings. She had hoped her eyes would grow used to the darkness, but they hadn't. The way sounds echoed suggested a room as large as the hull of the raiders' ship. The floor was cold stone, but she hadn't gathered the strength yet to find out if the walls were too.

She could only assume hours had passed. It was impossible to measure the passing of time here. In her home her people could tell what time it was by looking at a time lamp. The oil reservoir was marked at every hour. Or they could use the many tide measures to calculate the time. Wherever there was a tidal pool there was a time measure carved into the side.

Her stomach rumbled. She thought back to the platter of food the nice landwalker had fed her from. He had left it there and she had slowly finished off the contents over the next few hours. The salt water had soothed her skin. She had begun to feel better.

Now she only had a large pot full of salt water to splash herself with. It stood next to her in the darkness.

*Why?* she thought. *Why am I here?*

She thought of the argument between the nice landwalker and the nasty one. The nasty landwalker must have seen or heard the nice one planning to rescue her. He had moved her in order to keep her for himself.

*But why does he want to keep me? Does he want me to work for him, like the raider and the sea-bell fishermen?*

At the thought of sea bells she felt a stab of pain. *I hope I never see a sea bell again,* she thought. *I hate them. I shouldn't have left the city. How could I have been so stupid?* She rolled onto her back and blinked back tears. *I should have thought about the dangers outside the city. That's my problem. I don't think before I do things.*

*I've got plenty of time to think now.* She frowned. *Maybe I can think my way out of this. How likely is it that my father, or some handsome warrior, is going to find me? He doesn't know where I am. Neither does that nice landwalker. I should stop waiting for someone else to rescue me, and rescue myself.*

She sighed. *But what can I do? I don't even know where I am. All I know is that I'm in a room somewhere.*

Maybe she could find out more if she explored the room. Maybe if she made a noise, someone would come and find out what it was.

Slowly she pushed herself into a sitting position. She was still terribly tired. Forcing herself to her feet, she staggered forward. It was hard to keep her balance in the darkness and she nearly fell several times. Finally her outstretched hand met a hard surface.

It was stone. Feeling around, she noted channels in the stone and guessed they were mortared gaps between bricks. Around the room she went, feeling the surface for any change. After passing two corners, she came upon the door.

This was wooden. She could feel metal hinges on the inside. Drawing in a deep breath, she let out a yell that echoed deafeningly in the room. At the same time she pounded on the door with her fists.

A few yells later she had to stop. He head was spinning and her arms ached. She slumped against the door.

From outside came the sound of approaching footsteps.

Hope flared inside her and strength came back. She yelled with renewed enthusiasm. There were voices just outside the door. It vibrated as the lock was worked. She backed away as the door opened. Two men appeared.

Her heart sank. One was her captor, the other was a stranger. As the newcomer stared at her with inhuman, greedy eyes all hope fled. Her legs buckled. She flinched as her knees met the stone floor.

The two men ignored her and began to talk in low voices. Her captor gestured at something on the floor outside the room. The greedy man stooped to pick it up.

It was a sack. As he started toward Imi, she shrank away, but there was nowhere to go. When she struggled he cuffed her, speaking with words she didn't understand but in a warning tone she did. Once she was inside the sack, he picked her up and carried her away. She felt herself moving upward, then saw sunlight through the weave. She was put in a dark place again and the floor began to move.

Dizzy with weakness, she listened to the strange sounds about her. They multiplied and grew louder. Voices overlaid everything. She felt a surge of terror. Landwalkers surrounded her. It was too easy to imagine they were all like the raiders and her captor, greedy and cruel.

*The nice landwalker was different,* she reminded herself. *There must be more like him out there. Perhaps in this crowd.* What if she yelled for help? What if she managed to get out of the sack and the vehicle?

She struggled against the sack and felt her leg touch something. That something recoiled, then slammed into her calf. She gasped in pain. A voice muttered something angrily.

If she yelled he would hurt her again, but it might be worth it. She gathered her strength for another effort but paused as she felt the floor stop moving.

Another voice came from close by. It and the greedy man talked cheerfully. Hands grabbed and lifted her. She recognized the smell of the sea at the same time as she heard the too familiar creaking and splashing of a ship.

They carried her upward, then downward, then put her on a hard floor. She lay still, conscious of a familiar rocking motion. It made her feel queasy. Above her people were shouting. People on ships were always shouting. She heard the footsteps draw closer. The sacking moved, then drew back. She struggled free, eager for fresh air.

Looking up, she froze in surprise.

Instead of the greedy man, two women stood over her. Both wore many-layered black clothes and silver pendants. They smiled at her.

"Hello Imi," the older one said. "You are safe now, Imi."

Imi stared at her in astonishment. *She spoke my name? How does she know my name? And how can she be speaking Elai?*

The woman leaned forward and extended a hand. "Nobody is going to hurt you any more. Come with us and we will help you."

Imi felt tears spring to her eyes. At last, her rescuers had come. They didn't look anything like what she'd imagined. Neither was her father, or a great warrior—or even the kind landwalker. Just two women.

But they'd do.

# ❦ 26 ❦

The sky was every color. At the horizon it was a pale yellow. A little higher it gained a warm blush. Higher still, unexpected colors formed; greens that deepened into blues then shifted into an intense dark blue that stretched overhead and became the black, star-prickled night sky.

*A pretty sunset is supposed to be a sign of good weather,* Emerahl mused. *Better be or I'm in for another rough ride.*

The storm that had raged these last few days had been the kind that could easily have wrecked ships. When it eased a little she had searched for and found the staircase. It was steep, narrow and overgrown. Descending, she had wondered if she would find someone in the cave Gherid had told her she would find. Perhaps a victim of the storm. Perhaps The Gull himself.

The cave had been empty. The storm had worsened again, but no refuge-seekers had arrived, nor The Gull. It trapped her there, but she did not mind; she was in no hurry. The cave was not luxurious even by a poor man's standards, but it was dry. She could imagine The Gull here. She imagined she could smell him—a mix of sweat, salt water and fish—in the crude furniture made of driftwood and sailcloth.

The Gull himself. Immortal. Mysterious. A fellow Wild.

It was possible he was aware that his sanctuary had been invaded and was staying away. It was tempting to wait a little longer and see if he turned up. There was a store of dried foods in the cave and she could fish.

But she did not want to touch the stores. Gherid had told her this place was a refuge for those The Gull saved. She was no stranded shipwreck survivor so she felt she had no right to use any of the supplies here.

*No, it is time I moved on,* she thought. *The chance that he might happen by while I was here was slim anyway. I will do as I planned: leave a message and continue on my way.*

She considered the contents of her message. Not being much good at riddles, yet reluctant to write anything too specific—even in an ancient dead language—she had opted for symbolizm she hoped The Gull would understand. She had gathered up a hank of the stringy white weed called "old woman's hair" and twisted it into a rope. Onto this she had strung a moon shell with markings in the shape of a crescent moon. Knotting the rope into a loop, she had hung it on the wall at the back of the cave.

The string was meant to tell him: "I am The Hag," and the shell indicated the phase of the moon she would return at. Sometimes she thought it was a tad obvious. Other times she worried whether he would understand it. Or even find it.

The sky was now mostly black with a warm glow at the horizon. She crossed her arms and leaned against the side of the cave entrance.

Many things had occurred to her while she had been here. For a start, Gherid's mind and the minds of others who had met The Gull were not shielded. Anyone able to read their minds would know The Gull still existed. That meant the gods knew he was alive. So why hadn't they killed him?

*Perhaps because he is too hard to find,* she thought. *They need to work through a willing human. If he can evade their human servants, he can avoid them.*

*Or perhaps they've decided he is no danger to them. They may even approve of him, since he does save the lives of Circlians and has never encouraged mortals to worship him.*

She frowned. *Is he any different to me, in that regard?*

*I heal people. I'm no real threat to the gods. I have never wished to be worshipped. Maybe I fear them for no reason. Maybe they'd let me live if they knew where I was.*

*If that is true, why did the priests hunt for me when they found there had been a suspiciously long-lived sorceress living in the lighthouse? Why did the gods give a priest the ability to read minds, so he could better find me?*

They might not have intended to kill her, just question her.

*Not likely.* She snorted softly. *The gods hate Immortals. They always have.* Which brought her to another matter she had been considering. A question she had asked herself many times in the past.

*Why do the gods hate us? They have nothing to fear from us. We can't harm them. We might work against them, but our efforts have rarely had much effect. Could it be that they have a reason to fear us?*

She shook her head. It was easy to read more into the gods' hatred of immortals than was actually there. *They kill us because they want complete control over mortals. They want their followers to go to priests and priestesses for cures, not me or Dreamweavers.*

A brightness had appeared at a different stretch of the horizon. She pushed all thought of the gods aside and watched the half-moon rise. When it had floated free of the sea she looked around. It gave her enough light to sail by. She picked up her bag, gave the cave one last look, then started up the staircase to the top of the Stack.

It was narrow, and where it turned out of the light of the moon darkness blotted out all detail, forcing her to create a small light. The grassy surface of the top seemed much smaller now it was not veiled by rain. To her relief, her boat was still there. The ropes had kept it in place throughout the storm. She untied them, pulled out the pegs and dragged it to the side of the Stack. Stepping inside, she took a few deep breaths and cleared her mind.

Taking in magic from the world, she lifted the vessel into the air, out over the edge of the cliff, then slowly down to the water.

When she felt the caress of the sea on the boat's hull she released it. At once a current began to draw her away. She watched as the Stack slowly diminished in size, thinking of the message she had left and wondering if The Gull would believe it.

*And if he does, will he answer it?*

Moderator Meeran of the Somreyan Council drew in a deep breath and let it out again. The meetings of the council often left him exhausted these days. He did not like this sign of his encroaching old age and always forced himself to remain and chat with those who lingered afterward.

The grand old Council building faced toward the port of Arbeem. Tall windows allowed a grand view of the city and bay. Tiny lights moved on the water, each cluster indicating the position of a ship. Two figures stood by one of the windows, talking quietly.

Meeran blinked in surprise. A white circular garment hung from the shoulders of one of the figures. The other wore humbler clothes: a leather vest on top of a plain woven tunic. Meeran narrowed his eyes. It was not often that the Dreamweaver and Circlian Elders of the Somreyan Council were seen together. Usually those two coming together resulted in the need for his hasty intervention. This time, however, they appeared to be chatting amiably.

Appearances could be deceiving, and could rapidly change. Meeran decided it would be prudent to investigate. Nobody intercepted him as he crossed the room. His suspicion that this was because others had noticed the pair at the window was confirmed when Council Elder Timbler caught his eye and smiled sympathetically.

As he neared the window Arleej turned to regard Meeran. She smiled crookedly.

"We were just discussing our new neighbors, Moderator," she said.

He glanced out of the window and saw the object of their attention. A large ship was tied up to the docks. Its hull and sails were black. Distant figures were moving off the vessel, each well burdened.

"They are fools if they think they can convert Somreyans so soon after the war," High Priest Haleed muttered.

Meeran looked at the old man. "So you do believe that is why the Pentadrians are here?"

"Why else?" Haleed replied sullenly.

"Of course it is." Arleej gave Haleed a mocking glance. "They are convinced their gods are the only true gods. We already know how single-minded those with such beliefs can be."

Haleed's chin rose. "They will fail," he said. "Our gods are real. Theirs are not. They must be more forceful or clever to convince others to join them. In the attempt they will cause much trouble."

Arleej made a disbelieving noise.

"You disagree?" the priest asked.

"I agree that they will cause strife here," she said. "What I wonder is how you can be so sure their gods aren't real."

"Because the Circle has told us they are the only ones."

Her eyebrows rose. "The only ones to have survived the gods' war, that is. Perhaps the Pentadrians' gods have risen since."

"The Circle would have noticed."

"Perhaps they didn't."

Meeran raised his hands in a pacifying gesture, though the conversation did not appear to be leading to an angry exchange. "We could argue this all night. I am more interested to know what you both think the consequences may be of the Council's decision to allow them to settle."

Haleed looked down at the ship and scowled. "Trouble, as I said. First we allow them to enter our country, then what? Will we give them a place on the Council?"

Arleej smiled. "If they gather enough followers to become a legitimate religion we cannot refuse them a place. It is our law and tradition."

"Perhaps it is time we changed that law," Haleed said darkly. "Or increased the required number of followers."

A shadow passed over Arleej's face. *She's concerned the hatred of Pentadrians would convince Somreyans to agree to that,* Meeran realized. *The Dreamweavers are few in*

*number compared to the potential number of Pentadrians
that might come here. A law like that would rob her of her
place on the Council but not prevent the Pentadrians gaining power.*

"The people will never agree to that, no matter how
frightened they are of our visitors," Meeran assured them.

"So we're stuck with them," Haleed growled.

"Not necessarily," Arleej said quietly. "They have only
to undertake one act of aggression and we can throw them
out. *We* get to decide what an act of aggression is."

Haleed looked at her, his expression one of begrudg-
ing respect. She smiled back at him. Meeran looked from
one to the other, then shook his head. Their strengths had
been refined through years of resistance to each other. The
thought of what they might do united was more than a little
disturbing.

"They do claim to be here to make peace," Meeran reminded them. "Dubious as that claim may be, I think we
should at least give them a chance to prove it."

The two Elders looked at him, and though their faces
clearly showed that they disagreed, both nodded.

There was snow on the northern mountains already, Auraya
noted. Small patches of it reflected the light of the moon,
giving the mountains a dappled look. Soon those patches
would grow in size, join together and the mountains would
be clothed with white.

She frowned as she considered the effect an early and
hard winter might have on the Siyee if they were weakened
by Hearteater.

*It will not be so bad if I can stop the disease spreading,*
she told herself.

But that was not always easy. While healer priests and
priestesses understood a little about plagues, ordinary
people regarded the spread of such illnesses with fear and
superstition. She had discovered today that the Siyee were
no different.

The family that had left the North River tribe had refused
to leave the Open voluntarily, despite being offered bowers

close by and assurances that they only need stay away long enough for all to be sure they weren't sick. When Sirri ordered them to leave they had obeyed, but resentfully.

The Siyee living about the Open had mixed reactions to the situation. Some reacted fearfully, and Auraya suspected Sirri would have her hands full keeping those people from leaving. Others thought the North River family was being treated unfairly and did not hesitate to voice their anger.

Fortunately, none of the visitors showed signs of the illness. The messenger, however, was feeling more wearied by their journey back to the North River tribe than he ought to. She looked across at Reet and frowned.

*He must have left the priests' bower not long after I did,* she remembered. *I can sense that he's hungry. He could not have eaten much and didn't rest at all. Perhaps weariness is all that is wrong with him.*

He had left hours before she had, but she had caught up with him easily. Now she was torn between flying on ahead and remaining with him. What if the sickness came over him quickly? What if he passed out and fell to his death?

What if he was just tired and she arrived too late to save one of the tribe?

It was an impossible choice. If only she knew what was happening in the village—if anyone would suffer because of the delay.

Perhaps there was a way to find out. There was someone she could ask. He might not answer her call, he might not even answer her questions, but she could only try.

*:Chaia.*

She waited for several heartbeats then called again. When no familiar presence touched her senses she sighed and thought about her dilemma again. Perhaps she should consider what she *did* know about the situation she was in. *All I know is that Reet is dangerously tired.* So she must decide based on that.

*I will stay with him, just in case, or until I know more. Chaia may still turn up.*

She felt a shiver run down her back at the thought of

being in the god's presence again. So much had changed in the last few days.

*I don't miss Leiard any more,* she thought, smiling. *Chaia was right about that.*

She had never felt such pleasure before. Her experiences with Chaia were like a dream link, but far more sophisticated. Dream links relied upon the memory of physical pleasure. Her time with Chaia was one of discovery and of ecstasy she hadn't felt before. His touch could only be the touch of magic, but that changed when their mind and will united. Magic could become sensation. He was able to respond to her slightest desire, yet at the same time he could stimulate her in ways she had never imagined were possible.

She had expected the world to seem subdued in comparison to her encounters with Chaia, but instead it was as though her senses had been enlivened. Every object was fascinating. Every living thing, beautiful and vibrant.

Fortunately this effect faded. She did not want to be distracted by the beauty of an insect while trying to discuss important matters with the Siyee. Seeing them with her senses awakened had only strengthened her wish to protect them.

Yet she was also more conscious of the differences between them and herself now. Her height and winglessness. Their mortality. Being so conscious of the differences between herself and them saddened her. Had she come closer to a god only to move further from mortals? It was a disturbing thought.

*But it is nice to look forward to night again,* she thought. *And there's not much point worrying about it right now.* Smiling to herself, she put all worries aside and drifted into daydreams of her next encounter with Chaia.

# 27

"I am Genrian!" Devlem Wheelmaker shouted. "You can't do this to me!"

"You may be Genrian," Reivan replied calmly, "but while you live in Avven you must live by our laws. You have resided here long enough to know we forbid the enslavement of any but criminals."

"She isn't *human*," he insisted. "She's an animal—a creature of the sea. You only have to look at her to see that."

She stared back at him. "You have only to *speak* to her to know she is human. And what a tale she tells about you." She shook her head sadly. "It is you I'd describe as inhuman."

A cry of rage broke from him. He lunged forward. Reivan flinched backward, but his groping hands never reached her. They met an invisible barrier.

Magic. Reivan looked at Servant Kikarn. His disapproving expression softened as he met her eyes. The corner of his mouth quirked upward. Recovering from her surprise, she nodded in gratitude.

"You can't make me a slave!" Devlem bellowed. "My family has links with the noble houses in Genria!"

"Send in Servant Grenara," she ordered.

The Sanctuary slave-keeper was small in stature, but every step and gesture suggested he was a man who was used to being obeyed. He made the sign of the star to Reivan and Kikarn then turned his attention to Devlem, his eyes narrowing as he assessed the merchant.

"Come with me, Devlem Wheelmaker."

Devlem glared at the man. "If you think I'm going to just follow you out of here like a mindless arem you're . . . you're . . ."

The man shrugged. "That is up to you. Some accept it with dignity, others have to be tied up and dragged."

At the word "dragged," Devlem's angry glare faltered. He took a step back from the slave-keeper, then straightened his back and stalked out of the room. Grenara followed him out.

When the door had closed, Reivan let out a long sigh.

"Thank you, Servant Kikarn," she said.

He looked at her in mock puzzlement. "For what, Servant Reivan?"

She smiled. *It seems I've earned myself an ally here.*

"That's more than enough work for today. I'll see you tomorrow morning."

Kikarn inclined his head and made the sign of the star. Leaving him to tidy the room, she left by the second door.

The corridors of the Lower Sanctuary were all but empty. Most of the Servants had retired for the evening. Though Reivan longed for rest she did not head toward her rooms.

Several corridors and stairs later she reached the Upper Sanctuary. Torches lit the way to the main courtyard. Emerging into the night air, Reivan paused to muse at the sight before her. In the center of the yard, where a fountain cooled the air during the day, a large tent now stood. Lamps inside the tent cast the shadows of a woman and child on the cloth walls. Voices within formed strange, highly pitched incomprehensible words. Reivan moved to the tent flap.

"May I come in?" she called.

"Yes," Imenja replied. "We were just talking about Imi's home. It sounds like a fascinating place."

Reivan pushed aside the door flap and stepped inside. The Elai child was resting her elbows atop the wall of the fountain, which was now full of sea water carried up by slaves. Her skin looked even darker in the lamplight. When

Reivan recollected the drawings of sea folk in the Thinkers' books she was amazed at their inaccuracies. This child had no fish tail or flowing locks of hair. She was completely hairless and had a pair of normal legs.

*Almost normal,* Reivan corrected. Imi's hands and feet were disproportionately large, and between her fingers and toes was a thick webbing. Other distortions in the girl's body suggested further differences. Her chest was broad for a child. Reivan would not have been surprised to learn that the Elai had much larger lungs than normal humans.

The artists who had drawn such fanciful illustrations would have been disappointed by Imi. All in all, the distortions and hairlessness did not make for an attractive race. Not even the pretty tunic she now wore could hide that. As the girl smiled, displaying slightly pointed white teeth, Reivan had to suppress a shudder.

"Reivan," Imi said, speaking slowly.

"Imi," Reivan replied. "How are you feeling?"

Imenja translated. The girl glanced at her peeling skin and a look of sadness clouded her face as she replied.

"She is feeling stronger," Imenja told Reivan. "She has certainly been through a lot. Captured by fishermen then by pirates, both who made her work for them. Then she was sold to the merchant—is it done?"

"Yes. He claims she is an animal, so he wasn't breaking any law. He left with the slave-keeper."

"Good. Stupidity is no excuse for cruelty. None of her captors attempted to talk to her. They fed her only raw fish and left her to dry out. The Elai—"

Imi said something. Imenja smiled and spoke to the girl, then turned back to Reivan.

"The Elai need to spend some time in salt water each day. They eat a variety of food, like we do. Not just produce from the sea." She paused. "You'll never guess who she is."

Reivan chuckled. "No, I'd say that's unlikely."

Imenja turned back to regard Imi. "She is the daughter of the Elai king."

Surprised, Reivan looked down at the child. The girl smiled uncertainly.

"How did she come to be captured by humans?"

"She slipped away from her guardian to go looking for a gift for her father."

"Does he know she was captured?"

"Maybe. Maybe not. What is certain is that he won't be the only Elai celebrating when she is returned to her people."

"Unless her capture was arranged by his enemies."

Imenja frowned. "That is possible."

"You'll have to be careful when you return her."

"Me?" Imenja's eyebrows rose. "Why do you think I'll be taking her home?"

"Because she is a king's daughter. She was sold to someone living in our land. If she returns and tells her story, we will be blamed in part for her ordeal unless a great demonstration of apology is made. And," Reivan smiled, "because the Elai were never involved in the war, there is no lingering resentment barring you from introducing them to the Five."

Imenja stared at Reivan in surprise and approval. "You're right." She looked at Imi and smiled. "I should take her back myself. And you will have to come with me. I'll have to convince Nekaun, of course, but the possibility of gaining an ally will probably sway him. If we are successful nobody will dare object if I make you my Companion."

Imi stared back at Imenja. She spoke, her strange words forming a question. Imenja's reply brought a relieved smile to her face.

"She is tired," Imenja said. "We should let her rest." She spoke a farewell to the child, then rose and led Reivan out of the tent.

"I will speak to Nekaun now. You may as well go to bed. If he agrees you'll have a sea voyage to organize for us in the morning."

"More work!" Reivan groaned, pretending to be dismayed by the prospect. The Second Voice laughed and shooed her away. Smiling, Reivan started toward her rooms.

*I'm going to see the land of the Elai,* she found herself thinking. *The Thinkers are going to be so jealous!*

*     *     *

Mirar took a deep breath and jumped off the platform. For a fraction of a heartbeat he dropped downward, then he felt the rope about his chest and back tighten and take his weight. The thicker rope that his sling was attached to flexed, bouncing him up and down. When it had stopped moving he began to pull himself along it.

Hanging ropes between platforms had been Tyve's idea. The boy's impatience at the time it took for Mirar to climb down from one platform and up to another had led him to consider several ideas for transporting a landwalker between trees quickly. His first idea had been to have several Siyee fly across, carrying Mirar in a net, but he'd realized how implausible it was when he discovered how much Mirar weighed.

The boy had been determined to find a way. He'd kept muttering things like "Tryss could do it" and "What would Tryss do?" Tryss—the Siyee who had invented the hunting harness—appeared to be Tyve's hero and inspiration.

Ropes had been hung between most of the trees now. Making them had kept the healthier Siyee, confined to their platforms, occupied. Tyve was the only one Mirar allowed to move about, and then under strict instructions to neither touch others nor come close enough to risk breathing in the infected air exhaled from their lungs.

Not that it would have made much difference. Most of the Siyee were now ill.

None had died so far. Speaker Veece had come closest, but Mirar had brought him back from near death with magical healing. The old man's body was still disinclined to fight the disease, however. This left Mirar with a dilemma.

It was better for the patient if his or her body learned to fight the disease. Mirar could use magic to ease the symptoms and give the patient strength, but he was always reluctant to use it to expel the disease itself. If he did, the patient was vulnerable to catching the disease again. In a village where the disease was spreading so easily, that was a likely fate. If a patient's body was incapable of learning to fight the disease, magical expulsion and then isolation was the only option. Mirar would do it, if he must, but only as a last resort.

He was nearing the other end of the rope now. Lamplight illuminated a small platform supporting a single bower. The previous platform had been larger, and sat a little higher than this one. As Mirar reached it, he found himself hanging just above the wooden floor. He raised his arms and let himself slip out of the loop.

At the thump of his landing a child rushed out of the bower. She stared at him, then grabbed his arm and pulled him inside.

A woman lay on a mat on the floor, her eyes closed. Tyve was sitting beside her, holding her hand. A bowl of water steamed nearby, its surface swirling with oil. The sweet, crisp smell of brei essence filled the air.

"How is she?" Mirar asked.

"Her breathing is doubled," Tyve said. "It sounds a little bubbly. Her fingers are cold and her lips are starting to turn blue. I've given her some mallin."

*He's learning fast,* Leiard noted.

Mirar could not help smiling, but he quickly smoothed his expression as Tyve looked up at him.

"I know you said not to touch anyone, but she took my hand. I didn't mean it to happen. When it did, it was too late already."

Mirar nodded. "Compassion is a strength in a healer, never a weakness." He looked pointedly at the child holding his arm. "Just remember to wash your hands."

He extracted himself from the child's grip and kneeled beside the woman. Placing his hand on her brow, he slipped into a healing trance and sent his mind out into her body.

Her body was fighting it, he saw with relief. She just needed a little help. Drawing magic, he used it to ease some of the inflammation in the lungs and encourage the heart to beat faster in order to send more blood to her extremities.

Though her body was fighting the disease, he could not guess whether it would have won without his help. Hearteater did not have such a devastating effect on landwalkers. Was it a stronger version of the disease? If it was, landwalkers would face a terrible plague if it spread beyond Si. The Siyee could be more vulnerable to Hearteater, however. The disease had spread through landwalkers' lands before, but this might be the first time the Siyee had encountered it. Did that mean a race of people could become *used* to a disease?

It was an interesting idea, but not one that bode well for the Siyee.

He drew his mind from the Siyee woman's body. She was breathing easier now and her face was no longer pale. Tyve caressed her hand.

"Her fingers are warm," he said, looking up at Mirar in wonder. "How do you do that? It's . . . it's . . ." He shook his head. "I'd do anything to be able to do that."

Mirar smiled crookedly. "Anything?"

Tyve glanced at the woman and nodded. "Yes," he said.

*Here we go again,* Mirar thought, remembering similar moments over the centuries. Young men or women caught up in the wonder of helping save lives. Later, when the elation died and he told them what the life of a Dreamweaver involved, most changed their minds.

*If Tyve doesn't, will you teach him?* Leiard asked.

*There's not much else to do here,* Mirar replied. *It'll keep me occupied while I'm trying to stay away from the White.*

*What about Jayim?*

Mirar winced as he thought of the boy Leiard had begun training in Jarime.

*Arleej will have arranged for someone to finish the job. I certainly can't do it.*

*No, but if you are forced to abandon this boy's training you cannot rely on Arleej to take over,* Leiard pointed out.

*I could. Arleej might not like it much, but I could send Tyve to Somrey. She might curse me for giving her another student, but she will recognize the advantages of having Siyee Dreamweavers.*

*The White won't like that much,* Leiard warned. *If the gods hear that a Dreamweaver is training a Siyee, they will investigate. They will realize that Tyve is being trained by someone whose mind they can't see, and grow suspicious about your identity.*

Mirar considered. *Should Tyve decide to become a Dreamweaver he will have to understand and accept that it must be a secret, and that I may be forced to send him to Somrey to complete his training.*

*Where it would no longer need to be concealed. You'd like that, wouldn't you? You'd like the White to discover that while they were making themselves the first Siyee priests and priestesses, you were making the first Siyee Dreamweaver.*

*It would be satisfying,* Mirar admitted.

"Wilar?"

He looked up at Tyve.

"What do I have to do?" the boy asked.

Mirar smiled. "I will tell you, but not now. We must continue with our work."

Tyve nodded. He looked at the girl child, who was sitting cross-legged to one side.

"She is showing the first signs. What should we do?"

Looking at the girl, Mirar beckoned.

"Come here, little one. What is your name?"

# 28

A glow warmed the eastern horizon but the air was chill.
Auraya turned to look at Reet, but he wasn't beside
her. She felt a stab of alarm and searched all around. He
was flying below her. To her relief he wasn't succumbing
to weariness or Hearteater, but was descending toward their
destination.

She followed him down, dropping through a gap in the
leafy canopy of the forest and dodging branches of enormous trees.

A whistle burst from Reet. A few weak replies came.
Looking around, Auraya saw bowers built upon platforms
high among the tree branches. The messenger swooped
down toward one of these.

He chose the tribe leader's bower. Landing a moment
after the young Siyee, Auraya smiled as an old woman
shuffled out of the bower. She was the Speaker's wife, she
read from the woman's mind. Her smile faded as she recognized the symptoms of disease.

"I have brought help," Reet said tiredly. He turned to
Auraya. "Auraya of the White has come to help us. This is
Speaker Veece's wife, Tryli."

The old woman smiled wearily. "Welcome, Auraya of
the White. Veece would welcome you in the traditional way,
but he is ill. So it falls to me to thank you for coming."

Auraya nodded. "How many are ill?"

"Most of us, but we have not lost anyone since the healer
came."

Reet straightened and grinned. "Tyve persuaded him to come!"

Auraya blinked in surprise. Looking into the woman's thoughts, she read that a man had come to treat the sick.

"A landwalker?" she asked, alarmed. Had one of the Pentadrians remained? Had the Pentadrians given the Si the disease?

"Wilar," Tryli said, nodding. "He arrived the day before yesterday and has worked two nights and a day without rest. Your arrival is well-timed. I feared what would happen to him if he did not stop to rest, but also what would happen to us if he did. And Tyve—"

Her words were lost behind a piercing whistle. All turned to watch as a young Siyee swooped toward them.

"Tyve!" Reet called, relief giving his voice strength. As the newcomer landed, Auraya smiled. Even if she hadn't been able to see Reet's thoughts she would have known the approaching Siyee was his brother. They looked so alike.

"Reet!" Tyve replied. "You made it. Wait!" He held out his hands to stop his brother from embracing him. "We have to be careful. I've been around many of the sick. I might have picked up the disease. I wouldn't want to give it to you."

Reet stared at Tyve in horror. "You have it . . . ?"

Tyve shrugged. "I don't think so, but Wilar says we have to be careful not to touch or breathe on each other, just in case." His eyes slid to Auraya. "Welcome, Auraya of the White. Have you also come to help us?"

Auraya nodded. "I have. Tryli was just telling me of the healer who is helping you. Would you take me to him?"

Tyve grinned. "Of course. Follow me."

As Tyve dove off the edge of the platform she leapt after him. Ropes had been strung between the platforms and they had to swoop over and under them. Reading his mind, she learned that he had come up with the idea of a sliding sling that allowed the healer to move from one platform to another easily.

A familiar updraft enabled Tyve to soar a little higher. He swooped around a branch and glided to a large platform with three bowers. Landing, he paused to wait for her to arrive, then led her to the entrance of one of the homes.

The interior was dimly lit, the only source of illumination a single lamp. Two Siyee children lay in low-slung beds and a woman lay in another behind them. Standing before them, with his back to Auraya, was a Dreamweaver.

*Of course,* she thought. *He had to be a Dreamweaver. Who else would bother travelling into wild and distant places to heal others?*

There was something strange about him. It took a moment before she realized what it was.

*I can't read his mind! I can't sense anything from him! I can't . . .*

The man turned to face her and she froze in shock.

*Leiard!*

His hair was black and he was clean-shaven. He had put on weight. But it was definitely him. Her stomach sank, yet at the same time her heart lifted. Somehow a part of her managed to remain detached enough to find this contradictory reaction amusing. *Am I happy to see him—or not?*

She did not need to read his thoughts to see he was dismayed to see her, however. His stare was cold. His mouth had slowly twisted into a humorless smile.

Tyve gestured toward him. "This is Wilar the Dreamweaver," he said, enjoying the importance of the introduction. "Wilar the Dreamweaver, this is—"

"Auraya of the White," Leiard said quietly. "We've met."

Tyve radiated surprise and curiosity. "You know each other?"

"Yes," she replied. "Though he went by a different name then." *And his hair wasn't dark,* she added silently. *It does not suit him.*

"A name I have put behind me," he replied. "Along with the mistakes I made. I would prefer you did not use my old name," he told her. "I am Wilar now."

"Wilar, then," she said. *Mistakes? Does he mean our affair, or his unkind method of ending it by fleeing into the arms of a whore?* She felt a sullen anger rising, but pushed it aside. *It doesn't matter. I'd prefer the Siyee did not know about our past, so if he wants to be called Wilar that's good enough for me. I've hardly got the time to dwell on it anyway. There are sick Siyee to attend to. They are more important.*

She crossed her arms. "So, Wilar the Dreamweaver. What state is this tribe in, and where would my help be of most benefit?"

A strong southwesterly wind had sent Emerahl along the coast of Genria in what she would have said was good time, except she was in no hurry and had no particular destination in mind. The steady wind seemed to want her to speed along in that direction, and she was still reluctant to spend more than a day or two in any seaside town, so she had given herself up to its will. Her only concern was that if she travelled too quickly, and The Gull, having found her message, was following her, he might not be able to catch up.

The sun was baking her from high above when Aime appeared around a bluff ahead. Like Jarime, the city had grown around an estuary, but this was a river mouth of a much larger scale. The tributaries of the river were too wide for bridges—or at least nobody had been successful at building one since the last time Emerahl was there. As more of the estuary came into sight she saw that the water was just as crowded with ferries as it always had been.

On each point of land was a cluster of buildings. She could only suppose that matters were still the same here: with each cluster so independent of the others that they may as well be considered cities themselves. Each had its own docks, market, laws and ruling family.

As another group of buildings appeared Emerahl smiled in recognition. The Isle of Kings hadn't changed, though there might have been a few more buildings in the garden area. Colorful banners painted with an ancient design told her that the King of Genria still lived in there, though it looked as if there was a different ruling family in charge.

*Everything looks the same,* she thought. *I expect the language has developed, as the Toren one has. The money-*

*changers will give me a terrible exchange rate—that never
changes. What is . . . ?*

She sat up straighter as something completely unfamiliar
appeared. A large ship with black sails was moored in the
estuary. On its side had been painted a large white star.

*Pentadrians! What are they doing here?* She directed her
little boat toward the strange vessel. Maybe the Genrians
had captured it. As she drew closer she saw two black-robed
men on deck, talking to four well-dressed locals. Tied close
to the hull was a smaller Genrian vessel. Workers were lowering boxes from the ship into the boat.

*This is some kind of trade,* Emerahl mused. *Less than a
year since the war and already everyone's friendly enough
for a business transaction or two.* Changing direction, she
headed toward the nearest docks. *Maybe not that friendly,*
she amended. *The ship is a long way from land. The king
may have forbidden them to dock. His position might not be
strong enough for him to outlaw trading with the Pentadrians, however. I wonder which family decided to, and if they
did so because the goods are worthwhile or just to annoy
the king.*

She directed her boat toward the leftmost edge of the
city, selecting one of the smaller mooring areas where
wooden piers had been built for minor craft like hers. Several fishing vessels were tied up and all was quiet, since
their occupants would have left for the markets hours before. As she neared the wooden structure a cheerful-looking
round man stepped out of a building and walked to the edge
of the pier.

"Good morning," she called. "Would you be the master
of moorings?"

He grinned. "I am. My name is Toore Steerer."

She smiled. "Greetings, Toore Steerer. How much for a
mooring?"

He chewed on his bottom lip. "How long you staying?"

"A few days. I'm hoping to earn some money with my
healing skills before I move on."

Toore's eyebrows rose. "Healing skills, eh? I'll put the
word about that you're here. What's your name?"

"That's kind of you. My name is Limma. Limma Curer."

He chewed on his lip some more. "Two coppers a day. Mind you, don't tell anyone, though, or they'll come asking why I'm selling moorings so cheap."

She put a finger to her lips. "Not a word of it will escape these lips."

Toore grinned. "Can I give you a hand up?"

"Yes, thank you." Stuffing the last of her belongings into her bag, she took his hand and let him help her onto the pier. She slung her bag over her shoulder and started toward the shore, the dock master beside her.

"How much for your services, lady?" he asked. "Do you think you could do anything for my leg?"

She turned to regard him. "What happened to it?"

"Got caught between a ship and the wharf, a long time ago. Managed well enough until these last few years, when it gets to aching."

"I can sell you something for the ache," she told him. "Maybe do a bit of healing on the leg, but I won't know if that'll work until I see it."

They reached the end of the pier and stopped. Looking out at the estuary, she saw that the Pentadrian ship was putting on sail. The man followed her gaze and frowned.

"About time they left," he muttered. "Nobody's been happy with them around, like a black cloud over the city. Hope they never come back."

"They will," she said.

He looked at her, one eyebrow raised. "Why are you so sure?"

"They found a buyer for whatever they brought. I saw them loading it as I came in."

The man scowled. "Against the king's command! Who was it, did you see?"

She shook her head. "I haven't been to Genria in years. I wouldn't know a member of the ruling families if I tripped over one."

"What were the boat's colors?"

"It had blue and black stripes around the middle of the hull."

"Aha! The Deore family. Of course." He looked at her and smiled. "They're a powerful lot. Only ones powerful enough to defy the king."

Deore was a family name she hadn't heard of. It was probably a new branch, less inclined to follow tradition and ambitious enough to stir up trouble. "I hope I haven't visited Aime at a bad time."

He laughed. "No, this is normal life here. The ruling families are always trying to aggravate each other. You're only staying a few days, anyway."

"Yes," she said. "Do you want me to look at that leg now?"

"If you don't mind," he said. "And if the price is right, maybe we can skip the mooring fee."

She chuckled. "That depends on the treatment. Let's sit down and have a look."

Tyve landed just as Wilar emerged from the bower. The Dreamweaver did not look at Tyve, but glanced around at the other bowers.

*He does that all the time now,* Tyve thought. *Always looking for Auraya.* Tyve had taken messages back and forth between the Dreamweaver and the White all morning. The two landwalkers hadn't spoken to each other since she arrived. *They don't appear to like each other, and Wilar seems annoyed that she is here. I wonder . . . should I ask him about it? I get the feeling it's not something he wants to discuss. And I don't think I should ask a White such personal questions, though she seems friendly.*

Tyve took a step toward Wilar, then stopped as a wave of dizziness upset his balance. He drew in a deep breath, but it didn't help. Something caught in his lungs and suddenly he was coughing.

"Tyve. Sit down."

Steady hands held him as the world spun around him. He sank to his knees. The urge to cough gradually subsided, but the discomfort was replaced by dread. He looked up at Wilar.

"I've got it, haven't I?"

Wilar nodded, his mouth set in a grim line. "Looks like it. Don't worry. I'm not going to let you die."

Tyve nodded. "I'm not worried." In fact, he wasn't as frightened as he thought he'd be. It helped that he understood more about the sickness and knew he'd probably survive it. What he felt most was disappointment.

"I can't help you any more, can I? I'll spread the disease to others."

"No, but not for that reason. There's not one family here that doesn't have a sick member now so there's not much chance anyone is going to escape it. We just had to slow down the spread in order to have time to treat them all."

"So I *can* help you?"

"No. You're going to lose strength rapidly. What if you passed out in mid-flight? You might drop to your death."

Tyve shuddered. "It's good Auraya's here, then, or you'd have no helpers."

The Dreamweaver's lips twisted into a crooked smile.

"I'm not sure she'd make a good helper. The White aren't good at taking orders, except from their gods."

There was bitterness as well as humor in his voice. Tyve felt himself flush at his mistake.

"I meant Auraya can help—"

"I know what you meant," Wilar assured him. He looked away and sighed. "Your village needs all the help it can get. The drawbacks of having her here are mine alone. The damage, if any, is done. For now . . ." He turned back to regard Tyve again. "For now I need to find another messenger. Do you have the strength to fly back to your family's bower, Tyve?"

Tyve considered. "It's downward a little. I can get there mostly by gliding." He rose, took a few steps and turned. No dizziness bothered him. "Yes, I can make it."

"Good. Go there and rest. Sent Reet to me when he wakes up—if he is well."

Tyve moved to the edge of the platform. He glanced back to find Wilar watching him closely. "Perhaps when you come to treat me, you can tell me how I can become a healer."

Wilar's eyes brightened, though he did not smile. "Perhaps. Don't expect Auraya to like the idea, however."

"Why not?"

The Dreamweaver shook his head. "I will tell you later. Now go, before I come and push you off myself."

Tyve grinned. Turning away, he leaned forward, stretched his arms out and felt the rush of air over his wings as he glided away.

# 29

Imi eyed the platter and decided, regretfully, that she could not eat another mouthful. She looked at the servant standing nearby and gave a little dismissive wave at the food—a gesture she had seen Imenja make. The woman stepped forward, picked up the tray, bowed, and carried it away.

Imi sighed contentedly and sank back into the pool. She was feeling much better now. It wasn't just the food and the salty water. These black-robed people were so nice to her. It felt much better to not be frightened all the time.

The flap of the tent opened. Golden light from a setting sun silhouetted a familiar female form. Imi sat up and smiled as Imenja walked to the edge of the pool.

"Hello, Princess Imi," she said. "How are you feeling?"

"Much better."

"Are you strong enough to walk?"

Imi looked at her in surprise. *Walk?* Imi flexed her leg muscles. *I probably could, if we didn't go too far.*

"I could give it a try," she said.

"I'd like to take you somewhere. It's not far," Imenja told her. "First Voice Nekaun, the leader of my people, wishes to meet you. Would you like that?"

Imi nodded. She was a king's daughter. It made sense that the leader of this land would want to meet her. But her eagerness withered as she imagined herself meeting this important man. Suddenly she wished she was older and more grown up. What should she say? What *shouldn't* she say? Nobody had ever taught her how to behave around other countries' leaders.

*I guess father didn't think I'd ever have to*.

Slowly she got her feet under her and stood up. Her legs felt a little weak, but no worse than when she had first been in the raiders' ship. She stepped over the edge of the pool onto the dry pavement, then looked expectantly at Imenja. The woman smiled and offered her hand. Imi took it and they walked out of the tent side by side.

The courtyard looked no different to how it had when she had first arrived, except now it was nearly night. Imenja led her to a balcony on one side and through an open door. The interior was cool. Pools of light from lamps filled a long corridor. They walked down this to some stairs. The climb was short, but Imi found herself breathing hard by the time she reached the top. Imenja paused by an alcove to tell Imi about the special technique used to make the carving inside it. When they moved on, Imi was able to breathe properly again.

Another corridor followed. Stopping at a large, arched doorway, Imenja gestured inside. "The First Voice is waiting in here," she murmured. "Shall we go in?"

Imi nodded. They stepped through the doorway into a large room with a domed ceiling. Imi drew in a quick breath in amazement.

The roof, floor and ceiling were painted in vibrant colors. The dome was blue with clouds and birds and even some odd-looking Siyee. The walls were different landscapes, and the floor was half garden, half water. Pictures of landwalkers in gardens and houses, travelling in boats or being carried by slaves, were everywhere. Animals both familiar and ordinary, unfamiliar and fantastic, occupied gardens, forests, seas and rivers. Imi looked closer and saw that the pictures and designs were actually made up of countless tiny fragments of a shiny substance.

Hearing a sound, she looked up and jumped as she saw that a man was standing in the center of the room. Dressed in the same black robes as Imenja's, he was admiring the pictures, but as Imi noticed him he looked up and smiled.

"Greetings, Princess Imi," he said in a warm, pleasant voice. "I am Nekaun, First Voice of the Gods."

Not knowing what to say, she copied his manner of speaking. "Greetings, Nekaun, First Voice of the Gods. I am Imi, Princess of the Elai."

"How are you feeling?"

"Better," she said.

He nodded and his eyes seemed to twinkle like stars. "I am glad to hear it," he told her. "I was going to visit you tonight, but I thought it might be more pleasant, if you were strong enough, to show you this place. There is something here I think you may find interesting." He beckoned.

She walked toward him, concentrating on being dignified and all too conscious of her large feet and hands.

"I've only recovered thanks to Imenja and Reivan," she told him as she reached his side. "And thanks to yourself, for allowing me to stay here."

He met her eyes and nodded, his expression grave. "I must apologize for the ill treatment you suffered before Imenja found you."

She frowned. "But that was not your fault."

"Ah, but I do bear some of the responsibility for what happens to visitors in my lands. When the laws we make to discourage wrong-doings fail, then we have failed too."

Her father would probably feel the same way if a visitor was harmed by his people for no reason—especially an important visitor. She decided she liked this man. He was kind and treated her with respect, as if she were an adult.

"Then I thank you for your apology," she said, wondering at how grown-up she was sounding. "What do you want to show me?" she asked.

He pointed at the floor. "Do not be offended; it is the fancy of an artist who had never seen your people."

She looked down. They were standing on a picture of the sea, shown from above on a day so still the water was perfectly clear. Fish filled the blue space, some swimming on their sides to show off their colors. Corals and weeds grew inaccurately from the edge of the shore. At their feet was a landwalker woman with a fish tail instead of legs. Her hair was a pale yellow color, and it swirled around her body to hide her breasts and groin.

*This is what they think we look like?* A giggle escaped her and she quickly covered her mouth.

Nekaun chuckled. "Yes, it is very silly. Few landwalkers have ever seen Elai. All they know is that you live in the sea, so they imagine you are half-fish, half-human." He shook his head. "That is why the man who bought you treated you as something less than human."

She nodded, though she didn't understand why this drawing would make a person think another person wasn't human. Surely if they had fingers, wore clothes and could talk they were human. She had never mistaken a landwalker or Siyee for an animal.

Nekaun took a step to one side. "Come this way. There is something else I want to show you."

Imi walked beside him as he strolled toward a doorway in one of the walls. Imenja followed a few steps behind.

"People of other lands believe strange things about my people as well," he told her. "They see that we keep a few slaves so they assume we enslave anyone we wish. We only enslave criminals. To enslave an innocent is a serious crime. The punishment is slavery. The man who bought you was not of this land, but he knew the law."

"Is that what happened to him? Was he enslaved?"

"Yes."

She nodded to herself. Her father would approve.

"We have other customs foreigners misunderstand. Some of our rites require that we respect the privacy of the participants. Because we keep these secrets, foreigners think the rites must be of a disgusting or immoral kind." He looked at her, his expression sad. "Remember this, if you hear such rumors about us from other landwalkers."

Imi nodded. If any other landwalkers told her Nekaun's people were bad, she would tell them otherwise.

They passed through the door into a plainer room. The pictures on the walls were of groups of people. Each contained a man, a woman and a child. Each wore slightly different clothing and had different skin and hair coloring. One family had large feathered wings. Suddenly she understood why the Siyee in the other room had looked odd to her. She put a hand to her mouth.

"Yes," Nekaun said, though she hadn't made a noise this time. "We only recently learned how wrong that picture is. I'm considering whether to have it fixed or not." He looked down. "Though that is not what I brought you in here to see. Look down. This floor design is a map of all Ithania."

She did as he said and drew in a breath of wonder. Large shapes floated in the center of a blue floor. The shapes were filled with pictures of mountains, lakes, strange cities open to the air and dry roads between them. Nekaun pointed at a large shape like a spearhead.

"That is Southern Ithania." He walked over it to the place where the spearhead shape met a much larger shape and pointed the toe of his sandal at a city. "This is where we are: Glymma."

"Where is Borra?"

"I don't know exactly. I was hoping you could tell me."

She shook her head. "I've never seen the world from above. It's all . . . I've never seen something like this before."

He frowned. "Then we may not be able to return you to your home as quickly as we hoped."

"Why don't you ask the raiders where they found me?"

He chuckled. "If only we could, but we have seen no sign of them in Glymma's port. Either they left after selling you, or news of your rescue and the trouble it caused your buyer warned them to keep away. We need you to tell us where your home is, Imi."

She examined the map closely, looking for anything familiar. Pictures of Siyee in an area covered in mountains caught her eye. She moved to the coastline. Si was a few days' swim from Borra.

"Somewhere in the ocean south of Si," she told him.

"South is that direction," he said, indicating.

Looking at the vast area of blue, she felt her heart sink.

There weren't any islands marked. How was she supposed to tell them where Borra was if it wasn't on the map? *But of course it isn't on the map,* she thought. *If it was they wouldn't have to ask me to find it!*

"Have your people met the Siyee?" Imenja asked.

Imi looked up at the woman and nodded. "We trade with them."

"Would they know where your home is?"

"Maybe. If they don't, I could wait with them until the next visit by Elai traders. I . . . I don't know how often they travel there." Imi looked down at the map and felt a pang of longing. She had come so far, and now she was free to go home she wasn't sure how to get there.

"Then that is what we shall do," Imenja said.

Imi felt hope returning. "Will we?"

"Yes. We'll get you home, Imi," Nekaun assured her. "As soon as we can. Imenja says you'll be recovered enough to leave in a few days."

She looked up at him eagerly. "That soon?"

Nekaun smiled. "Yes. Imenja will take you on one of our ships. She will do everything she can to reunite you with your father and your people."

Blinking back tears, Imi smiled at Imenja and Nekaun, overwhelmed by gratitude.

"Thank you," she breathed. "Thank you so much."

The man's breathing was painfully labored. Auraya sat back on her heels and let out a long breath. She had expected a stronger version of Hearteater, but not one this virulent. Every member of the tribe was or had been seriously ill. Some had overcome the worst of it, but only with help from Leiard.

*Wilar,* she corrected.

Now that she had recovered from her surprise at finding him in Si she had started to question his presence here. He could not have known about this plague before he entered Si. The Siyee had been sick no more than a week or two, and it would have taken him months to reach the village from outside Si. He must have been here already.

*Why? I can understand him staying away from Jarime*

*and Juran, but surely he didn't need to change his name
and appearance and live in one of the most remote places in
Northern Ithania? Did he fear that our affair would become
common gossip and people would try to harm him? Did he
fear that I would seek to punish him for his infidelity?*

She wanted to ask him so many questions, but that
meant bringing up painful subjects. The answers ought to
have been easy to learn. She should have been able to read
his mind, but she couldn't. His mind was shielded. She
had never encountered anyone who could do that. Had he
always known how to do it, or learned it recently? Could
other Dreamweavers learn it from him? What if all Dreamweavers learned to hide their thoughts? An advantage the
White had over them would be lost.

Remembering the hospice, she felt a pang of guilt. Knowing that she was working toward disempowering Dreamweavers made it harder to face Leiard. It was another reason
she had avoided him, sending messages via Tyve then Reet.

She had been sending for Leiard more often than she
wanted to. One of the medicines Leiard was using worked
better at breaking up the mucus in the lungs of victims than
any she had brought. A few hours earlier a patient, delirious
with fever, had insisted on being treated only by "the dream
man." Now she must send for him again.

The patient before her, a middle-aged father, was sinking
fast. His body's struggles to fight the disease were pitiful.
She expected him to die soon and it seemed prudent to reassure the Siyee that the healer agreed with her assessment. If
a patient she was attending died, they might all decide they,
too, only wanted to be treated by the Dreamweaver.

Hearing a thump behind her, she turned and looked out
of the bower. Reet stood on the platform outside, coughing quietly. His attention was on Leiard, who was hanging
from a sling looped around the thick ropes stretched between the platform and another somewhere to the right. The
Dreamweaver was hauling himself along by grasping the
thick rope and pulling. As he reached the platform, she saw
that his hands were red and raw. His bag hung from a rope
around his waist.

Reet helped him up onto the platform then out of the sling. Wasting no time, Leiard marched into the bower. His eyes met Auraya's for a moment, but his grim expression did not change. He crouched beside her, placed a hand on the man's forehead and closed his eyes.

Unbidden, a memory rose of the few times she had watched him sleeping. A forgotten longing crept over her and she gritted her teeth. *It is just an echo of the desire I once felt. I don't love him any more.* She made herself think of the nights of pleasure Chaia had given her. Then she shook her head. That was too distracting, and she ought to be concentrating on her patient.

Looking down, she felt a thrill of surprise and hope. The man's skin was still pale, but the blue tinge had gone from his lips and fingers. His labored breathing had changed to a slightly easier, deeper sound.

*How is this possible?* she thought. *I gave him what strength magic can provide, but his body wasn't fighting the disease. It had ravaged him. Leiard can't be creating new flesh where it has been eaten away. He can't be making the body fight the disease. He can't be killing the disease itself . . .*

Or could he? The Dreamweavers' healing skills were greater than Circlians'. Leiard had only taught her about cures when she was a child, not of the healing methods of Dreamweavers. Since then no opportunity had presented itself for her to observe a Dreamweaver treat a man as sick as this.

She felt a thrill of excitement. If Dreamweavers knew how to re-create damaged flesh, make a body fight a disease or kill the disease itself, her priests and priestesses could learn the skill from them. Circlian healers could save countless lives.

*Maybe I shouldn't be avoiding Leiard,* she thought. *Maybe I should be recruiting him . . . again.* She grimaced at the thought. *It is a pity I can't read his thoughts, or I would know right now what he has done and I could continue avoiding him.*

Leiard drew in a deep, slow breath and let it out. Removing his hand from the man's brow, he stood up. From out of the shadows, where she had been waiting quietly, the man's wife appeared. The woman had barely recovered from the disease herself. In her hands was a round, flat loaf of bread.

"Eat, Wilar," she said to him. "Reet tells me he hasn't seen you eat or rest once."

Leiard looked at the woman, then glanced at Auraya. The woman followed his gaze.

"You too, lady, of course," she added.

Auraya smiled. "Thank you." She looked at Leiard critically. Dark shadows lay under his eyes. "He does look like he needs it."

Leiard hesitated, then turned to Reet.

"Check on Veece," he ordered. The boy nodded and flew away.

As the Dreamweaver sat down the woman broke the bread and handed pieces to them both. It was stale. No doubt she hadn't had a chance to cook for days. Many of the Siyee would be running out of fresh supplies.

*We must do something about that,* Auraya thought.

"What can I do for him?" the woman asked, looking at her husband.

"Continue applying the essence," Leiard told her.

"Will he live?"

"I have given him a second chance. If he does not improve, I might have to isolate him until the rest of the tribe are recovered."

"Why?" Auraya asked.

He turned to regard her. "He will be in danger of catching it again."

She held his gaze. "So you are killing the disease in his body?"

"Only when it is necessary," he said, with obvious reluctance.

"I know of no other healer who can do that. You're more skilled than I was aware of."

He looked away. "There are many things you do not know about me."

At his sullen tone, the woman's eyebrows rose. She rose

abruptly and left the room. Auraya regarded Leiard. His aloof expression annoyed her.

"Like what?" she asked. "Or should I ask: what else?"

He turned to regard her, his eyes cold, but as she stared back his expression softened.

"I am sorry," he murmured. "I knew you would look for me. I should have been more . . . considerate about how and where you might find me. It was the only way I could be sure you would not approach me. I did not trust . . . myself. I did not trust myself to have the will to leave."

She stared at him in surprise.

He was *apologizing*. And what surprised her more was to find herself accepting it. Not that it didn't still hurt that he had run from her, that he had run into the bed of a whore, but now she had to admit that she had understood all along why he had done it. She had been as incapable of ending their affair, despite knowing the harm it would bring.

*Am I forgiving him? And if I am, what does this mean for us?* She looked away. *Nothing. We cannot start again. We cannot be together. Why would I even want to? I have Chaia.*

Leiard was watching her closely. The room was tense with expectation.

Movements in the next room reminded her of the Siyee woman's presence. *Can she hear us?* Auraya concentrated and sensed curiosity and speculation. The woman didn't understand the little she had heard.

"I . . . understand," she said. "It is in the past. So . . . Lei—"

"Wilar," he interrupted.

"Wilar, then. Why is your mind blocked?"

His expression was suddenly guarded. To her annoyance she felt a small thrill of attraction. *It is his mysteriousness,* she thought suddenly. *It intrigues me. Everyone else is so easy to read. I can know everything about them, if I want to, but with Leiard I always had this sense there was more to discover about him even though I could read his mind. Now that I can't read his mind I'm even more curious.*

"An old friend taught me the trick. I never felt it necessary to use it until recently."

*An old friend?* She smiled as she guessed who he was talking about. "Is Mirar still lurking in the back of your mind?"

His lips twitched into a wry smile. "No."

"Ah. That's good. You wanted to get rid of him."

He nodded. He was watching her closely. A thump outside the bower drew their attention. Reet stood outside.

"Veece is failing again."

Leiard frowned and rose.

"Thank you for the food," he called to the woman. Then, without a word of farewell he strode outside, stepped into the sling Reet had held up for him, and slid away.

# 30

The room Reivan had been given as a full Servant was twice the size of her previous one—which meant it still wasn't particularly big. It was late and she longed for sleep, but no sooner had she entered her rooms than a knock came from the door. She sighed. It had been a day of interruptions. Returning to the door, she opened it, determined to tell whoever was out there to come back in the morning.

Nekaun stood outside. She stared at him in surprise.

"I have a few questions for you, Reivan. May I come in?"

She gathered her wits and held the door open. "Of course, holy one."

As he walked into her room she felt an unexpected thrill of excitement. What would other Servants say about her prestigious visitor? Her stomach sank as she realized they might suspect an amorous encounter. She glanced over her shoulder as she closed the door. Nekaun was even more good-looking in the light of the single lamp she had used to light her way through the Sanctuary. Her heart began to race. *What if he has come for more than just to ask questions? Would I mind?*

She shook her head. *Don't be ridiculous—and stop thinking about it!* she told herself. *He can read your mind, you fool.* Embarrassed, she hurried to light a second lamp, filling the little room with a reassuring brightness.

"Please sit down, First Voice," she said. "Would you like some water?"

"No," he replied as he folded himself onto her only chair. "Thank you."

She poured herself a glass of water then perched on the edge of the bed. He smiled at her warmly and she looked down, suddenly self-conscious.

"I wanted to ask you about the Siyee," he said. "It appears they believe they were created by one of these Circlian gods. Do you think they would ever be persuaded otherwise?"

Reivan frowned. "Perhaps. It will be far more difficult to convert them, but with effort and time they may see the error of their belief."

"Effort and time. A long investment of effort or a better-timed effort?"

She looked at him. "I suppose eventually the rest of Ithania will be worshipping the Five. It would be easier to coax the Siyee out of their heathen ways then."

Nekaun's gaze was thoughtful. "It might be worth the wait, so long as they don't prove a threat to us in the interim."

"What else could you do?" she asked.

He paused, then abruptly rose and began pacing the short space of floor between the chair and door. Two steps there. Two steps back. "Many Siyee died during the war. They are vulnerable right now."

"You would *attack* them?" she asked, surprised. This was uncharacteristically direct and warlike for him. His plans so far had been subtle and bloodless.

"I'd rather not," he said. "Not least because it might start another war."

"It *might* start a war?" She shook her head. "It *would* start a war."

He stopped pacing and turned to regard her with narrowed eyes. After a moment his face relaxed and he smiled.

"Ah, Reivan. Imenja was right to single you out. You are so refreshingly frank. I am tempted to take you as a Companion for myself."

She felt her face warming and looked away, her heart racing at the thought. *Me! An unSkilled woman! Companion to the First Voice!*

But it wasn't just ambition that set her pulse racing. Breathing slowly, she willed herself into a calmer state.

"I'm . . . flattered," she said. "It would be a great honor."

He chuckled. "Imenja is determined to keep you and is taking you away with her to Elai. I will have to find someone else to provide frank and direct opinion when I need it." He moved toward her and held out his hand. She took it and was drawn to her feet, but he did not step back to make room for her. Standing so close that she could feel the warmth of his breath on her face, he smiled. "Thank you for sharing your thoughts with me."

Her voice froze in her throat. She nodded, avoiding the eyes that sought hers. Her heart was beating quickly again, but this time she was unable to calm it. He reached out and touched her cheek lightly.

"I will not keep you up any longer. Good night, Reivan." Letting go of her hand, he strode across the room to the door. He opened it, paused to smile at her, then stepped outside.

As the door closed she slowly let out the breath she hadn't realized she'd been holding. *There is absolutely no chance that he doesn't know how he affects me,* she thought. She laughed wryly at his words. *'Thank you for sharing your thoughts with me.'* Had he been making a joke?

She sighed and sat down. *What are the odds that I can make myself get over this infatuation while I am away? Surely a few months at sea will be enough for me to come to my senses.*

*It better be,* she told herself. *Or this is going to make life in the Sanctuary very, very uncomfortable.*

*I must be crazy,* Mirar thought as he slid along the rope. *I should have realized Auraya would come here the moment news of Hearteater reached her. I should have left before she arrived.*

*But would you have?* Leiard asked.

Mirar frowned. *It would have meant abandoning the Siyee. Those who cannot fight the disease would have died without my help.*

*Yes. Which is why you stayed after she arrived.*

*I wouldn't have got far. She would have found me. And if I'd left before she arrived she would have heard stories of a Dreamweaver and come looking for me.*

*She would have been too busy healing Siyee to look for you,* Leiard pointed out. *Just as she will be if you leave now. So why do you stay?*

Mirar sighed. *The damage was done. Auraya must have noticed my mind was shielded the moment she met me. She ought to have been suspicious.*

*She wasn't. She was puzzled, but not suspicious. Your explanation satisfied her. She doesn't understand the significance of the mind shield.*

*Either the gods haven't told her or she's hiding her suspicions well.*

*Why would she do that?*

*Because she needs me. All she knows is that I'm capable of hiding my mind.*

*And can heal magically in a way only immortals can. Why did you reveal that?*

*Because the only other choice was to let someone die. Again, she seemed amazed by the healing, not alarmed. I don't think she understands the significance of it either.*

*But the gods do.*

*Yes. But they only know I'm a Dreamweaver who happens to be powerful enough to heal magically. They don't know if I have actually learned to stop myself aging as well. If I behave as if I have something to fear they'll guess I know more than I should. That's why I can't run.* He started pulling himself along the rope again.

*They won't take the risk that you haven't become an immortal,* Leiard warned. *They're biding their time. You're useful to them right now, but the moment the Siyee are safe the gods will have you killed.*

*By who? Auraya? It would be a bit much to ask their newest White to kill her former lover, don't you think?*

*You are taking an immense risk. If she knew your true identity she would not hesitate to kill you.*

*And I'm not foolish enough to tell her. Neither am I*

*foolish enough to stay here longer than I need to. Once the Siyee are well I will leave.*

Reet, as always, was waiting for Mirar at the next platform. As Mirar hauled himself along the rope the boy hovered at the edge, then when he reached the platform the boy stepped forward to help him up.

Abruptly, Reet turned away and a rough sound escaped him. Mirar placed a hand on Reet's shoulders and felt them shake with every cough.

"Go inside and rest."

Reet grimaced. "If I lie down I might not get up again."

"That will be true if you don't rest."

"Who will check on people? Who will take messages to Auraya?"

"There are other Siyee well enough to take over the task. Now, let's see how your brother is faring."

"He's better," a voice said from the bower.

He turned to find Reet's mother slouched against the entrance. Shaking his head, Mirar walked toward her.

"You should be resting, too," he told her.

"You said I was recovering," she replied.

"Not that quickly."

"Someone has to feed the boys."

He took her arm and guided her back inside, helping her climb back into her bed. When she had settled he left Reet talking to her, and moved into the other room. Two sling beds hung to one side, one empty. The boy in the occupied one was sleeping, his breathing slow and unhampered, his skin pale but not bluish.

*It appears your prospective student has overcome the disease,* Leiard said.

*Yes,* Mirar replied. He turned and called to Reet.

Reet's footsteps were hurried. He looked at his brother anxiously.

"He has beaten it," Mirar told him. "In a few days he'll have recovered his strength enough to walk." He pointed to the empty bed. "Now it's your turn. Rest."

Reet hesitated, then reluctantly climbed into the sling. Moving closer to Tyve, Mirar pretended to examine the sleeping boy while he watched his brother. Reet sighed, coughed a little, then his breathing slowed and he sank into an exhausted sleep.

"Has Reet got it?"

Mirar jumped at the voice. He looked at Tyve and found the boy watching him.

"Do not fear for him," he murmured. "I will make sure he recovers."

Tyve nodded. He closed his eyes and a faint smile crossed his face. "I know."

"You're past the worst of it," Mirar told him.

"I'm so tired. When will I be able to fly?"

"In a few days you can start building up the strength in your arms again."

Light footsteps brought Mirar's attention to the room's entrance. The boys' mother entered, carrying a bowl of water. He sighed and crossed his arms.

"What will it take to make you stay in bed?"

"How long is it since Reet ate?" she countered.

He felt a pang of guilt; he did not know. She searched his face and nodded.

"I thought so. The White lady brought food and fresh water. I hear she is not as good a healer as you, but she can fly. That's . . . useful."

Mirar took the bowl from her. "How do you know what the villagers are saying?" he asked, worried that people had been visiting each other secretly.

"Reet has been carrying gossip as well as messages for you."

He chuckled and turned back to Tyve. The boy took the bowl and drank all the water thirstily. It appeared to give him some strength.

"How is it you knew Auraya before now?" Tyve asked.

"That is something I wish to keep private," Mirar replied.

Tyve's eyebrows rose, then drew together into a frown. "You don't like her."

Mirar found himself shaking his head. "That's not true."

Taking the empty bowl, Mirar handed it to Tyve's mother. She left to gather more.

"You hate her, then?"

"No."

*Nosy, isn't he?* Leiard observed.

"What *do* you think of her?"

Mirar shrugged. "She is a capable woman. Powerful. Intelligent. Compassionate."

Tyve rolled his eyes. "That's not what I meant. If you don't hate her, what do you feel?"

"Neither friendship nor animosity. I suppose I feel respect."

"So you do like her?"

"If 'respect' means 'like,' then I guess I do."

Tyve made a small, dissatisfied noise and looked away. His eyes narrowed.

"If I was your student would I get to travel the world?"

Mirar laughed. "Who says you're going to be my student?"

"Nobody yet. But if I was, would I meet more important people like Auraya?"

"I hope not."

The boy frowned. "Why wouldn't you want me to?"

"Important people are always either beset by troubles or are the source of strife themselves. Keep away from them."

*You sound like me,* Leiard injected.

Tyve's eyes brightened. "Is that what happened to you? Did Auraya bring you strife of some kind?"

Mirar took a step toward the door. "That is none of your concern. I hope you recover your respect for elders and visitors when you recover your strength, Tyve. Otherwise I fear you'll turn into a shameless gossip." He turned away and walked to the door, and heard Tyve's bed creak as he sat up.

"But—"

Looking over his shoulder, Mirar placed a finger to his lips and looked at the sleeping form of Reet meaningfully. Tyve bit his lip, then subsided into his bed with a sigh.

Mirar met the boys' mother in the next room.

"You're right," he said. "Tyve is better. I fear you'll have trouble keeping him in bed. Try to stop him from flying until his strength is fully returned."

She nodded. "And Reet?"

"Watch him closely."

"I will." She moved past him with the refilled bowl.

Stepping outside the bower, Mirar moved to the sling. He paused to consider who was well enough to replace Reet as messenger. From behind came the thud of feet on wood. He turned to see Auraya standing a few steps away.

"Lei-Wilar," she said. "Speaker Veece is failing again. He needs your help."

Mirar found himself simultaneously dismayed and pleased. He was concerned by her news, and at the same time not sure why he should be happy that she'd sought him out. Perhaps only because she had acknowledged that his skills were greater than hers.

*No,* Leiard said. *That's not it. You're vain, but not that vain. It's because she's no longer avoiding you. You like her.*

"I'd better get myself over there," he muttered. Moving to the sling, he shrugged into it. In his mind he plotted a path to the Speaker's platform. It was at least three rope journeys away. He realized Auraya was still watching him.

"I'll meet you there," he told her.

She nodded, then moved to the edge of the platform and leapt off. Though she did not have to, she glided in an imitation of the Siyee's graceful flight, reaching the Speaker's bower in moments. She did it so easily, so naturally, that he could not help feeling an echo of his old, abandoned admiration for her.

*Not yours,* Leiard corrected. *Mine.*

*I admired her, too,* he retorted. *Just not to point of becoming a besotted fool.*

Dropping off the platform, he began to pull himself toward the next. It was an uphill climb, and soon he was breathing heavily with the effort. His hands hurt where they had been rubbed raw on the harsh rope.

*Still, it's better than climbing up and down ropes all day and night,* Leiard pointed out.

Reaching the next platform, Mirar slipped out of the sling and moved to another rope. Shrugging into the second sling, he slid down to a smaller platform. From there it was a harder journey to the Speaker's home. Auraya was watching him, which only made him conscious of how awkward and graceless he must look. He settled into the third sling and started hauling himself along.

Suddenly the sling began to move of its own accord. Looking up, he saw Auraya standing on the platform ahead, one hand outstretched.

*Moving you with magic. Now why didn't you think of that?* Leiard asked.

*I was concerned the ropes would be damaged if I travelled too fast,* Mirar retorted. *You know that.*

*Fast or slow, the wear would be the same,* Leiard said. *I know you know that.*

Mirar scowled. *You win. I didn't think of it. I'm an idiot. Satisfied?*

As he neared the platform he saw that Auraya was smiling. He felt his stomach flip over.

*She is wonderful,* Leiard murmured.

*Don't start this again,* Mirar warned.

Then his feet were on the platform and Auraya was helping him out of the sling. Her smile was gone, replaced by a frown of anxiety.

"His body just can't fight it," she told him. "This may be one of those times of last resort you spoke of."

He nodded. "I agree."

"I . . ." She paused, then shook her head.

He turned to look at her. "What?"

She shook her head again, then sighed. "I have to ask. When I think of how many lives might be saved, I can't let . . . other things . . . get in the way." She straightened her shoulders. "Would you teach me how to kill a disease within a body?"

He stared at her. She held his gaze.

*She can't know the significance of the healing,* he thought.

*No, she must think that what she's asking for is one of the Dreamweavers' greatest secrets,* Leiard said. *I think she'd understand if you refused.*

*Yes,* Mirar agreed. *But can I? When I think of the future . . . The Circlians are here to stay, whether I like it or not. There is only one of me in the world and I am not free to go where I am needed. She is right that she could save many lives. I would not be revealing anything more about myself than she knows already.*

*But surely the gods will not allow it!*

*Why not? She's already immortal.* He paused. *They must have some other way of making her ageless. If she can defy time as we immortals do, then she should already be able to heal magically.*

*So if her immortality is gained by other means than ours, you can't assume she'll be capable of healing magically,* Leiard concluded. *Perhaps that is why the gods have not already given her this Gift. Which is strange. Surely being able to heal people would be a great advantage to a White. There may be a reason why they don't want them to, and if you teach her it might anger them and . . .*

Auraya was frowning now. He realized he had been staring at her for some time, and looked away.

"I . . . I will consider it," he told her.

She nodded. "Thank you."

Then she turned to the bower and led him in to see Speaker Veece.

## 31

Aime had been a profitable place for a healer to visit. Emerahl had not expected it to be since there were priests aplenty, the Temple was not far from the market and she had even seen a few Dreamweavers about. It appeared few of either were female, however. Her customers had been women of all ages, too shy or embarrassed to consult a male healer about their more personal ailments, or women who simply preferred to be treated by another woman.

She had rented a room from the master of mooring, who had been keen to help her out after she had freed up the blood flow in his leg where scar tissue had restricted it. After several days she had a purse heavy with coin, but the moon had waned and appeared again as a thin crescent, and she had to leave in order to make it back to the Stack in time.

Last night a short storm had forced her to seek shelter in a bay. It was large enough to support a substantial fishing village, where she rented herself a room. She was making her way back to her boat when she felt a tug on her sleeve.

She turned, expecting to find a customer had approached her. The skinny, dirty boy in well-patched clothes at her elbow was not what she was anticipating.

"How can I help you?" she asked, hiding her dismay. This was obviously a street child and it was doubtful he, or whoever he might be approaching her on behalf of, would be able to pay her.

"Come see," he said, still tugging at her sleeve.

She smiled. "See what?"

"Come see," he repeated, his gaze overly bright.

All she detected from him was purpose and urgency.

"Is somebody hurt?" she asked.

"Come see." He continued tugging at her sleeve.

She straightened. He might be a simpleton, sent by someone to find a healer. The bags of cures on her belt were a clear advertisement of her profession that even an idiot child would recognize.

She nodded. "All right. Show me."

He took her arm and led her away.

It was just as well she was leaving. Whoever had sent the child probably wouldn't have any money but perhaps they could pay her some other way. Countless times in the past she had found that if word got around that she would cure the poor and helpless for no charge, hoards of sick and poor would somehow track her down. Soon after, customers that could afford to pay started demanding they get free healing too. It didn't matter how small or large the town, the situation could become difficult in mere hours.

The boy had led her into an alley so narrow she had to walk sideways in places. In doorways she caught glimpses of thin faces and eyes noting her passing speculatively. She drew magic and surrounded herself with a light barrier.

They emerged in another street. The boy turned down this and they descended several staircases. A wider street followed then they emerged onto grassy dunes that followed the arch of the bay. He started down a track, still holding her arm, toward a rocky point.

As they drew closer, she grew aware of the booming of the sea. The boy took her off the path and let her arm go. He hurried toward the rocks, jumping from boulder to boulder.

*Has someone hurt themselves falling off these rocks?* she wondered. *Or drowned, perhaps. I hope not.* Sometimes those with limited minds didn't comprehend when others were dead. They thought them merely sick.

The boy turned to look at her and beckoned. His voice was barely audible over the roaring.

"Come see."

She lengthened her strides. He waited until she was closer before continuing on. The rocks grew larger and more jumbled. It took most of her concentration to make her way over them. The roaring of the sea grew louder. When she judged she was about halfway to the end of the point the boy suddenly stopped and let her catch up with him.

From a few steps away a spout of water roared from the ground.

It rose up twice the height of a man, floated for a second, then splashed back down into a wide depression where it drained down a hole in the rocks. Emerahl found she was stiff with shock, her heart pounding.

The boy was grinning widely. He moved to the highest of the surrounding piles of boulders and climbed up to the top. Sitting down, he beckoned to her.

*Is this all he brought me here for?* she thought.

"Come up," he called.

Taking a deep breath, she pushed aside her annoyance and started climbing. When she reached the top he smiled and patted the rock beside him.

"Sit down, Emerahl."

She paused, frozen by the shock of both hearing her name and the realization that he had spoken in a language long dead. As it dawned on her who this was, she found all she could do was stare at him. He smiled up at her. His overly bright gaze was not that of a simpleton, but of a mind much, much older than his body appeared.

"Are you . . . ?" She left her question deliberately unfinished. No sense giving him a name to give back to her, if this was not the one she sought.

"The Gull?" he said. "Yes. Do you want me to prove it?" He cupped his hands together and whistled.

A moment later something whisked past her ear. A sea bird hovered over his cupped hands for a moment, wings beating, and she saw an object drop from its claws before it swooped away. He held up his hands. In them was a moon shell strung onto a rope of "old woman's hair." He picked out a strand of weed, then let it float away on the wind.

She sat down.

"We thought you were dead," he said.

Emerahl laughed. "I thought *you* were dead. Wait . . . you said 'we.' Are there other immortals left from the past age?"

"Yes." He looked away. "I will not say who. It is not up to me to reveal that."

She nodded. "Of course."

"So why have you revealed yourself to me?"

Drawing in a deep breath, she let it out slowly while considering where to begin. "I spent most of the last century living as a hermit. I'd still be there if a priest hadn't decided to visit me. I slipped away and haven't stopped travelling since."

"The Circlians chased you," The Gull said.

She looked at him in surprise. "Yes. How did you know that?"

"The gossip of sailors spreads faster than the plague," he quoted.

"Ah. So you know I evaded them."

"Yes. They lost you in Porin about the time the news came that the Pentadrians were invading. Where did you go then?"

"I . . . ah . . . I followed the Toren army."

His eyebrows rose. "Why?"

"I joined a brothel. It was the best hiding place at the time." She noted that there was no dismay or disapproval in his expression. "The brothel travelled behind the Toren army and I figured it was a good way to escape the city unnoticed."

His eyes brightened. "Did you see the battle?" He sounded eager, like an ordinary boy excited by the idea of watching real warfare.

"Most of it. I left at the end after I met . . . an old friend. I spent some time in Si before deciding to seek you out."

"Old friend, eh?" His eyes narrowed. "If you've been a hermit for the last century, this friend must be old indeed."

"Perhaps." She smiled. "Perhaps it is not up to me to reveal that."

He chuckled. "Interesting. How ironic it would be if this friend turned out to be the same friend as mine."

"Yes, but that's not possible."

"No? So more than a few of us evaded the gods."

Emerahl nodded. "By different means."

"Yes. For me it was easy. I have been hard to find for a long time. I simply became harder to find."

She looked at the boy. "Yet you sought me out."

"That's true."

"Why?"

"Why did you seek me?"

"To know if other immortals survived, and how. To offer help if you ever needed it. To see if I could ever ask for help in return."

"If you have survived this long, I doubt you need my help," The Gull said quietly.

She shook her head. "I cannot live like a hermit for the rest of eternity."

"So you seek company."

"Yes, as well as the possible benefits of powerful friends."

He grinned. "You are not alone in that. I would like to count you as one of my powerful friends."

She smiled, more pleased and relieved than she had thought she would be. *Perhaps I am lonely, after all those years living by myself.*

"However," he continued, his expression suddenly grave. "I cannot say whether my friend would agree. If my friend disagrees, I will follow their advice. I value it greatly. You must gain their approval. Otherwise . . ." he grimaced apologetically ". . . we cannot speak to each other again."

"How do I gain their approval?"

The boy pursed his lips. "You must go to the Red Caves in Sennon. If a day passes and you have not met anyone, approval has not been granted."

"And if it is?"

He smiled. "You will meet my friend."

She nodded. Sennon was on the other side of the continent. It would take months to get there.

"You don't meet your friend often, do you?" she asked wryly.

"Not in person."

"If they approve, how will I contact you again?"

"They will tell you how."

She laughed. "Ah, this is all wonderfully mysterious. I shall do as you say." She looked at him and sighed. "I don't have to leave straight away, do I? We can chat for a bit?"

He smiled and nodded, his gaze somewhere in the distance. "Sure. In just a—"

His words were drowned out as water once again shot out of the ground. When it crashed down he chuckled.

"The locals tell visitors this is called Lore's Spitbowl, but they have an even cruder name for the spouts of water."

Emerahl snorted. "I can imagine."

"They take it for granted that it will always be here. Eventually the water will wear away the rock, and there won't be enough constriction in the cave below to force the water up. There was a spout in Genria once that dwarfed this."

"Ah, I remember that." Emerahl frowned. "What happened to it?"

"A sorcerer thought that by making the hole larger he'd create a bigger spout." He shook his head. "Sometimes the greatest Gifts come to the greatest fools."

Emerahl thought of Mirar and the antics he was famous for, and nodded. "Yes, they certainly do."

Auraya climbed into the hanging bed and lay still until it stopped swinging. It was early evening, but signs that the Siyee village was stirring into life still reached her. Those that had recovered enough were resuming their old routines. Washed clothes snapped in the wind. The smell of cooking wafted to her nose. The laughter of children reached her ears.

She closed her eyes and drifted toward sleep.

*:Auraya.*

At once her eyes were wide open, and her longing for sleep forgotten.

*:Chaia! You've been gone for days.*

*:I was busy. So were you.*

*:Yes. I think the worst is over. We've isolated those whose bodies can't fight the disease. Once everyone is cured, we'll allow them to rejoin the tribe. They will still be in danger of falling ill again if anyone carrying the disease visits the tribe.*

*:You cannot stay here just in case they do,* Chaia warned.

*:I know. Leiard might stay, however.*

*:He was here when you arrived?*

*:Yes.* She paused. *I cannot read his mind. Why is that?*

*:He is blocking you. It is a rare Gift.*

*:His ability to heal is extraordinary.*

*:Yes. He is more than he first appeared to be. Such powers of healing are also rare.*

*:It is a pity he did not become a priest.* Auraya closed her eyes. *A powerful healer priest. He could have helped many more people. I have asked him to teach me this healing Gift. Do you approve?*

Chaia did not answer straight away, then he spoke quietly.

*:I must think on it. How do you feel about him now?*

She frowned.

*:Different. I'm not angry any more. He apologized. That changed more than I would have expected.*

*:How so?*

*:I don't know. I like him better for it. I think . . . I think I would like us to be friends—or at least remain in contact.*

*:You are still attracted to him.*

*:No!*

*:You are. You cannot hide that from me.*

Auraya grimaced.

*:Then you must be right. Are you . . . do you mind that?*

*:Of course, but you are human. So long as you have eyes you will admire other men. That does not mean you will pursue them.*

:*No. I definitely won't be pursuing Leiard. That is a mistake I will not make again.*

:*Good. I do not want to see you hurt. Now sleep, Auraya,* Chaia whispered. *Sleep, and dream of me.*

## 32

As the tent collapsed, Imi felt a fluttering inside her stomach. She drew in a deep breath, then let it out in a rush.

*I'm going home!*

As her excitement subsided she was surprised to feel a little regret. The Pentadrians had been so nice to her. If all of her time away had been like this she would not have wanted to go home immediately. She had discovered so many wonderful new things: delicious food, pretty things she'd never seen before, wonderful musicians and entertainers. The Elai palace was going to seem ordinary and boring in comparison, but she missed her father, Teiti, and the guards and children she played with.

Imenja moved away from the servants, who were now carefully folding the tent, and crossed the courtyard to Imi's side.

"Are you ready?"

Imi nodded. "Yes."

"You have all your belongings?"

Looking down, Imi pointed at the small box near her feet. Inside were the presents Imenja and Nekaun had given her. "I put them in there." She bent to pick it up, but Imenja put out a hand to stop her.

"No, you are a princess. You should not have to carry your own luggage." She looked up at Reivan, who smiled and bent to pick up the box. How Reivan understood what Imenja wanted, Imi could not guess. Sometimes she wondered if they had some silent code of gestures that they communicated with.

Imenja turned to a nearby door. "Let us depart."

Many corridors and staircases followed. Most led downhill, to Imi's relief. Though she was much stronger now, she still tired easily. They passed through a large courtyard and entered a hall full of black-robed men and women. Through the arches of the far wall she could see many landwalker houses beyond. She could hear voices—many, many voices. There must be a large crowd outside.

She dragged her attention away. A familiar man in black robes stepped forward to meet her.

"Princess Imi," Nekaun said. "It has been an honor to have you in our Sanctuary."

She swallowed and thought quickly. "First Voice of the Gods, Nekaun. I thank you for your hospitality and for rescuing me."

He smiled, his eyes sparkling, and without looking away beckoned to the people behind him. Two men stepped forward carrying a large chest between them. They set it down beside her, then stepped back.

"This is a gift for your father," Nekaun told her. "Will you accept it on his behalf?"

"I will," she said, looking at the chest and wondering what was inside. "I will make sure he gets it."

Nekaun gestured at the chest. Imi blinked as the lid opened by itself. *No, by magic,* she corrected. *He can use magic, like Imenja.*

She forgot all else as she saw what was inside. Gold cups and pitchers; fine, brightly colored cloth; jars of the sweet dried fruits she had grown to love; and beautiful glass bottles that, judging from the smells coming from the chest, were full of perfume.

"Thank you!" she breathed. She turned back to Nekaun and straightened her back. "I accept and thank you on behalf of King Ais of Elai."

He nodded formally. "May your journey home be swift, the seas gentle and the weather fine. May the gods guard and protect you." He moved his hands over his chest, tracing the pattern Imenja called a "star," and the rest of the Pentadrians followed suit. "Farewell, Princess Imi. I hope to meet you again."

"And I you," she replied.

He gestured to the two men, who picked up the chest. "I will escort you to the litters."

With Nekaun walking on one side and Imenja on the other, she moved toward the arched openings. As they stepped out of the building she caught her breath.

A wide staircase led down to a mass of people. They crowded between the houses, an endless sea of faces. As Nekaun, Imenja and Imi emerged, the people shouted and waved their arms, their combined voices a roar that was both thrilling and frightening. She had never seen so many people in one place before.

Imi hesitated, then made herself continue down the stairs. At the bottom, bare-chested landwalkers stood beside a glittering platform covered with cushions. Imenja smiled at Imi and ushered her onto the platform. As she lowered herself onto the cushions, Imi followed suit. Nekaun remained on the stairs.

The bare-chested men bent to take hold of poles jutting out from the sides of the platform. Another man barked an order and the platform rose. Imi clutched at the sides. Though the men moved smoothly and steadily she could not help feeling uneasy about being carried so far off the ground.

Now two columns of black-robed men and women descended the stairs and walked past the platform on either side. The crowd parted to allow the men to carry Imenja and Imi down the road. Imi looked back at Nekaun, who raised a hand in farewell.

As she began to lift her hand in reply a flurry of bright objects burst around her. She flinched, then laughed in delight as a shower of flower petals landed on the platform.

"Do they always do this?" she asked as more petals fluttered around her.

"It depends on the event," Imenja replied. "People tend to gather here when they know there's a chance of seeing one of the Voices, especially Nekaun. We don't get flowers, however. They are in your honor."

"Why?" Imi asked, flattered and amazed.

"You are a princess. It is a tradition to make a fuss of royalty. In times past, a monarch and his family were expected to throw coin in return, but that tradition ended when the last Avven king died almost a century ago."

"You do not have a king?"

Imenja shook her head. "Not since then. That king had no heirs, and the people chose to be ruled by the Voices instead. We also rule Mur, to the north, through a Dedicated Servant that the local Servants elect. In Dekkar, which lies south of here, the people still follow a High Chieftain—though his successor is chosen by the gods, not by direct lineage."

"How do the gods tell the people which man they've chosen?"

"The candidates must undergo tests of skill, education and leadership. The one who passes all the tests becomes High Chieftain."

"So the gods make sure the one they like passes."

Imenja nodded. "Yes."

"I wonder why I never thought to ask about this before," Imi said. "They seem like things a princess should know. I guess I'm not a good princess."

"You are a wonderful princess," Imenja told her, smiling. "You haven't been taught to ask these sorts of questions because your father never expected you to need to."

Imi grimaced as she thought of her father. "He's going to be so angry with me."

Imenja's smile widened. "Why?"

"Because I broke rules and got myself into trouble."

"I don't think he'll care about that at all. When he sees you he'll just be happy to have you back."

Imi sighed. "I'll be happy to be home. I don't care if I have to stay in my room or take extra lessons for a year, I'll never break a rule again."

The platform turned. Imi saw that they were being carried into a different street. In the distance she could see the sea and the tiny shapes of ships. Another shower of petals fluttered around her and she felt her heart lighten.

*I wish father could see this,* she thought. *He might change his mind about landwalkers. They're not all bad.* Then she smiled. *When he meets Imenja, he'll find that out for himself.*

Speaker Veece walked out of the bower as Auraya landed.

"Thank you, Auraya of the White," he said, as she handed him skins of water and baskets filled with fruit, cold meat and bread.

She smiled. "We can't have you dying of starvation after all the work we put in." Bright, dappled sunlight covered the platform and bower, making it hard to see inside the dim interior. "How is everyone?"

"Well. Wilar says we are all cured. We must wait until the rest of the village has recovered before we venture out, and we must stay in the village and avoid all visitors until the disease is gone from Si."

"He's right." She grimaced. "It is hard to be patient, but you can be sure that if any of you catch this disease again it will kill you. You have to be cautious, especially of visitors."

He sighed and nodded. "We will be. We do not want your efforts to go to waste, as you said earlier." Moving to the edge of the platform, he looked out at the other bowers. "You have saved us, you and Wilar. We owe you a great debt."

She shook her head. "You owe me nothing. I—"

*:Auraya?*

*:Priest Magen?*

*:It is I. How fares the North River tribe?*

*:They are recovering well.*

*:I have just received bad news. The Siyee have brought three sick children to me. All have Hearteater. It seems they visited their sick friends, the ones we isolated just outside the Open, and caught the disease. I fear they have spread it further.*

Auraya sighed.

*:Then I had best return.*

*:You may wish to take a detour,* he added. *A Siyee from the North Forest tribe arrived just now. He reported that his people are sickening, too. I haven't been able to discern whether it is the same disease or not.*

*:This is what I feared. Very well. I will visit this tribe on the way back. Will you and Danien be able to deal with the outbreak in the Open?*

*:We will try.*

*:Thank you, Magen.*

Turning back to Speaker Veece, she managed a grim smile. "I have to leave," she told him. "The disease has emerged in the Open again and the North Forest tribe is also sickening."

The old man paled. "What will you do?"

"Talk to Leiard—I mean Wilar. I will return."

Moving to the edge of the platform, she leapt off. As she searched for Leiard she sent out a mental communication.

*:Juran?*

*:Auraya. How do the Siyee fare?*

*:The North River tribe has almost recovered, but I have just received news of two new outbreaks. I'm hoping Leiard will agree to deal with one.*

*:It is fortunate, then, that you are both there—though I still wonder at his reasons for entering Si. Have you considered that he might have gone there in the hopes of meeting you secretly?*

She felt her face warm. She had avoided mentioning Leiard to Juran for as long as possible, not wanting to face questions like this.

*:He did not greet me warmly, and he has not attempted to renew . . . anything.*

*:Good. I must go.*

Leiard had just emerged from a bower. She dropped down to land beside him and he jumped with surprise.

"I just received some bad news," she told him.

"What is it?"

"The North Forest tribe has a sickness. They don't know if it's Hearteater or not."

His expression was grim. "And you want me to go there."

"Yes. It has also reappeared in the Open, despite the best efforts of Sirri and the priests."

He frowned. "So you want me to teach you to heal magically."

She paused. Until she had Chaia's permission, she hadn't planned to ask again. Still, if Leiard was willing and she had time to ask Chaia again . . . "Yes."

"Have you considered the possibility that the gods did not give you this ability because you weren't meant to have it?" Leiard asked.

She blinked at him in surprise. Had he learned to read minds as well as hide his own?

"It is possible. I would have to consult them."

He nodded. "If they agree, I will teach you."

Her heart lifted and she smiled. "Just give me a moment."

*:Chaia?*

She waited for an answer. Leiard had taken a step back, and a look of dismay had crossed his face, to be replaced with resignation. She called again and felt a powerful presence stir the magic of the world.

*:Auraya.*

It was not Chaia, but Huan.

*:Huan,* she said, surprised. *Thank you for answering my call.*

*:You wish to learn this Dreamweaver's healing Gift,* the goddess stated.

*:I do.*

*:I wish it were possible, but we cannot allow it. Magic of this nature upsets the balance of life and death in the world. If people understood what it could achieve and knew the White could perform it, their demands on you would be unreasonable.*

Auraya's stomach sank with disappointment.

*:But the Siyee . . . ?*

*:Will not all die. It is an unfortunate price they pay in order that the balance of life and death be maintained. You can only act swiftly to prevent the spread of this disease.*

*:And Leiard? Does he upset the balance of life and death?*

*:Yes, but he is but one Dreamweaver and, unlike you, not in a position of authority. The damage is minimal.*

*:He could teach others.*

*:He would fail. Few are capable of learning this Gift. You may be, but the consequences would be far greater.*

She sighed. *Then I must refuse his offer.*

*:Regretfully, yes.*

As the goddess's presence moved away, Auraya looked up at Leiard.

"They refused," he stated.

"Yes." She grimaced. "You were right. I was not meant to have this Gift." She shook her head sadly. "I will go to the Open. It will take someone of authority to stop the disease from spreading there. The North Forest tribe is closest to this one. You had best deal with it." She noticed he looked troubled. "What is it?"

He looked away. "I was planning to leave Si."

She smiled in sympathy. "Hearteater has spoiled my plans too." Then she frowned as she saw wariness in his gaze. "You still mean to leave? Oh . . . you were leaving because of me."

His shoulders rose. "I am under orders to stay away from you."

"Don't be ridiculous!" She put her hands on her hips. "Juran would never want you to abandon the Siyee for the sake of . . . and I won't be in the North Forest tribe anyway. Surely he didn't tell you to leave whatever country I happen to enter."

Leiard looked at the ground, then up at her. His eyes were hard. "Not exactly. He wasn't all that specific." He paused. "If I go to the North Forest tribe—if I stay in Si— will you promise me that I will not be harmed?"

She stared at him. Did he really fear retribution that much?

"Of course you won't be harmed."

"Promise me," he said. "Swear it on the gods."

She did not reply for several heartbeats, too dismayed at

his distrust to speak. *If this is what it takes for him to stay and help the Siyee . . .*

"I swear, in the names of Chaia, Huan, Lore, Yranna and Saru, that while Leiard the Dreamweaver remains in Si helping the Siyee fight Hearteater he will not be harmed."

Now it was his turn to stare at her. Slowly his face relaxed and he smiled.

"I can't believe you did that," he said. "For me."

She let out a quick breath in exasperation. "I can't believe you asked for it. Will you go to the North Forest tribe?"

He nodded. "Yes. Of course. I will pack my bags—and I had better tell Tyve." He lifted a whistle hanging from a string around his neck to his lips and blew hard. Auraya hid a smile. Tyve appeared to be happy to be summoned thus, but she wondered how long that would last.

"Wilar!"

She turned to see Tyve swoop down to land on the platform.

"Pack your bags," Leiard told the boy, smiling. "We've got another tribe to treat." Tyve's eyes widened as he comprehended what that meant. "Auraya must return to the Open and deal with the illness there."

Leiard met her eyes and a faint smile curled his lips. She thought of the coldness that had been in his gaze when she had first arrived in the village.

*I'm glad that changed,* she thought. *It is better we part friends.*

"I will tell Speaker Veece of our plans," she offered. "Take care of yourselves."

Leiard nodded. "We will. Good luck."

"Thank you."

She moved to the edge of the platform and leapt into the air.

## 33

Glymma's towers and walls had disappeared in a haze of dust not long after the ship set sail. The low pale line that was the Avven coast passed on their left, while the right horizon was flat and indistinct. Reivan leaned on the ship's railing and thought of what lay beyond.

*The low mountains of southern Sennon,* she thought. *Then desert, then mountains, then the lush lands of the Circlians.*

Not that all of Northern Ithania beyond the mountains was fertile, useful land. A dry wasteland existed at the center and the mountains of Si were near impassable. Circlians had far more usable land than the Pentadrians, however. Mur was crowded between the escarpment and the sea, Avven suffered droughts, and Dekkar's riches came from cleared jungle, but the soil quickly turned to useless dust within a few years.

*What will Imi's homeland be like?*

Reivan had picked up some information from Imenja. "Borra is a circle of islands," she had said. "But they don't venture out to them often for fear of raider attacks. They live, instead, in a city accessed by an underwater tunnel."

*So how are we going to get in?* Reivan wondered.

"There is another entrance, above ground."

Reivan jumped, and turned to find Imenja at her elbow.

"I see," she replied. "That's good to hear."

"Oh, we probably won't use it. The Elai don't trust land-walkers, so I doubt we'll be welcome in the city at all."

"How will we meet the king, then?"

"On the islands, perhaps." Imenja shrugged. "We'll see when we get there."

"Has Imi settled in?"

Imenja smiled. "Yes, she is in the pavilion, changing her clothes for something more comfortable. She'll join us soon, I suspect. It seems even the Elai suffer from seasickness. How are you feeling?"

Reivan grimaced. She was trying to ignore the queasy feeling that nagged at her. "I could be worse."

"You'll be fine in a few days." Imenja turned to face the sea. "I have a task for you."

Reivan looked at her mistress in surprise. What could Imenja possibly want her to do? They were stuck on this ship for the next few months.

"What is that?"

"I want you to learn Imi's language. It would be better for us all if I was not the only one who could communicate with the Elai."

Relieved, Reivan smiled. "I can do that, though how well I learn it depends on how much time I have. Is Imi willing to teach me?"

Imenja nodded. "Yes. We've discussed it. It'll give you both something to do while we travel."

"And I brought all those books thinking I would have plenty of time to read," Reivan said, sighing.

The Voice smiled. "There'll be plenty of time for reading, too. You have to keep me from going mad with boredom as well."

"Definitely can't allow that." Reivan looked at Imenja sidelong. "Being stuck on a ship with an insane Voice doesn't sound at all pleasant."

Imenja chuckled. She looked out at the sea again, then drummed her fingers on the railing.

"Imi hasn't yet realized I can read her mind. She is puzzled that I knew her name and can speak her language, but she hasn't worked out how."

"Are you going to tell her?"

"Not yet. I suspect knowing I can read minds will make

me seem even less trustworthy to the Elai than ordinary
landwalkers."

"It could. Although Imi may work it out in the future.
She may think you avoided telling her deliberately in order
to deceive her."

"Yes." Imenja frowned. "It would take a lot to shake her
trust. I must come up with a plausible explanation."

The ship suddenly heaved upward under a wave. Reivan
felt her insides shift in an unsettling, uncomfortable manner.

"I think I may throw up," she found herself saying under
her breath.

Imenja laid a hand on her shoulder. "Keep your eyes on
the horizon. It helps."

"What am I supposed to do at night, when I can't see
it?"

"Try to sleep."

"Try?" Reivan laughed, then clutched the railing as the
ship plummeted down the other side of the wave.

"One other thing," Imenja said. "Don't lean too far over.
You might lose your pendant. Or fall in."

Reivan looked down at the silver star hanging from the
chain around her neck. "You'd just make me another one,
wouldn't you?"

"I can't," Imenja said. "Inside each pendant is a tiny
piece of coral, carefully grown by secret methods known
only to Voices and a chosen few Servants. The coral's natural habit is to send out a telepathic signal to other corals,
on one night each year, triggering a mass release of coral
seeds. We've bred one special type of coral that allows us to
channel our own signals—or thoughts—on any day of the
year. That is what allows us to communicate via the pendants." Imenja chuckled. "I don't have any spare pieces of
coral on me, so don't lose the pendant."

Reivan lifted the star and turned it over. The back was
smooth but for a small indentation in the center, filled with
a hard black substance. She had often wondered what it
was, but her old habit of investigation as a Thinker had lost
against the fear of meddling with something sacred to the
gods.

"Coral," she said. "I wonder what the Elai would think of that?"

"They will not find out," Imenja said firmly. "It is a secret, remember."

"Of course." Reivan let the pendant swing back against her chest.

Imenja drummed her fingers on the railing again.

"So, which books did you bring? They're not all Thinkers' books, are they?"

Rolling her eyes, Reivan took a step back from the railing.

"Come on, then. I'll show you."

Mirar chuckled to himself.

*Feeling smug, are we?* Leiard asked.

*That promise I extracted from Auraya solves all our problems,* Mirar replied. *I don't have to leave. I can stay and continue helping the Siyee. She won't break a promise she made in the gods' names.*

*Won't she? I thought I was the overly trusting one.*

*You are. You wouldn't have asked her to make the promise.*

*Because I know she would break a promise if the gods ordered her to.*

*A promise made in their names?*

*Who would know? There were no witnesses.*

*Auraya would know. They would lose her respect.*

*And you will still be dead.*

*Not unless I give them reason to kill me. So long as the Siyee are sick, I am safe. Once this plague has passed I will attempt to disappear again. And I have a chance of succeeding if Auraya is elsewhere.*

Mud oozed up around Mirar's feet at every step and it was growing deeper. The air stank of rot. He cursed Tyve under his breath. No doubt the boy had sent him into this ravine because it ran in the direction of the North Forest village or was otherwise easier going than the terrain around it. Unfortunately Tyve could not have seen past the dense vegetation to the boggy ground beneath.

Taking another step, Mirar felt his foot slip and grabbed a tree trunk to prevent himself sliding down into the mire. He found himself sitting in a shallow pool of mud.

He cursed again and clambered to his feet. Looking ahead, he saw an endless forest of thin trunks snaking out between tussocks of grass. The ground between glistened.

*You have to go back,* Leiard said.

Mirar sighed. The grass was floating on top of the mud, making the ground look more solid than it was. He looked down at himself. Mud caked his trousers and dripped from the lower edge of his Dreamweaver vest.

*If Auraya could see me now . . .* he thought.

*. . . she'd have a good laugh at our expense,* Leiard finished.

*Yes.* He found himself smiling. Shaking his head, he turned and started back the way he had come.

*You like her,* Leiard said.

*I've never said I didn't.*

*No, but this time you know it for yourself. You have come to that conclusion without my influence. You know these are your own feelings, not mine.*

Mirar considered this and nodded.

*Yes. I see what you mean.*

The way forward became steeper. He thought of the slippery descent into the ravine and the trouble he'd probably have getting out, and groaned.

*Auraya has probably already arrived at her destination,* he thought wryly.

A memory rose of Auraya leaping off a platform, then speeding upward at an angle the Siyee would have found impossible to emulate. He had watched her until she had vanished behind the tree tops, wondering how it was that her ability could still amaze him.

*You admire her,* Leiard stated. *That's why.*

Mirar shrugged. *Yes.*

It was not just the ease with which she used her unique gift, but the way she set out to do whatever she needed to do. Competent, but not vain about her skills. Efficient, but not without compassion.

*She's not unattractive,* he added. *But, of course, the White wouldn't choose ugly people to be their representatives.*

Yet her beauty wasn't obvious. Some would say she was too sharp-featured.

*People who prefer round, busty women,* Leiard agreed.

She wasn't all angles either. She had curves.

*You noticed her curves, then?* Leiard asked.

*Yes.* Mirar snorted. *I'm a man; I notice curves. Are you jealous?*

*How can I be? I am you.*

He felt a chill. Looking up, he made himself examine the steep slope of rock and plants before him. Everything was wet and slippery. He sought hand- and foot-holds and began to haul himself up.

*If you're me, then you don't love Auraya,* Mirar found himself thinking.

*Ah, but I do.*

He shook his head. *So I do too?*

*Yes.*

Climbing was like walking on hands and knees up a half-collapsed wall. Mirar shook his head in exasperation, both at having to climb it and at Leiard's ridiculous conversation.

*Why don't I feel it, then?*

*You won't let yourself. You've buried your feelings.*

*Oh, really? That's a fine thing to claim. I could spend the rest of my life searching for feelings I don't have, and you could keep using that explanation each time I fail to find them. Just look a little deeper, you'll say. Just search a little harder.*

*But you* haven't *searched for them,* Leiard pointed out. *You have the skill as a Dreamweaver to explore your subconscious, but you haven't. You're afraid of the consequences. What would it matter if I am right? You can't pursue her anyway.*

*If you're right it will only cause me pain. Why should I risk that?*

*Because you'll never be rid of me until you do.*

Mirar paused. He was close to the top now. *I should be concentrating on climbing,* he thought.

Instead he closed his eyes and slowed his breathing. He sent his mind into the dream trance, entering it slowly and reluctantly. He made himself think of Auraya. A stream of memories flowed into his mind. Auraya healing. Auraya flying. Auraya talking, debating, laughing. He saw the past, both distant and recent, even as he continued climbing. He remembered their conversations about peace between Dreamweavers and Circlians and felt respect for her. He recalled humorous moments when they had played with Mischief and he felt affection for her. He pictured her powerful and skilled and felt awe and pride. He saw her flying and . . . remembered a suspicion he'd once had about this ability. It almost distracted him from his purpose but he made himself push it aside. If he was to do this properly he must allow himself to relive only those moments of closeness they'd shared, like the experience of intimacy, of pleasure and exploration, of deeper feelings, a feeling of belonging, of not wanting to be anywhere else. Of connection. Of trust.

Of love.

He found himself standing at the top of the slope, gasping with exertion and a terrifying, exhilarating realization of the truth.

*I understand. Emerahl was right and yet she was wrong, too.* To become Leiard he hadn't *created* new characteristics within himself. No, he had blocked those he felt were most identifiable to others. In doing so he had released others he had pushed aside for years. *Leiard is me. I am Leiard. He is what I became when I suppressed those parts of my character that once held back feelings I thought were dangerous. Feelings like love.*

Feelings he had learned to distrust. Love had only ever brought him—an immortal in a world of mortals—endless pain. By becoming Leiard, he had freed himself to love again.

*I am Leiard. Leiard is me.* He pressed his hands to his face. *I love Auraya.*

He laughed bitterly at the irony. Centuries ago he had built a hard wall around his heart to prevent himself falling in love with yet another mortal woman doomed to die. Now he had fallen in love with an immortal. An amazing, beautiful, intelligent sorceress with astonishing Gifts, who had once loved him in return.

"But she's a cursed high priestess of the gods!" he shouted.

The sound of his voice jolted him out of the trance to a full awareness of his surroundings. He drew in a deep breath and let it out.

*You did say it would be painful,* he thought at Leiard.

No reply came. Perhaps Leiard was playing a little joke on him. He waited a little longer. Nothing.

*Perhaps he is gone.* He shook his head. *No. Not gone, but no longer separate from me, or me separate from him.*

He looked around, then started walking. There was nothing to do but keep going. Alone. He felt a pang of regret. Somehow he knew he would not be hearing from Leiard again.

*I think I'm going to miss him. I can't have Auraya and now I don't have Leiard to talk to.*

The thought should have been funny, but instead it left him feeling empty and sad.

In the topmost rooms of the White Tower, Juran paced. Each time he passed the windows he glanced down at the city. Long ago he had given up trying to keep a picture in his mind of the way Jarime had looked at the beginning, or at different times in the last hundred years. He might not age physically, but his memories were as prone to fading as any mortal's.

Which was the source of his dilemma now.

*:I can't remember,* he said. *It has been too long. It's like trying to remember what my parents' maid looked like—and I probably saw her thousands of times more than I saw Mirar when he was alive. Why do you want me to remember what he looked like?*

*:A suspicion. Either Mirar lives, or we have another Dreamweaver in the world with abilities normally restricted to immortals,* Huan said.

Juran felt his heart turn over.

*:I'm not sure what would be worse. You do not recognize him, then?*

*:I cannot see him except through another's eyes. I cannot recognize him unless the viewer does. You are the only person alive who can recognize him.*

*Surely you would know if he was Mirar from his mind . . . ?*

*:I cannot see his mind.*

Juran stopped pacing and a chill ran down his spine.

*:Would this Dreamweaver be Leiard?*

*:Yes.*

*:Leiard can't be Mirar! I've seen into his mind.*

*:A mind which is now completely hidden. If he can do that, he may have been able to conceal parts of his mind before. He can also heal in a manner that immortals can,* Huan added. *As Mirar could. And there is one more suspicious factor.*

*:What is that?*

*:He has Mirar's memories and admitted to hearing Mirar's voice in his mind.*

*:But he can't be Mirar! I would have recognized him!*

*:I wonder if you can. A hundred years is a long time. We have not observed the effect of memory loss in immortals we have created until now. Are there any portraits of Mirar left?*

*:Most were destroyed, but there may be a few in the archives. But . . . We found his body.*

*:You found a body that had been badly crushed. It may not have been his.*

*:What if Leiard isn't Mirar?*

*:He may be a new Wild.*

*:And that makes him dangerous?*

*:Yes.*

*:Is Auraya safe?*

*:Chaia is watching over her.*

Juran moved to the window and looked down at the city again. If Leiard was a new Wild and they were forced to kill him, Auraya would be devastated. Perhaps not as grieved as she would have been when she was still in love with him, but she would find the gods' reasoning that all Wilds were dangerous hard to understand.

*:We did not find all of the Wilds. Those that evaded us haven't caused us any trouble,* he said.

*:Not yet. Remember, power is a corrupting force. Immortals do not recognize our authority. They believe their souls will never need to transcend the death of their body, so they feel no need to obey us. They are powerful and can do great harm. Better to be rid of them now, than wait until they fulfil their potential.*

*:What would we do if a Circlian became immortal— without your help?*

*:Perhaps, if they were loyal, we would allow them to live.*

Juran pressed his forehead against the cool glass.

*:So we must execute Leiard. We have no choice.*

*:If he is, indeed, a new Wild.*

*:How are we to confirm it?*

*:We will watch him closely. Do not alert Auraya to the possibility that he is a Wild yet, or the other White. Leiard has offered to teach her how to heal magically. That would require a linking of minds that may allow us to see past the shield hiding his thoughts. We must know if he is Mirar before we strike.*

*:When will this happen?*

*:We haven't yet decided. There are risks. We will seek other means to discover his true identity first. When we have decided, we will let you know. Good night, Juran.*

Moving away from the window, Juran headed for the cabinet he kept drinks for guests in. He poured himself a glass of Toren tipli. Though it would not make him drunk, he tossed it down and poured another. The tart flavor was both bracing and refreshing.

*:I hope, for Auraya's sake, that you are wrong, Huan.*

The goddess did not reply.

# PART
## THREE

# 34

From above, the blue lakes of Si looked like glittering gemstones strung together with silver threads. The lake Auraya was heading for was shaped like a crescent moon. Looking closer, she noted little boats on the water. She had been surprised at first to discover that the Siyee were as competent at sailing and fishing as landwalkers. They were a people of the sky, but that didn't mean they could not sail a boat or net a catch.

More unusual was the sight of flat, cultivated land around the lake. The Blue Lake tribe lived well within Si borders so hadn't needed to reclaim their tillable land from Toren settlers. It looked as if the area had been cleared of forest long ago in order for crops to be grown. The rows were dark green with the leafy winter crop the Siyee dug into the soil each spring to improve it.

For the past two months Auraya had watched as the land and its people prepared for winter. Food was stored carefully, bowers were repaired, warm clothes were woven. The bowers here did not rely on a tree at their center for support. She headed for the largest one, guessing that it might be a meeting place or at least the home of the village Speaker.

She must have been seen, as whistles filled the air and Siyee began to leave the fields and bowers, their faces turned toward her. They headed for a raised platform made of wood, so she altered her course for this.

Whistles and cries of welcome filled the air as she landed. To her relief, most of the tribe looked well. The

Speaker emerged out of the large bower, which, she read from his mind, was a storeroom for the tribe's produce.

"Welcome to the Blue Lake village, Auraya of the White. I am Speaker Dylli." The leader took a cup of water from one of the village women, then the traditional cake of greeting from another, and gave them to Auraya.

She ate the cake and sipped the water. "I am relieved to see you are all looking healthy."

The Speaker's expression grew serious. "We grieve the loss of nine tribesmen, women and children, but would have lost many more if we had not followed the advice you sent on preventing the illness moving to others—and if the Dreamweaver had not come."

Auraya smiled. "Wilar. I'd heard he'd travelled here, which is why I did not come sooner. You are in capable hands. I'd like to see him."

"Then I will take you to him."

He beckoned and led her away from the platform. Seeing her glance at it curiously, he chuckled.

"Most tribes live in trees, or on uneven ground like at the Open. Our land here is level. The oldest of us find it exhausting getting off the ground so we built this for them."

Auraya nodded in understanding. While the Siyee could become airborne by running and leaping into the air, it took a lot of energy. Dropping from a tree branch or cliff was much easier, especially for the elderly. The platform would serve the same purpose.

The crowd followed them, the children chattering among themselves. At the edge of the fields three new bowers had been built. The adults in the crowd stopped several paces away and told the children to stay with them. Auraya and the Speaker continued on.

"I haven't been ill, so I must stay away," he told her. "Please give Dreamweaver Wilar my regards."

She smiled and nodded. "I will. If there's anything I can do to help, I will do it."

He bowed his head in thanks. Turning away, she walked the rest of the way to the bowers slowly, searching for minds. The discomfort, pain and fear of the sick Siyee was a shock after the cheerful health of the rest of the tribe. After a moment she found what she was looking for: a mind aware of the presence of a man she could not sense. She stopped outside the bower.

"May I come in?"

There was a pause, then a familiar voice replied, "Of course, Auraya."

At the sound of his voice she felt her heart lighten. She pushed aside the door-hanging and stepped into a dimly lit space. Four beds hung between a thick central pole and the outside supports of the bower, two on either side. Leiard stood beside one, spooning liquid from a bowl into a woman's mouth. He glanced at her once and kept working.

"Look around," he invited.

She moved from bed to bed, checking the health of each patient. They were in the worst stage of the disease but their bodies were fighting it, even if sluggishly.

"Those who are recovering are in the bower to our left, and those whose bodies cannot resist the disease are in the other," Leiard murmured.

Hearing his footsteps, she looked up. He dropped spoon and bowl into a large stone dish of water, then paused to stare at it. The water began to steam, then bubble. He left it gently boiling, moved to the door and glanced over his shoulder at her.

"Do you want to see?" he asked.

She nodded. Following him out, she noted Siyee children watching at a distance as they moved to another bower.

It took Auraya a moment to take in the scene inside. Unlike the previous bower, this one was filled with furniture. A healthy-looking Siyee sat cross-legged in the center of the room, working on a dart harness. Another sat before a loom, his hands moving quickly as he worked. Two women were preparing jars of preserved fruit, and a boy and girl child were playing a game at the back of the room. All looked up as Auraya and Leiard entered.

As Leiard introduced her, Auraya slowly understood why these people were here. She had been expecting sick Siyee, but these people were obviously fully recovered.

Leiard had killed the disease within their bodies, but they couldn't mingle with other Siyee for fear of catching it again. They could, however, continue doing domestic tasks—even cooking.

"How long must they stay in there?" she asked him as they left the bower.

"I have told them they can go once no other member of the village is ill. They know there can be no certainty that they will be safe then, but they can't keep themselves separate forever."

Auraya nodded. "Do they know how lucky they are? All those in their situation in the Open, and in other villages, die."

Leiard winced and met her eyes. "How many so far?"

"About one in five."

He grimaced and shook his head. Walking away from the bower, he sat down on a log at the edge of the forest, frowning. Auraya sat beside him. She considered his profile. His face did not look as weathered as it once had, she noted, though there were still smile wrinkles around his eyes. The dye in his hair had partly washed out, leaving it a dark blond color.

"I have come here to see if your offer still holds," she told him. "Hearteater is everywhere. The toll is too great. I have come from Temple Mountain. The Siyee there haven't been the most cooperative of the tribes and their cave system is too small for so many people. All that close contact . . . not good for preventing the spread of a disease."

He smiled crookedly. "No." His eyes moved away, then returned to her and narrowed. "So the gods no longer forbid it?"

"No. I may only use your healing Gift with the gods' permission. Only in times of great need, such as now."

He nodded. "A compromise."

She turned to look at him, but found herself lost for words. In the last few months, in desperation, she had experimented on dying Siyee without success. She found she could not kill a disease that she could not easily sense as a separate entity to the body it attacked.

"Can you return tonight?" Leiard asked. "Tyve is out gathering cures and I need him to tend to the sick while we work."

"Of course. How long will it take?"

He shrugged. "That depends on whether you have the ability to absorb the concepts and how quickly you learn to apply them. Perhaps an hour. Perhaps several nights."

Auraya nodded. "There is another tribe I need to check on, but I can return by tonight."

"Then we will begin then. Keep in mind that few can grasp the concepts involved. It is not a question of magical strength, but of mental ability. You may not have the ability."

"I can only try," she told him, smiling wryly. "There's never been a Gift I could not learn."

His eyebrows rose. "Is that so?"

"Yes."

"What will you do if you fail, I wonder."

"Try to take disappointment gracefully."

The corner of his mouth twitched. "That will be interesting to observe."

She met his eyes. "It may depend on whether you taunt me about it or not."

"Do you believe I would?"

"I don't know."

He chuckled. "I will endeavor to be sympathetic." He rose and looked toward the bowers. "If you have time, I will introduce you to the third group. They're still in the early stages of the disease. There's a woman among them who knows more about the medicinal plants around here than anyone I've encountered. I think you'll like her."

"Will I?"

"Perhaps."

"Let's go and find out." Smiling, Auraya stood up and followed him back to the bowers.

Reivan leaned on the rail and gazed at the distant mountains of Si. The ship's captain had kept the coast in sight for the last few days, a situation Reivan found both reassuring and frustrating. There was something disconcerting about being so far out to sea that no land could be seen, but the sight of it, dry and still, was all the more tantalizing when it was land they could not set foot on without risking angering its inhabitants.

She considered the reception the Servants who had travelled to Si had received from the Siyee. Not surprisingly, the sky people hadn't welcomed the Pentadrians' overtures of peace and friendship.

*I wouldn't welcome a visit by the people who had invaded my allies and killed my people, no matter what they said their intentions were,* she thought. *If the White sorceress does have mind-reading abilities she'd have worked out that peace wasn't all the Servants were there to find.*

Reivan was inclined to agree with Nekaun that attempting to convert the Siyee wasn't worth the trouble for now. If they believed they were created by one of the Circlian gods, they weren't going to embrace the idea that their creator wasn't real and they should be worshipping the Five instead.

*I wonder how they came by the notion? I wonder how they actually came to exist?*

The slap of bare feet drew Reivan's attention from her thoughts. She turned to find Imi, her black skin glistening with water droplets, walking toward her. The girl had put on some weight in the last few months. She walked with confidence, no longer weak and easily unbalanced by the ship's rocking.

"Greetings, Reivan," Imi said gravely.

"Greetings, Princess Imi," Reivan replied.

The girl paused, then grinned. "You called me that because I was being too serious, didn't you?"

"It is your title. I should be getting used to addressing you that way, now that we are getting close to your home."

"Are we?" Imi asked anxiously. "I suppose we are closer than we were."

Reivan nodded toward the line of mountains. "That is Si. Any day now we may see Siyee. When we do, we can go to shore and ask for . . . for . . ."

"Directions," Imi finished. In the last few months Reivan had gained enough grasp of the Elai language to hold conversations, but her vocabulary was still limited.

"Yes," Reivan said. "Though I am worried that the Siyee will refuse to help you because you arrived here with us."

"Why would they do that?"

Reivan sighed. "Because of the war."

"Ah, yes." Imi frowned. "The Siyee are allies of the White sorcerers. They must consider Pentadrians their enemies."

"Fourth Voice Genza travelled to Si before the war to discover what she could of the Siyee, but before she could learn whether they would make good allies or not, the White sent one of their own sorceresses there. The one they sent has an unusual Skill that allows her to fly. Genza could not win them after that."

Imi looked up, her eyes shining. "That's the same sorceress that came to Elai. She offered to help us get rid of the raiders if we helped her people in return." Her eyes widened. "If we had, we'd be your enemies too. I'm glad my father sent her away."

Reivan felt a thrill of excitement. "He did?"

"Yes. Father doesn't like landwalkers. He didn't trust her."

"Will he trust us, do you think?"

Imi shrugged. "I don't know. He'll be happy that you brought me back." Her eyes narrowed. "Are you thinking of asking him to be your ally?"

Reivan smothered a smile at the girl's shrewd question.

"Maybe. We don't ally ourselves with just anyone."

The girl's mouth set into a determined smile. Reivan looked away, hoping her expression didn't betray her amusement.

"Will you try to make friends with the Siyee again?" Imi asked.

Reivan shook her head. "If we do, it won't be for a long time. They are too set in their ways."

"It would be good if you did. The Siyee and the Elai have always been friends. We have more in common with each other than either of us have with landwalkers. We both

have troubles with landwalkers." She paused, obviously
considering this. "And we were both created by Huan."

"The Elai believe they were created by a Circlian god?"
Reivan asked, turning to regard Imi closely.

The girl shrugged. "That's what the priests say."

"How interesting." Reivan hoped she looked more
thoughtful than alarmed. Her heart was now beating a little
faster. Had Nekaun known of this? Surely, if he had, he
would not have thought Imenja taking Imi home in an attempt to woo the Elai was worth the trouble.

*If Imi had thought about it, he or Imenja would have
known about it. So if they don't know then Imi must not
have thought about it—or at least not in their presence.*
Despite all that had happened to the girl, her mind must not
have turned to her god often during her stay at the Sanctuary. Perhaps religion wasn't important to the Elai.

"Do you pray to this god?" Reivan asked.

Imi's nose wrinkled. "Not unless the priests make me.
I used to when I was little, if I wanted something, but the
priests say Huan is too busy to arrange for little girls to get
the presents they want. I decided I'd only pray if I needed
something important."

"Did you pray when you were a prisoner?"

"A few times." Imi's expression was sad. "I guess I was
out of practice. Father doesn't pray much—and sometimes
he says angry things like if Huan cared about us she would
stop the raiders keeping us from living on our own islands.
He says she abandoned us years ago."

Reivan nodded in sympathy. She opened her mouth to
voice her agreement, but stopped. How could she frown
upon the inaction of another god—even if this god did not
exist—when her own gods had allowed her people to be
defeated in war?

"The gods are mysterious," she found herself saying
instead. "We don't always understand their reasons for
doing—or not doing—something. Their view of the world
is like that of a parent. Sometimes the actions of a parent
seem cruel and unfair to a child, but later they understand
those actions were for their benefit."

Imi nodded slowly, her face tight with the intensity of her thoughts.

"Ah! Company!"

The voice was Imenja's. Reivan turned to find the Second Voice walking toward them. Imenja pointed above their heads, at the sky.

"They're coming to inspect us," she said.

Imi glanced in the direction Imenja had pointed and gasped. Following her gaze, Reivan saw five large birds gliding toward the ship.

*Not birds: Siyee.*

"You had better conceal yourself, Imi," Imenja said as she reached them. "We don't yet know how they will react to us—or to you for associating with us. Let's not reduce your chances of gaining their help."

The girl reluctantly allowed the woman to usher her into the pavilion at the center of the ship. Imenja returned to Reivan's side. The Siyee were close enough that Reivan could see the ovals of their faces.

"Imi just told me the Elai believe, as the Siyee do, that the Circlian goddess Huan created them," Reivan told her.

"I know," Imenja replied.

"You do?"

"Of course."

"I'm surprised Nekaun allowed us to make this journey, then."

Imenja laughed quietly. "Nekaun doesn't know."

Reivan stared at Imenja. She doubted Nekaun would regard Imenja favorably for neglecting to tell him something like this. "Why not?"

"You said yourself, Imi is a princess and she should be escorted home with great fuss and ceremony by someone no less important than a Voice."

"I didn't say that."

"Not exactly those words, but the meaning was the same."

"That's not the reason you've concealed this from him, is it?"

Imenja smiled. "Who's the mind-reader here?" Then

her smile faded a little. "I am not as easily dissuaded from exploring a chance at alliance with the Elai. They may be small in number and they may worship a false god, but until we have met them we cannot know their full potential. Consider the Siyee and how effective they were in battle. We might benefit as much or more·from sea-warrior allies. Who cares what they worship?"

"Our gods would surely—"

The whoosh of wings drew Imenja's attention upward. The Siyee had reached the ship. They circled, their fierce faces creased with frowns of suspicion. The contraptions strapped to their chests looked flimsy, but Reivan knew well how lethal they could be.

"They are brave coming so close," Imenja breathed.

Reivan glanced around the ship to see that some of the crew were holding bows.

"Do not attack or retaliate," Imenja called out. "Unless I give the order."

After circling the ship three times, all but one of the Siyee swooped away toward the shore. The remaining man flew directly toward Imenja and Reivan. An object shot from the Siyee's harness. Reivan took a step backward but Imenja remained still. The missile landed with a thud, embedding itself in the deck at Imenja's feet. The Siyee flapped hard to avoid the rigging, then curved away toward the mountains.

Imenja nudged the dart with the toe of her sandal. "What do you make of that?"

"A warning," Reivan replied, her voice wavering a little. "And a reminder. We are not welcome in Si."

"I agree," Imenja said. "The trouble is, we have to get Imi to shore if she is to find out where her home is. How are we going to do that?"

"Perhaps we should ask her."

Imenja looked at Reivan and smiled. "Of course. We'll discuss it with her tonight."

# 35

Sitting down, Mirar rested his elbows on his knees and his chin on his fists and thought about Auraya.

Until she had visited that morning, he had not seen her for two months. While he had hoped they would encounter one another again as they battled Hearteater, he also knew there was nothing to be gained from a meeting except danger. The hopeless infatuation for her that had come with accepting Leiard as a part of himself wasn't easy to live with. In fact, it was a great nuisance. He constantly told himself to get over it—the sooner the better. Yet when she had called out to him, when she had walked into the bower, his heart had performed all manner of acrobatics, and he knew it would take more than two months' separation before he had full control of it again.

The last thing he had expected was for her to come seeking his magical healing technique. Since leaving the North River tribe, Mirar had cursed the gods many times for not allowing her to learn it. As the disease attacked Siyee in more and more tribes, many, many Siyee had died that she might have saved.

*Why now?* he asked himself. *Why have they changed their minds?*

The answer was clear. The disease had become a plague. Perhaps the Siyee had heard of his healing ability and started to wonder why the Gods' Chosen did not have it.

*If that is so, why don't the gods teach her?*

He'd pondered that question all day. The only conclusion

he could come to was that they couldn't. They were beings of magic. Perhaps beings with no physical body could not heal physical bodies, even through a willing human.

There was a danger in teaching her this technique. It was similar to the method all Wilds used to prevent themselves aging. Auraya might realize this. The gods certainly would.

*I can't bring myself to believe she will harm me if she suspects I am immortal. A suspicion is not a truth, and she is not one to act on mere suspicion. She promised I would not be harmed. Also, she will feel she owes me something in return for giving her the ability to save lives. Perhaps only the chance to leave Northern Ithania.*

When he had told Emerahl, through dream links, of his encounter with Auraya, she had urged him to abandon the Siyee and flee. She suggested he go to Southern Ithania, where Dreamweavers were tolerated and even respected. When he had told her he had offered to teach Auraya his healing method she had called him an idiot, but she couldn't come up with a reason why he shouldn't—other than those he had already considered.

He heard the sound of feet meeting the ground. Looking up, he saw only darkness, then Auraya came out of the gloom like a beam of moonlight taking form. Mirar felt a shiver run down his spine. The hem of her priestess's circ flared outward as a breeze stirred it. Her unbound hair blew across her face and she lifted a hand to catch and hook it behind one ear.

*Look away,* he told himself. *If she catches you gazing at her she might suspect you're still smitten.*

He drew in a deep breath and rose.

"Greetings, Auraya of the White."

One of her eyebrows quirked upward in amusement at his formal manner.

"Greetings, Dreamweaver Wilar."

He directed her to one of two blankets he'd set on the ground outside the bowers. She sat down and watched as he moved to the middle tent. Inside, Tyve was sitting beside a Siyee man lying unconscious on a stretcher. The boy stood up, stooped to pick up one end of the stretcher and helped Mirar carry it outside.

After they had placed the stretcher on the ground between Auraya and the other blanket, Tyve returned to the bower. Mirar sat down.

Auraya leaned forward and placed a hand on the man's head. Her eyes grew distant as she accessed the Siyee's condition. A grim twitch of her lips told Mirar she had seen the damage the disease had done. She looked up at him expectantly.

"What now?"

"I could explain to you in words and guide you toward discovering the Gift for yourself, but that would take months, or years, and neither of us have the time to spare. We must engage in a link."

Her eyebrows rose. "A mind link?"

"Not exactly. We will link hands, but unlike a mind link there will be no need for you to open your mind. It is similar to a dream link, but easier since you do not need to be in a trance or part-asleep. Physical contact removes the necessity for that. I will project my instructions to you. You will answer in the same way. Are you willing to do this?"

The corner of her mouth twitched upward as she considered. After a moment she nodded to herself and held out her hands to him. He was not surprised. She had accepted dream links before, despite their illegality, and would have decided what he was going to teach her was worth bending the law for.

He took her hands and closed his eyes, then sought and found a sense of her presence before him. From her came a feeling of both anticipation and uncertainty.

:*Auraya.*

:*Leiard? Or should I call you Wilar?*

:*Whatever you wish,* he answered.

:*I don't think of you as Wilar, so I'll call you Leiard. But . . . you seem different.*

:*I am changed?*

:*Yes and no. You seem more yourself. That sounds*

*strange, I know, but before you were so . . . so uncertain of yourself. Now you are not.*

He felt oddly pleased about that.

*:It is true. I am not the person I was.*

*:I was probably the source of all that uncertainty,* she continued sadly. *Perhaps we should not talk of it.*

*:Perhaps. Perhaps not,* he answered. *It could do as much harm as good.*

*:True.* She fell silent, then before he could think of a way to change the subject she spoke again.

*:I forgave you,* she told him. *I was angry, but not any more. Not since we worked together at the North River. I would like it if we could be friends.*

*:I would like that too,* he told her, perhaps with too much feeling.

*:Do not fear that it will bring you or your people any trouble. The gods know where my heart lies now.*

Mirar felt a twinge of surprise. She had found another lover? He struggled to hold back a feeling of jealousy. *No,* he told himself. *Accept it.* He examined the feeling then pushed it aside. *Better that she is happy. Better that I am not making her miserable, anyway.*

Then he realized that she might not have been referring to a lover at all. She might simply have meant her heart was for the gods. There was one way to find out . . .

*:I hope he is worthy of you,* he said.

A wave of embarrassment came from her. He smiled; he had guessed correctly.

He was only sensing embarrassment, however. She ought to be betraying some feeling of happiness or joy. She wasn't. *It won't last,* he found himself thinking with satisfaction. This time he did quash his feelings. It was time to direct their attention elsewhere.

*:Magic can be used in healing in many ways,* he told her. *Dreamweavers divide these into three levels of difficulty. The first level is the simplest: the use of magic to hold or heat or move. The second uses the same Gifts but in more challenging situations as well as using magic to boost a body's strength. The third is so difficult it requires*

*great concentration and a sure knowledge and experience of all processes of the body. It enables a Dreamweaver to influence tissue within a body to a degree of detail where flesh and bone may be realigned and persuaded to heal immediately.*

Mirar paused. No feeling of confusion came from Auraya, so he continued on.

*:What I will try to teach you is a step beyond the third level. It does not require drawing a great deal of magic, or even gaining a great knowledge and experience of bodily systems. What it requires is a mind capable of sensing and understanding the body from the finest detail to the greater whole. Once you understand, you can influence.*

He guided one of her hands down to the Siyee, setting it upon the man's chest.

*:Watch.*

To show her he had to lower the shield around his mind that prevented her seeing his thoughts. He took care to let it fall only while he was concentrating on healing, opening and closing the shield like a shutter and passing what he saw and did to Auraya in images and ideas.

The man's body filled his awareness. The damage within it, and the effect it was having on the whole, was obvious. He detected something out of place—the tiny but dangerous life that should not be there, and he communicated all that he sensed to her.

*:Now you.*

She did not send what she was perceiving to him. For a long time she was silent, then he felt a thrill of excitement from her.

*:I see it! I can see the disease! Show me how to kill it.*

He concentrated on the man again, showing her how to focus magic in a way that killed the intruding malaise but did not harm the body. Now he saw her actions by watching the effect she had on the Siyee. He was surprised and pleased to see that she had understood everything he had told her.

Her attack was not ordered, however, and he found himself demonstrating how to work systematically through the body so she left no trace of the disease alive. They began working together, each responding to complement or support the other's actions. It was like a dance. It was exhilarating.

*She does this naturally,* he thought suddenly. *It is like an innate Gift. She must be Gifted enough to become immortal without the gods' assistance.* The thought of what they could have been sent a thrill through him. Immortal lovers . . . *But that's not going to happen. It would make her an enemy of the gods she loves. And I am the hated Mirar. Even if she could forgive the deception . . .*

She was engrossed in the healing. He let her continue alone while he watched. Since this healing method was new to her, she could not be using it to stop herself aging. Perhaps the gods, through the ring she wore, were keeping her from aging without her being conscious of how it was done.

*I wonder how long it will be before she makes the connection,* he wondered. *Is that why the gods do not teach the White to heal?*

*:The disease is gone!* she said.

He examined the Siyee closely.

*:Yes,* he told her.

*:That was . . . easier than I thought. This way you have of sensing the body is . . . amazing. And logical. I cannot understand why I have never done this before. But . . . this man is still dying.*

*Yes, there is more to do.*

He led her attention back into the Siyee's body. Taking energy from stores of fat, he used them to help speed the regrowth of lung tissue. She followed suit. With the lungs restored, the blood began to improve and then the strength of the heart. Circulation enlivened, the fingers, toes and other extremities warmed. He could sense Auraya's amazement and joy.

Finally he moved to the man's hand. A finger had been broken and badly set long ago. Mirar carefully straightened it, shuffling the fibers of the bone into new positions. The amazement he sensed from Auraya changed into a bright excitement.

*:You could heal anything this way,* she said. *You could give sight to a man who had been blind all his life. You could restore a cripple. You could revive a dead man.*

*:Yes, but with the last it must be immediate. Memory deteriorates within minutes of death and cannot be restored.*

*:Can I heal myself the same way?*

*:Of course,* he told her. He needed to steer her away from this chain of thought. *You've learned exceptionally fast and well.*

*:You thought this would take longer.*

*:I did. As always, you've exceeded expectations. If only all my students learned so quickly.*

*:If that is all I need to know, then I should return to the Temple Mountain tribe immediately. There are many there who may die tonight if I do not bring them this healing.*

*Then I won't delay you any longer.*

Their hands parted and the sense of her presence vanished. Opening his eyes, he found her looking at him, smiling broadly. He felt his heart skip a beat and quickly looked down at the Siyee.

"Thank you, Leiard. Every life I save with this Gift will be a life you have saved."

He glanced up at her. "Don't go telling the gods that. They can be unpleasant to be around when jealous."

She opened her mouth to reply, then her eyes dropped to the Siyee.

"He's awake."

Mirar looked down at the man, who was regarding them curiously.

"Good evening," he said. "Auraya and I have cured you, but you will have to live in the first bower until the rest of the village is well. You will be tired for a day or two. Sleep and regain your strength."

The man nodded weakly and closed his eyes again.

Auraya climbed to her feet. "I'll help you carry our friend here back into the bower, then I must go."

Together they lifted the man and carried him to the bower of cured Siyee. Auraya stepped outside again. Standing in the entrance, Mirar watched as she walked a little way from the bowers. She smiled at him once, then rose up into the air and disappeared into the night.

He sighed. She had started to see the potential in the Gift within moments of learning it. It would not be long before she returned with questions.

Imenja's ship was bigger than the raiders.' It was a different shape, too. Reivan had explained to Imi that this ship had been built with a narrow hull so it would travel fast. Most ships were used to carry things to trade with, so they had wider hulls in which to store goods. This ship only had to carry them, a crew, and their supplies.

The entire ship was made of a black wood from a place in the southernmost part of the southern continent. The star shape that Imenja and Reivan wore had been painted in white on the hull. The sails were also black with a white star. Imi could imagine how formidable this large, narrow vessel would look to traders and raiders. She almost wished they would encounter the raiders that had captured her. Maybe Imenja would punish them with her magic.

Where there had been a large hole in the deck of the raider ship to allow access to stolen goods stored in the hull below, Imenja's ship had a shallow depression which created a sort of low sitting area, covered by a kind of tent. There Imi, Imenja and Reivan slept or sheltered whenever it rained. The rest of the time they sat on deck and tried to keep out of the way of the crew. Imi had been inside the hull a few times. There was a bucket down there for bailing out water, but the ship was so well made it didn't leak much. The time she'd spent in the raiders' ship felt like a distant memory or a story she'd been told, though she occasionally had nightmares about it.

The hull was full of stores. It was half as full as it had been when they had set out a few months before. The food they ate was far better than what she'd been given as a prisoner, but not as good as what she'd enjoyed in the Sanctuary. Tonight the meat they had eaten had been too salty and there had been only dried fruit and nuts to go with it. She found herself daydreaming of dried sea grass rolled around fresh crawler meat and smiled at herself for craving what she had once considered boring food.

A crewman was clearing away the plates and utensils now. Imi looked up to see Imenja unrolling a large map. She had seen it before many times, but it always intrigued her. It was the way the world looked to a Siyee, yet it was useful to landwalkers.

The captain unrolled his own maps, which were covered in lines that made no sense to Imi, and weighed them down with various objects. Lamps within the tent swung back and forth to the swaying of the ship, throwing moving shadows over everything. The captain pointed to a place on his map, then to one on Imenja's, and spoke.

Reivan glanced at Imi, then translated. "He says we're about here, far enough from shore that we can no longer see it from the mast."

"Could a boat be rowed to shore from here?" Imi asked the captain, with Reivan translating quietly.

"Yes, but it would take many hours. Worse if there are currents against us."

"What is the risk of being seen?"

"Always high during the day."

"And at night?" Reivan asked.

"The moon is near full," he reminded them. "We won't be able to see if there are any reefs closer to shore, either."

"You don't have to take me all the way in," Imi told him as soon as Reivan had finished translating. "I can swim some of the way."

They turned to regard her, each wearing a frown.

"Are you strong enough for that?" Reivan asked.

The captain said something in a warning voice.

"He says there might be sea predators. Spinerakes, which I think you call flarkes."

Imi felt a rush of fear, but she straightened her back. "The only really dangerous sea creatures are flarkes and they like smaller prey. They'll only attack people that are hurt, or if there's no other food. If the Siyee see you they'll try to kill you. That's more of a risk for you than this is for me."

As Reivan translated Imi's words, the captain smiled crookedly. He looked at Imi with what she thought might be admiration.

"We have to hope there are Siyee on shore to find," Reivan said.

"I only have to swim along it to find them. Getting back to you will be harder. How will I find you if the ship and the boat can't be seen from shore?"

Imenja and Reivan exchanged a glance.

"We must agree on a time and place," Reivan said. "We take Imi toward shore in the morning and pick her up at night."

"How will I find you in the dark?" Imi asked, shivering as she considered what it would be like swimming in darkness. "I'd rather swim during the daylight."

Imenja smiled. "Then we'll take you at dawn and pick you up in the late afternoon instead," she said. "If you don't find Siyee that day, we'll sail farther west the day after and try again."

Imi nodded. "That will work."

Reivan translated this for the captain, who nodded. He turned to a crewman waiting nearby and spoke. The man disappeared, then returned carrying a flask and some small, thick glasses. Imi struggled to stop herself grimacing. The drink served at the end of formal meals was too strong and sour for her, but she always made herself sip it for fear of causing offense. It did make her pleasantly sleepy, however, which was better than tossing and turning in the "tank" bed they had made for her in the hull. The tank kept her wet, but it wasn't easy to relax in water that constantly moved with the ship.

Tonight she probably would lie awake, despite the drink, thinking of the adventure ahead. Would there be any Siyee on shore? Would they help her?

*And what will we do if they don't know where Borra is?*

As Juran opened the door to his rooms, Dyara felt instantly on edge. Though he looked calm, there were lines on his face that only appeared when he was in great distress. He stepped aside and gestured for her to enter, saying nothing. Rian and Mairae were already there. Both looked bemused.

Sitting down, she waited as Juran paced the room slowly, clearly gathering his thoughts. She knew him better than the other White, but that was to be expected. They had worked together for seventy-six years. Every sign of his agitation worried her more, and it took all her self-control not to demand he hurry up and tell them what was bothering him.

"For the last few months Huan and I have been watching a . . . a certain individual," he began. "We have been waiting for a sign that our suspicions about him are right, or not. Tonight we found that they were."

"Who is this person?" Dyara asked.

Juran stopped pacing and looked at her. He took a deep breath and his expression hardened. "The man we have been watching is Mirar."

Dyara stared at Juran in disbelief. The room was silent for several heartbeats.

"He's dead," Rian stated.

Juran shook his head slowly. "He isn't. I do not know how it can be true, but it is."

"You're certain of this?" Dyara asked.

"We are now."

"But you found his body."

"We found a body that had been crushed. It was the right height, the hair coloring was correct, but nobody could have recognized his face. He wasn't seen leaving the collapsed house, and plenty were watching."

"But there was no way to prove the body belonged to Mirar," Dyara finished.

"No."

Mairae leaned forward in her seat. "How did you discover Mirar was alive?"

Juran sighed and moved to a chair. "I should explain how this all came about. Auraya discovered Mirar in Si a few months ago, though she didn't know it was him of course. He was treating the Siyee and—"

"Does she know who he is?" Dyara interrupted, alarmed. "Is she safe?"

Juran smiled. "She does not know, but she is safe enough. Chaia is watching over her."

"She thinks Mirar is an ordinary Dreamweaver," Rian guessed.

"Yes."

Dyara nodded to herself. *Of course.* Then a possibility occurred to her and she looked up at Juran, but his attention was on Rian.

"She asked him to teach her his method of healing," Juran continued. "At first Huan forbade it, but recently she decided it was a risk worth taking in order to confirm our suspicions. There was little dangerous information he might learn from Auraya's mind, but much for us to learn from his."

"Wait," Dyara interrupted. "Both Auraya and *Huan* can't read his mind?"

Juran grimaced. "No. It is shielded."

"No wonder you were suspicious of him," Mairae said.

"Yet you encouraged her to learn from him?" Dyara added.

Juran met her eyes and nodded. "We had to know if my suspicions were correct. Today Mirar agreed to teach her. Huan and I linked with Auraya through the lesson . . . though she was not aware of it."

Mairae drew in a quick breath. "Why didn't you tell her what you were doing?"

"To learn the healing Gift she needed to link with Mirar. If she had suspected who he was, or knew that Huan and I were watching, Mirar might have learned of it."

"If he could learn that from her, what else might he have learned?" Rian asked quietly.

"Nothing," Juran assured him. "We were ready to break the link, but it wasn't necessary. She kept her own mind well guarded. What Huan and I saw of his, however . . ." He shook his head. "While Auraya's attention was on what she was learning, Huan and I saw glimpses of Mirar's thoughts. At one point, while Auraya was distracted, he even considered what she would do if she learned he was really Mirar."

Dyara's mind was spinning with questions. *How has*

*Mirar survived? Will Juran have to kill him all over again? Or will the gods have mercy on him and send me or Rian to do it? Or Auraya, since she is in Si.*

Then she remembered the possibility that had occurred to her earlier. "Why would Mirar be teaching something like that to one of *us*? Why would he help or trust Auraya?"

Juran looked at her, the lines of sorrow deepening. "He knows her well and we know him. He is . . . he is Leiard."

The room fell into a stunned silence. Dyara nodded with a bitter satisfaction. She had guessed right.

"Leiard!" Mairae exclaimed. "How is that *possible*? We've all met him. We've all read his mind. How did we not discover his real identity?"

Juran spread his hands. "I don't know. If he can hide his mind from the gods, who knows what other Gifts he has? Perhaps he has gained the ability to hide his identity behind a false one."

"But you know what he looks like," Rian said. "Why didn't you recognize him?"

"He did not look as he did when I knew him." Juran sighed. "It has been a hundred years and my memory has faded." He moved to a table and picked up a sheet of parchment. "After Mirar's death nearly all of the statues or paintings of him were destroyed. I sent priests all around Northern Ithania to find what they could. This is a sketch of a carving found in the ruins of an old Dreamweaver house a few years ago."

He handed the sketch to Dyara. As she saw the face she drew in a quick breath. The face was smoother and fuller than Leiard's, and was beardless, but it was still recognizable. She handed the sketch to Rian, who scowled as he, too, identified the face.

Dyara leaned back in her chair and thought back to when Leiard had arrived in the city, and before. He had known Auraya as a child. He had sought her out once she became a White. She had made him Dreamweaver Adviser. As the implications of Mirar being in such a position of influence over Circlians occurred to her she groaned.

"How far back does it go?" she asked aloud. "Did he

know she would become a White? Was it a coincidence or did he arrange for her to come here, his unwitting tool?"

Juran turned to stare at Dyara. "Surely not."

"We must consider the possibility," she said.

"I doubt he arranged it that way," Rian said, "but when he heard what she had become he wouldn't have been able to resist the chance to meddle. He followed her here to gain her confidence and her trust."

"And her *bed*!" Dyara hissed. Anger filled her and she looked at Juran. "Truly he is the rogue you once knew. He used his influence over her to encourage acceptance of his people among Circlians." She felt a bitter thrill of triumph. "But he went too far. Taking her to bed was a mistake. After it was discovered he went to Si, knowing she would return there. Now he's seducing her all over again, using his magical knowledge as a lure." She looked at Juran. He shook his head in denial, but whether it was at Mirar's scheme or just the horror of the situation she couldn't guess.

He began to pace again. "What you say may be true, Dyara, but it may not be, either. When I confronted Leiard about his affair with Auraya I searched his mind and saw nothing to indicate he was Mirar, or any great plans of working against us. What I saw was a man in love with Auraya. A hopeless, fearful love, but a real one. He couldn't have invented that."

"And she loves him," Mairae murmured. "Or she did."

"What she loved was a lie," Rian pointed out.

"Then it is fortunate she doesn't love him any more," Dyara said. "Because she will have to kill him."

The room fell silent again. Mairae's eyes were wide with horror. She looked at Juran. "Surely not."

"She is in Si," Juran said wearily. "It would take months for any of us to reach him."

"You can't ask her to do that," Mairae insisted. "Even if she knows he is not the man she once loved, it is too cruel to make her kill him."

"When she learns who he is and how he has used her she will understand he cannot be allowed to live!" Rian said vehemently.

Dyara winced. She was inclined to agree with Mairae. "What do the gods want us to do?"

Juran smiled thinly. "They are deliberating."

"If they ask, I am willing to do the deed in her stead," Dyara said. "I agree with Mairae that it is a hard thing to ask of Auraya. There are other ways to do this. We may be able to use Auraya to lure him out of Si, for instance."

Juran nodded. "I will suggest that. Thank you."

The four of them fell silent then, all absorbed in this new revelation and its possible consequences. After a while Dyara stirred and looked around.

"We can only wait for the gods' decision. Let's return to our rooms and consult again tomorrow."

As she stood up, Mairae and Rian followed suit. They filed out of the room silently. At the doorway Dyara looked back. Juran smiled grimly. She felt a pang of sympathy for him as she stepped outside. He would get no sleep tonight. Truly his ghosts had come back to haunt him.

*He has never forgiven himself for killing Mirar,* she thought. *Now he knows he's been feeling guilty for a hundred years for something he never did.*

# 36

It had been many centuries since Emerahl had sailed up the Gulf of Sorrow. Sennon, with its deserts and drab towns, didn't appeal to her. In her long life she had never left the continent of Northern Ithania except to visit the island nation of Somrey, which nowdays was considered part of Northern Ithania anyway.

If she had been sailing along the middle of the gulf, and the air had been less hazy, she might have been able to see both Northern and Southern Ithania at once, but the need to stop for supplies from time to time kept her close to the Sennon coast. She could have tried to buy food in Avven but she didn't know what sort of reception she would receive on the southern continent, and knowing nothing of the local language would make trade difficult. Sennon, on the other hand, had barely changed from what she remembered. Even the language hadn't altered that much in the few hundred years since she had last visited.

The horizon in every direction was hazy with dust, blown up by the wind that drove her boat east. Ahead was the Isthmus of Grya, a strip of land that divided the Gulf of Sorrow from the Gulf of Fire. A city, Diamyane, lay at the point where the Isthmus joined Sennon. There her sea journey would end.

She chewed her lip and patted the tiller. The little boat had taken her a long way in the last few months. It had weathered more than a few storms as well as the unusual strain of being lent speed by the occasional push of magic.

She was going to miss it. The only way to get a boat past the Isthmus was to pay someone to haul it across, and she doubted she had enough money for that. Once she sold her boat, she could join a trader caravan travelling east, or, if she could afford it, buy passage on a ship.

Pushing aside regret, she reminded herself that she had made this decision months ago and there was no point changing her mind. She could have sailed right around Southern Ithania, but that would have added months to the journey. She might also have sailed around the top of Northern Ithania, but that would have taken her past Jarime and she would prefer not to travel past a country the White ruled.

Mirar had warned her in a dream link that the Siyee were watching their coastline closely after the Pentadrians had landed and been sent away again months before. He had also warned her that Auraya was in Si. Passing by one White was better than passing by four, Emerahl had reasoned. She had taken plenty of supplies so she could avoid landing in Si. No flying white-clad sorceress had come to visit her, and the winds had been in her favor most of the way. Until now she hadn't had reason to regret her choice.

Unnaturally regular shapes began to appear in the dusty haze ahead. As they emerged they revealed themselves to be buildings. Emerahl directed her vessel toward them. She did not hurry, prolonging the moment she had to give up the boat. All too soon she was drifting up to a mooring and tossing rope to the dock boys, who pulled her boat in close and bound it to the bollards with practiced speed. She climbed up onto dry land, dropped coins into their hands and asked where the boat haulers were.

They had set up a shop by the docks. As she walked in she sensed the hauler's mood change to gleeful greed. Over several cups of a hot, bitter local beverage she convinced them that a woman could barter as well as a man, but while her senses told her she had forced them down to a reasonable price, it was still too high.

Next she sought a buyer for her boat and discovered that craft as small as hers weren't in demand. The main use for boats here was to transport goods, and hers was too small

for that. One man was prepared to pay her a paltry amount
for the craft, however. She arranged to meet him later in the
day so he could inspect the boat.

Hours had passed. She sought the local market to exchange some money for the local coin, the canar. There
she bought food and a measure of kahr, the local liquor,
then half-heartedly tried to sell her services as a healer.
Several healers already working the market regarded her
with hostile stares. She knew she would not be able to stay
here untroubled for long. In Sennon all were free to live as
they wished and worship who or what they wanted so long
as they did not break any of the essential laws of the country. On her way to the market she had seen a Dreamweaver
House and plenty of Dreamweavers. In Toren people had
approached her for help; here they ignored her, clearly satisfied with the amount of local healing available.

*So I must get their attention with better or less common
products,* she told herself.

"Cures for infertility," she called to the crowd. "Removal
of scars. Aphrodisiacs."

A man and a woman turned to look at her. The woman
carried a baby and the man was holding the hand of a small
boy. They exchanged a glance and hurried toward her. Emerahl wondered which of the three services they wanted.
They didn't appear to need fertility treatment. They might
want aphrodisiacs, but scar removal was just as likely.

"Are you Emmea, the healer who wishes to sell a boat?"
the man asked, using the name she'd given the boat haulers.
She had stopped using the name 'Limma' once she reached
Sennon. Using a different name when she was on the other
side of the continent made her less traceable.

Emerahl blinked in surprise, then nodded. "Yes. Do you
wish to buy one?"

"No," the man replied. "Let me introduce myself. I am
Tarsheni Drayli and this is my wife Shalina. We wish to buy
passage for us and our children."

Disappointment followed his words. "Oh. I can't help
you. I'm not going west."

The man smiled. "We do not wish to go west. We want to go east."

"I still can't help you," she told them apologetically. "I can't afford haulage."

"Ah, but you do not have to buy haulage," he told her. "There is a small tunnel through the Isthmus. It was opened a few years ago. Only small boats can go through. The fee is much less than haulage."

"Is that so?" Nobody had told her about this tunnel, but it was not surprising that haulage sellers would neglect to tell her of it. "How much does it cost?"

"Twelve canar per boat," the man said.

Emerahl nodded. She sensed no dishonesty from him. Twelve canar was still too much, however. She could manage it, but would have no money left to buy food—unless she did take these people east. She silently cursed herself for not pricing passage on a ship. She had no idea how much to charge these people.

"My offer is this," the man said, forestalling her. "We will pay the fee to go through the tunnel. In return you will take us east to Karienne."

Emerahl smiled. "That's reasonable. Passage on a ship will cost a lot more than twelve canar."

He nodded and she detected no emotions associated with deception from him—just hope.

She pursed her lips as she considered the deal. The man, Tarsheni, regarded her patiently.

"You must bring your own food and water. I have no money to pay for your basic necessities," she warned.

"We will, of course," Tarsheni replied.

"And while I don't believe you have any plans of stealing my boat from me, I should warn you against coming up with any such ideas in the future. My Gifts are not inconsiderable."

Tarsheni smiled. "You have nothing to fear from us."

Emerahl nodded. "Likewise. I have one more question. What is the reason for this journey?"

The couple exchanged a glance and Emerahl sensed apprehension. She crossed her arms and stared at them expectantly. The man's shoulders slumped.

"You may find this foolish," he said. "We have heard of a man in Karienne who knows wise and wondrous things. We are travelling there to hear him speak."

Emerahl sensed no dishonesty, but guessed they were withholding something.

"What is so special about this man?" she asked.

"He . . ." Tarsheni began.

"Are you Circlian?" his wife asked.

Emerahl regarded the woman—Shalina—with cautious surprise.

"No," Emerahl admitted, hoping she had not just lost herself the deal.

"You're not Pentadrian," Shalina said, her shrewd eyes glittering. "Are you a heathen or a non-believer?"

Emerahl held the woman's gaze. "Does this man you want to see follow one of the dead gods?"

Shalina shook her head.

"He says the gods were created by a greater being," Tarsheni said. "Maybe he is wrong. That is what we are going there to find out."

"I see," Emerahl said. "What an interesting idea," she added, genuinely intrigued. If the idea became popular, it might be the first new religion to manifest in millennia, if she did not count her own long-dead unscrupulous and unwanted Followers of The Hag.

"So," she said, bringing her attention back to the family, "when do you want to leave?"

The couple grinned broadly.

"We have only to pay the boarding house and fetch our belongings," Tarsheni told her. "And buy some food. How much should we purchase?"

Emerahl smiled. They were young and inexperienced travellers who were probably used to living comfortably. They would probably find the journey rough going. She had better make sure they were well-prepared.

"Take enough to last a few days—you can never be sure how long it will take to get to the next village. Take nothing perishable and make sure everything is well wrapped. It can be hot out on the sea and everything will get wet if a storm blows in. Have you got any oilskins? No? You had better take me back to the boarding house with you. I'll look over what you're bringing and tell you how to pack it. And you'll need something for seasickness . . ."

Feeling more cheerful than she had all day, Emerahl led the family out of the market. She didn't have to give up her boat, and she might even make a profit out of transporting this family to Karienne.

Six more Siyee were sick from Hearteater at Temple Mountain by the time Auraya returned, and another two Siyee had reported members of their families sickening since then. Auraya had used her new healing Gift many times already, but the Temple Mountain Siyee were less willing and able to keep separate from each other. There were already signs of re-infection.

At the same time, news had come of sick Siyee in tribes that had escaped the disease so far. She was all too aware that her efforts would be more effective in tribes that were less crowded and more cooperative, but she was determined to leave the Temple Mountain tribe in a better state than at present.

"This disease is determined to test every one of us," Speaker Ryliss said resignedly as he topped up the oil heater.

"It will, if given the freedom to spread," Auraya agreed.

"How can we stop it?"

"Send everyone who has recovered from the disease away."

He frowned. "You said people could not catch the disease from those who had fully recovered from it. I'd be sending away people who are of no risk to others here."

"Yet they take up too much space, preventing us from properly isolating the sick. If you sent away those who have not been ill, you risk that some of them may be sick and not showing symptoms yet."

"But sending people away . . . is that necessary?"

"Your village is overcrowded," she told him, not for the first time.

"No more than others, surely."

"Most villages have reduced in size in the last year, having lost members in the war. Many of the Siyee here have moved to this tribe recently, haven't they?"

Ryliss nodded. "Yes. They came here to learn about and serve the gods."

She looked up at him in surprise. "Why didn't they go to the priests in the Open?"

He shrugged. "They came here before the priests arrived. And . . . not meaning to give offense, but some Siyee feel they should learn Siyee ways of worshipping from other Siyee."

She smiled. "I can understand that. Would it help if priests came here? Would the Watchers be willing to teach alongside landwalkers?"

"I will ask them."

"Thank you." Moving away from one patient, Auraya approached the next. "These newcomers are young and strong. Their bodies are fighting the disease." She straightened and met his gaze. "So will you send some of the people here away?"

His face wrinkled with reluctance, but Auraya did not hear his answer. Another voice filled her mind.

*:Auraya. Come to the Temple.*

As abruptly as it had arrived, Huan's presence flashed away. Ryliss was still talking. Still making excuses, she noted.

"I'm sorry, Speaker," she interrupted. "I must leave you now. I have been summoned by Huan."

His eyes widened. "Best not keep her waiting."

"No." She strode out of the room and into a corridor. The cave system was shallow, and she reached an opening to the air in a few moments. She glanced upward, making sure no other Siyee was about to leap from an opening in the cliff face above and collide with her, then concentrated on her sense of the world and propelled herself toward the closest mountains.

Wind buffeted her face, cool and pleasant. As she drew

closer she was able to make out the Temple. Though she had seen it several times now, she always felt wonder at the sight of the small structure carved out of the mountain peak. How it had been made was a mystery. Ryliss had told her it was far older than the Siyee race. Whoever had made it must have been either a talented climber or capable of flight. Why they had done it was an even greater mystery.

Five columns supported a domed roof. Auraya landed in the center of the circular floor. She took a deep breath and looked around, her heart beating quickly with anticipation. Though she had grown used to Chaia's company, the prospect of being in the presence of the other gods was still both thrilling and daunting.

*:Huan, I am here,* she called.

Auraya concentrated on her sense of the magic around her. She felt a presence approaching at a rapid speed. The magic in the world roiled in its wake and she had to resist an instinctive urge to back away. It stopped abruptly just a few steps from her and the air about it began to glow. The light formed the figure of a woman, her expression stern. Auraya prostrated herself.

*:Rise, Auraya,* Huan said. *We have a task for you.*

"What must I do?" Auraya rose to face the goddess.

*:We have discovered a great mistake, made long ago. You must correct it—but be warned: it will not be easy or pleasant. We have discovered that an enemy we believed long dead is alive. Not only does he still live, but he has been meddling in the affairs of the world.*

Auraya's heart skipped as she realized who this enemy must be. "Kuar! But how did he survive? How am I to defeat him?"

*:It is not Kuar. If Kuar had survived we would not set you against him. He was more powerful than you. This is a lesser enemy and an older one. Juran was the last to face him. His name is Mirar.*

Auraya stared at Huan in astonishment.

"Mirar? How can this be?" Then she realized what the gods wanted her to do and felt her heart sink. *Oh, Leiard. Will you ever forgive me?*

*:He won't,* Huan told her. *Leiard is Mirar.*

"*Leiard?*" Auraya exclaimed. For a moment she could not think. Then she laughed in disbelief. "That can't be. I've seen his mind. Well, I did before he—"

*:Mirar is Leiard. He deceived us. He deceived the White and, worst of all, he tricked and used you. We are not sure how he managed to hide behind the persona of Leiard, but we* are *certain of his true identity. When you linked with him to learn his healing Gift, I saw the truth.*

"You were there . . . ?"

*:Yes.*

Auraya shook her head in disbelief. She had caught glimpses of Leiard's thoughts during the link. None of what she had seen had revealed anything but healing knowledge.

*:While you were distracted he let his guard down, believing he was safe.*

She searched her memories of Leiard. First she recalled him as he had been when he had lived in the forest near her village, teaching her about cures and the world. Had there been any sign that he was really Mirar? She couldn't recall any.

Next she considered the man who had been her adviser in Jarime. He had been so uncomfortable in the Temple. She had assumed any Dreamweaver would be. Was his fear of all things Circlian an indication of his true identity? He had overcome that fear and become Dreamweaver Adviser. It hadn't been his idea, however; it had been hers. Dreamweavers had benefited from his work, but there was nothing unusual or wrong in that. Any Dreamweaver would have aimed to do the same.

Unless he had somehow used his position to gain other advantages without her knowledge . . .

*:You are not seeing the depth of his deception, Auraya. Leiard does not exist. He never did. The man you knew was an invention designed to manipulate you.*

Auraya frowned. She was looking for something unusual in *Leiard's* behavior. She should consider what *Mirar's* behavior had been. If he had set out to deceive her by inventing Leiard, he had succeeded. He had gained her friendship and trust, then her love. She thought of the dream links, the declarations of love, the promises. None of it had been real. She shivered. She had . . . done things with a man she didn't really know, whose intentions couldn't have been good for her, the gods or Circlians.

*What was Mirar's real intention, then? Did Juran ruin his plans by discovering our affair and sending him away? Did Mirar come to Si hoping to encounter me and resume our affair?*

As the possibilities occurred to her she felt a rising anger. *I was willing to risk so much for Leiard! But I saw that he had changed,* she realized. *When we linked so he could teach me, I sensed a difference. What did he say again? "I am not the person I was."*

*:Now you do see the truth,* Huan said. *It will cause you pain. We wish that it were not so. Better that this mistake had never been made. Hold on to your anger. You will need it to do what must be done. The other White are too far away to act. You are close, and have the advantage of surprise. He will not expect you to be the one to execute him.*

"Execute him?" Auraya went cold to the bone.

*:Yes. You hesitate to kill. That is good; we would be disappointed in you if you did not. But he must die—properly this time. I will guide you.*

"When?"

*:Now.*

"But the Siyee . . . ?"

*:It will not take you long, Auraya.*

"Oh." She felt strangely disoriented. *I'm not going to have time to get used to this, am I? I'll have to sort out what it all means afterward.*

*:Yes. You must not let anything distract you,* Huan warned. *He is strong. It will be difficult. He will try to manipulate you. He will try everything to stop you.*

*Of course he will,* she thought. *I doubt he wants to die.*

*:I will guide you. Go, Auraya. Find him.*

# 37

The breath of the rowers misted in the air, yet Imi was warm. She had wondered at first why Imenja was not heating the air around the crew with her magic, but then as she noticed sweat glistening on their brows she realized that they were hot enough already from their exertions. If they'd been inside Imenja's area of warmth they'd have been uncomfortable.

Clouds were visible at the horizon to one side. They muted the light of the coming dawn. The sea, the boat, even the tanned faces of the rowers were an unhealthy gray. All color seemed to have been leeched from the world.

The coast was a dark mountainous line emerging from the night sky, separated from the dark water by a band of pale sand. Imenja turned to Imi. Her eyes were steady and she did not smile as she placed a hand on Imi's shoulder.

"This is as far as we can come without risking being seen," she said. "Are we close enough to shore?"

Imi nodded. "I think so."

"Don't take unnecessary risks."

"I won't."

"We'll return here this afternoon. Good luck."

Imi smiled. "I'll see you then."

She moved to the side of the boat. It was rocking too much with the waves for her to leap off into the water safely. She decided the best way to get into the water would be to sit on the edge, move her legs over, then drop from there when the boat tipped her way.

It worked well enough, though it was hardly an elegant exit for a princess. The water was deliciously cold. Taking a deep breath, she dove under the surface and started swimming toward the coast.

The distance had looked small from the boat but it took longer than she expected to get to shore. The water was murky and the pre-dawn light was still too faint to reveal much below the surface anyway. Imi had rarely been in such an open place, and never alone. She could easily imagine something emerging from the gloom around her. Something large and ponderous. Or maybe something smaller and quicker like a flarke, seen only a moment before it attacked.

She felt on the brink of a shiver, like the feeling that she had sometimes when she felt she would sneeze soon, but never did.

Suddenly the water lightened. She surfaced, expecting to find the sun had risen, but nothing had changed. The beach lay ahead, now forming an arc around a shallow bay. Looking down again, she realized that she could see the pale sea floor beneath her. She swam on.

Soon the water around her began to push and pull. It roiled above her, curling and twisting. She had heard of surf before, but had never tried to swim in it. A water dancer had told her about it once. He'd said you could ride the waves, if you knew how. Swimming up one of them, she sought the right part to ride. She knew she had found it when she felt the force of the wave catch and propel her forward.

The wave's rush was exhilarating and ended too soon. She found sand under her feet and stood up. Looking back, she considered swimming out to ride another wave.

*No, I must start looking for Siyee. I don't know how long it will take to find them.*

Wading out of the water, she continued up the sand to where the grasses began. The sun finally emerged in the gap between cloud and horizon, bathing all in golden light. She climbed a dune and found more dunes beyond, stretching out as far as she could see.

The Elai traders who had told her stories about the Siyee

had said the winged people lived in strange houses that
looked like half-buried bubbles. She doubted those traders
would have travelled far from the water for fear of drying
out, so she was hoping the Siyee houses would be visible from the beach. She began walking along the shore,
following the wide arc of the bay to a rocky point, then
around to a larger bay. After a while she grew thirsty and
drank from the flask Imenja had given her. Though the sun
was covered by cloud and the air filled with mist from the
surf, Imi eventually felt her skin becoming uncomfortably
dry. She returned to the water and swam parallel to the
beach.

*I could walk for hours before finding any Siyee,* she
thought. *Maybe I should swim instead, stopping in the
middle of every bay to look for Siyee. That way I won't dry
out and I can ride the waves in each time.*

For the next few hours she swam along the coast. Gradually the spit of land between each bay became rockier. She
gave the water around these points a wide berth. Seeing the
waves crashing against the rocks, she knew if she swam too
close they might throw her against the rocks as well.

Otherwise, there was little variation between one bay
and the next. The clouds kept a jealous veil over the sun,
but she felt the day growing older. Stopping to survey yet
another stretch of grassy dunes, she sighed and shook her
head.

*I'm going to have to turn around soon or it'll be dark
before I get back to the place Imenja left me.* She frowned,
then felt a stab of panic. *How am I going to recognize the
bay?*

The wind whistled and fluttered around her. She looked
up . . . and jumped as she saw the figures circling above.

*Siyee!*

They looked just as the traders had described them.
Though small, she could tell these two were adult men.
One had gray hair while the other was younger. She felt her
heart lift and waved her hands in what she hoped they'd interpret as a friendly, beckoning gesture.

The two Siyee circled lower and landed in a spray of

sand. They straightened and regarded her with both caution and curiosity.

"Greetings, sea lady," the older of the Siyee said slowly in the Elai tongue. "I am Tyrli, Speaker of the Sand tribe. My companion is my grandson, Riz."

"Greetings, people of the sky," she replied. "Please forgive me for trespassing uninvited in your land. I am Yli, daughter of hunter Sei."

Imenja had warned her against telling the Siyee she was a princess. They wouldn't want to let her go home alone. If she couldn't go back to the ship she would have to wait until the next group of Elai traders arrived. She might have to anyway, if the Siyee could not tell her where Borra was, but it would be so much nicer if her father had a chance to meet Imenja and Reivan.

The man smiled. "You are forgiven, sea lady. May I ask you why you are here alone?"

She bowed her head. "I am lost," she admitted. "It is my own fault. I slipped away when my elders were not looking. Raiders caught me, but I escaped. Now I find I do not know the way home. I've never travelled this far before. I hoped to find Siyee who could tell me." It was the truth—or close enough. She saw sympathy in the Siyee's faces.

"You are lucky," Tyrli said. "Lucky the raiders didn't kill you and lucky you escaped."

"The White should do something about them," the young man said, scowling.

"You are also lucky to find us," Tyrli continued. "We are a few hours' flight from our village, patrolling the coast for Pentadrian invaders. It would have taken you days to reach our tribe."

"Do you know where Borra is?"

"I can give you rough directions."

She sighed with relief. "Then I am lucky indeed."

He chuckled. "You must be tired and hungry. We have made camp not far from here. Come and eat with us. You can rest in safety tonight and begin your journey home tomorrow."

"I'd love to but I have to get back to—" She stopped as

she realized she could not tell him she needed to return to meet Imenja. She could think of no good reason why she must swim back along the coast again.

He smiled at her warmly. "You're anxious to get home. I understand that, but your home is still many days' swim from here and it will be dark soon. Stay with us tonight."

Perhaps she could slip away after they told her where her home was. Forcing a smile onto her face, Imi nodded. "Yes. I will. Thank you."

He gestured for her to walk beside him along the beach. Glancing out to sea, she fought a rising panic.

*Imenja is going to be so worried when I don't return to the boat, but what can I do? If I press Tyrli to give me directions now he might get suspicious.* She chewed on her lip. *But if I don't meet Imenja, she might come to shore to look for me.*

Tyrli patted her on the arm. "Don't worry," he assured her. "We'll help you get home."

As Auraya neared the Blue Lake tribe's village she slowed and felt her anger fade a little. Siyee were everywhere—in the village, fields, and, of course, the bowers where the sick were treated. It was too easy to imagine how confused and frightened they'd be if they saw her attack the Dreamweaver who was helping them.

*:Huan,* she said. The goddess had remained close, though silent.

*:I am here,* the goddess replied. *Ah, I see your concern. It would be better to avoid disturbing the Siyee. Find a way to lure Mirar away from the village.*

Auraya's relief was short-lived. He would not leave the sick Siyee and the village unless she gave him reason to. If she faced him he might somehow detect that something was wrong. Could she ask someone else to take him a message? What should it say?

*Only that I want to meet him privately,* she thought. She felt ill as she realized he might interpret that as an invitation to resume their affair. *It seems unfair, but so was deceiving me into believing he was someone else*. At that thought, anger flared again.

Concentrating on the minds below, she located Speaker Dylli inside his bower. She dropped to the ground beside the entrance.

"Speaker Dylli," she called.

"Auraya of the White?" he responded. She heard him coming to the door.

"Yes," she replied. As the hanging door opened, she smiled. "Could you have a message delivered to Wilar for me?"

He nodded. "Of course, but I cannot tell you when it will reach him. He left a few days ago to gather ingredients for his cures. Tyve is here. Can he help you?"

"No."

*Mirar has gone*. She felt a rush of emotion and found that it was relief. *I don't want to kill him*, she realized. *Even though he deserves it. I just don't like having to kill. Maybe I won't have to. He'll slip out of Si and it will be up to Juran to hunt him down*. But as soon as the thought came she knew she would not avoid the task so easily. "Do you know where he was heading?" she made herself ask Dylli.

He shook his head.

Auraya nodded. "He can't have gone far. I will just have to fly around until I find him."

The Speaker smiled. "Good luck, Auraya of the White."

"Thank you."

She propelled herself straight up into the sky and considered the village and surrounding lakes and forest. When the Siyee searched for animals to hunt they often flew in ever widening circles. She would try this, at the same time searching the thoughts of anyone who might have seen, or be watching, Mirar.

Searching gave her time to think. She considered everything Huan had told her. The goddess had detected Mirar through Auraya's link with him. *Strange that she didn't tell me at the time*, she thought. *It's also a little strange that Chaia hasn't spoken of it. Perhaps he doesn't want to sour*

*our relationship by making it obvious that he wants me to
kill my former lover.*

She considered her reluctance to kill Mirar. *It is because
I haven't fully comprehended that he is not Leiard,* she told
herself. *It is all too incredible. I don't have time to sit and
think about it, however. I must trust that what Huan tells me
is true. Perhaps it would be easier if I knew why Mirar did
it,* she thought. *I wonder if I can trick him into revealing his
plans to me.*

*:You would be unwise to believe anything he told you,*
Huan warned. *A true villain does not gloat about his
achievements or plans except to deceive. Accept that some
questions will remain unanswered.*

Auraya sighed. *Why me?* she found herself asking. *Why
did he target me? He would never have deceived the other
White so easily. I am a fool!*

*:No, Auraya. We do not choose fools to be our represen-
tatives. If we could not see through the deception, we could
hardly expect you to. That is why he must die. His abilities
and his hatred of us make him dangerous to mortals.*

Auraya winced. His abilities included an extraordinary
healing Gift—a Gift he had taught to her, that had saved
many hundreds of Siyee. Why would he do that? Was
there a hidden trap in it that might cause her or her patients
harm? Teaching her had led to his discovery. Had he known
this was a risk?

A movement caught her eye below the foliage of the tall
trees. She slowed and felt a chill run over her skin as she
caught a glimpse of a Dreamweaver robe. Mirar was following a stream that flowed down a narrow ravine, carrying
his bag and a heavy coil of rope.

Suddenly her heart was racing.

*:Don't be afraid,* Huan told her. *We made you strong
enough to defeat Wilds.*

*:I do not doubt that,* Auraya replied.

*:Yet you fear. He can only harm you with words. Hold
in your mind the knowledge of his deceit. Silence his lies
forever.*

Taking a deep breath, Auraya drew up all her anger and

determination. *He is not Leiard; he is Mirar.* Then another thought shot through her mind. *The Dreamweavers don't deserve to have their future and reputation ruined by this man.*

Auraya dropped down through the trees. She landed a few paces in front of him. As he looked up at her his eyes widened in surprise.

"Auraya," he said.

Then he smiled. It was such an easy, familiar smile. From somewhere deep rose all the indignation and anger she ought to have been feeling. She embraced it and felt it strengthen her resolve.

"Mirar," she replied coolly.

At the look of realization in his eyes she felt all lingering hope that Huan was wrong die. His smile faded. They stared at each other for a long moment.

"So you know," he said.

"Yes. You're not denying it."

"Would it do me any good?"

"No. Huan saw who you were during your healing lesson."

"Oh." He grimaced.

Suddenly she felt empty. She had hoped the gods were mistaken, that Leiard would come up with a plausible explanation and prove that he was not Mirar. But he had all but admitted it. He was not Leiard. The person she had loved had only existed as an illusion, a lie.

To her surprise the realization brought a wave of relief. She did not know this man. He was only the trickster sorcerer of legend, a man the world was once rid of and should be again.

*I can kill him,* she told herself. But instead of gathering magic to strike, she found herself blurting out a question.

"Why did you do it?"

His chin lifted. "You wouldn't believe me if I told you."

The challenge in his eyes sent a chill of warning down her spine. "No, because there is no way I can know if anything you say is true."

*Huan is right. My questions can only remain unan-*

*swered*. Suddenly she wanted only to get it done and over with.

*:Good,* Huan said. *Further talk will only leave you vulnerable to trickery. Attack him now.*

Auraya looked down as she drew magic to herself. As she did she considered how she should attack. He would have created a shield, but it might not be strong enough for an attack of great power. If he wasn't able to strengthen his shield in time it could be all over in moments. She heard him take a few footsteps closer to her.

"There is a way you can know—" he began.

Without looking up, she let loose a bolt of power. He gave a yelp of surprise and staggered backward. His shield held.

"Wait . . ." he exclaimed, catching his balance. "Auraya!"

She attacked again. Though she now knew who he really was, she could not help feeling surprise at his strength. She had known Leiard was powerful, but not *this* powerful.

"What of your promise?" he half-shouted at her. "You said I would not be harmed. You swore on the gods!"

She paused, then battered him with magic again.

"I swore that Leiard would not be harmed. You are not Leiard."

He wasn't fighting back. *He must know he has no chance of winning,* she thought. *I have only to increase the strength of my attack until it overwhelms him.* As she drew in more magic his expression changed to one of determination and she braced herself for a counter attack.

"But I *am* Leiard," he said quietly. "It is time you knew the truth."

Where there had been nothing suddenly there was a mind. She saw a flood of memories and images and felt intentions and emotions.

*:No!* Huan hissed. *Don't look!*

It was too late. The answers to all Auraya's questions were there for her to see. Mirar's mental voice spoke to her and she could not stop herself listening.

*:This is how I died . . .*

She saw Juran fighting and felt Mirar's disbelief and betrayal as his strength failed. He reviewed all he had done and could not see how any of it justified his execution. His only crime had been to annoy the gods. Nobody had died. Nobody had been harmed. He'd only encouraged people to question and offered them a choice. And in return . . .

She saw a great explosion of dust and stone and felt an echo of the agony of being crushed. She understood that Mirar had reached out for enough magic to sustain a fragment of himself, and how he had evaded the gods and Juran by suppressing his personality and creating another to replace it.

*:This is what I became.*

Not the man she had known as Leiard. Not at first. His body twisted and scarred, his memory gone, he had roamed the world a miserable cripple. Only after many years did his body recover. Only when he came to Jarime and became Dreamweaver Adviser did his true identity begin to stir.

*:This is why I remembered.*

His disguise had unravelled because of her. His instincts, created when he'd made Leiard, told him to stay away from Jarime, but the desire to stay near her was stronger. She felt her heart twist. Leiard *had* loved her. She had not been deceived. But Leiard was not real.

*:He is. This is what I have become.*

She saw what she had only glimpsed before. The link memories of Mirar were his real self returning, but Leiard had spent a century becoming a real person. After the battle he had travelled to Si with a friend. Glimpsing this beautiful young woman, Auraya felt a stab of jealousy. *Who is she?* The friend had helped him realize that Leiard could not be anything that Mirar was not capable of being. Accepting that if Leiard loved Auraya then he must too had been the moment he had become whole again. Knowing he could not be with her hurt, but so did the thought that he might cause her trouble, so he intended to leave Northern Ithania when the Siyee had recovered and to take himself far away.

*:I am Leiard,* Mirar said. *I am also Mirar. Neither of us are the same as we once were. But what we—*

*:No!* Auraya started as Huan's voice drowned out Mirar's. A glowing figure flared into existence beside her. *Whatever you have been this last century, you are no less guilty of the crimes you committed.*

*:What crimes?* he asked defiantly. *Being annoying? Giving people an option other than worshipping you blindly? Telling them the truth about your past? You and your companions are guilty of far worse crimes than I.*

Auraya frowned as she glimpsed terrible memories in Mirar's mind. He glanced at her as he pushed them aside.

*:I would show you,* he said, *but to do so would cause you great pain.*

Yet from what she had seen she knew that he believed the gods were capable of cruelty and injustice. He also believed he had done nothing to deserve death.

She also knew he had done nothing to her or the White out of spite or malicious intent. He had been bumbling about, struggling with the return of his true identity, and getting himself into strife.

*:Auraya.*

She turned to the goddess, numb from shock at all she had learned.

*:Is it a crime to deny a soul immortality? Mirar claims he offered mortals a choice, but he cannot offer them an existence after death. To lure a mortal away from us is to cheat them of eternity. You know this.*

Mirar shook his head.

*:Some would prefer that, rather than an eternity chained to your side. I might not be able to preserve their souls, but I also cannot use that end as a reward or punishment. Perhaps I should show Auraya some of the things you have done—*

*:Things I did in the distant past. The Age of the Many ended long ago,* Huan declared, her head high. *The excesses of that time are forgotten. Even you must acknowledge that we, the Circle, have created a peaceful, prosperous world in the last century.*

Mirar paused.

*:You have,* he admitted. *But if your past can be forgotten, then why not mine?*

Auraya felt a smile pulling at her lips. He had a point.

Then the glowing figure that was Huan suddenly flared brightly.

*:Because you continue to work against us, immortal. See, Auraya, how he turns our words against us!* She turned and walked toward Auraya. *He has befuddled you with twisted truths and hidden lies. Give over your will to me.*

Auraya's heart stopped. Give over her will ... Huan meant to possess her? She took a step back as the goddess drew close. Instead of colliding with her, the glowing figure passed through her. She found herself surrounded by light.

*:Give over your will,* Huan commanded.

Mirar was staring at her. Different expressions crossed his face: first horror, then fear, then resignation.

*:I must do as she says,* she told herself. *I must.*

It would be so easy to just give over the responsibility for Mirar's death to the goddess. It wouldn't matter that killing him was ... was ...

Unjust. Unfair. He had done things she did not approve of, but nothing deserving of death. Circlians did not execute people without good cause—at least not the law-abiding ones. There were alternative punishments for minor crimes. Imprisonment. Exile.

*:Obey me, Auraya.*

She put her hands to her face and groaned.

*:I can't. This goes against the laws that* you *laid down, and that you gave us the responsibility to uphold and refine. Killing without just cause is murder. I can't kill Mirar. I can't allow him to be murdered.*

She waited for Huan's reply, but none came.

"Auraya?"

Taking her hands from her face, she looked at the man standing before her. Whether Leiard or Mirar, he had brought her more trouble than anything else in the world. She wanted him gone. "Go," she found herself saying. "Leave Northern Ithania before I change my mind—and never come back."

*:Auraya!* Huan's voice boomed. *Do not defy me!*

As Mirar hurried away, his boots splashing in the stream,

she felt her knees weaken. She sank to the ground, feeling ill and desolate and yet also a bitter and disturbing satisfaction.

*If I just made the right just choice, then why do I feel so bad?* She shook her head. *Because I just disobeyed one of the gods and for a moment there I was proud of it.*

*And Huan can't have failed to notice.*

## 38

The Drayli family had so much luggage with them that Emerahl suspected they'd brought every possession they owned apart from their home. They had been dismayed to learn they would have to sell or throw away at least half of it.

"My boat is small," she had reminded them. "Not only will there be no room for you if we pack all this in, she'll probably lie so low in the water that the slightest wave will flood the boat, and you'll lose everything. Can you swim? I hadn't thought to ask until now."

Shalina had turned white, which told Emerahl her question had had the desired effect.

"They are only things," Tarsheni said quietly to his wife. "Possessions. We can't let mere objects get in the way of our search for the true deity."

The sorting out of their belongings had taken a frustratingly long time, then Emerahl had to accompany the family to the market to watch over the selling of them. Their friendly innocence and generosity made up for their expectation that she would help them in all matters. When the afternoon grew old, Tarsheni had insisted he pay for a meal and a room for her at the boarding house. They did not want to search for the tunnel in the dark, concerned that their children would be frightened.

Now, as she watched them climb tentatively into her boat, she found herself worrying how they would cope with a sea journey. She sensed determination and excitement from both adults and curiosity from their son. The baby was blissfully unaware of the adventure his family was undertaking. They gazed at the other water craft as Emerahl guided her boat out of the docks.

Leaning forward, she gave Shalina a small bottle.

"What is this?" the woman asked.

"It is for seasickness," Emerahl told her. "Take one capful each and a third for the boy. Give the babe a drop mixed with some water and let me know if she starts to redden."

"I don't feel sick at all," Tarsheni said. "I don't think I'll need it."

"You will when we get out into the waves. The cure takes some time to work and isn't as effective after you get sick, so best take it now."

They did as she said. Once free of the docks, Emerahl directed the boat in line with the Isthmus. The boy began asking his parents a flood of questions about sea-related matters. Emerahl resisted smiling at some of their answers.

"How are you moving us?" Tarsheni said suddenly. "The sail is down and you're not rowing."

"Magic," Emerahl told him.

His eyebrows rose. "A useful Gift for a sailor."

She laughed. "Yes. One tends to learn and practice what is useful to one's trade. Do you have any Gifts?"

He shrugged. "A few. I am a scribe, as all my ancestors were. We pass down Gifts used for preparing parchment and ink, sharpening tools, and to defend ourselves."

"Defend yourself?"

"Sometimes the letters we deliver are not well-received, even if we did not dictate them."

Emerahl chuckled. "Yes, I imagine that would happen occasionally."

"I hope to write down the words of the wise man of Karienne."

"You seem to know a lot about him already," she said. His quiet enthusiasm had impressed many at the boarding house the previous night. Emerahl had almost expected to find a string of boats following her to the tunnel today.

"Only what I have been told by others who have listened to him," he admitted. "Sometimes what is said is contradictory. If his words are written down, none can alter his meaning."

"In theory. Others might alter your work later."

He sighed and nodded. "That is possible. If there were a Gift I could use to prevent it, I would dedicate my life to learning it."

"You said last night that this god created the world, the gods, all creatures and every person. If it created humans, and they are capable of cruelty and murder, then it must either have intended that to be so, or made a mistake."

Tarsheni grimaced. "That is a question I wish to pose to this wise man."

"If it wasn't a mistake, I don't think I'd like this . . . Is that the tunnel, do you think?"

Emerahl felt the boat shift slightly as the family turned to follow her gaze. She had seen a fold in the steep side of the Isthmus ahead. As they drew closer she noted a path running down to the gap.

"It looks like it," Tarsheni answered.

"Yes," Emerahl agreed. "No—don't bring that into sight yet," she added as he drew out his purse. "Let's see what we find here first."

He looked anxiously toward the tunnel. "Do you think it is a trap?"

"Just being cautious."

The fold deepened, and as they reached it they could see lamps hanging from the walls on both sides of a tunnel and a half-circle of light at the other end. The walls were supported by brickwork, which looked like it had been recently repaired at the entrance. In what Emerahl guessed was the center, a large metal gate filled the gap. The path became a ledge that ran along one side of the tunnel.

She could see figures ahead and sense interest as they noticed her boat entering. Her skin pricked as their interest changed to greed and anticipation.

"How did you find out about this tunnel, Tarsheni?"

"A man told us about it. He said he could sail us north in exchange for the fee to get through the tunnel."

"Why didn't you?"

"We didn't like the look of him."

"Hmm. It seems to me that this tunnel ought to be busier or there'd be no profit in making and manning it."

"Perhaps it is too early in the day."

"Hmm."

She considered who might use the tunnel. Fishermen could find it useful, but the tunnel was too small for any craft except little boats like hers. Only travellers like herself, alone or with a few others, would seek out the tunnel.

"What else did he say about the tunnel?"

Tarsheni shrugged. "That there used to be many tunnels through the Isthmus, most carved by smugglers, but people began to worry that they'd collapse and the Isthmus would be washed away by the sea. They had them filled in."

Emerahl thought of the repairs to the brickwork around the entrance. Had this tunnel been blocked, then recently reopened?

"Did he say if anyone objected to this tunnel being reopened?"

"No," Tarsheni replied. He paused. "It's not likely to collapse, is it?"

Emerahl looked at the arched ceiling. "It looks solid enough."

As they neared the gate, Emerahl saw four men standing on the ledge. Their expressions reflected the avarice that spilled from their minds. Drawing a little magic, Emerahl created a defensive shield around the boat. She guided the vessel to a stop before the gate then met the eyes of each of the four men in turn.

"Greetings, gatekeepers. My passengers and I wish to buy passage."

A large man with missing teeth hooked his hands in his belt and grinned at her.

"Gree'ings, lady. Thi' your boat?"

"Yes."

"No' of'n we ged women sailors."

The other men moved forward, peering down at the family and their belongings. One started to step off the ledge down into her boat. The man's knee rammed against her barrier. He cursed in pain and stumbled backward.

"I don't allow anyone onto my boat uninvited," Emerahl said, turning to regard the toothless man again.

He narrowed his eyes. "You be'er invi'e us, den, or you won' be going frough."

"You don't need to come aboard," she told him firmly.

The toothless man puffed out his chest. "So you go' Gifs. Ameri here has doo." He gestured to one of the men, a thin, sour-faced young man. She nodded to him with feigned politeness and turned back to the toothless man.

"How about you reduce the fee to ten canar and I leave the gate standing?"

She realized she was hoping for a refusal. They probably did this to travellers all the time. While she couldn't put a stop to it completely without delaying her journey, it would be satisfying to ruin their little scheme—for a while at least.

The man's eyes narrowed. "Ameri," he said, without taking his eyes from Emerahl. "Make dem coopera'e."

The thin man extended a hand toward her and made a dramatic and ridiculous-looking gesture. Magic splattered off her shield. He was stronger than the average man or woman and his attack would have hurt or even killed most travellers. She glared at him, no longer amused by the situation.

When he stopped she blasted him and his companions with a force that slammed them against the wall and held them there. She turned to the gate and sent a wave of heat out. Soon it began to glow and warp. As bits of molten metal fell into the water, hot steam filled the tunnel. Her shield protected her boat, but the men began to scream. Releasing them, she let them flee back down the tunnel.

As the last of the gate sank into the water, Emerahl moved the boat forward, taking care not to bump it against the glowing walls of the tunnel. Only when it had emerged from the other end did she relax and turn to regard her passengers.

They were staring at her in amazement.

She shrugged. "I told you: my Gifts are not inconsiderable. And I don't have much sympathy for thieves."

Auraya moved from sling bed to sling bed, examining the Siyee yet again. Two of the sick were fighting Hearteater effectively, the other two were struggling. She did not want to use Mirar's healing Gift on them until she was sure they wouldn't defeat the disease by themselves.

*I'm calling it "Mirar's healing Gift" now,* she thought. *Not Leiard's. I suppose Mirar has been using it for hundreds, even thousands, of years. It is his more than Leiard's.*

Tyve watched her, his thoughts full of curiosity and worry. She could not make herself stop moving. She could only pace from bower to bower, trying to find a distraction to stop her thinking about what she had done.

*I disobeyed Huan. I disobeyed the gods I'm sworn to serve.*

The alternative had been to kill a man who did not deserve it. *That should not matter. I should trust the gods have reason to want him dead. Juran did, long ago.*

Instead of reassuring her, that thought only brought her more discomfort. *I can't believe Juran tried to kill Mirar without being sure it was justified.* Though she knew it was his duty to do as the gods wished, she found she thought less of him for doing so. *I wonder if he knows what has happened . . .*

One of the Siyee woke and asked for water. Tyve did not stir as she rushed to take a bowl to the woman. As she held it to the woman's lips a terrible feeling of dread welled up in her and she froze.

A familiar presence was moving toward her. Auraya let out a gasp of relief as she recognized Chaia.

*:Auraya,* he said.

*:Chaia!*

*:I can see I don't need to tell you that you're in trouble,* he said. His words were spoken lightly, but she sensed a deeper concern.

*:No,* she said.

A hand touched hers. She looked up, startled, to find Tyve taking the bowl away from her. He waved her away from the patient. Auraya moved toward the bower entrance.

*:Why did I do it?* she asked Chaia. *Or why* didn't *I do it?*

*:You have a conscience,* he told her. *You need to know your actions are justified. To you, being just and right is more important than obedience. It is a part of your nature I like. Unfortunately my view is not shared by the others.*

*:By all of the others, or just Huan?*

*:We vary in our opinions, but are united in our decisions, Auraya. It is not for you to know our individual views.*

She stepped outside. The sunlight was too bright. She headed for the shade.

*:You and the other gods must have known it was part of my nature. Why did you choose me to be a White?*

*:Because the White cannot all be the same. You each have strengths and weaknesses. When you work together your weaknesses are lessened and your strengths enhanced. Your own weakness—your compassion—is your strength. A leader who can kill without question is unlikely to have the empathy and compassion needed to negotiate mutually beneficial alliances and help other people resolve their differences.*

*:Then why did Huan choose me for this task?*

*:I'm afraid you are the wrong White in the wrong place at the wrong time. You should not be the one executing Mirar—and not just because you were once in love with a part of him.*

Auraya felt a spark of hope.

*:Am I forgiven, then?*

*:Not quite,* Chaia replied. *Some of us believe that the White must be obedient, no matter what is in their nature. If the White have different natures, then they are bound to disagree at times. When conflict happens they must look to us for a resolution. They must obey us, or their unity will be broken.*

Auraya felt her stomach sink.

*:Huan still wants me to murder Mirar.*

*:Execute, not murder.*

As her hopes were smothered she was surprised to find anger stirring.

*:And if I refuse again?* she found herself asking.

*:You will be punished. To what degree I cannot guess. It took me some time to persuade the others to give you a second chance. I also insisted that you be given a day to reflect on the task and the consequences of refusing or obeying. While you do, consider this: sometimes we face a problem where all solutions are unpleasant, where the least damaging option must be chosen. Consider which choice is the least damaging to the people you are sworn to protect.*

*:Mirar has no intention of acting against us.*

*:No? He may not now, but that does not mean he won't try in the future. He is powerful and clever—you know that. He hates us—you know that too. Can you gamble that if the opportunity comes to cause trouble, he won't take it?*

Auraya shook her head.

*:Consider what might happen if he decides to reclaim his role as leader of the Dreamweavers,* he urged. *He can influence and direct them from another land through dreams.*

Her stomach sank. Even exile wasn't a plausible alternative.

*:And consider the possibility that you may still love Leiard.*

*:I don't,* she told him.

*:No? I know your heart, Auraya. I know there is still attraction and affection there, confused and unresolved. He will keep you bound to him if he can, not just because he is still enchanted by you but because you will not harm him while you are unsure of your feelings. You will not be free to love again until those bonds are gone.*

Auraya wrapped her arms around herself. She felt ill. Wretched. Torn.

*:I cannot console you, Auraya, though I wish I could,* Chaia said sorrowfully. *I cannot be affectionate, or fend off your nightmares, lest the others think I am rewarding you for your disobedience. They agreed that I should speak to*

*you, as you know me better. I ask as your friend and lover,
do as Huan bids.*

He moved away. For a long time she sat alone, thinking
about all that he had said, then she rose and returned to the
bowers. She needed to think, but the Siyee needed her help
more.

## 39

Mirar drew magic and warmed the air around him. During the months he had treated the Siyee he had barely noticed the turning of the seasons, too caught up in his work. Now he felt the chill of winter in the air, especially in these last hours before dawn. He leaned back against a tree and closed his eyes.

Though he had travelled all day and most of the night, this stop wasn't for rest or sleep. Clearing his mind, he sent himself into a dream trance.

*:Emerahl?*

They had communicated through dream links every few days since she had left. Recently she had grown secretive about her location or destination. He hoped that meant she'd had some success finding other immortals, but couldn't yet tell him about it.

*:Mirar?* she replied.

*:How is my travelling friend?*

*:Much the same as before. Lots of sailing, more sailing, and a little sailing on top.*

*:Bored, are we?*

*:No. I have some interesting paying passengers. You?*

*:Life just got a lot more interesting,* he told her. *The gods know who I am.*

*:What! How?*

*:I taught Auraya how to heal. The gods must have been watching.*

*:You idiot.*

*:Yes. Disappointed in me?*

She was silent for a moment.

*:No. I'm not surprised. You should have left as soon as she appeared, but you didn't. I know you stayed because of the Siyee and I'm guessing you taught her for their sake.*

*:That's true.*

*:I suspect that's not your only reason for tossing aside all concern for your own safety. So how did Auraya take the news?*

*:She tried to kill me.*

*:Oh.* She was silent for several heartbeats. *She was prepared to break her promise, then.*

*:As she pointed out, her promise was to Leiard.*

*:Ah. Obviously she didn't succeed in killing you. Why not?*

*:Because I opened my mind to her and showed her the truth.*

*:And that dissuaded her? How interesting. Do you think killing you was her idea or the gods'?*

*:The gods. Huan appeared and urged her to do it.*

*:Auraya disobeyed her?*

*:Yes.*

*:Even more interesting. So did she learn it?*

*:Learn what?*

*:Healing.*

*:Yes.*

*:You do realize what that means.*

*:That she is Gifted enough to become an immortal. She already is immortal, Emerahl.*

*:Yes, but what is significant is that she could be without the gods' intervention. She is a Wild. What that means for her depends on why they hate us. If it is a pure hatred of all Wilds, they will kill her.*

Mirar went cold. Had he doomed Auraya to die just by teaching her to heal?

*:There is something else I must tell you. The gods may have seen more than I intended.*

*:You let some secrets slip out, then?*

*:Yes. When I explained how Leiard and I became one*

*person I thought of you, though only as my helper. I tried
not to . . .*

    *:You think the gods will guess who this helper was.*

    *:Yes. I am sorry. You may be in danger.*

    She said nothing for a long time.

    *:Not as much danger as you face. They know I still live,
but they do not know where I am. They know where you are.*

    *:Only that I am in Si.*

    *:Where are you heading?*

    *:Auraya told me to leave Northern Ithania. I am heading
for the coast.*

    *:Auraya may not be willing to kill you, but I wouldn't
rely on the other White having the same scruples if I were
you. Huan will enlist the Siyee to search for you and send
the White in once you've been found. Do you think you
could evade the Siyee?*

    *:If I travel at night, perhaps, but it won't be easy without
a light.*

    *:It's a pity you're not close to the coast already. You
could make a boat and sail out to sea. There will be a limit
to how far out a Siyee can fly. Once you have lost their pursuit, you can come to shore again. So long as nobody sees
you, the gods will not know where you arrive. But I fear
the White will be waiting for you by the time you reach the
coast.* She paused. *Eventually you will have to approach
water in order to leave Northern Ithania. Good timing will
be essential. Let me think about this. I will reach my destination in a few days. I may learn of a safe place for you to go.*

    *:Your destination, eh? There you go, being all mysteri-
ous again.*

    *:You have just revealed my existence to the gods. Do you
expect me to tell you where they may find me?*

    *:No. I expected you to flay my mind with telepathic
curses.*

    *:If I didn't think you will probably die—properly—any
day now, I would.*

    *:That's reassuring.*

    *:Is it? It's not meant to be. Now wake up and get your-
self out of Si.*

*:Yes, oh wise and holy one,* he replied mockingly.

She broke the link with deliberate abruptness, startling him out of the dream trance. As he began to stand up a memory of Auraya surrounded by light flashed into his mind. Had she refused to surrender her will to Huan, as he suspected? Would the gods punish her? Or would they kill her now that it was clear she was a Wild?

*She could be dead already,* he thought. *Because of me.*

He had to find out. There was only one way. He had considered and rejected it countless times during his trek. If he dream-linked with her, and she was still alive, would she talk to him? Would he put himself in any more danger? Or her?

*So long as I don't tell her where I am, I am safe enough.*

Closing his eyes, he sent his mind in search of the woman who had tried to kill him.

*:Auraya?*

She was slower in responding than Emerahl. The silence deepened his fear that she was dead. Then he heard his name spoken in surprise.

*:Mirar?*

*:Yes.*

*:Why are you dream-linking with me?*

*:I am worried about you.*

*:You're worried about me? I just tried to kill you!*

*:I may be a little different to the Leiard you knew, but I do still care for you.*

*:This is too strange.*

*:You think this is strange? I've woken up after a hundred years to discover I'm not the same person I was. I find I've done some stupid things: going to Jarime, working for the White, falling in love with one of the gods' most powerful servants. What is strangest is I don't regret any of it. All I regret is that I can't be with you. I fear what they will do to you for letting me go. Have they punished you?*

She was silent for a long moment.

*:Not yet.*

*:Will they?*

*:I don't know.*

*:Don't wait to find out. Come with me. We will leave Ithania and seek the distant continents.*

He felt amusement from her.

*:Abandon everything I have, the people I protect and the gods, for you? Abandon the Siyee just when the disease is at its worst?*

*:No? Oh well. It was worth asking.*

*:If I choose to disobey the gods, I will face whatever punishment they deem appropriate.*

*:Even death?*

She paused again, but not for as long.

*:No. They won't kill me for this. That would imply that they made a mistake in choosing me. If Circlians learned that I disobeyed the gods they would start to doubt the rest of the White. No, the punishment will be subtle. I fear . . . I fear they will remove my ability to fly.*

*Flight.* He felt a sudden and unexpected thrill of insight. *Her flying Gift! None of the other White have it! If Emerahl is right, and Auraya is a Wild, flight may be her innate Gift!*

*:If I left with you, however,* she continued, *the gods would be angry. Even if they didn't send the other White after me, they might still be able to punish me. Consider the ring I wear. If they can make me immortal through it, perhaps they can kill me through it too. I don't even know what effect taking it off would have. At the least I would no longer be immortal. I would age and die. Forgive me if I think staying here and accepting whatever punishment they choose is the better option.*

*:But you are . . .*

With an effort, he made himself stop. He desperately wanted to tell her that she could make herself immortal, that all it took was a different application of his healing method. He wanted to warn her that she was a Wild, and the gods might kill her just for that.

Yet he also realized that she was right: the gods would not risk that her death would shake Circlian belief in the gods' infallibility. They must have known she was strong enough to be a potential Wild. What did it matter when she was a White?

Once again he felt the excitement of a sudden insight. The gods knew that more Wilds were likely to arise over time. Powerful sorcerers tended to become priests and priestesses. Did this enable them to ensure Wilds never reached their potential? Had they chosen Auraya simply to control her? Were the other White potential Wilds, too?

*:I am what?* she asked.

His thoughts were racing. The other White hadn't manifested any unique powers. Only Auraya had. Now she had shown herself to be capable of rebellion. Worse still, she had rebelled in order to protect another Wild. The gods must be torn between the consequences of getting rid of her and the risks of letting her live. And she was aware of none of this.

Which might be the only thing that saved her.

He had two choices: leave her ignorant and gamble that the gods would not harm her so long as she was unaware of her true nature, or try to persuade her to flee with him. She was too distrustful of him and bound to the gods and the White. She would not believe him if he told her his suspicions—at least not straight away. Even if she did and left with him, he would be taking her away from the life she loved into a life of danger.

*:Mirar?* she asked. *What were you saying?*

*:That you are a braver person than I,* he said. *Thank you for sparing my life. I hope I can repay you one day.*

*:Don't thank me yet, Mirar,* she told him.

*:No? Are the other White coming to catch me?*

She did not answer.

*:All I can promise you is that if you are found your death will be quick. And permanent.*

She broke the link. Opening his eyes, he saw that he was surrounded by mist turned white by the faint light of the coming dawn. He shivered, but not from the cold.

Her last words were a warning. She could not help him. The other White were coming. He must get away, and quickly. The mist would hide him from any Siyee that might be searching for him. Standing up, he stretched and started through the trees.

\*   \*   \*

Sunlight glittered off the waves, setting Reivan's eyes smart-
ing. The night had been long and uncomfortable but the day
wasn't going to be any better, if the growing heat of the sun
was any indication.

*I'm grumpy,* Reivan thought. *It's lack of sleep and being
stuck in a small boat for most of a day. That would make
anyone grumpy.*

Whenever she thought of Imi she forgot discomfort and
weariness. The princess hadn't returned the previous afternoon so they had remained in the boat all night. Imenja sat
in the prow, silent and watchful. Now she turned to Reivan.

"What would you advise, Reivan?" Imenja murmured.
"Should we go to shore and search for her, or return to the
ship?"

Reivan considered. "We promised to take her home. We
also agreed to stay out of Si. That doesn't mean we can't
row in close to shore to look for her. So long as we don't
set foot on dry land they can't accuse us of invading."

Imenja chuckled. "No. I doubt the Siyee will see it that
way. They will . . ." She frowned and looked up. "Ah."

Reivan followed the Voice's gaze. Farther east, three tiny
specks moved in the sky toward the seaward horizon.

"They have seen the ship."

Reivan looked back. The ship was not visible.

"How?"

"They are higher up than we."

"Of course." Reivan shook her head. *I am tired,* she
thought. *I should have realized the Siyee would have a better view.*

"No matter. They are . . ." Imenja's eyes narrowed, then
she smiled. "They are hoping to distract us so we don't notice an Elai girl swimming toward her home."

"Imi."

"Yes."

"Has Imi left us? Did they convince her that we are the
enemy, and that she should go on alone?"

Imenja shook her head. "Those Siyee do not know she
was with us."

"Perhaps she told them she was going east so she could swim this way without drawing their attention to us."

"We can only wait and see. If she does not appear in the next few hours, we will know she has gone on alone."

They waited in silence. The distant Siyee returned to shore without noticing the small boat.

"I hear her," Imenja said suddenly.

Letting out a sigh of relief, Reivan searched the water around them. Every splash caught her attention. Suddenly a head appeared above the edge of the boat. The girl grinned, though she was breathing heavily.

"Sorry," she panted. "I couldn't . . . get away . . . They insisted . . . I stay . . . eat . . . rest."

"I understand," Imenja said, smiling. She rose and offered Imi a hand. The girl took it and yelped in surprise as the Voice lifted her out of the water and into the boat.

"You're strong!" she exclaimed.

"When I need to be," Imenja agreed. She ordered the rowers to take them back to the ship, then sat down again. "They told you the way to Borra?" she asked Imi.

"Yes." Imi grimaced. "They don't like Pentadrians much. They warned me to keep away from you."

Imenja nodded. "That is the unfortunate consequence of fighting against them in a foolish war," she said with feeling.

Reivan looked at Imenja, surprised the Voice would express such an opinion in the presence of others. Then she remembered that they were speaking in Elai; the rowers could not understand them.

"I wanted to tell them they were wrong about you," Imi said. "But I didn't."

Imenja patted her hand. "They will find out, in time."

"I hope so." Imi yawned widely.

"You're tired," Imenja said. "Lie down and sleep. I'll wake you when we get to the ship."

Imi nodded and stretched out on a seat. Taking a blanket, Reivan dipped it in the sea and then draped it over the girl to protect her from the sun. She looked up and found Imenja nodding approvingly. They exchanged a look of mutual relief, then fell into a weary silence.

*   *   *

As Mairae entered Juran's room she mused that the scene that greeted her was becoming a familiar one. Juran was pacing and Dyara was sitting on the edge of her seat, her back straight and her forehead creased with a frown. As Rian followed Mairae to the chairs, Juran stopped pacing, looked at them both, then sighed.

"I have called you here to report on the situation in Si," he said. "The gods decided that, since she was closest, Auraya should find and execute Mirar."

Mairae drew in a breath in surprise, which drew Juran's attention.

"She was closest," Juran repeated. "None of us could have got there quickly enough."

*Poor Auraya,* Mairae thought. *Wasn't it bad enough that her former lover turned out to be an enemy of the gods?* "So you're about to tell us she's feeling bad about it and we should give her our sympathies?" she asked dryly.

Juran winced. "No."

Mairae blinked in surprise. "She isn't? She's made of stronger stuff than I thought. I suppose if she was angry enough she—"

"She didn't kill Mirar," Juran interrupted. "She let him go."

"Oh." Mairae looked at Dyara. The woman's lips had thinned in disapproval. Rian was staring at Juran with what looked like both shock and anger. "Why?"

Juran shook his head. "Mirar opened his mind to her. He convinced her . . . of many things: that he smothered his own identity and invented Leiard in order to hide from the gods, that he didn't intend any harm and means to leave Northern Ithania, that he does not deserve execution." Juran sighed. "I cannot say if any of this is true. It may be that he is able to fill his mind with lies in a way that it appears he is offering up the truth. If he can or cannot is irrelevant. The gods ordered Auraya to kill him. She didn't."

The room fell silent. Mairae felt a pang of sympathy for Auraya, yet at the same time she was disappointed. It would not have surprised her to know Auraya had found it difficult and distressing to kill Mirar, but she had not expected to learn that Auraya had refused to do it.

"Wait . . ." she said. "Was she unable to bring herself to do it, or did she refuse?"

"What difference does that make?" Rian muttered.

"There's a difference between hesitation and refusal. An experienced fighter may hesitate in battle when confronted with something unexpected—that his enemy is his friend, for example. Whatever Mirar showed her, it made her hesitate. If she'd had time she might have dismissed it. She should be given a second chance."

"She has been," Juran said. "She has until this afternoon to consider her actions, then she must complete her task. Mirar can't have travelled far. Siyee have been sent out to locate him."

"If she refuses again?" Rian asked.

Juran grimaced. "She will be punished."

Mairae shook her head. "I still think this is too much to ask of her. She is still new to her role. One of us should go in her stead."

"She must prove her loyalty to the gods," Rian stated.

"He is right," Dyara said. "If people knew that she had refused their order—"

"Who is going to tell them?" Mairae asked. "This happened in a distant place," she glanced at Juran, "hopefully without witnesses. Nobody but us and the gods know about it."

Dyara's expression hardened. "If the gods ask this of her, it must be necessary. The gods see into our hearts and minds. They know when our loyalties need testing."

Mairae stared at Dyara. The older woman could be stern and domineering, but she was not usually this lacking in sympathy. She sounded more like Rian. "How easily would you kill your adviser if the gods ordered it?"

Dyara's eyes widened in surprise and anger. "Timare is a *priest,* not a . . . a filthy *Wild.*"

"How do you know? You didn't detect Mirar's mind behind Leiard's."

"I've known Timare for forty years. How well do you know your lovers?"

Mairae shrugged. "I don't. I don't need to."

"It seems to me there are a *lot* more people in this world that you may find yourself reluctant to kill."

"I use them for sex, Dyara. I'm not in love with any of them."

"Mairae!" Juran protested. "This is not getting us anywhere."

She looked up at him then smiled apologetically, knowing she was unlikely to gain Auraya any sympathy by arguing with Dyara. Juran was always more inclined to take Dyara's side over hers, anyway.

"What are we going to do?" Rian asked.

Juran turned to regard him. "We have to be ready in case Auraya refuses again, or needs our help finding and killing Mirar. You and Dyara will sail south. We know Mirar intends to leave Northern Ithania so he will probably travel to the coast."

Rian straightened in his seat.

"I will not hesitate. It will be a pleasure to serve the gods."

Mairae smothered a sigh. *I hope you find the resolve to do this, Auraya,* she thought. *Rian is going to be even more unbearable if he gets to kill someone as famous as the great Mirar.*

# 40

Morning light revealed ominous clouds obscuring the mountains around the Blue Lake village. The air was icy and the vegetation around the bowers was white with frost. Auraya drew magic and dried off a log with a blast of hot air. As she sat down she realized it had only been a handful of days since she had rested here beside Mirar. It seemed a lot longer.

*I suppose all those hours I've been awake thinking rather than sleeping make it seem longer.* Last night she had only managed to fall asleep an hour or so before Mirar had linked with her. Afterward she had woken up fully. Something had nagged at her. Finally, as the light of the dawn filtered through the membrane of the bower, she had realized what it was.

Seeing into Mirar's mind had been like seeing someone familiar and yet unknown. Like being reunited with someone she had known as a child, who had grown into an adult she didn't know. Seeking a hint of Leiard, she had only seen that he was no longer the person she had known. Leiard was in him, but only as a part of a person she didn't know—or love.

*You're wrong, Chaia,* she thought. *You see the remnants of the love I had for Leiard. You haven't had the chance to see that I'm not attracted to Mirar in the same way—or what Mirar has become.*

If Chaia didn't see that, then perhaps he didn't see that Mirar was not the person he had been a century ago. What he had done to survive had changed him—made him into a new person. As a new person he deserved to be judged on his own merits and character.

*Huan had said that the past should be forgotten. That is even more true of Mirar than the gods. The gods haven't changed. Mirar has. It's unfair to punish him for the past crimes of another person.*

But Mirar was not a completely new person, so she could understand that part of him was guilty and untrustworthy. However, when she considered what she had been told of his crimes she could not see how he deserved to be executed. Mirar had worked against the gods and the formation of the Circlian priesthood by seeding doubts about the fate of souls in the gods' hands and spreading stories of terrible acts of cruelty that the gods were guilty of. One of the ways he had communicated to these people was through dreams.

Looking into his mind, she had seen an acknowledgment that he had done these things. She had also understood that he had done them out of concern that mortals would be ruled by beings he believed were capable of evil. Dream links were not banned then; he had broken no law. The Circlians had spread lies about Dreamweavers and he had used dreams, as he always had, to reassure mortals of Dreamweavers' good intentions.

He hadn't encouraged anyone to kill priests and priestesses, yet she knew that some Circlians had preached a hatred of Dreamweavers that had led to thousands of Dreamweaver deaths.

Yet she was disturbed by his conviction that the gods had done terrible deeds in the past. He had not revealed exactly what they had done, however. *His fear that the gods would harm mortals through forming the Circlian priesthood proved unfounded,* she told herself. *They have done much good. Perhaps these evil deeds he accuses them of were only other ways in which the gods encouraged mortals to worship them—an aim he seems to think is wrong.*

She sighed. Discouraging people from worshipping the gods was wrong because it cost them an eternal soul after death. Mirar hadn't *forced* anyone to turn from the gods. He had given them an alternative. That was not a crime worthy of death. If it was, thousands of people would die every day. People resisted the gods' will in many small ways.

*How much easier is it to believe that resisting the will of the gods isn't a crime when you're guilty of it?* she found herself thinking.

The priesthood existed to guide mortals toward a lawful and pious life. The White were the highest priests and priestesses.

*That makes my crime worse than his. Mirar never vowed to serve the gods. If I don't deserve to die, he doesn't either. Perhaps that is why he thought the gods might have me executed. Perhaps he is right to worry . . .*

She shivered. *I'm not dead yet. They have offered me a second chance. I can find him and . . .*

Her stomach twisted and she went cold all over. Frustration rose. *Why can't I do this? Why do I feel such strong resistance to even the thought of killing Mirar?*

She bit her lip gently. How would she feel about herself and the gods if she did kill Mirar? Every time she considered this question she felt a chill of foreboding.

*I would feel like I'd murdered someone. No matter what the gods said. I would feel differently about the gods, too. I would fear what they would have me do next. I would not think of them as benevolent and just any more. I would not feel I was worthy of ruling others if I could be induced to commit murder.*

She frowned. *And how would this affect Circlians if they knew of it? I'm not fool enough to believe anyone would openly question the gods or argue with their verdict, but there would be a change. It would be clear to some that it was unfair to kill Mirar without a public trial and clear guilt. It would shake their belief that the gods were just, too. Those that believed the gods were always right would see that unjustified executions were acceptable. They might decide that they could mete out other unjustified executions themselves.*

Yet if people knew that one of the White had disobeyed

the gods, their belief in the gods and the White would also be shaken. They would wonder if the gods had chosen badly in selecting her, and perhaps start doubting the other White. They would reason that if a little disobedience now and then was reasonable for a White, it must be reasonable for Circlians, too.

*But there's no need for the people to know of my disobedience,* she thought. *Only the White and the gods will know. I have considered how I would feel if I obeyed them. What if I disobeyed them?*

There would be guilt, she knew. There would also be relief. She would respect herself for standing up for what she thought was right even as she disliked herself for failing to obey the gods. Yet it was better to feel disappointment in herself than in the gods.

*I don't expect the gods to hold a public trial, just let Mirar leave Northern Ithania. If he comes back . . . well, I will deal with him. If they punish me, so be it.*

She felt a little better at that thought. *Is this my decision?* she asked herself. *Am I prepared to accept any punishment?*

What punishment would they choose? She didn't believe they would kill her, as Mirar feared. They would not take away her position as White, either. That would shock the people as badly as if they executed her. No, every time she considered the worst punishment they could deal out she came up with only one: removing her ability to fly.

Just contemplating the possibility made her feel like her heart was being torn into pieces.

*If they do, you'd better appreciate my sacrifice, Mirar,* she thought. *You had better get yourself out of Northern Ithania and never return, because if you come back I will kill you.*

She closed her eyes and sighed. *I think that means I've made up my mind. What next? Should I call Chaia and—*

Her thoughts were interrupted by two Siyee landing several steps away. They hurried toward her, both radiating urgency and fear.

"Auraya of the White," the taller said, making the sign of the circle.

"What is it? What has happened?"

"A Pentadrian ship was sighted off the coast a few days ago," he said. "Within sight of the Sand tribe village."

"Did they land?"

"No. A ship was seen to the east a few days before that."

"Another ship, or the same one?"

"We don't know."

She rose. "I will fly south and investigate."

"Thank you," the taller Siyee said.

As they walked away toward the center of the village she hurried to the bower. Tyve nodded and smiled wryly as she told him she was leaving, wondering if he would ever learn what was going on between her and Wilar. Turning away quickly, she stepped outside.

As she propelled herself into the sky she felt a rush of sadness. *This might be my last flight. I had better enjoy it while I can.* Then she laughed aloud. *If Mirar's right, and the gods decide to kill me, removing my Gifts while I'm in the air would certainly do the trick.*

Imi had come up onto the deck when the first island had been sighted and remained at the rail despite the rain. So far all that the ship had passed were small outcrops of rock barely large enough to call islands. Now there were larger shapes ahead, familiar to her from the paintings in the palace.

"Stony Island," she said to herself as they passed an island bare of vegetation. In the distance was a low, shapely island covered in trees. "Maiden Island."

She heard footsteps behind her and turned to see Imenja and Reivan approaching. They joined her at the rail.

"Is this your home, Imi?" Imenja asked.

Imi nodded. "Yes." As the ship sailed farther past Stony Island it entered a ring of islands. "This is Borra."

"Is there anything left of the old settlements on the islands?" Reivan asked.

Imi shrugged. "I don't know. We haven't been able to live outside the city for a long time. Some people tried to, but the raiders killed them." She smiled. "But the raiders have never been able to settle either, because we burn their houses."

"Did your people build defenses around your settlements?"

"Defenses?"

"Walls. Perhaps something on the beach to stop boats landing."

"I don't know." Imi smiled. "That sounds like something you should tell my father about. Maybe if we could defend ourselves we would then find a way to get rid of the raiders."

To her surprise, Reivan shook her head. "So long as there is trade between Northern and Southern Ithania there will be thieves in these waters. The wind blows in favor of ships sailing past these islands but there are no major ports along the Si coast from which to base a force of ships capable of dealing with the raiders."

"It is a pity we can't negotiate an agreement with the Siyee to deal with these raiders," Imenja said.

Imi frowned. "Why haven't my people done that?"

Reivan shrugged. "I've heard the Siyee were a peaceful people before they allied with the White."

"They had their own problems with landwalkers," Imi said, remembering what Teiti had told her. "Are those problems gone now?"

"I don't know," Reivan said. She looked at Imenja, but the woman said nothing.

Imi decided she would ask her father. Looking toward the peak where she knew the lookout was, she felt a pang of longing. She wouldn't feel like she had truly reached home until she felt her father's strong arms around her.

"Will they come out to meet us, Imi?" Imenja asked.

"I don't know," Imi confessed. "They're scared of landwalkers. Maybe they will if they see me."

"We're a bit far away for that." Imenja drummed her fingers on the rail. "We should take you to shore."

"No." Imi shook her head. "I know how I'd feel if I saw landwalkers walking on our islands. It will make people angry and frightened. If I saw an Elai with them I'd think she was a prisoner."

"Then we'll row you closer to shore and wait."

Imi shook her head again. "No. I think I'm going to have to swim into the city." She looked at Imenja and smiled apologetically. "I'm sorry, but my people are suspicious of landwalkers. I'll talk to them; tell them what you did for me."

"Will they believe you?" Reivan asked.

"I'll make them." Imi frowned. "Though it could take some time."

"We'll wait," Imenja assured her. "You know your people best. If you must swim, then you must."

Imi smiled, then stepped forward and hugged the woman. Imenja chuckled and patted her back.

"Take care, princess. I will be sad if I never see you again."

"I will be too," Imi told her, pulling away. She turned to Reivan. "And you, Reivan. I will try to talk father into meeting you both. I'm sure he'll like you as much as I do."

Reivan smiled in the self-conscious way she had. "We'll see."

"Go," Imenja said. "The sooner you do, the sooner we get to meet him."

Imi grinned. She ducked under the rail and squinted at the water below. It was deep here, in the center of the islands, but she had learned since coming onto the ship that it was always a good idea to check for large sea creatures inspecting the hull before diving into the water.

Letting go of the rail, she felt herself fall forward. The drop was short but exhilarating and she relished the plunge into cool water. Surfacing, she waved at Imenja and Reivan before taking a deep breath and starting toward the city.

She was not entirely sure where the entrance of the city was, so she decided to swim along the rock wall around the area she thought it was in. Soon she saw a shadow swimming below and felt her heart lift as she realized it was another Elai. Keeping at a distance, knowing she would attract a lot of attention once she was recognized, she followed.

The shadowy figure vanished and she felt her heart sink, but then another pair of Elai appeared. Following them, she saw a great blackness appear in the wall ahead. The light-

fish were gone, perhaps a precaution against the landwalkers finding the city entrance. She realized it was possible,
having seen landwalker divers. But landwalkers couldn't
hold their breath long enough to get *into* the city.

Swimming into the darkness, she was relieved to see
light ahead. It led her to the pockets of air in the tunnel. She
managed to swim the entire length without coming up for
air at the same time as anyone else, so nobody recognized
her. Then a larger, brighter glow drew her upward, and she
surfaced in the Mouth.

For several minutes she floated there, gazing at the caves
and lights and people. It was a sight too good to be real.
She was afraid to swim forward in case . . .

As another arrival splashed up nearby she shied away.

*What am I afraid of?* she asked herself. *Am I still afraid
that Teiti or father will punish me for slipping away? Even
if I knew they would, would I swim away now?*

She shook her head and swam toward the edge of the water.

As she emerged she began to attract attention. Ordinary Elai glanced at her, then turned back to stare. Guards
frowned, then blinked in surprise. One, the captain, stepped
forward.

"Princess? Princess Imi?"

She smiled crookedly. "Yes."

"Where have you . . ." He paused, then straightened.
"May I escort you to the palace?"

Amused by his sudden formality, she nodded. "Please."

At once he began to bark orders. Three more guards took
their places with the captain, in front and behind her. Others
ran down the main stream toward the palace.

*They'll tell father. He'll know I'm coming.*

She felt her stomach flutter but forced her legs to move.
A crowd of onlookers had stopped to watch and now they
began to keep pace with her on either side. Stares had
changed to smiles. Voices called a welcome to her. Abruptly
she felt tears coming and blinked them away.

The distance to the palace seemed endless. She quickened her pace, then slowed as she saw the palace gates.
They stood open.

A man stood between them.

Her father.

The guards stepped aside as she started forward again. She barely noticed. All she saw was her father hurrying forward, then she felt her hold on her tears slip as she saw his own eyes glittering.

Finally, she threw her arms around him and felt his around her, familiar and strong. She realized she was apologizing, then laughed aloud as she realized he was too.

"What are you apologizing for, Father?" she blurted out. "I'm the one who gave Teiti the slip and left the city."

He pulled away to regard her. "I should have let you out more often. You would not have been so curious, and you would have had guards to protect you."

She smiled and wiped at her eyes. "I would have given them the slip, too."

He looked at her searchingly. "Where have you been? That rascal trader's son told us you'd been taken by raiders."

"That's true." She paused. "You weren't too mean to him, were you? I talked him into it."

He frowned. "Teiti had me lock him up."

Imi gasped. "Poor Rissi! She must have been so angry!"

Her father winced. "She was, but I was much angrier with her. You must tell me everything." He turned her toward the palace. "Does your return have anything to do with the ship outside?"

"It has, Father. The people on that ship rescued me and brought me home. I owe them my life."

He frowned, clearly unhappy to hear it.

"Not all landwalkers are bad," she told him.

His frown turned into a scowl. "You think so, do you? What do they want in return?"

"Nothing."

"Nothing!" He shook his head. "They always want something. They won't get anything from me!"

"Father," she said firmly. "They saved my life."

He paused, then sighed. "I should give them something in return."

She shrugged. "At least your thanks."

He stopped and looked at her strangely.

"What has happened to you, to make you so wise and brave?"

She grimaced. "A lot, Father. Let's go in, and I'll tell you everything."

He nodded, put an arm around her shoulders, and guided her through the palace gates.

# 41

There was little point in going over it again. He'd considered everything he'd done and what the consequences might be. He had spent fruitless hours considering how he could have done things differently.

But while travelling in Si took much of Mirar's concentration, it didn't occupy his mind completely. The part not concerned with endless climbing and walking insisted on circling around and around, and every time he tried to think of something else he soon found himself dwelling on Auraya, himself, the White and the gods.

*And Emerahl. Why did I have to go and think of Emerahl when I opened my mind to Auraya?*

He had only thought of her briefly, as a helper and friend. He had not thought of Emerahl's quest to find other immortals. If the gods had recognized her—and it was possible they hadn't—they would alert the White to her existence. They did not know where she was, however. So long as Emerahl didn't do something to attract their attention, or bump into one of the White, she was safe. The gods might search for her by looking into the minds of mortals, seeking someone visible to a human but invisible to them, but that would take time and they had a more pressing matter to occupy them—Auraya.

He hoped she was right that the gods would not kill her for fear of weakening their followers' trust in the White. He hoped he had not doomed her by opening his mind to her. It had been the only way to save himself, but he hadn't done it purely out of self-interest. He had wanted her to see the truth. Wanted her to finally know him for what he was—and that he loved her.

*Fool,* he thought at himself. *She's one of the Gods' Chosen. She can't love you in return.*

*But she could,* another part of his mind whispered.

He felt a stab of alarm. Was Leiard coming back? He sought a sense of other in his mind, but there was none.

*I am Leiard,* he reminded himself. *I had better accept that his weaknesses are mine and make sure I don't endanger others again. If I can't have Auraya, I had better take myself as far away from her as possible.*

The air in the steep, narrow ravine was humid and still. It set Mirar yawning and he considered stopping for a short sleep. He'd barely paused to rest since leaving the Blue Lake tribe and the weariness he'd pushed aside for so long suddenly seemed unbearable.

He stumbled. Looking down, he frowned as he saw the thin vines crossing his path. His heart stopped and he looked up and around, fear chasing away the muzziness encroaching on his thoughts.

The trees and forest floor around him were draped with sleepvine. Caught up in endlessly circling thoughts about Auraya and the gods, he hadn't noticed what the ravine had led him into. The smell of rotting flesh turned his stomach. Somewhere under the lush carpet was an animal corpse or two, victims of the sleepvine's Gift.

Now that he was aware of the insidious suggestion at the edge of his mind it was easy enough to block it. He started forward again, carefully stepping over the vines that crossed his path. It was a large, mature plant. The ravine was a natural corral and probably brought the plant many victims.

The ravine narrowed further, but the reach of the plant's vines soon ended. Breathing a sigh of relief, Mirar made his way down the narrow crevice. He had to climb or squeeze past several rocky outcrops.

*This better not lead to a dead end . . .*

If only Tyve had been able to come with him. He was sure the boy would have. But Tyve's mind was open to the gods and would have unwittingly betrayed Mirar's location to them.

The rock walls ended on both sides several paces ahead. Mirar could also see that the ground dropped away there, too. Beyond he could see the tops of trees swaying in the wind. As he reached the end of the ravine he found himself standing at a cliff edge. It wasn't a dead end, but climbing down would take time and a lot of concentration.

Before him rose mountains, and the climb he faced next was nothing compared to what he was going to have to tackle to cross those rocky slopes. Emerahl had suggested he head for the Sennon desert. Crossing the mountains was the shortest route. The easier route, though longer, would have taken him downriver from the Blue Lakes to the coast, but the coast was where the gods would expect him to go. It was where the Siyee would watch for him and the White would wait for him. They would not expect him to climb over a mountain then tackle a desert to get to Southern Ithania. At least he hoped they wouldn't.

Sighing, he sat down to eat and examine the terrain ahead. Though the forest hid much of the ground beneath, he could plot an optimistic path past more obvious obstructions.

A shadow passed over him. A large shadow.

He looked up in time to see a Siyee glide out past the edge of the cliff, then curve back out of sight.

Few Siyee lived in this part of Si. It was still Blue Lake tribe territory, but with so much usable land near their lake the tribe didn't need to roam far to find food or other necessities. *They could be after something they can't find locally,* he thought. *Rare plants, perhaps. Or maybe they're patrolling their land.*

*Or maybe they're searching for me.*

Standing up, he backed into the crevasse. Whether seeking him or not, any Siyee who saw him might reveal his location to the gods, if they were watching. He paused, considering if he should go back instead of climbing down the cliff.

The cliff stretched a long way in either direction, a natural barrier between him and the mountains. He would have to tackle it or go a long way out of his way.

A winged shape glided overhead. He sensed a smug satisfaction, and patience. His stomach sank.

*He knows I'm here.*

So he may as well let the Siyee watch him descend. After that, under the cover of trees, it would be much easier to evade pursuit.

No black ships were visible on the horizon as Auraya neared the village of the Sand tribe. Siyee were everywhere: among the bowers, on the coast and in the sky. When she was close enough she searched their minds and located Speaker Tyrli.

By the time her feet touched the sand a crowd of Siyee had gathered. One of the women from the village had brought two bowls with her, and Tyrli offered these to Auraya. One was full of water, the other filled with tart berries.

Auraya accepted the ritual welcome.

"I received your message, Speaker," she told him. "Where did you see the ship?"

He pointed a little eastward of south. "It was only visible from the air. The sails were marked with a star. My men flew out to it and saw Pentadrian sorcerers on board."

Auraya nodded. "Has it been seen since?"

"No." She caught a glimpse of a hairless, dark-skinned child in his mind. An Elai girl. He was worried that she might have encountered the Pentadrians, though it was unlikely. Auraya restrained her curiosity; there were more important matters to deal with.

"Did anyone follow the ship?" she asked.

He nodded. "At a distance, for as far as was safe. It sailed southeast, far out to sea. Toward Borra."

"They did not land?"

"No. Are the Elai in danger?"

Auraya shook her head. "I doubt it. The Elai are no threat to them, and they are too few to be of interest to the Pentadrians as allies. I suppose they might try to convert them, but the Elai were created by Huan. I doubt they'd turn from her."

Tyrli nodded in agreement.

*That doesn't mean the Pentadrians won't try,* she thought, remembering that Juran had told her of Pentadrians trying to settle in other lands. She sighed. "I should discuss this with Juran."

The Speaker smiled. "Come to my bower. My daughter will make sure you are undisturbed."

Auraya hesitated, then nodded. "Of course." He did not know she had reason to be reluctant to communicate with the other White.

*I can't avoid it forever,* she told herself.

By the time she had reached Tyrli's bower she had steeled herself for what she expected to be an unpleasant argument. Tyrli's daughter brought water and a more substantial plate of food, then left Auraya alone.

The walls of the bower glowed with the sunlight the membrane allowed through. Auraya took a deep breath, closed her eyes and sent her mind out.

*:Juran?*

There was a pause, then,

*:Auraya. Where are you?*

*:On the Si coast. The Sand tribe reported seeing a Pentadrian ship a few days ago.*

*:Did the Pentadrians land?*

*:No. They said it headed southeast, toward Borra.*

*:What would the Pentadrians want with the Elai?*

*:I don't know. There is no reason for them to attack, and the Elai are unlikely to embrace any offers of friendship. We know how suspicious they are of landwalkers.*

*:Yes.*

*:Should I investigate?*

Juran was silent for several breaths.

*:No. How well are the Siyee recovering from Hearteater?*

*:The disease has spread to all but the most remote tribes. The situation cannot get much worse.*

He paused again.

*:What are your intentions regarding Mirar?*

Auraya felt her chest tighten.

*:I can't kill him if I believe he doesn't deserve it.*

*:Not even if the gods order you to?*

She hesitated.

*:No. It makes all they represent—all we represent—worthless.*

There was a long silence.

*:Dyara and Rian are leaving for Si today. If they kill Mirar, will you feel they have rendered all we represent worthless?*

Her stomach sank at the question.

*:I might. I don't know . . .*

*:I executed Mirar over one hundred years ago with as little evidence of his guilt as you have now. Have you lost your respect for me, knowing that?*

She could not answer his question. To deny it would be dishonest, yet she still felt a great deal of respect for him.

*:Our situations are not the same,* she said. *Mirar did not open his mind to you. When you faced Mirar the gods had only just begun laying down the laws that we live by. The laws and principles that they are asking me to break.*

*:They asked me to trust them. Do you trust them?*

*:Perhaps not as much as I did before,* she admitted. *I cannot help it. When they asked me to do something unjust, I lost my trust that they would never ask me to do something unjust.* She felt a bitter amusement. *If I kill Mirar I will hate myself and question the gods' wisdom for all eternity.*

*:I fear you will now question the gods' wisdom anyway.*

She felt a cold stab of realization. He was right. There was no going back. She had lost a little of her respect for the gods and couldn't make herself pretend that she hadn't. *I am a White. A White should not doubt the gods he or she serves! If I can't regain my respect for them then . . .* She shivered. *Then I shouldn't be a White.*

*:Auraya?*

Her mouth was dry. She forced her attention back to Juran.

*:What should I do? Should I return to Jarime?*

*:No. Stay in Si. There is no point you returning here when the sky people still need you.*

He broke the contact. Opening her eyes, Auraya felt tears spring into them. All she had ever wanted was to be a priestess and use her Gifts to help people. To serve the glorious beings that were the gods.

*The gods I love,* she thought. *But not as wholeheartedly now as before. That has been tainted. Ruined. Perhaps my love should be more robust. Perhaps I should be like Rian, willing to do anything, whether right or wrong, in their name. Am I being selfish? Does it matter whether I believe what I do is just?*

But it *had* to matter whether the White cared if what they did was right or wrong. For it to be otherwise was frightening. And it did matter that the gods were good and just. Otherwise . . . what other abuses of power could the gods ask the White to perform?

*If Mirar is right and the gods have abused their power plenty of times before, what would prevent them from doing so again? What if the gods had created the Circlians and White in order to to do whatever they wished in the world, unchallenged?*

She felt her stomach clench. It was too frightening to consider. If the gods' intentions were evil, where did that leave humans?

*At their mercy.*

The safest path for her was to stay in their favor—to kill Mirar and be an obedient servant. She should be as loyal as Rian, except her unquestioning obedience would be motivated by fear, not love or loyalty.

The thought made her feel ill. Living in a constant state of fear and lies, forced into actions she knew were wrong, would only lead to misery. An eternity of misery.

*It might not come to that,* she thought. *No. The gods are not evil. They want Mirar dead because they fear he will harm mortals. Their viewpoint is too distant for them to see that he is no longer a danger. Mine is closer. I have seen inside his mind. I know better.*

But how could that be so? The gods were supposed to be wiser than humans. If she believed they were wrong, then she must believe they could make mistakes. *A White should not doubt the gods.* She put her head in her hands and faced the simple truth. *I am not worthy of this position.*

The crew scurried about the deck of the *Arrow* as if their lives depended on them getting their tasks done as quickly as possible. Rian looked over to the *Star*. The crew of the other ship was as busy. Dyara stood at the prow. Though the two ships would sail together, he would not speak to her except mentally for the next few weeks.

Footsteps echoed on the deck. He turn to see Juran approaching.

"Rian," he said. "Have you everything you need?"

"Yes," Rian replied.

Juran paused as a young priest carrying a wooden box hurried on board. The man approached them nervously, placed the box on the deck, then made the sign of the circle.

"The copies you requested, Rian of the White."

"Thank you," Rian replied. "You may go."

"So what did you ask the scribes to stay up all night to copy?" Juran asked.

"Sennon's Code of Law, some histories of previous emperors and a few studies I commissioned on the many cults practiced there. I will need some reading material for the journey, and did not want to risk taking originals."

Juran chuckled. "I would not have thought you'd have time for reading on the way to Si, with your mind occupied in speeding the ship through the water."

Rian shrugged. "No, but once Mirar is dealt with we may return at a more leisurely pace."

The White leader's expression became grim and pained. Rian had seen that look before. It appeared whenever Mirar's name had been spoken. He had guessed long ago that killing Mirar had been unpleasant for Juran. It must be frustrating to find that the heathen leader of the Dreamweavers had not died, and was manipulating mortals again. And immortals. The sooner he and Dyara rid the world of Mirar the better—for Juran as well as the world. However, talking about it was pointless and would only frustrate Juran further.

"I am beginning to think it will take years, perhaps centuries, to bring Sennon under our protection," Rian said, bringing the subject back to that land. "These people will worship anything. Have you heard of this new cult of the Maker?"

Juran's eyebrows rose. "No."

"It is based on the idea that the world, even the gods, were created by some greater being for some high purpose. This being is known as the Creator. The man who leads the religion offers no tangible proof of this, but uses twisted logic to convince people of the truth. The cult is small now, but it is growing at a disturbing rate."

"New cults usually do. Their followers' enthusiasm fails when they realize there is no advantage to be gained from a non-existent god—especially when death is close."

"Yes." Rian sniffed in disdain. "So few of them worship simply out of awe or respect. Always they expect something in return."

Juran smiled. "If awe and respect were all that was required, you could worship this Creator as easily as the true gods."

Rian shook his head. "I still require proof of their existence."

Juran's gaze had sharpened now. "And their goodness? What would you do if they asked you to do something you thought was unjust?"

Leaning back against the railing, Rian resisted a smile. This was about Auraya, he guessed. "No task is unjust, if they ask it of us."

"Even if it contradicts the laws and principles they have encouraged us to embrace?"

"They must have their reasons for contradicting themselves. There are always circumstances in which laws may be flexed."

"And if this wasn't one of those circumstances?"

"Then I would conclude that I do not know the true circumstances. If the gods do not offer a reason for acting against their law, I must conclude they cannot. I would have to trust that their decision was right."

Juran frowned and rubbed his chin.

"So you would not require them to explain their full reasons to you?"

"No."

Rian watched as Juran drummed his fingers against his arm, his expression thoughtful. Of the four White, Juran was the only one who welcomed religious debate. Dyara didn't have the patience for what she called "fruitless speculation," and the few times Rian had attempted to draw Mairae into the subject she seemed uncomfortable. He hadn't tried to talk to Auraya. Though the opportunity had come a few times in the past, he had let it pass by. It wasn't that she gave the impression she wasn't interested—more the opposite. But he suspected he would not find her opinions agreeable.

"Have the gods ever made a decision that you would not have agreed with, but you accepted only because you trust their wisdom?" Juran asked slowly.

Rian's heart skipped a beat. Should he admit to that? Before he could decide, Juran smiled.

"I think I can guess that your hesitation indicates that they have."

Rian nodded once. "But I came to see the wisdom of their decision later."

Juran's eyes narrowed. "You do not wish to tell me what that decision was."

At first Rian began to shake his head, but then he reconsidered. In light of recent events, Juran might need to know this small thing.

"In the past it would have been petty to speak of it, but now it may prove important."

"Yes?"

"I disagreed with Auraya's Choosing."

Juran's eyebrows shot upward. "But you say you came to see the wisdom of it."

"Yes, she proved useful."

"You speak in past tense."

Rian shrugged. "I cannot see the future. I do not know if she will be useful in the future."

"It almost sounds as if you see her as . . . expendable," Juran mused.

"I did not mean to."

Juran looked away and sighed. "She has only been with us for a year. Was killing Mirar too much to ask of her?"

Rian frowned. "What time limit would you place on obedience to the gods? She vowed to serve them the day she was chosen—and before then: the day she became a priestess."

Juran chewed on his lower lip. "Making that vow does not mean fulfilling it is easy."

"She killed Kuar."

"I have to wonder if Mirar would not recover again anyway. We do not understand his powers."

"I will burn his body to ashes and scatter them across the world," Rian assured him. "I doubt he'll recover from that."

Juran looked at him, his expression unreadable. "And what would you have the gods do with Auraya?"

Rian paused and frowned. "She disobeyed them. Perhaps she hesitated out of confusion or indecision, but they gave her a second chance and she still defied them. I find myself questioning her Choosing again, but I will accept whatever the gods decide."

Juran nodded, his expression thoughtful. Then he looked around at the crew. They were no longer rushing about, but pretending to work while they waited for the signal to leave. The crew of the *Star* was also waiting expectantly.

"Have a safe journey, Rian. Don't strain the ship too much."

"Dyara would never let me come close to risking a leak," Rian replied.

Juran chuckled. "No."

Rian watched the White leader leave the ship, then nod to the captains of both vessels. An earlier discussion with Juran and Dyara came to mind.

"Together you will be strong enough to repel an attack by one of the Pentadrian leaders," Juran had said.

"But not two," Dyara had pointed out.

"If that should happen, call on Auraya. She is the only one of us who can reach you quickly."

"And if she refuses to help?" Rian asked.

"She would never consider it," Dyara said indignantly. "She may be a fool when it comes to Mirar, but she would not abandon us."

"And if Mirar joins with the Pentadrians?" Rian asked.

Dyara and Juran had exchanged grim looks. "I feel that is unlikely," Juran had said. "There was no sign of such an alliance in his mind. If there had been Auraya would have . . . behaved differently. But if such a situation occurs I see no choice for you but to flee."

The two ships pulled away from the docks. *The gods will warn us,* Rian told himself. *And Auraya will have no choice but to come to her senses, or betray us all.*

# 42

The boat vibrated faintly as its hull scraped against the sand. An order was barked, and the rowers quickly stowed their oars, leapt out into the water, and began to haul the boat onto the shore. Reivan rose with Imenja and followed her mistress to the prow. They stepped onto dry sand then started toward the crowd of dark-skinned, hairless men.

It was not hard to distinguish the leader from the rest. The King of the Elai wore no clothing apart from a pair of short trousers made of a leathery material similar in color to his skin, but his body was draped and decorated with jewellery. From chains of gold hung medallions molded into the shapes of sea creatures, glinting with insct precious stones. Carved shells polished until they shone like rainbows had been linked together to form an impressive vest. The weight of the jewellery must have been considerable, but he held himself proudly, back straight and shoulders set. In one hand he held a spear that, despite embellishments of gold and jewels, looked as if it could easily withstand more than decorative use.

He was scowling.

Reivan suppressed a smile. Imi *had* warned them that her father was hostile to foreigners.

A protective circle of Elai warriors stood around the king, all wearing armor and frowns, and carrying spears. Imenja walked to the edge of this circle and stopped. The warriors nearest her stepped aside, allowing her and Reivan inside.

"Greetings, Ais, King of the Elai," she said.

"Greetings, Imenja, Second Voice of the Pentadrians," he replied.

"I have come here, as you requested. Did Princess Imi return to you?"

"Yes. She did."

Imenja smiled. "That is good to hear. I would have escorted her all the way to you, but I understand that you have reason to dislike unexpected visitors."

The king's eyebrows lowered even further.

"I am grateful to you for her return," he said stiffly. "I have asked you to meet me here so that I may offer my thanks to you for freeing her from those who meant her harm and for bringing her to us." He lifted his free hand. "As a reward I have brought you this."

The warriors behind him parted and several equally fierce-looking men stepped through carrying bundles. They moved past the king and stopped to unwrap their burdens, revealing an array of beautifully wrought gold and silver vessels, brimming with jewellery, unset gems, carved shells and, ironically, dried sea bells. Reivan felt a little thrill at the sight.

"These are beautifully crafted," Imenja told him. "You are generous in your thanks, but I am not sure if I can accept this. We did not come here expecting such a reward. Seeing Imi returned to her home is reward enough."

Both of the king's eyebrows rose. "Then why did you not leave once she had returned to us? Why did you stay here and not sail home?"

"I wanted to be sure Imi was safe. I could not leave without knowing she had been reunited with her family. Now that I have seen that this is so, I will leave satisfied that I have done what I promised. Before I do, I have some belongings of Imi's to return to her that she could not carry when she swam to the city." She turned and beckoned to the waiting rowers.

They lifted the chest of gifts from Nekaun from the boat and carried it forward. Reivan smiled at Imenja's claim they were Imi's. If Imenja had told the king they were for him, he could easily have refused them. Now he couldn't. Entering the circle of warriors, the rowers placed the chest before the king. One unlatched the lid and opened it, then all bowed to the king and backed away, returning to the boat.

The Elai king's eyebrows rose again as he saw the contents of the chest.

"This belongs to my daughter?"

Imenja smiled. "Gifts from the leader of my people, First Voice Nekaun. It is a custom of my land that gifts be given to guests of royal blood. For Imi it was a pleasure to follow that custom. And though the crime of abducting her was not undertaken by my people, she did spend some time as an unwilling captive in our land. For that, Nekaun felt she ought to be compensated."

King Ais nodded, his eyes still on the chest's contents and his expression thoughtful. He looked up at Imenja.

"In my land a good deed is rewarded. Take my gifts to your leader and give them to him with my thanks."

She smiled. "I will, and I offer thanks on his behalf. He will be as impressed by the skill of your makers as I am."

Beckoning to the rowers once more, Imenja ordered them to bundle up the Elai treasures and carry them back to the boat. When the men had left the circle she looked at the Elai king again.

"Imi told me of the raiders that cause you so much trouble. I would offer our help, if I thought you would accept it."

"How could you help us?"

"Perhaps by teaching you what we know of sorcery, warfare, or simply the construction of fortified villages. Perhaps by selling you weapons."

"What profit would there be for you in that?"

"These raiders prey on trade ships travelling between Northern Ithania and my lands. Our merchants lose much to them. Establishing a fleet of patrol ships would be impractical and expensive even if there was a suitable port to use as a base. If your people became strong enough to defend yourselves, you may eventually become a force able to help us control these raiders. I know our merchants would pay a healthy fee for such a service."

The king regarded her skeptically. "So you say. More likely they will rob us."

Imenja nodded. "You are wise to consider that possibility. The threat of being mistaken for raiders would keep most merchants honest, but in such an enterprise you would need to be both cautious and clever."

"Or not embark on it at all." He lifted his chin. "Thank you for returning my daughter, Imenja of the Pentadrians. You must leave before the midday."

"Then we will, of course," Imenja replied. "If in the future you wish to negotiate, look for a black-sailed ship. There will be a Servant of the Gods dressed as I am on board who will relay a message to me."

She turned and began walking away. Reivan followed, resisting the temptation to look back to see the king's expression. *He's probably still frowning and puffing out his chest,* she thought.

*:That didn't go too badly, did it?* Imenja asked.

Reivan glanced at her mistress.

*:I don't know. What did you read from his thoughts?*

*:Suspicion, mostly. He distrusts all landwalkers.*

*:Even those who rescued and returned his daughter?*

*:Especially us. Distrust is his strength. But I know what his weakness is.*

*:What?*

*:His daughter. He blames himself for her kidnapping. She has seen more of the world than he could ever imagine and returned better informed than he. Between feeling guilty, his old habit of indulging her, and realizing she will never be satisfied cooped up in the city, he is fighting quite a battle.*

*:A losing battle?*

Imenja smiled.

*:I'm counting on it.*

The city of Karienne looked, in character, much as it had the last time Emerahl had visited. Buildings of all shapes and sizes mingled to form a sprawling metropolis on either side of a modest and dirty river. That sprawl had nearly doubled in size in the last few centuries, if what she could see of it from the water was any indication.

"Where would you like to disembark?" Emerahl asked, turning to regard the couple and their children.

Shalina looked at her husband.

"Won't you be docking at the main wharf?" Tarsheni asked.

"I could, but it will probably cost me a hefty mooring fee. These smaller piers are usually less costly."

"From what I remember, the main wharf is close to the Great Square, where the Wise Man speaks, and we would like to board near there if we can. If we pay for your mooring, will you come with us to listen to him?"

Emerahl considered. Part of her itched to sail up the river to the Red Caves as quickly as possible, but another part was curious to see this Wise Man. It had taken her months to get here, what difference would a half-day delay make?

"Very well," she said. "I'll come and see what the fuss is about."

Soon they reached the edge of the main docks and found a mooring among the crowded piers and wharves. She helped the couple carry their belongings off the boat and into the city. The streets were narrow and many were covered to ward off the desert sun. They ran in all directions in a pattern that was unrecognizable to her or Tarsheni. Homes, warehouses, shops, temples and barracks mingled. None stood parallel to another, so all the streets varied in width.

Fortunately the residents were friendly and happy to give directions. Emerahl and the family emerged from a narrow, crowded street to find themselves in an open space.

The Great Square was not big compared to some in other cities, but it seemed large after the congested streets. A crowd had gathered at one corner. Tarsheni's eyes glowed with excitement. The couple found a boarding house nearby and haggled down the price to a barely reasonable fee, impatient to finally see the man who had inspired them to travel so far.

With their belongings stowed in a room, they left the boarding house and strode across the square toward the crowd. Both adults were tense with expectation. Their son was merely overwhelmed by all the activity around them, and the baby blinked sleepily.

The crowd was thin at the edges. Tarsheni slowed and moved deeper. Emerahl could not see the object of the crowd's attention, but she could hear him easily.

"We are all creations of the Maker," he boomed. "You, me, the priest over there, the arem that hauls your goods and the reyner that you ride are its creations. The bird that sings and the insect that bites are its creations. The lowly beggar, the successful merchant, the kings and emperors of the world, the priests and followers of all gods, the Gifted, the unGifted, all are its creations. Even the gods themselves are—"

The voice stopped and Emerahl heard a fainter one.

"No!" the Wise Man continued. "That is not true. I have studied the texts and sought the wisdom of all religions, and no god has ever claimed to have created the world. But it must have a creator. A Maker—"

Emerahl almost caught the next question. She decided to move closer, leaving the family listening with rapt attention.

"The existence of the world is proof enough! Only a being of higher . . . Yes, that is right. The Maker made creatures that we consider evil. But why do we consider them evil? Because they kill? A carmook kills and eats other living things, and we keep them as pets. A reyner eats plants. They are living things as well. We fear the leramers and the vorns because they can kill us, but they do not do so out of malice, but hunger. We dislike them because they eat our stock. That is inconvenience, not evil."

There was a pause, then a chuckle. As two men beside her shifted their weight, Emerahl unexpectedly caught a glimpse of a handsome young man standing on a wooden box, arms raised as he prepared to address the crowd again. She paused, surprised that the Wise Man was so young, then moved closer.

". . . be evil, too. Why do we prey upon ourselves? I do not know. Why is the world not perfect? Why can we not comprehend and understand every part of it from birth? Clearly the Maker did not intend that. The Maker made the world changeable. Perhaps so that we have a reason to strive."

Emerahl stopped as she found herself nearing several priests and priestesses. There was even a high priest in the group. While several of the Circlians were frowning, some were listening with interest.

"It has fallen to me to strive to understand the Maker," the Wise Man continued. "All are welcome to join me. I do not ask you to give up anything. Not family, wealth, profession, power or even religion. Believe in the Maker and together— man and woman, rich and poor, Gifted and unGifted—we may strive to unravel some of life's mysteries."

He continued in the same fashion. Listeners moved on and others replaced them, and questions began to be repeated. Emerahl made her way back through the crowd to the family. She saw that the Circlians had left. A pair of Pentadrians were also departing. *I don't see any Dreamweavers,* she noted. Tarsheni's eyes were shining with excitement.

"I must get my inks and papers," Tarsheni breathed. He turned to Emerahl. "What did you think?"

She shrugged. "An interesting idea."

"So you said before."

"I also said if he couldn't prove it most people wouldn't pay much attention."

"Isn't the existence of the world enough?"

"No," she replied honestly. "I don't think the Circlians like the idea that someone claims a greater being created their gods."

Tarsheni grinned. "Who cares what the Circlians think, eh?"

Emerahl laughed. "Indeed." She looked at each of them, then smiled. "I guess it is time for us to part."

"It was a pleasure travelling with you," Shalina said, with feeling.

"And you," Emerahl replied.

"Thank you for transporting us," Tarsheni said solemnly. "And for saving us from those thieves in the Isthmus tunnel."

"If you hadn't told me about the tunnel I'd have had to sell my boat," Emerahl pointed out. "So you saved me from being robbed as much as I saved you."

The couple chuckled. "Where will you go now?"

"Upriver."

"A family matter?"

"You could think of it that way. I, like you, am hoping to meet someone I've heard much of but never met."

"Then I hope you are as satisfied with your meeting as we are with ours," Tarsheni replied. "Farewell, Emmea. May the winds always blow in your favor."

"Farewell," Emerahl replied. "And remember my advice. If he starts asking for your money, don't give a coin more than you can safely afford. I've encountered false wise men before, and they can be cunning."

"We'll be careful."

Smiling, Emerahl turned away from the family and started back to the docks and her little boat, and the last leg of her journey to the Red Caves.

## 43

For once Auraya wished she could fly into the Open without attracting a crowd of welcoming Siyee. Their reverence felt wrong. Misplaced. She was not worthy of it.

As she landed Speaker Sirri met her and offered the traditional water and cake. But before Auraya could eat them something streaked across the ground and bounded into her arms, knocking bowl and cake from her hands.

"Mischief!" she exclaimed. "That was rude!" The veez wriggled with excitement. It was impossible to scold him convincingly. She hadn't seen him in so long, and it was suddenly so good to be the subject of simple, unconditional adoration.

"Owaya back," he said. "Owaya stay."

"All right, Mischief. Auraya stay. Now—bleargh! Stop that!"

She'd had a glimpse of a pink tongue headed for her, but too late to avoid it. Grabbing the veez, she held him at arm's length to stop him licking her face, then looked beyond him and saw that Sirri was holding a hand over her mouth to stop herself laughing.

Auraya chuckled ruefully, and looked around in surprise as the sound of laughter came from all sides.

"Sorry about that, Speaker Sirri," she said. "I've neglected his training of late and he has a talent for picking up new bad habits."

"I think he learned that from the children," Sirri said apologetically, removing a hand to reveal a wide grin. "They adore him."

Mischief began to struggle, suddenly intent on getting down to the ground again. Auraya let him go, but groaned aloud as he pounced on the piece of cake. At this the crowd of Siyee burst into laughter again. Auraya felt a wave of affection for them. Instead of insult at the interrupted ceremony they found humor in the situation.

"Are you staying?" Sirri asked. "Would you like to join me in my bower for a proper meal tonight?"

"I am, and I'd love to." Auraya picked up Mischief and set him onto her shoulders. "How are things here?"

"Let's discuss it on the way to your bower," Sirri said, stepping away. Auraya fell into step beside her. Sirri remained quiet until they had moved out of the hearing of other Siyee. "Messengers of the Sand tribe reported that a Pentadrian ship had been seen off the coast, and that they had alerted you."

Auraya nodded. "They did, but the ship was long gone by the time I got there."

"We have had several new cases of Hearteater since you left. They came from the Temple Mountain tribe, saying you sent them here. They have been isolated and the priests are looking after them."

Auraya groaned. "I told the Speaker to send only those who had been sick and had recovered away from the mountain. What of the other villages?"

"Even the most distant tribes are sending messages for help. I fear you cannot reach them all in time. I do not know what to do. And the Blue Lake tribe has sent news that Dreamweaver Wilar has vanished."

Auraya felt a shiver run down her spine at the name. From Sirri's thoughts she could see the Speaker didn't know the reason for Mirar's disappearance, but the Blue Lake messenger had speculated at the possibility that there had been an argument between Auraya and Mirar.

"I know that he has left," she said carefully. "And I know why, but I cannot speak of it except to say that I wish he did not need to and that there is nothing I can do to help him."

*Except do nothing,* she added silently.

Sirri was intrigued, but she did not voice any of the questions that came to mind. They had reached Auraya's bower. Mischief leapt off Auraya's shoulder and darted inside.

"That is a shame," Sirri said. "If you cannot help him, who can?"

"Only himself." Abruptly Auraya remembered the friend she had seen in Mirar's mind. Would the woman who had helped him regain his identity be able to help him again?

Sirri smiled and stepped away. "We have much to discuss tonight. What will you do next?"

"Convince Mischief to stay here, then visit the sick newcomers."

Sirri nodded. As the Speaker walked away, Auraya entered her bower. Looking around, she noted the bowl of fruit and fresh jug of water sitting on a table. She silently thanked whoever had kept the place ready for her return, including taking care of Mischief.

The veez had climbed up to the hanging basket he used as a bed. His nose peeped over the edge, then he climbed onto the brim and leapt onto her shoulders.

"I think you're heavier than before," she told him. "Are you getting fat?" She scratched him under the chin.

"Msstf fat," he agreed.

She laughed. He had recognized the Siyee word for "fat," though she could see he didn't understand it. People must have been saying it in his presence enough for him to associate it with himself.

"Have you been pestering people into giving you food?" she asked him.

He didn't answer. His eyes were closed in appreciation of her scratching.

"Now, Mischief, stay. Auraya go and—"

*:Where is she? Ah. Here she is.*

She froze. The voice was Chaia's. Her heart began to pound. Mischief leapt off her shoulders and turned to regard her, whiskers twitching. He could sense her agitation, but not the source of it. Then a glow began to form in the center of the room and the veez fled into the bedroom.

Auraya swallowed hard as the glow formed the shape of a man. Chaia was smiling, she saw with relief.

*:Hello, Auraya.*

*:Hello, Chaia,* she replied.

*:Did you miss me?*

She stared at him for a moment, unsure how to answer. It wasn't the question she was expecting. His smile was the sort of playful expression he wore during his more amorous moods, but for some reason that disturbed and repelled her. As he stepped forward she had to resist the urge to back away.

*:It's a little hard to miss someone when you're not sure if you'll like what they're going to do or ask of you when they return,* she said, perhaps too bluntly.

His smile widened and he reached out to touch her cheek.

*:It would be. But putting that aside, don't you miss our nights together? Don't you miss my touch?*

Where his fingers passed through her skin she felt a delicious tingling. A shiver ran down her spine.

*:Yes,* she admitted. *A little.*

*:Just a little?* He pouted. *Wasn't I attentive enough?*

She could not resist a smile.

*:You were more than attentive enough.* She stepped back out of his reach. *But that was just physical pleasure, Chaia. I miss it. I even crave it sometimes. But . . .*

*:But?* His eyebrows rose. *You didn't miss me, did you? You don't love me?*

She looked away. Now that he had confronted her with the question, she knew he was right.

*:Not in the way human lovers do. Not in the way . . .*

*:The way you love Mirar,* he finished, all humor gone from his face.

She felt a flash of anger.

*:No. Nothing like what I feel for Mirar. Is it pity you want?*

He stared at her, then smiled.

*:I believe I asked for that. And I know you do not love me as you once loved Leiard.* His eyes narrowed. *What do you feel for me?*

She considered.

*:Something between love for a god and the love for a friend. I think . . . I think we are too different.*

*:I have always treated you as an equal, when we were alone together. You have done the same.*

*:Yes, but it isn't about us pretending to be equals.* She shook her head. A movement in the bedroom entrance caught her eye. Mischief was looking out. *Maybe it is as implausible as expecting Mischief to feel romantic love for me. He is a veez, I am human. Gods and humans may be more similar than humans and veez, but not similar enough. There are so many differences in how we see the world. So much that we can't get from each other that we can get from our own kind. I . . .* She looked up at Chaia. *But you know this. You can see my mind.*

*:I can only see what is, not what you have yet to decide,* he told her.

She felt her heartbeat quicken.

*:Then you can see what I have decided in other matters. What are you and the other gods going to do?*

He shrugged, though his expression was now serious.

*:We haven't decided yet.*

She frowned.

*:Why not?*

His mouth twisted into a crooked smile.

*:We do not always agree on everything, Auraya.*

*:Then what options are you considering?*

*:Ah,* he replied. *That would be telling.*

And he vanished. She felt a surge of anger and frustration.

*:Chaia?* Her senses told her he was still in the room. *Chaia! I know you're still here. I can sense you.*

*:I know you can.* He drifted away, but before he faded from her senses words came to her like a distant voice blown to her on the wind.

*:I expected you to refuse, Auraya. Know that you have made an enemy of one of the gods.*

And then his voice faded to nothing. She turned around and around, wondering if he had been referring to her refusal to kill Mirar, or her admission that she didn't love him like a human. Which of the gods had she made an enemy of: Chaia or another?

Imi walked slowly around her room, touching everything. She had done this several times in the last few days, not sure if it was to reassure herself that she was truly home, or to remind herself how much had changed.

The carvings around the walls had never interested her as they did now. As a child she had liked them for what they represented: famous Elai, the goddess Huan, creatures of the sea. Now she saw the workmanship in them and she wondered how much landwalkers would pay for carvings like these.

And what else could the Elai sell them?

While she hadn't liked wearing the formal jewellery favored by adults before, now she carefully chose something from her chest every day. Her favorite toys she now displayed on a shelf, but she did not play with them. Instead she asked Teiti endless questions about Elai history, the landwalkers who had attacked or deceived Elai in the past, magic and the goddess. When her aunt could not answer her questions, she had sent the woman away to find answers, or demanded to see people who could tell her what she wanted to know.

"All landwalkers have Gifts—even small ones. Why don't we?" she had asked of the palace sorcerer, an ugly old man with a wheeze and loose skin that hung from his bones like cloth.

"The oldest records tell how Huan selected men and women with weak Gifts to become Elai," he told her. "They were less resistant to the changes she wrought in them."

"Resistant? Didn't they want to become Elai?"

"They did, but those with magic found they kept undoing the changes without meaning to."

"What of the Elai who have Gifts now? Do they undo themselves?"

He shrugged. "We do tend to sicken easily and age faster."

"Is it the same for the Siyee?"

He nodded. "They have fared better, however. They have a few sorcerers with moderately powerful Gifts. At least they did ten years ago, when I last visited."

"Why have they done better?"

"I don't know," he had admitted. "Why don't you ask the head priestess?"

She had followed his advice. The head priestess, a woman of Teiti's age, told her that the way things were was how Huan intended them to be.

"So she doesn't want us to change?"

"Not necessarily. We can change. But if we begin change in a way she does not want us to, she will intervene. She has done it before."

Imi had considered this, then moved to another question that had been bothering her.

"We only follow Huan. What of the other gods? Why don't we follow them?"

"Because Huan made us."

"And she doesn't let us follow other gods as well as her?"

The priestess's eyebrows had risen at that, but not in surprise. Imi had met her disapproval with determination.

"What are the other gods like?"

"Chaia was always known as the God of Kings. Lore was the God of War. Yranna the Goddess of Women and Saru the God of Wealth."

"You say that as if they aren't any more."

"They put aside their former titles after the War of the Gods. But these titles are still an indication of their natures. Chaia has the character of a leader, and is wise in all matters of holding and keeping power."

Imi nodded. "What of the Pentadrian gods?"

The priestess shrugged. "I know nothing of them. It is said only five gods survived the War of the Gods, and that in some lands people still worship dead gods as if they are real."

"Servant Reivan said that she once heard her god speaking in her mind. That sounds as if he is real."

"She may have imagined it." The priestess shrugged. "I

know nothing of these Pentadrian gods, nor do I need to
know anything. Huan is our goddess and creator. We need
no other."

"No. But it would be good to know all about other
people's gods."

"Why?"

"In case Huan decides we need to change," Imi replied.
"Or in case we begin to change and Huan doesn't stop it."

"I doubt she'd approve of us worshipping other gods."

"I don't think any Elai would want that. But other things
can change, sometimes without us wanting it. We should be
ready to face anything."

The priestess had smiled at that. "You'll make a good
queen one day."

Imi felt a wry pride at the memory. She had nearly
finished her circuit of the room. As she moved to the next
shelf there came a knock at the door, and she stopped.
Teiti emerged from her little "room" within Imi's cave and
opened the door. The woman frowned as she saw the boy
standing there.

"Come in, Rissi."

The boy sidestepped past Teiti and walked toward Imi.
He stopped a few steps away and bowed.

"Princess," he said. "I have come to report my findings."

Teiti nodded approvingly at the formality before returning to her room. Imi smiled at Rissi. After a day of
pleading, her father had finally agreed that several months'
imprisonment was enough punishment for the boy who had
led her out of the city and to the islands where she had been
captured. Rissi hadn't been angry with her for leading *him*
into trouble. Instead he apologized endlessly for failing to
stop or rescue her. He had come to the palace each day,
asking if there was anything he could do to make up for his
mistake.

Teiti had suggested Imi think of something useful for
the boy to do, as guilt—though undeserved—was obviously making him miserable. That had given Imi an idea,
and she had sent Rissi out on a quest for information. Her
father used the pipe room to listen in on the city populace

and gauge people's opinions on his rule. She would use the children.

Rissi had asked other children to pose a question to their parents. He was to tally the answers and give them to her.

The question was: "Should the Elai be friends with the people who had rescued Princess Imi?"

Imi smiled at Rissi. "What did they say?"

"It was even," he told her. "Some said the answer was 'yes.' Just as many said 'no.' A few didn't get an answer, or didn't understand the answer, or their parents couldn't decide."

"So half of the definite answers were 'yes' and half 'no,' " Imi mused aloud. "Without anyone trying to change their minds yet."

"You're not going to get your father to befriend land-walkers, are you?" he asked.

"You don't like the idea?"

He shook his head. "Landwalkers took you away and made you work like a slave. They're dangerous."

"Not all of them," Imi told him. "The Pentadrians were good to me."

He shook his head in disagreement, but said nothing.

"Why don't you believe me?" she asked.

He frowned. "It's not that I don't believe you, but . . ."

"But?"

His frown changed to a scowl. "It only takes one bad one among the good and we're all dead."

"Not if we don't bring them here. When we trade we should do it somewhere else. And insist that there only be a few of them. We could even have them leave goods some-where for us, and we could leave ours in return."

"And if they come back and attack us? If raiders come to take the goods?"

"We should have a quick escape route. They can't swim like us, remember. We have to stop running and hiding. We have to be able to stand and defend ourselves."

"We have our warriors."

"Who can only fight one on one. We need to do better than that. We need archers. And fortifications. And magic."

Rissi shuddered. "I don't like it. We've been safe living here for generations. Why change that?"

"Because we're not growing, Rissi. Look at the Siyee. There are thousands of them. We're crowded in here. We need to live on the islands again. We need space if we're going to grow." She sighed. "My father started talking about finding me a husband in a few years. I asked Teiti who he might choose, and there were only five boys or young men who were close to me in age, and they were all cousins, and I don't much like any of them."

"You might in a few years," Teiti offered from within her "room."

"Though he did say I might marry a warrior leader, if he was impressed enough with the man, in order to bring some new blood into the family," Imi added, ignoring Teiti's comment.

Rissi's expression was a mixture of amusement and horror. "A husband? Already?"

She nodded. "I think he was trying to change the subject from landwalkers to something else."

The boy chuckled. "I imagine he was. You haven't stopped talking about the Pentadrians and Elai trading with landwalkers since you got back, from what I've heard lately."

She frowned. "Do you think other people have heard? Do you think it would have affected their answers?"

He rolled his eyes. "Do you think about anything else?"

She straightened her back. "Not when I have the future of my kingdom to think of."

"Don't you play any more? Why don't you come down to the Children's Pool?"

She paused. "Father forbids it," she admitted. "He doesn't want me associating with foolish young men," she added, keeping her expression serious.

Rissi looked away, his face reddening. "Then I should leave."

Imi's heart sank. She missed the company of other children. He was a boy, but at least he was closer to her age.

"You don't have to," she said. "I didn't mean—"

He shook his head and moved back to the door. "I have to go. I have to go to the Warriors' Pool."

"Come back tomorrow," she commanded. "I have another question for you to get the children to ask."

He nodded. "I will, Princess. Goodbye."

As the door closed behind him, Imi crossed her arms and sighed.

*What did I do that for? Now I'm going to have to think of a good question to ask.*

# 44

After several days travel Mirar had given up on evading the Siyee's notice. They were diligent in their searching, and there was little chance of them failing to notice him once he reached the snow-laden slopes of the mountains, where there was no dense forest to hide him. He no longer even bothered to hide his tracks in the snow.

They did not approach him, however. Each night they disappeared into the forest below. Each morning he found them circling lazily above, watching him. He sensed no anger or conflict from the Siyee so he doubted they knew why they were tracking him.

Constantly sensing their emotions kept him on edge and he dreamed unpleasant dreams in which he was stalked by huge eyes with glowing white wings. One advantage in having the Siyee near, however, was that a change in the emotions he sensed might alert him to the approach of the White. He didn't expect that to happen for weeks, though. Other than Auraya, the White would find it hard to reach him in these mountains.

At the first sign of dawn each day he would wake, clear his mind, then put himself into a dream trance. First he would try to find Auraya, but she never replied to his calls. She could be ignoring him. The gods could be blocking him from reaching her. Or she could be dead. Sometimes during the day the thought of the latter tortured him. If the gods killed her, he must take some of the blame.

When he could no longer bear Auraya's silence he called

to Emerahl. Now, as she replied curtly, he could tell she was still annoyed at herself for accidentally revealing her location to him the previous night.

*:Yesterday was the same as the day before,* she told him this morning. *Except it's swampy now. The river splits endlessly and I wasted half of yesterday discovering the branches I'd chosen were dead ends. But last night one of the swamp people approached me. He said he had a message from The Gull's friend: "follow the blood of the earth."*

*:Blood of the earth,* Mirar mused. *Liquid and soil. Silt from the Red Caves?*

*:Yes. Rather obvious, really. I had noticed that the water ranged from a filthy black to a filthy red. As soon as the sun is high enough I'll set out again. How are you faring?*

*:My watchers are still watching,* he told her.

*:Do you think you can lose them?*

*:Not unless I find another forest on the other side. Then they are sure to patrol the edge of the desert and find me again. Once I have travelled far enough into the desert they won't be able to follow. They can't carry enough water.*

*:No, but neither can you. You'll have to stop at wells or buy water from caravans. Every mortal you meet could reveal your location to the gods.*

She was right.

*:They must have guessed by now that I'm not going to head for the Siyee coast.*

*:Yes. You will have to approach the coast eventually if you are going to get to Southern Ithania.*

*:Which I'll never reach if there's a White waiting there to meet me.*

*:Ah, but I have thought of a way you can improve your chances there.*

He felt a small thrill of hope.

*:How?*

*:Your people. If the coastal towns are suddenly full of Dreamweavers, how much notice will anyone take of another one arriving?*

It wasn't a bad idea, but it was not without drawbacks.

*:Do you have a clever idea for drawing enough Dream-weavers to the Sennon coast?*

*:Ask Dreamweaver Arleej to send them there.*

*:If I contact Arleej she will sense that I have changed. She might think me only Leiard gone mad.*

*:Yes. You'll have to convince her of the truth as you did with Auraya—without revealing anything about me this time.*

*:Of course. But if I allow the world to know I have returned there may be consequences. If Circlians knew that the supposedly wicked sorcerer Mirar had survived his just punishment, they might turn on Dreamweavers.*

*:Then tell only Arleej. Tell her to give the Dreamweavers some other reason for going to the villages. It will be better if the Dreamweavers who come to your aid don't know who they are aiding. They'll give the game away if the White read their minds. If you are not dressed as a Dreamweaver, but as an ordinary traveller, you will attract no attention at all.*

She was right. It would improve his chances considerably. He had not wanted to reveal himself to his people until he was sure it would do no harm. Arleej could be trusted to keep his return a secret. She had kept his and Auraya's affair to herself, despite her disapproval of it.

*:I think it will work. Thank you, Emerahl,* he said.

*:Anything for a friend.*

*:Anything?*

*:Almost anything,* she amended.

*:Have a nice day paddling in the swamp.*

*:Ha ha. Now go interrupt the sleep of a Dreamweaver.*

Her mind faded from his senses. He paused a moment to reorient himself, then called out a name.

*:Arleej?*

It would be about the same time of day in Arbeem as it was here in Si. There was a chance Arleej was already awake, but that might not matter. She had proven herself sensitive enough to detect someone calling to her months before, when he had sought her after Juran had sent him away.

*:Arleej?*

After several calls he heard a faint and sleepy reply.

*:Hello? Who is this?*

*:It is the one you know as Leiard.*

He sensed his connection with her waver as she nearly woke up from shock.

*:Leiard! But . . . you are not Leiard. You do not sound like him.*

*:No. I am him, and yet I'm not. There is much I need to explain to you. Do you remember the link memories I had of Mirar's?*

*:Yes.*

*:They were not link memories. They were real memories. I am Mirar.*

She paused.

*:How long is it since you linked with another Dream-weaver?*

*:This is not a delusion resulting from me losing my sense of identity, Arleej. I created Leiard and suppressed my own memories in order to live. Let me show you.*

He drew up the memories, feeling her react with sympathy, anger and wonder as she learned how he had survived. He explained how he had regained his identity yet also retained Leiard's. When he had finished, Arleej was silent for a long time.

*:So you are Mirar,* she said finally.

*:Yes. I'm back. And as always, I've made a complete mess of things.*

He sensed her amusement.

*:I imagine there was not much time to plan for the future while you were crushed and dying under the old House of Jarime. How could you have known the child you taught would become a White? She is an extraordinary person. This hospice she started in Jarime has been a great success.*

*:Hospice?*

*:Auraya has brought together Dreamweavers and priests in order to provide healing for the poor and encourage co-operation and tolerance.*

*:She never mentioned that.*

*:You've spoken to her recently?*

*:Yes, we have both been treating the Siyee, who have suffered badly from a particularly virulent plague of Hearteater.*

*:I hadn't heard. Should I send Dreamweavers there?*

He felt a pang of guilt. If he had contacted Arleej earlier, Dreamweavers might have made the difficult journey into Si in time to be of assistance. But he had been so concerned with keeping himself isolated and hidden, and since no other Dreamweaver was powerful enough to heal magically their help would have been limited. Still, even those Siyee whose bodies could fight the disease needed care while they were sick.

*:If there are any Dreamweavers willing to make the journey, send them. But Auraya may have the disease under control by the time they get there,* he told Arleej.

*:Will she? On her own? Her skills must be greater than I thought.*

*:I taught her all I know of healing with magic,* he assured her.

*:That was generous of you, what with her being one of the White!*

*:I know she will use it well.*

*:Yes. You are right. The hospice in Jarime is proof of that.*

*:There have been no protests? No trouble?*

*:Of course there has. But there's been a rumor going around that she did it to prove that the priests and priestesses are better healers, so people won't be tempted to join us.*

*:Which can't be true. She knows we're superior healers.*

*:But she can't have meant the opposite to happen, either.*

*:No,* he agreed. *She would not encourage people to join us. Juran would not approve of this unless there was something in it for the Circlians to gain.* He felt a chill. *Knowledge. They will gain healing knowledge from us.*

*:Yes, but not everything. I doubt they'll seek to learn any dream or mind-link methods.*

*:Wouldn't they?*

She hesitated.

*:What do you think?*

He considered.

*:In the long term, attitudes can be changed,* he said. *In a few decades, after she has encouraged the careers of healer priests who have open minds, the general attitude toward mind links will soften. It gives her time to work at changing the minds of other White, too. She is thinking like an immortal.*

*:I thought only that it was a chance to improve our standing among the people and . . .*

*:And?*

*:Sometimes I feel it is more important that our knowledge survive than that we survive. We have never held back from helping others, even if doing so was to our detriment.*

Her admission disturbed him. That the current leader of the Dreamweavers felt this way about her people ought to appall him, but before he could think of the words to reassure her realized that he had taught Auraya for similar reasons. He was not free to roam the world performing healing miracles, so he had given her the ability.

Perhaps it would be better if Dreamweaver knowledge was given to the world, then the cult allowed to fade out of existence. In this age Dreamweavers could only live a life of persecution and division. The gods, through the White, were too powerful.

The way of life of Dreamweavers, of refusing to make war, of tolerance and generosity, might be lost, but what would rise in its place? While Dreamweavers represented that philosophy people would reject it. If Dreamweavers didn't exist, some Circlians could take a similar philosophy to themselves without being accused of thinking like Dreamweavers.

*:Now that you are here we will grow stronger again,* Arleej said, perhaps interpreting his silence as dismay.

*:Not if I don't survive the next few weeks. When I taught Auraya I unintentionally revealed my identity to the gods. I am fleeing toward the Sennon coast.*

*:You can't return only to perish so soon! Is there anything I can do to help?*

*:Perhaps. The Siyee are tracking me, and keeping my location known to the gods and the White. When I get to the coast I mean to take a boat and sail out into the sea. The Siyee can't follow me far. It is my only chance to escape. But there is sure to be a White waiting for me at the coast.*

*:What can I do?*

*:Send Dreamweavers to the coast. Lots of them. Fill the streets of several villages with them. Hopefully I'll be able to slip through one of the villages unnoticed.*

*:It will take some time for them to get there.*

*:I know. We must time this carefully. The Circlians may work out what we are doing and drive the Dreamweavers away. There is a danger they may retaliate if I am successful, too.*

*:We are used to evading danger. And once Dreamweavers hear about you, I'll have too many volunteers to handle.*

*:No. They can't know about me, Arleej. If they do the White will read our intentions from their minds.*

*:You're right. I will create another reason for them to be there,* she said.

*:Thank you.*

*:If you do survive this, will we meet again?*

*:I hope so.*

*:Perhaps I will visit the southern continent. The Dreamweavers there lead a freer life than even those of us who live in Somrey.*

*:I won't be letting anyone know who I am,* he told her. *The Pentadrians might tolerate Dreamweavers in their lands, but they may not tolerate me. I will link with you again when I know which village I intend to pass through.*

*:Take care of yourself.*

*:I will. Goodbye.*

Drawing himself out of the dream trance, Mirar opened his eyes. The sky beyond the entrance of the crevasse he had sheltered in was dark and close, promising bad weather. There was no sign of the Siyee. He stood up, surveyed the ominous clouds, and cursed.

*Looks like a blizzard coming.*

He wouldn't be travelling far today, but at least it would

keep the Siyee out of the sky. For once he wouldn't spend the day with the nagging sensation of Siyee minds watching him.

Emerging from below deck, Reivan saw that Imenja was standing at the stern. The Voice was leaning against the rail, her head bowed. Reivan had found her like this several times in the last two days. She moved to stand beside her mistress and wasn't surprised to see that the woman was gazing down at the water.

"It's amazing how quiet the ship is now that Imi has left us," she said. "I think the crew miss her."

"Yes," Reivan agreed. "Or it might just be your moping."

Imenja turned to regard Reivan. "Moping?"

"Yes. You're always gazing off into the distance, or down at the water."

"Am I?"

"Yes. I'm guessing you're disappointed that we left without an alliance."

"You're guessing wrong," Imenja told her, smiling. "This is not over yet, Reivan. The king may have sent us on our way, but his people haven't seen the last of us." She glanced down at the water. "We are being followed."

Reivan felt a thrill of excitement and searched the waves, but could see no sign of Elai.

"Do they know you know they're there?"

Imenja laughed. "That's quite a mouthful. They suspect I have seen them, but they are not sure."

"Is this why only the main sail is unfurled?"

"Yes. I don't want us to outpace them."

"And why is that?"

"Just hoping fate will favor us with an opportunity. Well, to be truthful, research has as much to do with my plans as fate. Before we left I read the minds of several Elai who'd seen raiders. I learned the most common places where trade ships are attacked."

"And we're headed for them?"

"We're in one already. There is a raider ship to the south, beyond the horizon. I've caught the faint thoughts of its crew."

"You're hoping we'll be attacked?"

"No. I doubt raiders would attack us. This isn't a trading ship. Even if I ordered the sail changed to a plain one, raiders know how to recognize the shape of a hull."

"So you intend to find and attack them? Is that wise? What if the White heard we had destroyed a ship? They might not learn or care that it was a raider ship."

Imenja narrowed her eyes. "They would not hear of it, if there were no survivors."

"But there will be witnesses, if the Elai are still with us."

"I want them to be. I want to give them the opportunity to take part, if that is possible." Imenja frowned. "But I'm not sure how. What would you do to harm a raider ship, if you were an Elai warrior?"

"I'm not sure. What advantages do they have over their enemies? They can hold their breath a long time, so they could easily drown their enemy."

"If they can get to the raiders themselves. I want to know what they could do to harm a *ship*."

Reivan shrugged. "Elai can easily reach a ship's hull, and there's nothing stopping them from trying to damage it. Could they break through it?"

"Not with their bare hands."

"Nor with their spears, either. They need a weapon designed for the purpose. Or magic."

"Neither of which we can give them."

"Can't we?" Reivan grinned. "There must be woodworking tools on board this ship."

"Would they work fast enough, in a battle?"

"Maybe. Maybe not. It would depend how long the battle lasted, and how many tools were employed."

"How else could they fight raiders?"

They had reached the prow of the boat now. "Luring them onto reefs, perhaps?" Reivan suggested. "But I doubt that would work. The raiders must know these waters well. I'm sure I could think of something better, given time and—"

Imenja abruptly lifted a hand to silence her. Eyes half closed, the Second Voice stared at the horizon.

"I think our raiders have found themselves a victim. Yes, a merchant ship sailing west. You had better come up with some ideas quickly, Reivan."

"I thought you didn't want the White to hear of this. Or are you planning to sink the merchant ship too."

"No, I think it might be useful to us if a few merchants are grateful to have been rescued from their attackers by a Pentadrian ship."

Reivan chuckled. "We can impress two peoples in one fight. But will it come to a fight? Once the raiders see we are approaching they'll flee."

"And we will give chase. I will make sure we catch them."

A thrill of anticipation ran through Reivan. *But I must not let the prospect of a bit of magic and justice blind me to possible ill consequences.* "It's possible that, if the merchants hate us enough, they will claim we were the attackers."

"The White can read minds," Imenja reminded her. "They'd soon learn the truth. Look." She pointed to the south, where sails were just visible on the horizon. "The raiders." Turning to the east she narrowed her eyes. "The merchant is ahead of us."

She turned to the helmsman and ordered him to turn out of the wind. As he obeyed, the sails slumped and the ship slowed to a halt. Reivan looked at Imenja questioningly.

"The merchants haven't noticed their pursuers yet," Imenja explained. "And we don't want to put the raiders off yet. The Elai need some time to prepare."

"They do?"

"Yes. We're going to show them how to use woodworking tools."

"We are?"

"Yes."

"I'm sure they already know how. There are some impressive carvings among the gifts the king gave you."

"Yes, but just because they have talented crafters doesn't mean their warriors know how to use a mallet and chisel."

Imenja called to the captain, telling him to be prepared for chase and a battle. At the stern she stopped and called

out to the Elai by name. After several minutes two heads
appeared several strides from the ship.

"How much do you hate raiders?" she asked them, her
voice full of challenge.

The pair exchanged glances, but said nothing.

"There is a raider ship ahead, about to attack a merchant
vessel. I intend to stop it. Will you help me?"

"How?" one of the warriors asked.

"Let me show you." Imenja beckoned to one of the crew.
"Bring us carpentry tools. Chisels and mallets. Anything
that might be used to put a hole in the hull of a ship."

"Is that wise, Second Voice?" he asked. "What if they
decide to sink us as well?"

"They won't," she assured him.

As the man hurried away, Reivan looked at the Elai.
*They look more suspicious of us than enthusiastic,* she
thought. *They're going to take a lot of convincing.*

To Reivan's surprise, the crewman returned with several
chisels and mallets. She guessed that if a ship needed repair
in some isolated place, the entire crew were expected to
help in the work, and so they carried enough tools for all.

The two Elai had swum closer. Four more heads had appeared farther away.

"Demonstrate how they are used," Imenja ordered.

The crewman cast about, then grabbed a bucket, placed
it between his knees, and began chipping away at the wood.
Imenja turned to the Elai.

"I will give you these tools. Use them to break the bottom
of the raider ship. Water will flow in and the ship will sink."

"But we'd never catch up with it," an Elai protested.

"You will if you come aboard," she told them. "My ship
is faster than theirs."

The two Elai vanished under the water then reappeared
among the distant four. Several minutes passed, then four
of the heads disappeared and, a moment later, reappeared
beside the ship.

"We will come with you," one said.

As crew threw ropes over the sides for the Elai to climb,
Reivan turned to smile at Imenja.

"I can't believe you convinced them to come aboard," she murmured.

"They're young and, like Imi, frustrated by being cooped up in their crowded city so much of the time," Imenja explained quietly.

"Where are the others?" Reivan asked, looking out to where the two remaining Elai had been.

"They'll follow at a distance, in case this proves to be a trick." As the Elai reached the deck she stepped forward to greet them, drawing their attention to the raider ship on the horizon and telling them she would catch it in an hour or two. She then introduced Reivan to them.

The Elai warriors struggled to stay balanced on the rocking of the ship. If they were intimidated by Imenja, they hid it well. The crewman handed over the chisels and mallets. The Elai held them confidently and Reivan concluded she had been right: they knew how to use them.

The ship suddenly lurched forward. Reivan hadn't noticed the sails being unfurled. Now ropes and mast creaked as the wind in the sails increased. The crew stopped and exchanged surprised looks, but the Elai appeared to accept this change without question.

*They won't have boarded a ship before,* she reminded herself. *This improbable wind is just another bit of strangeness.*

Ahead, the raiders were bearing down on the merchant ship, which was too heavy and slow to outrun its pursuer. Every move in the distant struggle was laborious and deliberate.

"Have they seen us?" Reivan asked.

"Yes," Imenja replied. "They think they can rob the merchant and get away before we arrive. And no Pentadrian ships have ever attacked them before."

The closer they came to the raider ship and its intended victim, the faster they seemed to travel. Suddenly the raiders veered away from the merchant ship.

"They've realized we're travelling faster than they first thought," Imenja murmured. "Now the chase begins."

Time stretched out. They passed the merchant vessel close enough to see the confused and frightened crew watching them. Imenja raised a hand to them, then turned her attention back to the raiders.

The distance between them shortened steadily. When they were close enough to see the men on board, the raider ship abruptly—or as quickly as a vessel could manage—turned about.

"They have decided to fight," Imenja said. She spun around to face the Elai. "Now is your chance to strike your enemy. Take care. Once they realize what you are doing they will shoot arrows in the water."

The warriors nodded, then, without speaking a word, moved to the rail and dove out into the water.

"Stay by me, Reivan," Imenja said quietly.

The air thrummed with the sound of approaching arrows. Imenja darted to the side of the ship and spread her arms. The arrows bounced off an invisible barrier.

"This hardly seems fair," Reivan muttered. "They can't possibly defeat you."

Imenja laughed. "Would you have me stand back and let my people die for the sake of a fair fight?"

"Of course not," Reivan replied.

"Be assured these are thieves and murderers. We do not kill innocent men."

The raider ship passed a few strides away. A few grappling hooks were thrown, but Imenja's barrier blocked them and they fell down into the water. Reivan looked down, but she could not see far beneath the surface.

"How are the Elai doing?" she asked.

Imenja chuckled. "They're enjoying themselves. I cannot tell if they're making any progress because they don't know themselves. The raiders are worried, though. They can hear the tapping."

A man moved to the railing of the raider ship. He was dressed well, and gold glittered on his hands and chest.

"The raider captain," Reivan guessed.

"Yes. A Skilled one."

The man raised his arms and the air rippled. Imenja laughed quietly.

"It does seem unfair," she admitted. She glanced at the crew, who were holding bows at the ready. "Fire!"

Before the arrows met their target the raider ship lurched in the water. A few raiders scurried out of the hull. Their panicked shouts sent a chill down Reivan's spine. The sea began to nibble at the sides of ship, sucking it down. Her stomach sank as the raiders began to fight each other for a place on the small row boat. The raider captain abandoned his magical attack on Imenja to stake his place on the little vessel.

The ship tipped. Water spilled over the deck, then claimed it. Bubbles of air rose as the vessel vanished into the depths. A chill ran over Reivan's skin as she saw men thrashing in the water, clearly unable to swim. They soon disappeared. Then she realized that those who were swimming confidently were going down too, pulled beneath the surface by shadowy attackers.

Reivan shuddered and looked away. The desperate pleas and shouts of anger dwindled. An ominous silence descended and she heard Imenja sigh.

"It's over. No survivors. And the Elai did most of it themselves."

"No survivors?" Reivan turned to see the little row boat floating upside down. "What happened to the captain?"

"Our sea-folk friends took care of him."

Two dark heads suddenly appeared close by. The white teeth of the Elai warriors flashed as they grinned.

"Bravely done," Imenja called. "You gave us almost no chance to attack them ourselves! You've brought down a raider ship all by yourselves!"

"We couldn't have caught them without your help," one of the warriors called back.

"No, but they saw us coming," she told him. "You could have easily snuck up on them underwater."

"Do you want the cutters back?"

She shook her head. "Keep them."

Another dark head appeared. The warrior held up a gold goblet. "Look. Their ship is full of it."

"Stolen from merchants," Imenja told them. "It is yours now. So should be the treasure on any raider ship you sink."

The warriors' grins widened.

"But take care to be sure the ships you sink are raiders," she warned. "If you sink a trader ship there are landwalkers who would seek to punish your people for the crime. Powerful landwalkers with powerful magic. They would make raiders seem as dangerous as children, and my people could do nothing to stop them."

The grins had faded. Imenja raised a hand in farewell. "Well done, warriors of Elai. The sea is a little safer today, thanks to you. Go celebrate your victory with your people."

"Yes!" the warrior with the goblet agreed.

"Farewell, then," one of the warriors called. "Have a safe journey."

"Many thanks for your help!"

"Goodbye!"

The fourth Elai surfaced, gold chains around his neck. He looked around, saw his fellow warriors swimming away, and dove after them.

Imenja turned and gave the order for the journey to resume.

"Not too fast," she told the captain quietly. "When word of this reaches the Elai king, I don't want us to be so far away that an invite to return to his land can't reach me." The captain nodded. She looked at Reivan and smiled wryly. "That is," she murmured, "if he doesn't take exception to me urging a few young, naïve warriors to sink a raider ship."

# 45

Every night since Emerahl had entered the swamp, the local people had passed on a message to her. First there had been "follow the blood of the earth." That had been obvious, since the red mud that stained some of the tributaries could hardly be missed. Once all the water was the same color "head for the flat mountain" had kept her moving in the same direction. Not that she could go in a straight line. She had to wind between islands as small as waterlogged tussocks to large hillocks of solid ground, at the same time avoiding water too shallow for her boat to cross. This morning she had been struggling to "fight the fastest current," which, to her relief, followed a channel more than deep enough for her boat to move along without its hull scraping through mud.

Once the ground had become solid enough to support more than tussocky grass, the vegetation had grown tall, lush and dense. Trees grew thin and high, and creepers roped them loosely together. When they reached heights too ambitious for the sodden soil they slumped against each other or toppled completely, their enormous root systems flaring out of the soggy ground.

Imposing spires of rock occasionally appeared. Some were broad, some thin, and all were draped with vegetation. Once she had passed a spire that had fallen against its neighbor. The top half of the gap between them had been filled with the web of a spider the size of her hand.

It was beautiful and yet utterly inhospitable.

*And there are no signs of caves,* Emerahl thought. *There's just not enough rock around. I guess I have a long way to go.*

Even as the thought passed through her mind she saw that she was wrong. The river had turned and before her was a wall of rock barely higher than the trees. At the base of it the water had washed out shallow hollows—none large enough to be a cave, but there was potential for it.

Her heart began to beat a little faster. The river continued to follow this low cliff. She resisted the temptation to push the boat at a greater speed. There were still snags and shallows hidden beneath the opaque red water.

The wall undulated, luring the river into a winding path. After over an hour of following its twists and turns, she rounded a corner and let out a sigh of satisfaction.

The river widened ahead, forming a large pool before a latticework of hollows and caves. Ripples in the surface of the pool revealed the path of the current she was following. It led directly to a larger cave entrance. Emerahl followed it. Just before she reached the cave she glanced up at the sky and smiled grimly to herself.

*Caves. Why do we immortals always end up in caves?*

The muted light of the swamp forest quickly faded. Emerahl created a spark of light and sent it before her. The roof of the cave dropped until it was so low the mast would have scraped it, had she not taken it down the previous day to stop it tangling in overhanging vines. Her light revealed openings to either side leading into a maze of natural, half-drowned rooms and passages.

She followed the current deeper into the wall of rock. There were no turns, just the constant ripple of water. The air was heavy with moisture and the silence was intense.

Suddenly the roof ahead curved up out of the reach of her light, and walls and columns on either side ended. She slowed and approached this void cautiously, brightening her light until it revealed a large cavern. Only the ripples from her boat's passage disturbed the still water. The roof was a smooth dome. At the far side she could see a ledge just above the level of the water.

And on the ledge stood a large pottery pitcher.

*I guess that's where I'm supposed to disembark,* she thought.

She directed the boat to the ledge, grabbed the mooring line and stepped off. The pitcher was full of clear water. Emerahl looked around. There were two cave entrances nearby. Above the larger one was a symbol—two small circles joined with a line.

Feeling a tug on the mooring line, Emerahl turned to see that her boat was drifting away in the current. Casting about, she realized there was nothing to tie the line to. She looked down at the pitcher, looped the line around it and stepped back, ready to grab it if the pot began to move. The line pulled tight, but the pitcher remained standing. Emerahl nudged it. It seemed secure enough. Stepping away, she approached the cave marked by the symbol. She moved her light through. It illuminated a small room beyond.

The room was round. The walls were painted in an elaborate pattern of dots. Another pitcher full of water stood in the center. From the ceiling moisture dripped into the vessel.

*"Who are you?"*

The voice spoke in a whisper, in a long-dead language, and she could not judge what direction it had come from. It sounded as if two people had spoken, but that might just be an echo effect of the room.

Emerahl considered what name to give. "I am . . ." They might not know her real name, she realized suddenly. "I am The Hag."

*"Why are you here?"*

"To meet you," she replied.

*"Then drink and be welcome."*

Emerahl regarded the pitcher suspiciously. The water was so clear she could see the base of the pot inside. Was there anything here to fear? Surely The Gull would not send her into a trap. No, she was just being her usual over-cautious self. The invitation was probably a ritual of good manners. Dipping a hand in the water, she lifted some to her lips and sipped.

Immediately her mouth began to burn. She gasped and backed away, as if that would stop the pain. The sensation began to spread. She touched her face again, alarmed to find that it was swelling rapidly.

"What . . . ?" she tried to say, but her swollen lips could not form words.

*The Gull said his friend would ignore me if he or she didn't want to meet me, not kill me! Why would he . . . ? Why would they . . . ?*

*Shut up,* she told herself. *You've been poisoned! Deal with it.*

Backing out of the room, she staggered to her boat and collapsed into it. A lethargy was spreading through her body. She had no strength left to cut the mooring line.

Closing her eyes, she sent her mind inward.

The poison's effect was spreading from her mouth, throat and stomach. She halted its progress by blocking the pathways it was taking. Pushing as much as possible back into her throat, she forced it and the liquids it had mingled with out.

Spitting it out, she sent her mind after poison that had managed to contaminate her blood. A burning sensation led her mind through organs and limbs. She saw that it was too dilute to do much damage. Speeding her heart, she filtered the poison out through the waste organs, gathering it into a little droplet, which she guided out of her body.

Taking three deep breaths, she opened her eyes and sat up.

*"Congratulations, Emerahl the Hag. You passed the test,"* a female voice said.

"Surely you could have come up with something a little more . . . polite," Emerahl replied, scowling.

A laugh echoed through the cavern. Male and young. *So there are two of them,* she mused. The voice held no malice, but plenty of irony. She still could not judge where it had come from.

*"If we could have, we would have,"* the man replied. *"Please forgive us, Emerahl. We had to be sure you were who you said you were."*

Emerahl rose and stepped out of the boat. "I'd have preferred a riddle."

The man laughed again. "*Would you? I find them annoying and pretentious.*"

She looked around. "I don't even know who you are, though I have a few ideas. How am I to test you?"

"*Come through the other cave,*" a woman replied.

Emerahl moved to the entrance and paused.

"*Don't worry. We do not have any more tests for you.*"

Even so, Emerahl kept her barrier strong as she stepped into the room beyond. It was empty. An irregular stairway led upward. She climbed slowly.

She emerged in the center of a large cavern. The floor was uneven, and there were holes here and there. On some of the higher levels cushions had been arranged, woven in bright colors. Alcoves had been carved into the walls, holding a variety of homely objects including reed baskets, pottery bowls and wooden statues. There was even a vase of flowers.

"Welcome, Emerahl. Or do you prefer The Hag?" a woman said from behind her.

Emerahl turned. A man and a woman sat within two alcoves on the back wall, both pale-haired, handsome and simply dressed. They were so alike they had to be related, confirming her suspicions about their identity.

"You are The Twins," she said.

The man grinned broadly, while the woman's smile was dignified and almost shy. The sides of their faces wrinkled, drawing Emerahl's attention to scars that ran down their faces, necks and shoulders.

*Scars? If they are immortals, they should not have scars.*

Then she noticed that the scars, on the woman's left side, matched those of the man's, on his right side, and a wave of realization swept over Emerahl. These two had once been joined. The scars were deliberate, perhaps a reminder of their former union.

"We are," the woman replied. "I am Tamun."

"And I am Surim."

"Sun and Moon," Emerahl translated. "In ancient Velian."

"Yes. Our parents thought it might bring luck."

"Did it?"

The pair exchanged a glance, then Surim shrugged. "We grew to be unexpectedly Gifted. Some consider that lucky."

"Somewhat," Tamun agreed, smiling faintly. She looked at Emerahl and grew serious. "Are we forgiven for our little test? There are some tests only an immortal can pass, and we needed to be sure."

Emerahl spread her hands. "I guess I might have done the same, if I feared deception."

Tamun nodded. "We have heard reports of you from time to time over the centuries. Despite our rude welcome, we have been looking forward to meeting you."

"And I you," Emerahl replied. "It is odd that we should have lived so long, yet never encountered each other before."

Surim shrugged. "It is not wise to flaunt one's immortality, especially in this age. If we immortals all have one common trait, it is keeping to ourselves."

Emerahl nodded. "And yet I have felt compelled to seek other immortals."

"Paradoxically, it is the increased threat to our lives in this age that motivates us to seek our own company," Tamun said.

"And support," Surim added.

"So you, too, have sought out other Wilds?" Emerahl asked.

Tamun's nose wrinkled. "Wilds. That is what the gods call us. We called ourselves immortals before, and so we should now."

"Yes," Surim said in answer to Emerahl's question. "We have." He rose and walked to Emerahl. Taking her hands, he smiled warmly and gazed into her eyes. "We've been isolated from the world too long. We crave company."

"For the last hundred years we have watched the world through the minds of mortals, but that is not as satisfying as walking among them," Tamun agreed, standing up and stretching.

"Come sit down," Surim said, drawing Emerahl across

the room. He led her to a pile of cushions. Tamun settled down next to Emerahl. She drew a small loom close to her and began weaving, her fingers moving with the sure deftness of someone who had been practicing a skill for a long time.

"I always wondered what it was that you two did," Emerahl told him. "The reports I heard suggested you were prophets. Like The Seer."

Surim laughed.

"We never claimed to be able to see or predict the future," Tamun said. "Not as The Seer did. She couldn't, you know. She just used her mind-reading skills to learn what a person wanted to hear, then gave them ambiguous answers."

"She wrote the most appalling poetry and called it prophecy," Surim added, gesturing dismissively. "All this nonsense about lost heirs and magical swords. We all know swords can't be magical."

"Unless they're made of the wood of a welcome tree," Tamun pointed out. "Or black coral."

"Which makes them utterly useless as a physical weapon." Surim looked at Emerahl and smiled. "Ignore us, dear. We have been arguing like this for most of a millennia. Now, tell us about yourself, and the world. The Gull keeps us informed, but he hears only rumors and gossip. You have seen recent events with your own eyes."

Sitting down, Emerahl chuckled to herself. "No doubt The Gull told you. I have seen a few things. And not of my choosing."

And she began to relate how a priest had driven her from her lighthouse over a year before.

Auraya paced the bower.

For the last few weeks she had flown about Si to all the villages suffering from Hearteater. In each place she had ordered three bowers to be built, as Mirar had done at the Blue Lake tribe. She had taught Siyee in each village how to prepare cures and how to judge when a patient probably needed magical help in overcoming the disease. Now, whenever she visited a village, she could attend to those who needed her most before flying on to the next village.

But Juran had contacted her this morning to tell her the gods would be delivering their judgment later that day at the Altar. It had forced her to remain in her bower for hours, knowing that sick Siyee needed her help and at the same time giving her nothing to distract herself with. Suddenly she realized she was wringing her hands, as her mother used to do when anxious. She threw her hands apart and sighed in exasperation.

*Oh! Enough waiting! I wish the gods would announce their decision and be done with it!*

Her stomach fluttered as she paced the room. She remembered Chaia's words: *Know that you have made an enemy of one of the gods.* One of the gods. Not two. Of all the gods, she had given Huan and Chaia most reason to dislike her. Was disobeying Huan likely to make her an enemy? Probably. Was spurning Chaia's love likely to? Possibly.

She had considered the revelation that the gods did not agree about her fate many times. What side had each god taken? Chaia had hinted that Huan was the most angered by her refusal. What did the other gods think?

:*Auraya?*

Her stomach clenched as she recognized Juran's mental voice.

:*Juran? Is it time?*

:*Yes. Mairae and I are at the Altar.*

She nodded, forgetting that he could not see her, and moved to a chair. As she sat down Mischief scrambled out of his basket and climbed down the wall of the bower. He curled up in her lap. Now that the weather was growing chilly he was constantly taking advantage of any warm body that remained still for more than a few moments.

Concentrating on Juran's mind, she closed her eyes and let what he was seeing reach her. He was in the Altar. The walls had folded up. Mairae was in her seat. Auraya sensed Dyara and Rian link with Juran. When all were ready, Juran began the short ritual.

"Chaia, Huan, Lore, Yranna, Saru. Once again, we thank you for the peace you brought to Ithania, and the Gifts that you have given us. We thank you for your wisdom and guidance."

"We thank you," Mairae murmured. Auraya heard Dyara and Rian speak the words mentally and said them herself.

"You have indicated that you are ready to deliver judgment for Auraya's refusal to execute Mirar. Please appear and be welcome among your humble servants."

"Guide us."

From Juran's viewpoint Auraya saw four patches of air around the room begin to glow. The lights slowly took shape, forming the figures of Huan, Lore, Yranna and Saru. She wondered where Chaia was, then Juran turned his head and she saw that the god was standing at Juran's right.

:*Juran, Dyara, Rian, Mairae and Auraya,* Chaia said. *We have chosen you to represent us and act on our behalf in the world of mortals. Until now we have been satisfied with your work.*

:*We have taken care to give you only those tasks you are capable of,* Yranna added. She looked at Juran. *Once, long ago, we were forced to ask one of you to act against his heart. Recently we had no choice but to ask the same of one of you again.*

:*Only this time, the task was left unfulfilled,* Lore rumbled.

:*Twice we ordered for it to be done; twice we were denied,* Saru said.

Huan's gaze met Juran's and Auraya shivered as she realized the goddess was not looking at Juran, but at her. She felt herself trembling. Fear ate away at her resolve. How could she pit herself against the will of the gods, who she had always adored?

*How can I worship beings that can so easily throw away the laws and justice they established?*

:*We acknowledge that Auraya is new to her responsibilities,* Huan said, *but her inexperience should be no encumbrance to her ability to carry out her duties. Some of you believe that the task we gave her was unsuited to her character. We expect you all to perform unpleasant tasks when needed.*

*:Auraya believes our decision unjust,* Lore said. *We laid judgment upon Mirar a century ago and that judgment has not changed.*

Auraya resisted the urge to protest. *He has changed,* she thought. *He is not the same person.*

*:Time, even a century hiding behind another identity, does not negate the crimes he has committed in the past,* Huan said.

*They were crimes too minor to justify the punishment of execution,* she thought. But she stayed silent. The gods knew her mind. There was no point speaking out.

*:Auraya demands justice for the sake of her own conscience,* Saru added. *You cannot do this every time we ask you to execute a criminal.*

*:You must trust us at times like these,* Yranna said softly. *When the need is urgent and the justice in our actions difficult to see.*

Huan's gaze shifted upward and Auraya guessed she was looking at Chaia.

*:We have decided that Auraya must return to Jarime,* Chaia said. Was it her imagination, or did he sound weary and reluctant? *She must not leave Jarime for a period of ten years, unless Northern Ithania is invaded and she is accompanied by her fellow White.*

Chaia paused. Auraya waited for more.

*:That is our judgment,* Chaia finished.

Surprised, she let herself relax. *That's it? They did not take away my Gift of flight? I suppose ten years is a long time to be stuck in one place . . .*

*:Auraya must leave Si tomorrow and return to Jarime,* Huan said.

*Tomorrow?* Auraya went cold.

*:What of Hearteater?* she found herself asking. *Who will heal the Siyee when I am gone?*

*:They will have to deal with it themselves,* Huan said. *It kills only one in five. That is regrettable, but survivable.*

Aghast, Auraya could not think of anything to say to that.

*:Will you accept your punishment?* the goddess asked.

Auraya felt ill. So many Siyee would die. All because of her.

*:Auraya.*

She dragged her attention back to the goddess.

*:If I must. Yes, I will return to Jarime.*

Huan nodded, a gleam of satisfaction in her eyes. Then, without another word, the gods vanished.

Etim stood straight and stiff before the king. In one hand he held his spear, in the other he grasped the mallet and chisel the Pentadrians had given him.

"What did they ask for in return?" the king asked.

"Nothing, sire," Etim replied.

King Ais scowled. He turned to look at the young woman by his side, who had laid a hand on his arm. This must be the Princess Imi, Erim decided. She looked older than he had expected. It wasn't just the adult clothes, but the maturity in her gaze as she smiled at her father.

"Imenja could probably have sunk that ship herself, father. She asked our warriors to do it to prove a point. We *can* fight them without great risk to ourselves."

The king's brows sank even lower. "Your priestess has forced us into a war. Once the raiders know we destroyed one of their ships, they will come here in force."

*They don't know!* Etim thought. But he couldn't say that unless invited. Frustrated, he shifted his weight from one foot to the other.

The king noticed the movement. He looked at Etim and narrowed his eyes.

"You disagree?" he asked, his voice dark with warning.

Etim decided it would be better to simply state the facts than offer an opinion.

"We left none alive. None to tell the tale."

"None but the Pentadrians," the king finished.

"They won't," Imi said. "But I want the raiders to hear about it. I want them to fear us. I want us to cut holes in their ships and the fish to feed on their bodies and the city to be enriched by their loot." She smiled. "I want us to be respected by traders and feared by thieves. We can be that, with the Pentadrians' help."

The king stared at his daughter, but Etim could not tell if it was with amazement or dismay. After a moment the king looked away. He rubbed his chin, then looked up at Etim.

"What do you think of these Pentadrians, warrior?"

Etim considered how best to answer.

"I would prefer to be their friend rather than their enemy," he replied honestly.

A faint smile touched the king's face.

Imi chuckled. "That's what I want people to think of us."

"And in the meantime, we must trust these Pentadrian landwalkers," the king replied sourly.

Imi shrugged. "Even they cannot stop us boring holes in the hulls of their ships."

The king's eyebrows rose. Etim might have been mistaken, but he thought he saw a spark of interest in the monarch's eyes. Imi reached out and touched her father's arm again.

"Did you consider my suggestion?" she asked quietly. "Did you list all the terms you would want in an alliance?"

"They will not agree to them," he replied.

"Maybe not," she agreed. "But you won't know that until you ask them."

The king looked at her, then drew in a deep breath and let it out. He looked up at Etim.

"Bring me the First Warrior."

Wondering if he had just witnessed a great decisive moment in Elai history, Etim hurried from the room.

# 46

"Msstf, Owaya fly?"

Auraya looked at the veez, who was inspecting her pack hopefully.

"Yes, Mischief. Auraya and Mischief fly . . . to Jarime." She had been about to say "home," but the words didn't seem right. Jarime no longer felt like home.

Sighing, she sat down and patted the veez. Sirri had been dismayed to learn that Auraya was leaving. *Without my help many, many Siyee are going to die,* she thought. *But if the gods had removed my ability to fly instead, I would not be able to reach all the distant villages anyway.*

She had expected that, with the plague spreading throughout Si, whatever punishment the gods decided upon would not take effect until the disease was under control. By sending her to Jarime now the gods were also punishing the Siyee for her disobedience. That was unfair. Cruel, even. She felt her mood darken. Perhaps Mirar was right about them . . .

It was ironic that by persuading Mirar to teach her his healing Gift she had brought about events that forced the only two people who could help the Siyee to leave Si.

Mirar's words repeated in her mind. *"Come with me. We will leave Ithania and seek the distant continents."*

What he had proposed was absurd. It meant abandoning the Siyee. She looked down at the ring on her finger and smiled wryly. Even if she had been ordered to give away everything it meant—her position, power, flight, immortality—she would still prefer to stay and help the Siyee.

Looking up, she regarded the array of objects on the table. Gifts had started arriving as soon as the news of her departure began to spread. She couldn't take everything, her pack wasn't big enough even without a veez filling half the space. But she wanted to fill her room in the tower with Siyee-made objects so that every time the other White visited her they would be reminded about the fate of the Siyee.

She wasn't just abandoning the Siyee to Hearteater, but to the Pentadrians. If they tried to land here again, none of the other White could arrive in time to help. *And what use would I be, without flight or my powers enhanced by the gods?* She grimaced. *I supposed I could live on the coast. If I had a ship, we could reach the place the Pentadrians landed fairly quickly. Maybe my reputation would scare them off.*

It was almost tempting. Perhaps if Siyee, as soon as they showed signs of sickening, flew to her, she could help them. She could set up a healing place in the Sand tribe village. Maybe a few Siyee would be capable of learning Mirar's healing Gift.

Then her heart sank. She wasn't sure if she would still be able to use Mirar's Gift if she removed the gods' ring. She wasn't even sure she could remove the ring without something terrible happening.

*Perhaps I should ask Chaia,* a dark, quiet voice in the back of her mind said. Shaking her head, she stood up and moved to the table. *It's absurd,* she thought. *I'm not going to take off the ring or turn from the gods. I have to accept their judgment. I will make the best of it.*

In Jarime she could teach Mirar's Gift to others. There must be healer priests and priestesses capable of it. Perhaps the Siyee who chose to join the Temple could take the skill back. It would be too late to save most Siyee from Hearteater, but it might go some way toward them forgiving her for abandoning them.

Which she hoped they would. It would break her heart if,

ten years from now, she found she was no longer welcome in Si.

Someone was screaming. No—lots of people. Their wails were almost comically melodramatic. Mirar tried to feel concerned, but only became worried that he wasn't concerned.

*:Mirar?*

*:Emerahl? Are you making that noise? It's irritating.*

*:What noise?*

*:This noise.*

*:Oh. That. You're dreaming.*

He paused to think.

*:If I am, am I dreaming you?*

*:No. I'm trying to dream link with you. Get control of yourself, Dreamweaver.*

*Control. Of course.* He exerted his will on the dream, and the screaming became muted. It should have fallen to silence. Then he remembered.

*:It's the blizzard,"* he told Emerahl. *The noise of the wind must be so loud that my mind can't help registering it even in my dreams.*

*:How lovely for you.*

*:Yes. How are you?*

*:I've reached the Red Caves. I hope you don't mind, but I've told my hosts all about you. They're impressed at how you managed to change your identity for a century.*

Mirar felt a twinge of apprehension. She had told them *that*? What else had she told them?

*:Do I mind?* he replied. *Well, that depends who your hosts are.*

*:The Twins.*

Surprise nearly shook him from the dream state.

*:Is that so?*

*:Yes. Have you ever met them?*

*:Once, a long time ago. About fifty years before Juran was Chosen they warned me that the Dreamweavers would face bad times in the next century. I didn't believe them.*

*:They say they see patterns in the world. They constantly*

*skim the minds of mortals, watching the spread of ideas. They say human behavior is fairly easy to predict, most of the time.*

*:Well, they've been skimming minds a long time,* he reminded her. *I heard rumors of their existence only a few hundred years after I became immortal.*

*:Oh, they're older than that,* she told him. *They've watched mortals for many, many centuries before they learned to see patterns in their behavior, and became famous for their predictions.*

*:What do they see happening in the near future?* he asked.

*:They don't agree. Surim thinks there is some great change about to happen. Tamun does not think it likely, so soon after the rise of the Circlians and the Pentadrians. And that is interesting, too. They say the two religions formed and grew simultaneously. Surim thinks that there is nothing more to it than powerful beliefs rising to fill the voids left after so many gods died in their war. Tamun believes there is more to it than that—that the religions are linked.*

*:Do they know if the Pentadrian gods are real?*

*:They are. Too many Pentadrian worshippers can recall encounters with their gods for them not to be real. Nobody knows where these gods came from, however. They are different to the Circlian gods in that they rarely appear before mortals. They don't like to meddle too much in the affairs of their followers.*

*:Except to tell them to invade Northern Ithania?*

*:The Twins believe that was the decision of the former leader, Kuar.*

*:Interesting. I like the idea of non-meddling gods, but if the result is mortals making decisions like that . . .*

*:Don't tell me you've changed your mind and think we're better off with gods than without.*

*:No. Never. But mortals can make astoundingly stupid and cruel decisions, too.*

*:Even your own followers?* she asked.

*:Of course not. Dreamweavers are always unfailingly sensible.*

*:Ha!*

*:Well, most of them.*

*:Have you contacted Dreamweaver Elder Arleej?*

*:Yes,* he said. *She's making the arrangements you suggested.*

*:How did she take the news about you?*

*:She was surprised.*

*:I'm sure she was more than just surprised. The Twins told me something you'll find interesting and maybe even useful in the future. There are more voids in the world. Most are of no use to anyone, but there are a few in remote locations that might be good places for you to hide.*

*:Do they know what caused them?*

*:No. Only that a great magical event must have happened to drain that much magic from one place in the world. They had never heard of them before the War of the Gods.*

*:That certainly qualifies as a great magical event,* Mirar remarked.

*:Yes. I'd always thought it strange that a war between such beings has never affected the physical world. All that changed for mortals was that gods no longer appeared, or they lost Gifts their gods had bestowed upon them.*

*:I wonder if the voids are dangerous to the gods. They are beings of pure magic, after all.*

*:Only if they blundered into one, I suppose.*

*:Yes. I wonder if we could arrange that.*

Emerahl's amusement came to him in a gentle wave of humor.

*:It's gone quiet,* she said suddenly.

Mirar paused and listened. It took a moment for the meaning of the silence to occur to him. The sound of wind had stopped. Either his subconscious had finally blocked it, or the storm had ended.

*:I had best wake up and be civil to my hosts,* Emerahl told him. *Happy travelling, Mirar.*

*:Thanks,* he replied, thinking of the treacherous snow and rugged mountains he still had to cross.

Her mind faded from his senses. He drew in a deep

breath and pulled himself into full consciousness. To his relief the wind *had* stopped screaming. Opening his eyes he saw only darkness, so he drew magic and created a spark of light. His relief changed to dismay.

The entire mouth of the enormous cave he had been sheltering in was completely blocked by a wall of snow.

That was why he couldn't hear the wind any more.

# 47

A day after the Elai had sunk the raider ship, Imenja ordered her vessel to moor near a collection of little islets. Though more rock than anything else, those just beneath the waves were covered in bulfish. The islets were too far from Borra for the Elai to be relying on them for food, and too dangerous for anyone without magic to approach. Imenja had ventured out with a few daring crewmembers every day to collect bulfish, and they had feasted on the delicacy for two days.

All except Reivan. Unfortunately, she was the only person on board who didn't like these bulfish. Some of the crew even preferred to eat them raw. Just the thought of that turned her stomach. The ship's cook, however, had taken Reivan's dislike as a personal challenge. Each night he prepared them in a different way, trying to find one that might win her over. Under Imenja's watchful eye she had tasted them seared, roasted, in soups, and even mashed into a paste, but the strong, pungent, fishy taste left her gagging.

She longed for the ship to move on, but culinary pleasure wasn't the only reason Imenja was dallying in this place. The Second Voice had to give the Elai warriors time to return to their city, give the king their news, and for a messenger to return—if the king decided to send one.

"I think I'm growing to like this life on the sea," Imenja said. "Maybe I should put aside ruling the world and become a trader."

Reivan turned to regard Imenja. "I suppose it wouldn't

be a great change for you. You'd still get to boss others around and negotiate with peoples of many nations. I think I prefer the simple comforts of the Sanctuary, though."

"There's much more room there," Imenja agreed.

"And there's no . . . oh, no. Here we go again."

She had spotted the cook approaching the pavilion. He held a wooden board covered by an upturned dish.

Imenja chuckled. "He only seeks to please you."

"Are you sure he's not trying to make me ill?"

The cook entered the pavilion. He traced the star over his chest quickly, then lifted the dish off the wooden board with a flourish. Reivan sighed.

A shallow stone bowl lay on the board, filled with bulfish. Their shells had been removed and they steamed invitingly. A delicious smell of herbs reached Reivan's nose, but it did nothing to boost her confidence.

The cook held out a fork.

"Try."

Reivan shook her head.

"Just try it, Reivan," Imenja said, in the tone of someone who would not be refused.

Sighing, Reivan took the fork and skewered one of the slimy-looking fish. She regarded it fatalistically, then forced herself to put it in her mouth.

The sickeningly pungent flavor she expected to assault her senses did not come. Instead, a mild flavor mixed with the pleasantness of the herbs filled her mouth. Surprised, she chewed cautiously, sure that doing so would release the flavor she disliked. It didn't, and she swallowed almost reluctantly.

The cook was grinning. "You like it."

She nodded. "It's better. Much better."

"Really?" Imenja took the fork from Reivan's hands, then plucked a morsel off the board. She popped it into her mouth and chewed, and her eyes widened. "It is. It's subtle and delicate. You steamed it?"

The cook nodded.

"Remember what you did," she told him. "I wonder if we can get bulfish shipped home to—"

Her expression changed suddenly. With furrowed brows she waved the cook away, rose and stepped out of the pavilion. Reivan followed as her mistress moved to the ship's rail and stared out at the sea.

"I think we are about to receive a visit from the sea folk," she murmured. "Yes. There."

She pointed. The water was all black shadows and the red light of the reflected sunset. Staring out at the waves, Reivan saw a head-sized object moving up and down with the waves. After a moment it disappeared. She sought another sign of the Elai, but in vain.

"Throw over a rope," Imenja ordered a crewman nearby. He hurried to obey. As the rope unfurled, Reivan peered over the rail.

A head appeared and two milky eyes stared up at them. The inner eyelids of the Elai warrior slid back. He grasped the rope and began to climb.

When he reached the rail, he paused and looked at the crew nervously. He was older than the Elai warriors who had sunk the raider ship. As Imenja stepped forward to welcome him, he turned to regard her, his expression serious.

"I have come to give you a message," he told her. "King Ais, ruler of Borra and the Elai, invites Second Voice Imenja, Servant of the Pentadrian gods, to consider this proposal."

He spoke slowly and carefully, and had obviously memorized the message from the king. Reivan smothered the urge to smile in triumph as she realized this was a treaty proposal.

"The king suggests his people and yours meet to trade goods in the future, but not at the islands of Borra. Islands a few days' sailing from Borra might be suitable, if they are not overrun by raiders.

"In return for help with Elai defenses, King Ais will help Pentadrians fight raiders, but only if the risk to his warriors is not too great. All valuables taken from raider vessels would become the property of the king. Training of Elai in fighting, magic or building defenses would also occur away from Borra."

Imenja nodded. "Am I right to guess that the signing of such a treaty will occur on one of these remote islands as well?"

The messenger nodded. Imenja looked away as if considering.

*:What do you think, Reivan?*

*:I think this is the only offer we'll get. There will be no discussion of these terms. If we attempt it, we will not hear from him again.*

*:And what of the terms?*

*:The only part that sounds unreasonable is that they get all the loot. It would not take long for it to occur to them that if they wait until a trader has been attacked, they will get more loot from the raider.*

Imenja turned back to the messenger.

"I agree to these terms on behalf of my people. If you tell me the location of the islands you spoke of, we will sail for them tomorrow."

The messenger looked surprised, but not displeased. He gave her directions, then, bowing respectfully, he bid them farewell and moved to the edge of the ship. Unlike the younger warriors, who had leapt into the water, he climbed down carefully and slipped into the sea with barely a splash.

Imenja beckoned to Reivan, who moved to her side.

"You still fear they'll replace raiders as the greatest danger for traders in these waters," she said quietly. "Don't worry. I will make them think twice about that."

A warm weight lay between Auraya's shoulders. After long hours of flight, Mischief had grown bored, yet he understood, perhaps instinctively, that he could not leave the protection of her pack. Instead he did something she envied him for: sleep.

The night landscape below was coy about revealing its features. Different shades of darkness marked different areas: forest was darker than fields, water was blacker still. From time to time the moon found a gap in the clouds and Auraya was able to make out roads and houses.

Now there was an aberration below. An interruption of the natural pattern, poised at the meeting of land and water. As moonlight once again bathed the world it showed hard angles and a jumble of interconnecting lines. Two buildings caught the light and seemed to throw it back. The Dome shone like a second moon, half-buried in the ground. The White Tower stretched up, like an accusing finger.

Moving toward the Tower, she considered once again the reception she might receive. Would all four White meet her? Would they be sympathetic or angry? Would she be expected to apologize or explain herself? As she descended she braced herself for a meeting that was probably going to be awkward, if not unpleasant.

As her feet touched the roof her surroundings darkened. She looked up to see that the clouds had covered the moon again. No one stepped out to greet her. She waited for several heartbeats, then laughed quietly.

*I assumed the gods would let Juran know I was coming. Looks like they didn't.* She moved toward the door, amused to feel a faint disappointment. *They might be waiting inside, or in my room.*

She entered the building, opening and closing the door to the roof quietly. Moving down the stairs, she did not meet anyone—not even a servant. Reaching the door to her rooms, she paused to listen. No sounds came from within. She opened the door and found her rooms dim and empty.

Putting her pack down, she created a spark of light. A sleepy Mischief crawled out. He blinked at her then jumped onto a chair and curled up. She patted him, then looked around.

Everything was how she had left it, yet it did not feel like the place she had left. She felt no lifting of her spirits at familiar surrounds. Walking from room to room, she wondered if her lack of relief at returning home was because it was going to be something like a prison for the next decade.

She sat down on the edge of her bed and twirled the ring on her finger.

During her long flight, with nothing to distract her, she had spent a lot of time thinking. At first she had decided there was no point agonizing over her future. It was set and there was nothing she could do to change it. But something nagged at her and eventually she had admitted to herself that she did have choices, even if they were foolish or ridiculous. She began examining them, weighing up the consequences, in order to convince herself they were not ones she wanted to make.

By the time she had reached Jarime she had come to the realization that some of these choices weren't as foolish as she'd first thought. That she might be happier, or at least more useful to the world, if she made them.

At the same time they frightened her. She had decided she needed to sleep before making any decision. And there was something else she needed to know.

Lying back on the bed, she let herself sink toward sleep. When she judged the time was right, she spoke a name.

*:Mirar!*

There was a long silence, then a familiar mental voice replied.

*:Auraya? Is that really you?*

*:It is. I have a question for you.*

*:Yes?*

*:Will I be able to teach your healing Gift to others?*

*:Only in rare circumstances.*

*:What circumstances?*

He did not answer.

*:Mirar?*

*:Have the gods chosen a punishment for you yet?* he asked.

*:Yes.*

*:What did they decide?*

She hesitated. If he had any intention of causing trouble, knowing she couldn't leave Jarime might encourage him.

*:That is none of your business,* she told him.

*:Isn't it? Consider it an exchange of information. I will tell you the circumstances which limit the teaching of healing for the gods' decision on your punishment.*

She felt annoyance, but pushed it aside. She could give him part of the truth.

*:They sent me back to Jarime.*

*:Ah. So the Siyee are without a healer, which explains your question about teaching. They've punished you by punishing the Siyee. I guess they didn't have much else they could take from you.*

*:You did not expect them to remove my ability to fly?*

*:No. I've suspected that ability is your own since the day I taught you healing. Now I am sure of it.*

A shiver ran down her spine.

*:What do you mean?*

*:You were already a powerful sorceress when you joined the Circlians. I saw the potential in you long before that. Doesn't it seem odd to you that the other White were not given this ability?*

*:Yes, but they weren't meant to go to Si.*

*:Weren't they? You discovered your ability yourself. If the gods meant you to have it in order to befriend the Siyee, wouldn't they have given it to you in a ceremony, with great fanfare, so that people adored them for it?*

*:But if Juran is more Gifted than me then surely he could learn it.*

*:Did you try to teach him?*

She paused. Juran's efforts had come to nothing.

*:But that would make me more Gifted—stronger—than him!*

*:Not if the gods are holding you back. They put you in third place, but since you started showing signs of growing beyond the limits of your position they've had to suppress you.*

*:How do you know this!* she demanded.

*:I don't. I am guessing. But I do know that you are stronger than you think. Stronger than the gods intended you to be. I felt it the day you tried to kill me.*

Auraya felt a stab of frustration.

*:You haven't answered my question: What circumstances will stop me teaching others your healing Gift?*

He paused before answering.

*:Only powerfully Gifted sorcerers will be able to learn it. Perhaps your fellow White can, perhaps not.*

She felt her heart sink. There would be no priests or Siyee returning to fight Hearteater.

:*What other circumstances are there?*

:*Did I say there were more?*

:*You spoke in plurals.*

:*So I did. There is this: if you did manage to find someone Gifted enough to learn my healing method, the gods may have them killed. Remember that Huan said it was forbidden.*

:*Why?*

:*That I cannot tell you.*

:*Cannot or will not?*

:*Will not.*

:*Why not?*

:*I can't tell you that either.*

She felt her frustration growing and took a deep breath.

:*So why don't they kill me?*

:*You're a White.*

:*So if I wasn't, they'd kill me?*

:*Yes. Or maybe not. It depends if you're speaking of yourself before you were a White or not. If before, then yes.*

:*And if I were a former White, no?*

:*I'm not sure. Are you thinking of quitting?*

She paused, knowing he would sense the lie if she denied it.

:*Because if you are,* he continued, *the gods might be so angry that they'll kill you anyway. Not that they'd find it easy to kill someone so powerful. You might escape them. But I know what it's like to be hunted and despised by the gods. You don't want that life, Auraya.*

:*No,* she said. *I have no intention of making myself an enemy of the gods. Thank you for answering my question, Mirar, even if not fully.*

:*I answered it as fully as you answered mine,* he replied. *Good luck.*

As he broke the link she sighed. *He is too shrewd. But shrewd or not, he doesn't know everything.*

He also knew much that she didn't. She had learned a few things from their conversation, though she had to consider if his claims were true. It was unlikely she would get much sleep before morning.

Yet by the time Mischief leapt softly onto the bed and curled up beside her, she had made the journey from waking to slumber.

Stepping into her sleeping pool, Imi splashed her body. She sighed with relief as the cool water soothed her skin.

*How does father do it? He listened as that merchant droned on for hours and hours, and all the weaver woman did was whine and complain.*

When Imi had asked her father if she could sit with him as he dealt with the requests, protests and reports people brought to him, he had agreed, but only if she stayed there as long as he did. She soon discovered that he spent many more hours there every day than she had expected, and that most of the time it was utterly boring.

But she suspected her father had insisted she must stay the whole time so that she would lose interest and leave him be. He was testing her resolve. Or perhaps he simply wanted her to begin learning how to run the kingdom. That thought filled her with both fear and anticipation. And sadness, because the day she took charge of Borra would be the day her father died.

Her resolve hadn't broken and her determination had finally been rewarded. She had realized that many traders and warriors, and even some of the courtiers, would have much to gain from a treaty with the Pentadrians, and she had pointed these reasons out to her father whenever he asked what she had thought of a visitor. When her father had decided to send the messenger to the Pentadrians, her heart had sung with victory.

Now that she'd had time to think, doubts had begun to weaken her confidence. Imi stepped out of the pool and began to pace the room.

What if the Pentadrians did prove untrustworthy? What if they came back and forced their way into the city somehow? What if her people were killed, and it was all her fault?

*Imenja would never allow it,* she told herself. *She's a good person. And powerfully Gifted. Nobody would dare disobey her.*

When Imi was not worried about the future she had set in motion for her people, she worried if it would come about at all. The Pentadrians might not agree to the restrictions her father had placed on them. They might decide that the Elai had nothing worth trading, or that the Elai were too weak to be useful allies.

*Even if that is true, even if the alliance doesn't happen, things have changed for us.*

She remembered the bright light in the eyes of the warriors who had sunk the raider ship. *Father won't easily stop them trying that again. Or trying out other ways to harm the raiders. He can order them not to, but they won't like it.* She frowned. *Is that the only reason he sent the messenger? Is he afraid people will resent him, or even turn against him, if he refuses them this chance to strike back? Did he feel he had no choice?*

*Is that my fault?*

*No,* she told herself. *Even if he thinks he has to give in to the warriors, he doesn't have to involve the Pentadrians at all. We don't need them in order to fight the raiders.*

But if the raiders proved too powerful an enemy, the Elai will need an ally like the Pentadrians to help them.

*If this. If that. So many ifs.*

From the door came a knock. She watched as Teiti emerged from her room to answer it. As Rissi stepped past Imi's aunt she sighed with relief.

"Hello, Princess."

"Rissi," she replied. Here was a welcome distraction. She wondered if he could stay long. Perhaps they could play a table game. Anything to keep her mind from these worries. She ushered him toward some chairs. "Teiti, would you send for something to drink? Maybe something to eat, too?"

Her aunt narrowed her eyes at Rissi, then nodded and left the room. As Imi sat down, Rissi gingerly took a seat. There were dark, bluish patches on his arms.

"What's wrong with you?" she asked.

He grimaced. "I've been practicing."

"Practicing what?"

"Fighting."

"What for?" She frowned. "You boys aren't playing at wars again, are you?"

He grinned. "No. Me and a few others are having warrior lessons."

"Oh." She shrugged. "Aren't you a bit young for that?"

He scowled. "No."

She bit her lip as she realized she'd offended him. Boys were like that. Always wanting to be older.

"Of course you aren't," she said apologetically. "Is this something all traders' sons do?"

He looked away. "We have to be able to defend ourselves, if we go outside the city."

She looked at him closely. There was more to it than that. He glanced at her, then shrugged.

"And besides, I don't want to be a trader. I want to be a warrior."

Surprise slowly changed to alarm. If he became a warrior now, when warriors were going to be attacking raiders, he might be killed. And this, too, would happen because of her.

"The First Warrior has promised me I will have a place among the recruits when I'm old enough," he told her. "If I pass the tests. Father doesn't like it, but he can't stop me."

"Why?" Imi blurted out.

He spread his hands. "Because he wants me to take over trading."

"No, I mean why do you want to be a warrior?"

He stared at her silently, then slowly began to smile. "Because, Princess Imi, I'm going to marry you one day."

Teiti saved her from trying to think of a reply to that. The door to the room opened and the woman bustled in with a tray of food balanced on one hand and a jug held in the other. She placed both on a table next to Imi and Rissi, then straightened.

"The *king* sent a message for you, *Princess*," Teiti said.

She always used and emphasized the titles when Rissi was visiting. "The messenger has returned from the Pentadrians. They have agreed to all terms."

Imi jumped up. "They have! That's wonderful. I have to talk to father now!"

And ignoring Teiti's protest that she had just brought them food, and Rissi's confident smile, Imi seized the opportunity to escape.

Hurrying through the palace, she felt a flash of annoyance. *I should be overjoyed, but Rissi's gone and spoiled that. I didn't know what to say. I've never been so embarrassed! And where did he get the idea that becoming a warrior would mean he could marry me?*

Then she remembered. She had told him. She'd told him her father would probably marry her off to someone of royal blood, *unless he decided a warrior leader of impressive standing would bring new blood into the family.*

*It'll take a lot to impress father,* she thought. *But he's willing to give it a try.*

And that was quite flattering, she realized. Would any of her cousins, second cousins and distant relatives do that? She doubted it.

Smiling, she slowed her stride and started considering where her father was likely to be.

# 48

"Ah, here he is," Tamun said, looking away from her loom toward the cave entrance.

Emerahl turned to see Surim climbing the stairs. Around his neck was an enormous snake, its body as large as his thigh and so long he had draped it around his shoulders twice. He carried it to the side of the cave where they always prepared meals, and shrugged it off his shoulders.

He looked at Emerahl and grinned. "Dinner. We will have a fine feast tonight."

Emerahl regarded the snake in horror.

"A fine and boring one, if that's all you've brought us," Tamun replied.

"I have more," Surim said defensively. He reached into a woven bag that had been concealed by the snake and drew out several objects, all of plant origin, Emerahl noted with relief. She looked at the snake, lying motionless on the floor.

"Have you eaten takker before?" Surim asked.

Emerahl dragged her eyes from the reptile. "No."

"They're delicious," he told her. "Rather like breem in texture, but slightly meatier in flavor."

"You should have caught something more conventional," Tamun said disapprovingly, her eyes not leaving her work. She glanced at Emerahl and smiled. "You don't have to eat it. It took us a while to adapt to this place, but we've grown accustomed to some unusual additions to our diet. You are our guest, and, her eyes narrowed as she turned to regard Surim, "should not be expected to eat such things."

One of his eyebrows rose cheekily. "No, she should be treated with special generosity. Given the best. Rare delicacies like roasted takker, for example."

"I'll give it a try," Emerahl said quickly, hoping to head off another endless argument. It wasn't that their banter was hurtful, but it could and often did go on for hours. "And if I don't like it, I'll happily eat the vegetables instead."

Surim smiled broadly. "Thank you, Emerahl. Or you might like to try this instead . . ."

From the bag he drew a spider at least twice the size of his hand.

"You are kidding me," Emerahl found herself saying.

"He is," Tamun growled. "Stop it, Surim."

He pulled a face. "But it's so much fun. I haven't had anyone to play with for so long. Tricking someone as old as you isn't easy."

Emerahl looked at Tamun. "You've put up with this for how long?"

"Nearly two millennia," she replied calmly. "You'd think after all this time he'd realize his pranks aren't funny. It's like being told the same joke over and over. Some would call it torture."

"Being old doesn't mean I have to lose my sense of humor," he told her. "Unlike *some* people."

"I'm amused by you every day," she said dryly.

Emerahl shook her head. "You two never stop, do you?"

Surim grinned. "Not for a moment. Not even after we separated ourselves."

The Twins paused to look at each other, their faces open and full of affection. Emerahl glanced from one to the other, wondering . . .

"A century ago," Tamun said suddenly, turning to meet Emerahl's eyes. Her expression was serious. "To escape the gods' determination to rid the world of immortals."

Emerahl stared at her in dismay. "Did you just . . . ?"

"Read your mind? No." Tamun shrugged and returned to her weaving. "But we know that expression well." She smiled. "Don't worry. We're not offended by your curiosity. Ask away."

Emerahl nodded. "How did separating save you?"

"The gods, as you may already know, cannot easily affect the physical world," Surim told her. He had dragged the snake up onto a table and was gutting it. "They must work through a mortal, preferably someone Gifted in magic."

"So they need their priests and priestesses to do their work," Tamun continued. "After Juran dealt with Mirar, he went after the rest of us. The Seer was easy to find . . ."

"Bet she didn't predict *that*," Surim muttered.

". . . and The Farmer was taken by surprise. We learned of the gods' orders too late to warn him. The only immortal we were able to warn was The Gull."

"He is older than all of us," Surim said, pausing in his work to meet Emerahl's eyes. His expression was full of respect.

"His habit of moving about constantly, concealing his identity and appearing to be nothing more than a scrawny ship's boy saved him."

"And folk of the sea protect their own," Tamun added.

"We, on the other hand, were both well-known and particularly recognizable. Of course we tried to hide—and succeeded for a while. Then the gods declared that people like us are 'abominations' and should be separated or killed at birth. All joined twins of all ages were taken to Jarime. Most attempts to separate them failed."

"But there were a few successes," Tamun said with deliberate brightness. "Or so we told people. The fact that we had been separated suggested that we'd been examined by Circlians and found acceptable, so we could not possibly be the famous Twins."

Emerahl scowled. "Cursed gods."

"Oh, don't be angry on our behalf," Tamun said, smiling. "We'd always meant to do it. We just didn't have the courage. What if we didn't like it? What if we couldn't put ourselves together again?"

"We have no regrets," Surim assured Emerahl. "And some good did come of the separations. Healer priests and priestesses are better at it now. More children survive."

"But the ones they kill . . ." Tamun frowned and shook her head. "For that, I hate the gods."

"Among other things," Surim muttered.

Emerahl sighed. "I, too, though they have done no more to me than force me into hiding. I hate them more for what they did to Mirar." Emerahl sighed. "If only we could be free of them."

"Well, they can be killed," Tamun said.

Emerahl turned to stare at the woman. Tamun shrugged. "Before the War of the Gods there were many gods; after it there were five."

"Ten now," Surim corrected.

Tamun ignored him. "So the question is: Is killing a god something only another god can do?"

"And if it is, can we persuade, bribe or blackmail a god to do it for us?" Surim chuckled. "Tell her about the scroll."

"Ah, the scroll." Tamun smiled. "Over the last century of skimming minds we've occasionally encountered rumors of a certain scroll. It is said to contain the story of the War of the Gods, told by a goddess to her last servant before she was killed."

Emerahl felt her heart quicken. "Where is this scroll?"

"Nobody knows," Surim said, his eyes widening theatrically.

"But certain scholars in Southern Ithania have collected hints and undertaken searches over the years. Of all people in the world, they would be the ones most likely to find it."

"Unless someone else finds it first."

Both Surim and Tamun turned to regard her, their faces both wearing the same expectant, meaningful expression. Emerahl laughed.

"When it comes to giving hints, you're both as gentle as a Dunwayan war-hammer. You want me to find it." She paused as a delicious smell caught her attention. "Is that takker I can smell cooking?"

Surim chortled. "It might just be."

"Smells good." She shifted into a more comfortable position and turned to Tamun. "So what else can you tell me about this scroll and the scholars of Southern Ithania?"

\*    \*    \*

The island was farther out to sea than the islands of Borra. Several rocky islets had led the way, each reminding Reivan of tiny drowned mountains. Now, as the ship sailed into the sheltered lagoon the Elai king had chosen as their meeting place, Reivan suddenly realized they were sailing into a crater not unlike those she'd seen in Avven. These islands *were* drowned mountains. Like soldiers standing in lines, the great mountain range that divided Northern Ithania stretched not just from Dunway to Si, but into the ocean.

A narrow beach edged the lagoon. At the center stood a small crowd of dark figures.

"Imi is among them," Imenja said.

Reivan smiled. "Good. I was hoping we'd see her again before we returned home. Even if just to make sure she's safe and well."

"We know she's safe and well."

"Yes, but I can't read minds."

"Don't you believe me?"

Reivan chuckled. "Of course I do. But that's not like seeing it for myself. It's like someone telling you something tastes good, but not tasting it yourself."

Imenja looked at Reivan sideways. "Like bulfish?"

Reivan decided she didn't need to answer that. She nodded toward the beach.

"Is the king there?"

"Yes."

"What does he make of all this?"

"He's still suspicious of us, but he can see advantages. He's pleased with himself for gaining the restrictions he wanted, too. And he's both proud and a little scared of Imi."

"Scared?"

"Yes. Her adventures have changed her. It's hard for him to accept that his little girl came back all grown up. He's the sort of man who doesn't like change." She paused. "There's another with him. A priestess. She is wondering if the king will change the treaty in the way she suggested."

"How?"

Imenja smiled. "She fears the Elai will be seduced by

our gods, so she wants him to forbid us from teaching their ways."

"What will you do?"

Imenja didn't reply. The captain was approaching. He told Imenja the boat was ready. The Second Voice nodded and looked at Reivan.

"Do you have everything?"

In reply, Reivan lifted the oilskin bag she had packed with parchment, ink and various scribing tools.

"Then let's go and make a little history."

They climbed down into the boat. As soon as they had settled the crew began to row. Nobody spoke. When the hull scraped against sand the men jumped out and hauled the boat from the waves. Imenja and Reivan stepped out. The crew waited by the boat as they strode toward the Elai.

As on their previous meeting with him, the king stood within a ring of warriors. Imi waited beside him and an old woman stood at his other side. The stranger wore gold jewellery and fine clothes, and Reivan might have mistaken her for a queen if she hadn't known Imi's mother was dead. No, this must be the priestess. Another man stood a few steps behind the king. At his feet were two slabs of stone.

"Greetings, King Ais, ruler of Borra," Imenja said.

"Welcome, Imenja, Second Voice," the king replied.

Imenja turned to Imi. "Greetings, Princess Imi. How are you settling into your home and life again?"

Imi smiled. "Well, Second Voice."

Imenja glanced at Reivan and smiled. "That is good. Now, shall we discuss the terms of our treaty?" she asked of the king.

He nodded. Reivan listened carefully as they began to examine the issues of warfare and trade. As they decided how to word each part of the treaty she wrote notes on small pieces of parchment with a gray stick. Each point was considered carefully and it took some time before the subject of religion came up.

"My people are content to follow Huan," the king told them. "But we also understand that the new can be seductive, and that even small religious disagreements among a people can cause strife. I must also ask that you do not attempt to convert any Elai, neither by endeavoring to teach the ways of your gods, nor by granting any request for such lessons."

"My people will keep their practices to themselves," Imenja assured him.

Reivan managed to stop herself glancing at Imenja in surprise. She touched the pendant around her neck.

*:If you agree to that, Nekaun will not see much value in this treaty.*

*:No, but he will see, in time, that the more forbidden something is, the more certain individuals will want it.*

"I have my own restriction to place on this treaty," Imenja said aloud.

The king's eyebrows rose. "Yes?"

"Certain of my people at home have expressed concern that your people might seek to rob traders, either by waiting until raiders have attacked merchant ships before attacking the raiders themselves, or by attacking traders directly. I have assured them that you will not, but they want your promise on this."

"They have my word that any of my warriors found to be indulging in such practices will be punished."

Imenja bowed her head in acknowledgment. "Change 'warrior' to 'Elai' and specify the punishment and they will be satisfied. And also note that, if we discover your people have begun preying upon non-raiders in this manner, this treaty will be considered broken by my people."

The king nodded. "That is reasonable."

Imenja held his eyes. "I *will* learn of it," she told him. "In the same way I learned that the merchant who bought Imi from the raiders was guilty, and your warriors were following my ship, and that there is a second entrance to your city, where watchers keep a lookout for raiders. What I cannot see with the Skills the gods have given me, they tell me of themselves. I will know if your people turn into thieves."

The king's frown slowly faded as he realized what she was saying. He turned to Imi, who suddenly looked a little frightened. The girl straightened.

"I told you she was a sorcerer," Imi said to her father.

"But you didn't know this," he muttered.

She shook her head.

The king turned back to Imenja and narrowed his eyes. "How do I know you won't return with more ships and take my city?"

Imenja smiled. "I have no interest in taking your city. Not only is it too great a distance from my home, but what use would an underground city the size of an Avven village be to us? I *can* see the value of trade, and of keeping these seas safe for it.

"We both have taken a risk in doing this," she continued. "For you, it is trusting that we have no interest in harming your people. For us, it is that you won't turn what we teach you to ill use. I think it worth the risk."

The king nodded. "I had my doubts. I admit I still have them. But my people cannot remain as they are, and they are willing to take this risk."

He turned to the man behind him. Reivan saw that one of the stone slabs was covered in Elai writing. "Bring them forth and we shall watch you carve our words into promises." He looked at Imenja. "We will set down our treaty in both languages."

"And in the manner of both peoples," Imenja agreed. She glanced at Reivan. Nodding at the unspoken order, Reivan opened the oilskin bag and drew out parchment, ink and a board to write against.

"That will never survive the water," the Elai scribe murmured.

Reivan smiled and drew out a message tube, oilskin wrapping, wax and a coil of rope. "Yes it will," she assured him.

He looked unconvinced. With a shrug, Reivan settled cross-legged on the sand and began to write.

Between Mirar and the thin spread of trees at the edge of the forest was a smooth, steep blanket of snow. The easiest way to descend would be to cross back and forth, he decided. Going straight down would make it hard to keep his footing.

*Would that be such a bad thing?* he asked himself. *It might be faster to slide.* He looked at the trees below. Though smaller than those deep within the forest, their trunks were just as hard. Sliding out of control and in a flurry of snow, he might not get a clear view of his path. He might not see a tree in time to use magic to stop himself crashing into it.

*Yes,* he told himself. *That would be a bad thing.*

Looking back up at the mountain, he sighed. Few times in his long life had he ventured into such high, inhospitable places, and always in the company of others. The views had been breathtaking, but the way had been treacherous in places. It had taken mere brute magical force to get out of the buried cave, but avoiding falling into snow-covered crevasses had been a much greater challenge.

Starting out across the open slope, he moved slowly. The snow was lightly packed but not deep. It cascaded down the slope at each step. Halfway across, he paused to look around.

After a moment he realized he was still moving. The whole slope was moving.

His heart skipped a beat then began to race. The smooth surface began to ruck and ripple. The instinct to flee turned him around and sent him hurrying back, but his path was all but obscured as snow above it folded over the snow below.

It tangled his legs. He struggled to stay upright and failed. As he landed on his side and began to slide, snow swept over him like breaking waves.

*Don't panic,* he told himself. *It'll just carry me to the bottom. The only danger is suffocation and those trees below.*

Drawing magic, he surrounded himself with a barrier, adding extra space around his face so he could breathe. He felt himself hurtling downward. Then his descent abruptly slowed and he stopped. Snow covered him. The weight of it against his barrier grew.

*I'm being buried.*

Memories of being crushed flashed into his mind. From somewhere deep within a terror began to rise. He fought it, forcing himself to breathe slowly. The pressure on his barrier felt powerful enough to crush him. If he lost concentration for one moment the barrier would fall and . . .

*Why not let it?*

A numbness began to replace fear.

*Why not let go of this life? Find out what's beyond. The gods' servants might find and kill you in a few weeks, when you reach the coast. Why let them do the deed? Die here and deny them the satisfaction. Imagine how they will always wonder where you got to . . .*

The cold of the snow was nothing compared to this empty despair.

*What's there to live for? My people are dwindling, and I can't let them know me without endangering their lives. The woman I love is as far from my reach as any could be. This is the Age of the Five, and I have no place in it. I should just . . .*

"Stop being so bloody melodramatic," he said aloud.

Closing his eyes, he pulled a great stream of magic into himself, then channelled it. There was a dull boom. The whiteness above him flew upward and fragmented to all sides. As it pattered down around him he sat up and looked at his surroundings.

He now lay in the middle of a large crater. Standing up, he climbed one side of it and turned back to regard his handiwork. The hole was quite impressive. He smiled.

Then a shadow streaked past his own and his smile faded. Looking up, he glimpsed two Siyee gliding away.

Sighing, he turned away and began trudging toward the forest.

# 49

Auraya stopped and looked up at the Altar. The five sides were upright, closed to the world. Scenes from the day played through her mind.

Mischief had announced her return, somehow slipping out of her room to find Mairae's veez, Stardust. Soon after, she had been summoned to Juran's room. Mairae had been there, with both veez.

"Why didn't you tell us you had arrived?" Juran had asked.

"I expected the gods would tell you when I arrived. I was surprised you weren't there to meet me." She shrugged. "It was late and I decided not to wake anyone."

He had nodded at that. "I want you to tell me everything that happened, from the moment you first discovered Mirar, as Leiard, was in Si."

So she had related everything. It had taken some hours. She was interrupted from time to time with questions from the other White. Dyara and Rian were listening through a link to Juran.

When she finally finished, Juran had spoken of the gods' punishment and asked if she was willing to accept it.

"For myself, I am," she had told him. "But I find it hard to accept that the Siyee are being punished for my actions."

*:You should have thought of the possible consequences to the Siyee before you disobeyed the gods,* Dyara had said.

"I would never have guessed the gods would be so, so . . . would make such a decision," Auraya answered.

*:You still question the gods' wisdom,* Rian said.

"Yes," she replied. He had made several such lofty comments. "If the ability to question was not a requirement of being a White, the gods would not have chosen me. And it certainly would have reduced the candidates at Choosing Ceremonies."

Auraya remembered seeing Mairae smile at that, but when Juran had turned in her direction she had schooled her expression to one of stern disapproval. *That was when I realized they all felt they must behave as if I were a disgraced child. That they must quash any sympathy they felt, whether for me or for my decisions.*

*:Those worthy of serving the gods are few,* Rian had said next.

She had winced at that. *I know I have been a fool,* she thought. *I don't regret it, since the only other option was to be a hypocrite and a murderer. I only wish being a fool hadn't had such an impact on the Siyee. I would do anything to make up for that.*

Juran had stepped in then, saying that they should endeavor to cooperate and avoid unnecessary conflict. That matters should return to how they had been before. Mairae had looked at him with an expression of sadness and pity.

"I doubt matters will ever be the way they were before," she had murmured.

Auraya wondered who Mairae had been referring to. Herself, perhaps? Had the gods' decisions caused another White to question? Or was Mairae referring to all the White? *Or just me.*

She obviously wasn't referring to the Siyee. Nobody seemed at all concerned about the sky people. When Juran had finally ushered Auraya from his room, she had turned back and asked him if he wanted to learn Mirar's healing Gift. He had shaken his head as if the idea appalled him.

A faint sigh of air drew Auraya's attention back to the Altar. The five sides were beginning to hinge open. She felt her heart stop, then begin racing.

*I am about to take an enormous risk,* she thought. *I might lose everything.* But as Mairae had said, matters would never be the same. *I have already lost a great deal. If I lose the rest, I'll just have to accept that.*

Hurried footsteps echoed in the Dome. She turned to see Juran and Mairae striding toward her. Turning away, Auraya walked up to the Altar's table and sat in her chair.

"What have you called us here for?" Juran demanded as he reached the Altar.

"I have a question to ask the gods," she replied, meeting his eyes. "One that you may wish to hear the answer to."

He stared at her, clearly annoyed that she had called a meeting without consulting him first. "Which is?"

"You will hear it just as soon as you begin the rite, and the gods appear."

He hesitated, then Mairae put a hand on his shoulder.

"Go on. I doubt we'll get it out of her any other way."

Sighing, Juran took his place. Mairae slid gracefully into her chair, her eyes aglow with curiosity.

"You're certainly keeping us entertained, Auraya," she said approvingly, in a near whisper.

Auraya managed a smile. She looked at Juran expectantly. He sighed again, then closed his eyes.

"Chaia, Huan, Lore, Yranna, Saru," he intoned. "Once again, we thank you for the peace you brought to Northern Ithania and the Gifts that have allowed us to keep it. We thank you for your wisdom and guidance."

"We thank you," Auraya murmured along with Mairae. She concentrated on the magic around the Altar, but felt no sign of the gods.

"Auraya wishes to ask of you a question. If you will allow her an answer, please appear before us."

"Guide us," she murmured.

Juran opened his eyes and leaned back in his chair. Meeting his gaze, she saw disbelief in them. He did not expect the gods to respond. But as she stared back at him she felt presences at the edge of her senses. They moved toward her.

Five glowing figures slowly appeared around the Altar. Chaia appeared beside Juran. He looked at her and smiled, but then his smile faded as he saw what was in her mind.

*:What is your question, Auraya?*

Huan had spoken. Auraya felt a sudden trepidation. This was the goddess she had defied. This was also the one who demanded unquestioning obedience.

Forcing herself to face Huan, Auraya gathered her courage.

"Will you allow me to resign from my position as White?"

Juran gasped and Mairae drew in a sharp breath.

"No, Auraya!" Juran said. "That is not necessary."

"We were all a bit harsh on you today. You can't take Rian too seriously," Mairae added.

Auraya kept her gaze on Huan. The goddess's eyes narrowed.

*:Where will you go?*

"To Si."

Huan looked at her fellow gods.

*:We must discuss it. Remain here.*

The five figures vanished. Auraya drew in a deep breath and let it out slowly.

"Auraya," Juran said sternly. "You said you would accept the gods' punishment."

She turned to stare at him. "And I have. But I cannot accept their abandonment of the Siyee."

He frowned. "Are they worth giving up your position, your immortality—your power of flight? How can you help them without that?"

"I will do what I can," she told him. "I . . ." She shook her head. At the limits of her senses was a buzzing. Concentrating on it, she was surprised to find she could make out words.

*: . . . warned you this might happen, but you insisted on testing her again and again.*

It was Chaia, she realized. He was angry.

*:No more than we have tested the others,* Huan replied.

*:After many years in service!*

*:She was the last White. She was never going to have the luxury of time to get used to her role. Now we can find a more worthy replacement. What say the rest of us?*

*:Agreed,* Lore said.

*:Yes,* Yranna added.

*:Give her what she wants,* Saru agreed. *Then we can get rid of her.*

*:Only if she turns against us,* Chaia corrected, his tone firm. *I say we should keep Auraya a White.*

*:You are out-voted, but we will let her go to Si. The shock of her resignation will be damaging enough, though knowing she left to help the Siyee will reduce the . . . Wait. She can hear us!* Huan exclaimed.

*:I warned you. You know she can sense us when we're close,* Chaia said, perhaps a little smugly. *Does this change your mind?*

*:No,* Huan said.

The gods drew closer and moved into their positions around the table. Auraya realized she had been staring blankly at Juran, and looked away. The five gods reappeared.

*:We grant you your request,* Huan said.

*:There are conditions,* Chaia added. *You must not seek to rule a land or people for yourself. If you set yourself against us or the White, or our work, or if you ally yourself with our enemies, you will be regarded as our enemy.*

"That is reasonable. I accept your conditions."

*:Remove the ring.*

Auraya's heart lurched again. She held out her hand, then slowly drew the white ring off her finger. Standing up, she turned to face Chaia.

"Serving you has been the greatest joy and honor, but it is clear you need someone in this position more worthy of it. I do not wish to turn from you. You still have my respect and love, and I will continue to serve you as a priestess if that is acceptable to you."

Chaia looked at Huan.

*:That, as always, will be a decision for the White to make,* he said.

Huan's eyes narrowed slightly. Auraya glanced at Juran, then looked down at the ring. Taking a deep breath, she placed it on the table. She felt nothing—no wrenching loss, no change at all. Taking a step back, she straightened and looked up at Juran again.

He regarded the ring with a grim expression. *Well he should,* she thought. *The White are vulnerable without a fifth member. But I'm sure the gods won't leave them so for long. I doubt they'll wait another twenty-five years to replace me.*

She looked at Mairae. To her surprise, the young woman smiled and nodded. There was a friendly respect in her eyes. She doubted the other White felt the same. Dyara and Rian were sure to be watching through Juran and Mairae. *Dyara will be disappointed,* Auraya thought. *Rian, however, will be overjoyed.*

*:Your decision cannot be reversed,* Huan said. *However, there is no need for you to remain in Jarime. You may return to Si.*

Auraya nodded and made the formal sign of the circle. "Thank you."

The gods vanished.

Auraya paused, uncertain what to do or say next. Juran was still staring at the ring. Slowly he reached out and picked it up. His eyes rose to hers.

"You sacrificed everything for the Siyee," he stated.

She smiled. "Yes." She thought of Mirar's belief that her Gift of flight was her own.

"But maybe not everything," Mairae said.

Auraya looked at the woman in surprise.

"I can read your mind now," Mairae explained.

"Of course." Auraya shook her head. "I didn't think of that."

"Well, are you going to try to fly?"

Auraya looked at Mairae, then focused her mind on her sense of her position in the world. She could still feel it. Drawing magic, she lifted herself upward. Mairae gave a laugh of triumph.

"Yes! You can still help the Siyee."

Relief rushed through Auraya and she found herself grinning. "I can reach them. All I have to find out now is whether I can still heal them."

"Then I guess you will be leaving as soon as possible," Juran said. He looked tired. Auraya dropped to the ground again.

"Yes. I only need to pick up Mischief and a few belongings."

He nodded, then stood up. "Take care of yourself, Auraya. I don't need to tell you to avoid Pentadrian sorcerers. I . . . I must consult the others before deciding if you may remain a priestess."

"I understand."

"Drop by now and then, so we can catch up," Mairae added.

Auraya smiled. "You must both come to Si some time. Perhaps you could sail to the coast. I think you'd like it there."

Mairae looked at Juran. "We should make the effort."

He nodded, then led the way down the Altar to the Dome's floor. "We should. And it may be of great advantage to us to have a priestess living in Si who can reach us quickly."

Auraya looked at him sideways. "I would like to continue working with you, too, Juran of the White."

He looked at her, then for the first time since she had returned, he smiled.

Her boat was just where she had left it. Emerahl turned to Surim and Tamun.

"Thank you for your hospitality," she said.

Tamun smiled and opened her arms wide. To Emerahl's surprise, the normally reserved woman stepped forward and embraced her.

"I should be thanking you for coming here and giving me someone to talk to."

"Other than me," Surim added.

"You're not such bad company yourselves," Emerahl said.

As Tamun stepped back, Surim gave Emerahl a hug, squeezing the breath out of her.

"Take care of yourself, Old Hag."

"You take care of each other."

"Oh, we're good at that. We've always looked after each other."

"For better or worse," Tamun added. Then she cleared her throat. "That's enough, brother." Surim released Emerahl and stepped back, grinning.

"But it's been so long since I had another woman in my arms."

Tamun made a low noise. "A few weeks, from what I recall."

"A few weeks is a long time." He looked thoughtful. "Hmmm, and I think it's probably time I did another trip downstream."

"That swamp girl takes too much of your attention," Tamun said disapprovingly.

"She's a little old to be called a girl, though I'm sure she'd be flattered by it."

Tamun made a low noise, but said nothing. She handed Emerahl a bag—the one Emerahl had been watching her making.

"This contains food and clean water, and those local cures we talked about."

"Thank you."

"We'll try to contact you every night," Surim told her. "In dreams."

"And I will contact you if I learn anything new."

They both nodded. Surim frowned. "We would go ourselves, but you know the world that exists now much better than we do. Though we skim the minds of mortals every day, we cannot be sure what we have learned will enable us to survive."

"And if we did go, we ought to separate." Surim didn't say how much they didn't want to. He didn't have to. His normally bright voice was strained.

"We will be of better use skimming minds and feeding what we learn to another."

Emerahl smiled and raised her hands. "Stop it. I understand your reluctance. I want to do this. Even if we don't find a way to kill the gods, knowing more about them—especially their limitations—is always a worthwhile pursuit."

"It's your quest," Surim said, chuckling. "That's what The Seer would have called it, anyway."

Emerahl laughed. "She would have called it 'The Quest for the Scroll of the Gods.' "

Tamun nodded. "And she would have written some appalling poetry and called it 'prophecy.' A green-eyed sprite will find the scroll; save the world and everyone's soul."

"Stop. Please." Still chuckling, Emerahl turned to the boat. She unwound the mooring line from the pottery urn and stepped aboard. At once the vessel began to drift away from the ledge and The Twins.

"The current will take you out," Surim called.

"Good luck," Tamun added.

Emerahl set down the bag and looked over her shoulder. Already the current had taken her halfway across the cavern. The brother and sister waved. She raised a hand in reply.

Then, as her boat reached the cave entrances on the other side, she turned to the front and guided it into the main tunnel.

She chuckled to herself. *The Quest for the Scroll of the Gods has begun.*

Nothing had been said since they had left the island. Nothing could be said, since they swam the whole way with only a few short rests. When Imi had begun to lag behind, warriors had caught her hands and pulled her along, which would have been fun if everyone hadn't been so serious.

Now, as Imi emerged from the water beside her father, she found just wading through it took an immense effort. Her whole body ached. Her legs hurt from so much swimming and her shoulders were sore from being hauled along. She was relieved when her father, having reached the edge of the Mouth, stopped.

"My people. Citizens of Borra."

She looked up, surprised by her father's voice suddenly booming loudly from beside her. Seeing the crowds of Elai

milling around the edge of the Mouth, she realized that
many had gathered to await their return. And for news.

"Today I have made a great gamble, but one I know
many of you support. I have struck an agreement with the
Pentadrians. They will trade with us, they will teach us—
and you all know they have much to teach—and they will
come to our aid in times of trouble.

"There is danger in such an agreement, and it relies on
trust and integrity on both sides. But it also offers great
benefits. I believe, with the Pentadrians' help, we will grow
stronger. Perhaps strong enough that we will no longer need
to hide here in this city. Perhaps strong enough that not
only will we no longer need to fear landwalker raiders, but
we will rid the seas of their filth."

He looked around at the faces before them. Some were
frowning, but most looked pleased. He glanced at Imi, then
took her hand.

"Together we will grow proud and strong, and live to occupy the islands once more!"

Someone cheered, then more voices joined in. Imi felt
her weariness fade. She looked up at her father and grinned.
He smiled at her, and for the first time it was not a wary
half-smile, but one of determination.

And, together, they began to walk through the crowd
toward the palace.

Danjin settled into a chair beside his wife. Silava smiled at
him and put aside the letter she was reading. Rising, she collected a jug of tintra that had been warming by the brazier
and poured some into a goblet for him. Returning to her
chair, she picked up the letter again.

"Which daughter is it this time?" he asked.

"Your eldest," she replied in mock disapproval at his
tone. "Your granddaughter had a fever, but she appears to
have recovered. Do you think we could visit them again
this summer?"

"That depends whether—"

A knock interrupted him. Their servant appeared and

hurried to the main door. Danjin caught a glimpse of a white-clothed man before the door closed again.

"A message for Fa-Spear," the servant said respectfully, handing Danjin a metal cylinder.

Silava glanced at the message. "Off to the Temple again?"

He regarded the metal cylinder in puzzlement. "They usually just tell me to come. This is formal."

"Perhaps it is an invite to a special ceremony."

"Perhaps." He examined the seal. It was unbroken. The cylinder was no fake, as far as he could tell.

Silava drummed her fingers on the arm-rest of her chair. "Are you going to open it?"

"Eventually."

"Why not now?"

"You haven't nagged me enough yet."

He ducked as she threw her empty goblet at him. Laughing, he broke the seal and tipped out the scroll inside. Silava rose to collect her goblet and refill it with tintra. Danjin uncurled the scroll.

His eyes moved across the words, but his mind refused to comprehend them. Or so he wished. When he had read the message three times he laid it aside, then stared at the brazier as he struggled with disbelief.

"What did it say?" Silava asked.

"Auraya has resigned."

He saw Silava's head come up abruptly. She said nothing for a moment.

"Did it say why?"

"No, but it said she has returned to Si. She came here. To Jarime. She didn't tell me."

"Of course not. If people had known what she was going to do there would have been an uproar."

"I suppose so. I would have kept it a secret, but if she didn't want the other White knowing her plans she might—"

Another knock came from the door. This time Danjin rose and answered it. A white-clothed messenger solemnly handed Danjin another message cylinder, made the sign of the circle, then strode back to a Temple platten.

Danjin had the seal broken and the scroll in his hands before he reached his chair. When he saw Auraya's graceful writing he felt a rush of relief. She hadn't forgotten him.

*To Danjin Spear,*

*I have little time to linger in Jarime, so I must make this regrettably short. Today I made a difficult decision, but one that I do not regret. I have resigned from the White in order to dedicate myself to helping the Siyee.*

*I wish I could deliver this news in person, but each moment I linger more Siyee may die of Hearteater. I want to thank you for all your advice and assistance this last year and a half. You have been as much a friend as an adviser and I will miss your wisdom and humor. I will recommend that the White instate you as the adviser for my replacement. I know you will do well.*

*A good future to you,*
*Auraya Dyer*

"That's nice," Silava said. "She sounds rushed."

Danjin looked up to find his wife standing by his shoulder. He shook his head at her. "This might have contained secret information."

She patted his shoulders. "It might have. I took a risk. What will you do with the ring?"

He looked down at his hand. "I expect they'll ask for it back."

"Probably. It might not even work any more."

"No." He slipped it off his finger and cupped it in his hand. Looking at it, he felt a pang of sadness. "She was a good White. Too good. She's given it all up to help the Siyee."

"I know," Silava said soothingly. "Let me take that and put it somewhere safe for now."

He handed her the ring. Her footsteps moved away, then stopped and she returned. Taking the jug from the brazier, she topped up his goblet.

"Drink. It'll warm you up. And think of this: it's going to be months before they find a new White. We'll have all that time to ourselves."

He looked up at her. "And we'll be free to visit our daughters for the summer, too, I suppose."

She pretended to be surprised. "I hadn't thought of that . . . but you're right."

As she walked away, he chuckled. At least his wife was happy. Looking down at the letter he felt a wry amusement. Since Auraya had first met the Siyee she had been enchanted by them. *I hope that means you're happy too, Auraya,* he thought. *I hope the sacrifice is worth it.*

*And I guess I should welcome you back to the world of mortals.*

# EPILOGUE

Looking back toward the coast, Mirar chuckled. Arleej had been true to her word. The town had been crowded with Dreamweavers. In his battered, dirty clothes, he had been too ordinary and uninteresting to attract more than a cursory glance.

Unfortunately, it had also meant there was no shortage of healers, so he had nothing to trade. He had been forced to steal a boat. It was a small craft—too small for the swells of the ocean—but with his limited sailing experience he doubted he could manage anything larger.

Throughout the night he had kept it moving and upright mainly by magic. Now, just before dawn, the water was calmer and he was exhausted.

*I can't sleep yet. I have to get Emerahl to teach me how to keep this thing afloat,* he told himself. *Otherwise I won't sleep at all for the next few days or weeks.*

Lying down, he fell into the dream trance easily.

*:Emerahl.*

After his third call, he heard a reply.

*:Mirar. Where are you?*

*:In a boat.*

*:What? How did you . . . oh! You got past them!*

*:Yes. Last night.*

*:Well done.*

*:Thank you. Arleej did a fine job of filling up the coastal villages with Dreamweavers. I think she spread a rumor about a plague starting there. The locals will be making a*

*fortune out of charging Dreamweavers for beds and meals, though hopefully they'll also be robbing the Circlian priests and priestesses the White brought with them.*

*:Did you see any of the White?*

*:No, but I heard someone say they were close by. The Siyee followed me right up to the village.*

*:When was this?*

*:Yesterday.*

*:So what are you doing asleep? You must get as far from the coast as you can. The Siyee can fly a long way in a day.*

*:I know. But this boat is small and it takes all my concentration to stop it capsizing. I need your help.*

*:What sort of boat did you get?*

He sent her a mental image.

*:You got a DINGHY! You IDIOT!*

*:There wasn't much choice. I had to steal it. With so many Dreamweavers in town, nobody was going to exchange a boat for dubious cures from a vagabond traveller.*

*:I suppose not.*

*:You've got to help me. Teach me to sail.*

*:Via dream links? I can't lie around all day. I'm on a Quest.*

The way she said it, he knew there was a capital letter.

*:But I'll drown!*

*:Very well. Between you and The Twins I'm spending half my day on my back . . . Hmm, that wasn't the best way of phrasing that. Oh! That reminds me. I have some important news for you.*

*:Yes?*

*:The Twins tell me the rumors have spread like a summer fire across Northern Ithania.* She paused for dramatic effect. *Your Auraya has quit the White.*

Mirar felt his entire being come apart then fly back together again. How could so few words hold so much meaning, both thrilling and terrifying?

*:Is she alive?*

*:Apparently so. She has returned to Si. According to the Siyee The Twins have skimmed, she's been there for a few weeks.*

*:Which means she can still fly.* His heart was racing now. *It's her innate Gift, Emerahl. She's close to becoming an immortal. I know it!*

*:You can't be sure.*

*:I am. She learned to heal with magic too easily for it not to be true. Just one small step, one nudge, and she will become an immortal.*

*:The gods will hardly approve of that.*

*:No, but the only alternative is to let her grow old and die. I must teach her.*

*:How do you plan to get her to come to you?*

He frowned. Auraya would never leave Northern Ithania and venture into the land of the Pentadrians, even if the Siyee didn't need her.

*:I'll have to go to her.*

*:You'll die. Even if you managed to avoid Siyee, Auraya doesn't know how to hide her thoughts. And I thought she told you never to return. That doesn't sound like someone who'd welcome you back, let alone trust you to teach her something that will probably make the gods want to kill her, too.*

He felt a pang of pure frustration, then the answer came to him.

*:Someone else must teach her.*

*:Who?*

*:You must teach her, Emerahl. You must go to the cave you took me to, then send for her. While she is in the void you can teach her to hide her mind. She won't be leaving Si, so the gods won't be too suspicious about her movements. Yes, that would work.*

Emerahl was silent for a long moment.

*:But . . . what about my Quest?*

He felt a wave of affection for her. If she had been going to refuse, she would have answered more forcefully. Yet he paused before answering. She was so keen to follow this Quest. He liked that she now roamed the world with confidence.

But who else could he call upon?

*:It can wait, can't it? I wouldn't ask but . . . you're her only chance.*

Emerahl was silent for a long time.

*:I'll do it. She had better be a quick learner.*

He smiled.

*:She is. Believe me, she is. Thank you, Emerahl.*

*:You had better make it up to me.*

*:I will,* he promised. *I will.*

# GLOSSARY

VEHICLES
platten – two-wheeled vehicle
tarn – four-wheeled vehicle

PLANTS
dembar – tree with magic sensitive sap
drimma – fruit of Southern Ithania
felfea – tree of Si
florrim – tranquilizing drug
formtane – sophoric drug
fronden – fern/bracken-like plants
garpa – tree. Seeds are a stimulant.
heybrin – cure believed to protect against stds
hroomya – coral that produces a blue dye
kwee bulbs – the edible fruit of a seaweed
mallin – herb that promotes circulation
mytten – tree with wood that burns slowly
rebi – fruit found in Si
saltwood – wood that is resistant to decay
sea tube – ink-producing coral
shendle – plant on forest floor
sleepvine – uses telepathic compulsion to trap prey
smokewood – bark with stimulating qualities
velweed – cure for hemorrhoids
wemmin – fleshy flower
winnet – tree that grows along rivers
yan – tubers on forest floor

# ANIMALS
aggen – mythical monster that lives in mines
amma – believed to be giantfish tears
arem – domestic, for pulling platten and tarn
ark – predatory bird
breem – small animal hunted by Siyee for food
bulfish – shellfish that lives on rocky outcrops
carmook – small pet native to Sennon
dartfly – stinging insect of northeast mountains
fanrin – predator that hunts gowts
flarke – sea predator
garr – giant sea creature
giantfish – enormous sea creature
girri – wingless birds, domesticated by Siyee
glitterworm – insect that glows in the dark
gowt – domestic animal bred for meat and milk, resides
      in mountains
kiri – large predatory bird
leramar – predator with telepathic ability
lightfish – fish that glows in dark waters
lyrim – domestic herd animals
moohook – small pet
ner – domesticated animal bred for meat
reyer – animal for riding and pulling platten
shem – domestic animal bred for milk
shrimmi – freshwater shellfish
spikemat – spiney creature of reefs
spinerake – landwalker name for flarke
takker – large snake
tiwi – insects that make a hive
veez – cute, telepathic pet that can speak
vorn – wolf-like animals
woodfish – tasteless fish
yern – deer-like, limited telepathy
yeryer – venomous sea creature

# CLOTHING
circ – circular overgarment worn by Circlian priests and
      priestesses

octavestim – garb of the Priests of Gareilem
tawl – overgarment worn draped over shoulders, fastened
     at throat
tunic – dress for women, shirt for men
undershift – undergarment for women

## FOOD
wafercakes – fried, flakey pastry
firespice – spice from Toren
nutmeal – paste made from nuts, Si
flatloaf – dense bread
rootcakes – patties of boiled and fried roots

## DRINK
ahm – drink of Somrey, usually warmed and spiced
drai – Elai drink
jamya – ceremonial drink of Pentadrians
kahr – Sennon drink
teepi – Siyee drink
teho – drink of Sennon
tintra – Hanian drink
tipli – Toren drink

## DISEASES
hearteater – disease that attacks lungs
lungrot – disease that, funnily enough, rots the lungs
woundrot – the festering of a wound

## BUILDINGS
wayhouse – place for travelers to stay in
safehouse – place where Dreamweavers can stay
blackstone – stone that is dark colored
whitestone – stone that is pale colored

## OTHER
canar – Sennon coin